Passage to 2838

Frank Muhm

This is a work of fiction. Many of the names, characters, places and incidents are the product of the author's imagination or used fictitiously. In the great Irish Storytelling Tradition, the author reserves the right to create information, characters or situations etc. that enhance the story being told.

Passage To 2838

ISBN-10: 1-893937-62-3
ISBN-13: 978-1-893937-62-8

For more information about this book, please contact the author at: frankmuhm@att.net

Printed in the United States by
Independent Publishing Corporation
Chesterfield, Missouri 63005

This Book is Dedicated

To My Wife Jeanette

FOREWORD

I had two Mothers and two Fathers. My mother was Bridget Walsh. She married Tim Kelley. They lived on a small farm near Jerseyville, Illinois. They had three children, two boys and a girl. My mother, Bridget died giving birth to me in 1927. My siblings were sent to the orphanage in Alton, Illinois as they were too young for my father to take care of while he worked the farm. I was taken by my mother's sister, Estella Muhm and her Husband, Emil to be raised in St. Louis. Stella and Emil became my Mom and Dad.

In later years I developed a keen interest in my family history. I was told at some time that my maternal Grandfather, Thomas Walsh was born on an English ship coming from Ireland to this country in the year 1851. I have the "coffin" ship that he and his parents and his brothers were aboard docking in New Orleans and proceeding up the Mississippi on a steamboat to St. Louis.

This is the year that my story begins and most of this part is fiction with historical facts.

The second part begins after an epilogue bringing the story to my mother and father's farm in the spring of the year 1927.

This part is told by a young boy who grows up Irish with a German name among nuns, priests and a multitude of hard working, beer drinking, Irish relatives and interesting roomers in the three story, nine room house at 2838 Eads Avenue in St Louis during the age of Lindbergh, Flappers, forty acre farms, the Gas House Gang, the Browns, Joe Louis and the Hoovervilles, alleys and ash pits.

This is not a perfect work but now that I am well past the age that most of my relatives lived it is all that I am willing and able to perfect at this time.

It is my hope that the story will bring some enjoyment to the reader.

Francis Leo Kelley Muhm

Book One

≈

The Voyage

~1~

Ireland

Richard Walsh stood on the side of the road with his back to the cart upon whose side seat sat his wife, Rose, and their two young sons, Edward and Daniel, huddled underneath blankets. Their trunk and what little else that they had was piled between the benches and behind the driver, Mr. Courtney.

On this chilling morning the twenty-eightieth of April in 1851, a fast moving shower had glistened the landscape. Droplets still hung from the leaves and anxious rhododendron buds that overhung this narrow road near Rinvyle, County Galway, Ireland.

Mr. Courtney ran the only public transportation system in the area. He picked up passengers occasionally from towns in and around Clifden and took them to Galway and back. These days, very few of his passengers returned. The passenger business had been slow, at least for the live ones. His carts were also used to carry the dead up the hills to their final resting place. The carts were compact narrow affairs with two large wheels in the rear and somewhat smaller ones in front. The benches on each side seated a total of six people, the seat up front, center, was for the driver, and the middle was for luggage. The carts were hauled by four horses, which always seemed in need of shoeing and nourishment. One of the horses pawed at the ground impatiently, and tossed its head about, creating a bit of tension on the reins.

"Tis about that time, Mister Walsh," said Mr. Courtney.

Richard Walsh raised his hand in response. He continued looking out at the Atlantic. His eyes ignored the gentle slope of the land from the mountain behind him continuing down toward the ocean. Today he did not see the different shades of green housed in stone-walled plots of all shapes and sizes. The low clouds cast their moving shadows, creating even more darker hues of green. He no longer saw the small, whitewashed houses with their snug thatched roofs scattered about, or the blues, aquas and foamy whites of the surf, creeping and receding slowly upon the wide expanse of beach, or the small mounds of offshore islands. All he could see was the savage, bloody hell that had befallen his family, friends and neighbors ever since the first potato crop failure six years ago. He saw people crawling on the beach, looking for any kind of seaweed to eat, not caring that the salt would hurt them. He saw them searching for shellfish, small periwinkles, sucking what little food was inside, along with the sand and more sea water. Their minds and sense of reason had ceased to work properly when their hunger pangs started. They dug in the sand with their raw, swollen hands for anything that looked like food. Some died where they lay, only to be washed out to sea with the high tide. Where before, dogs ran frolicking in and out of the surf, now there were none anywhere. In time, the family pet would be traded to another family for theirs, each family unable to bear the thought of eating their own. All the dogs and cats were gone and so were most of the people. He saw families die off one by one, with the last one of the family being carted off and buried on only a straw mat, their predecessors being buried in crates fashioned out of whatever furniture remained in their possession after their eviction.

Squire Lawrence Bentley foresaw that rent payments would be late coming, if at all, and he took advantage of the opportunity to clear his vast land holdings of these people, who in the past, with their church's absolute rule of propagation of the faithful, multiplied like flies. The dirty, simple-minded, unread people. They leased their small plots of ground and raised their families and their extended families in the same small area. They built small snug homes out of existing rock and mud, white wash, and thatch made from reeds, and the scraps of lumber that weren't good enough to be shipped off to England by Squire Bentley. The floors were of dirt, sometimes covered with sand and slate or any other flat rock. Rooms or spaces were added as the families grew, as they were sure to do, contributing to the crowded living conditions and overuse of the land.

In some ways, Squire Bentley envied these "croppies", as they were called. They had such a sense of humor and seemed to make the best of any situation, except now. The potato failures were too much for them to endure. Their solitary crop was this precious plant. It provided food for them, and money from the excess of the harvest paid the rent on the land, and for purchases of other staples such as the grains for bread, the seeds for cabbages and the feed for a few chickens and perhaps a pig or two. In each of the last six years, save one, the potatoes turned black, and rotted, and produced an unbearable smell.

The English land owners, Squire Bentley included, and their agents were able to grow the grains and raise livestock on their vast holdings with Irish labor. The hungry Irishman would watch the grains and the cattle shipped to England to pay the land owner's bills, even during the famine years.

Squire Bentley's profit had dropped during these turbulent times, and the only way for improvement was to plant more grain and raise more cattle. He needed the land that was occupied by these rent-overdue, sickly and dying tenants, so he hired Richard Walsh to help muscle them off his land.

Richard Walsh was big and strong and had kept order in some of the public houses in the area. He was different from most of his people; his mother taught him to read and he devoured every printed and written paper he could lay his hands on. He became a good listener and learned much in the public houses, besides the proper time to throw a punch if one was necessary.

The agreement between Squire Bentley and Richard Walsh was that the Walsh family would be well fed, and when Squire Bentley's land was cleared to his satisfaction he would provide suitable passage for him and his family to America. The other part of the bargain was for Squire Bentley to hire Richard's brother, Fergus, to manage his herd of livestock when that time came.

Richard Walsh considered it a pact with the Devil, but a necessary one. His family was well fed and survived through the worst of the famine years. Many times Richard would carry with him on an eviction a large package of food that Rose had prepared, stuffing it among the hopeless people's belongings. They had smuggled other provisions out from time to time, as much as they could without being discovered.

These small acts of generosity and risk pleased Rose but did nothing to alleviate the un-displayed distaste Richard felt with each eviction.

Now that Squire Bentley had cleared his land of most of the tenants, and the walls of their cottages were torn down so they would not come back again, he paid off Richard Walsh, as previously agreed, forty pounds sterling, and arranged passage for him and his family to America.

By 1851 two million people had died of starvation or the "fever" associated with starvation. Another two million or more emigrated. The propagation of the faithful came to a halt. For once they had other things on their minds- food and emigration.

The Walshs relatives, most of them, were no different. Half of them died, the rest emigrating. Richard and his wife Rose and their two sons stayed, trying to believe that the land was all important and that things would get better. So did Richard's brother, Fergus, who now was working in Liverpool, bringing money home with him about every three months to his wife, Anne who was pregnant with their fourth child. Anne and Rose were sisters. It was not uncommon that a large percentage of families intermarried.

~2~

Foley's Armada

"Father, it's time now," pleaded Rose.

Richard Walsh turned and walked toward the cart, and then stopped and turned around again. He spat defiantly upon the ground, turned again and jumped up on the seat beside his wife. Mr. Courtney tapped his horses gently with his whip. Their long journey had begun.

Along the road they passed many destitute people. Mr. Courtney and the Walshs had learned to look blindly upon them, as they had for several years; in time they had learned that there were too many to even think of helping. Survival of one's own was foremost. Richard saw faces too familiar, faces that would haunt his dreams and thoughts forever, faces of those he helped evict, of those prior to his working for Squire Bentley that he had fought with over food. His reward for these acts was that he could look upon his own small family, as he did now, with the faint hint of a smile, overwhelmingly tempered with the realization of the price he had paid and would forever pay in his unwanted dreams and thoughts.

"So you'll be going to the land of milk and honey, will you now?" started Mr. Courtney cheerfully.

"Aye, that we are, Mr. Courtney. Finally," responded Richard.

"Are you aware now of all the schemes and pitfalls that might befall you? Where are you bound, lad?"

"A place called New Orleans, and yes, I've heard the problems of those that went before us. That is one reason we waited. To test the water, so to speak. My cousin wrote me that he shipped to New Orleans and was told that it was only a few miles from Boston, and that when his ship docked only half of the people that had boarded walked off, the rest died during passage and were buried at sea. What else can you tell me, Mr. Courtney?"

"Oh, I've heard a lot, not that it's all true, now. Most of the folks went to Liverpool first and shipped out from there, but not before their pockets were picked, and their luggage stolen and they found out that there was no such ship for which they were sold passage and had to labor in workhouses to earn enough to eat and purchase their passage a second time. Our people are a simple lot, you know. We were trusting you know, at least among our own kind; a spit upon the hand and a shake was all that was needed to seal an agreement between two Irishmen, but not anymore. The times have changed men's souls as any terrible times will with men everywhere. But we learn quickly, we do, by hearsay and experience, not by books, mind you now; the bloody English and our own Church have seen to that."

"You're starting to sound like a preacher, Mr. Courtney."

"Aye, I'm not one to hold back an opinion, whether it be here or in some pub. I'm better in a pub, I am. What ship are ye booked on?"

"The name is *Foley's Armada* ; is there such a ship?" Richard asked quickly.

"Aye, you're alright there, lad. James Foley and his brothers have three ships. *Foley's Armada* was their first. They thought it would be their only ship, but business being so good, they built two more, all under English registry. They're all but fair, but much better than the others sailing out of Galway. I see you haven't much luggage, and that's good. If you have to wait awhile before you go aboard you can sit on it lest someone steals it when your back is turned. Never let anyone carry any of your things. That big trunk you have there will give you a bit of trouble."

Mr. Courtney continued to give his advice. They passed by the remains of the old Gaelic, Renvyle Castle; and later they passed through the village of Tully Cross, a crossroad that brought back memories of better times to Richard and Rose. Crossroads in Ireland were the gathering places for the people to celebrate the harvest or a wedding with dancing, singing and drinking and games for the children. He and his wife first met here and danced under the watchful eye of Father Ryan and everyone else. Now, clumps of people lie beside the road with their hands extended, pleading, with their open mouths displaying the green from eating the grass.

They passed through the town of Letterfrack, then bumped along the road between the pine forest that ran up the side of the mountains. They rode past the peat bogs in the lowlands to their right before subjecting the horses to their strenuous task of pulling their passengers up through the mountains and then straining to hold the carts from a runaway descent through the glens until they arrived in the town of Clifden.

Clifden was nestled in a glen with a small river rushing into an inlet of the Atlantic. The town was favored by English gentlemen as a seaside summer resort and many lavish manors were built. The Irish were there to serve and labor. In Clifden a woman and her two young daughters joined the Walshs. After the horses were given time to feed on the grass and drink they moved on toward Galway, sixty miles away.

Galway was a mass of confusion with people moving, sleeping, sitting everywhere, and the closer they got to the quay the more compact the people were, gathered around their meager possessions, waiting for their ship to leave if they had tickets or waiting for someone in their group to earn, beg, or steal enough money for passage. The going rate for passage on an immigrant ship was a mere three pounds sterling per person, but to those who didn't have it, it was a fortune.

Mr. Courtney drove his cart as close to the quay as the crowd would allow and helped Richard Walsh and his wife unload their luggage.

"There she is, lad, *Foley's Armada*, not the biggest or the best, around seven-hundred tons, I'd say. Drag your things as close to the ship as you can, and remember, don't leave them. Good luck to you, now, Mister and my lady. May God be with you."

"Bless you, Mr. Courtney," responded Rose, as her husband heaved one crate on his shoulder and started dragging the other toward the frigate, upon which he could see the rushed activity of its crew underneath the three, tall mast, holding furled, dingy, white canvas.

The emigrants boarded the ship as the sun lowered across the bay. Soon after, the ship was towed away from the quay. The crew shimmied up the mast like monkeys, crawling along the yards and booms, untieing, and dropping the sails, making them flap and billow out catching the wind and jerking the ship forward.

Richard Walsh watched the crew with interest and admiration. Three hundred and nineteen other passengers crowded the deck viewing their homeland for the last time. The sun had set and now the subdued light of the moon shimmied across the bay bouncing off the bare stone Aran Islands.

The passengers were reluctant to go below at the crew's beckoning and did so only after the last glimmer of light faded from shore.

For the next thirty-four days this ship would be their home. The ship was outfitted to allow twelve square feet per person, but because of the overwhelming demand for passage out of their country, all immigration ships were dangerously overcrowded. The Walshs had less than eight square feet to hold them and their belongings. The bunks were arranged three high allowing space for three adults on each bunk. Many families had a stranger sleeping next to them.

These emigrants were in too jovial of a mood to complain. They were on their way to the land of milk and honey. They were tired from their trek into Galway, the waiting and the hauling aboard of their possessions, but not too tired to sing and dance, and that they did, this first night only.

~3~

Sometime during the night, Rose Walsh turned her in bed and still half asleep stroked her husband's hair and kissed him gently on the back of his neck. Her hand caressed his cheek and when her fingers reached and felt along a long scar, she suddenly realized that something was wrong. This wasn't her husband! She withdrew her hand from the man's face and remained stiff. Her eyes opened wide. Who is this and where am I, and what have I done. She inched away from this body and moved against that of her husband. Richard continued snoring undisturbed. In gathering her scattered thoughts she remembered where she was and that after the dancing and singing she slid into the wide bunk with Richard following. The children clambered to the bunk above them. She remembered there being some space on the other side of her but thought nothing of it. In the dim light she tried to make out who lay to the right of her. If it could only have been one of her boys, but she knew better. If only she was dreaming, but—-. She listened and watched carefully to ascertain if this stranger was awake and if, God forbid, he was aware of what she had done. The stranger even smelled different than Richard, how could she have done such a thing. How would she tell Richard, or should she. She wanted to turn over and embrace her husband, but she couldn't move. She had sinned and she prayed for forgiveness and pleaded that the last few minutes could be erased from reality. She shut her eyes but remained awake and in the same position for the rest of the night being careful not to move with the roll of the ship. The stranger remained motionless, but smiled and closed his eyes and went back to sleep anxious for morning to come so that he could see who had kissed and caressed him.

When morning came, Daniel and Eddie climbed upon their mother and father urging them to arise and begging for permission to go above and explore the ship. When Rose opened her eyes she saw that whomever had laid beside her had gone.

The steerage passengers were crowded together. People stood in clusters or sat upon their crates and bundles containing clothing, cooking utensils, chamber pots, and for those more fortunate and with foresight, a supply of food staples and tobacco.

"I have to go, Father," pleaded Daniel.

"So do I," added Eddie.

Richard looked around at the arising masses and observed a man nearby relieving himself in a chamber pot that he held before him. Another man held up his coat to shield his wife as she squatted over their pot and as she dressed. Pipe smoke drifted above the rumpled carpet of humanity. The smell of damp cedar that they experienced the night before was quickly mixed with that of tobacco, body odors and human waste. *Foley's Armada* hauled lumber on the return trips from New Orleans and rough bark and small pieces of cedar were scattered throughout the deck.

A small stocky man wearing a dark stocking cap and a heavy black sweater jumped upon a crate banging away at a wash pan and hollered for attention.

"My name is Mr. Kyle. The captain wants all of you on deck in ten minutes. Everyone. Get a move on you, now! Ten minutes. There are water closets up on deck. Get up, now, up with ye!"

Daniel and Eddie were climbing the steps before the mate finished his sentence. Some of the elderly passengers had trouble ascending the ladders and had to be assisted. Other passengers voiced concern about leaving their belongings unattended. The sun was rising from the cloudless horizon. The air, carried by a strong wind, was bracing. Those without heavy clothing shivered, especially when covered with a fine sea spray. People had trouble walking confidently on a deck that seemed to move beneath them between their every step as the ship cut through the rising and ebbing waves of ocean. The passengers spoke to each other mostly with questions, their voices nearly drowned out by the wind passing through the riggings, the creaking of wood, the straining of ropes and the flapping of sail.

~4~

Four men, all wearing dark caps and sweaters, climbed upon the quarter deck followed by a tall gangly man with black curly hair down to his shoulders, and heavy black eyebrows above his slightly sunken blue eyes. He wore a uniformed black coat and trousers with a yellow stripe down the pant legs. He stood in the middle of the four mates, puffing on his pipe, waiting for the crowd to settle down and notice him.

"I am the Captain of this ship. My name is Dermot Lynch, Captain Dermot Lynch. Now listen all of ye to what I have to say. Each of you have been assigned living quarters. Learn where it be. Those of you that are starboard forward are——. That's fore-starboard, fore-port, aft-starboard and aft-port", Captain Lynch pointed out quickly with his walking stick.

"There are rules of this ship that must be followed. There are to be no exceptions. *Foley's Armada* will be your home for the next fortnight." Mr. Kyle, the first mate, turned to the captain quickly with a quizzical look on his face.

In a low voice out of the side of his mouth Captain Lynch addressed his mate, Mr. Kyle, "You don't think I'm going to tell them that it be more like forty days, do ye, after their agents told them twenty four? They'll all jump overboard after the first ten."

"Now then", continued the captain, "We will be together for the next fortnight. We are sailing to New Orleans which is a bit farther than Boston or New York. If we run into foul weather it could take longer. Cooking will only be permitted up here on the main deck, weather permitting. One cast iron stove for each section. You will take turns with your cooking chores. You will keep your living area clean at all times. Chamber pots will only be used when the weather prevents ye from coming up on deck. When they are used, they are to be emptied on the leeward side of the ship as soon as possible and cleaned immediately with salt water. Is that understood? All washing of clothing and bodies is to be done with sea water. The water closets have been set up fore and aft and are to be cleaned out daily. There will be no gambling or drinking allowed on board. Your quarters are small and there's no privacy. I can only rely on each of you to abide by your moral teachings."

Rose stiffened at this, and her eyes shifted from side to side. She observed a man several groups away smiling at her. She pretended not to notice him but she looked for a scar. Her heart pounded and her face flushed.

Captain Lynch continued, "On a long voyage as this, everything must be rationed if we are to survive. Each person will be allotted one quart of water a day to be used for drinking and cooking only. You must have your own containers."

"Your access up here on deck will be limited to only certain sections and you are not to venture beyond them. My sailors are not to be interfered with and my mates here, one of each, will be assigned to your section. They will act as Captain of that area and they must be obeyed. Any complaints or desires will be directed to them."

"When do we eat, Captain?", shouted one of the emigrants.

"Quiet! I haven't finished! Some of you will not make it to New Orleans alive. You should have realized the risk before you came aboard. As far as I know, there hasn't been an emigrant passage without deaths. Some were not fit to travel, others became sick or were washed overboard. Cleanliness is the best prevention for disease. On our last voyage we lost eleven passengers." The crowd moaned. "But we gained four. Is there a priest aboard?"

"Aye, Captain. My name is Father Daniel Healy", responded a slight of build young man wearing the collar, standing to the rear of Rose.

"Fine, Father. You will be needed, and so will Mr. Carey, your ship's surgeon. Doctor, come up here."

The plump old man needed help climbing the steps and stood beside Captain Lynch coughing and continually pushing his glasses back up his nose after every cough.

"Doctor Carey has a limited supply of pills and medications and will see to those in dire need and not able to tend themselves. Now, about food. You were instructed to bring what you could with you. There will be no food distributed until tomorrow evening——"

The crowd roared its disapproval.

"Quiet. You wont starve! Now go below where your mate will give you further instructions."

Lines formed quickly for the water closets. They consisted of three kegs on each side of a partition which separated the men from the women. Both were enclosed by lumber only shoulder high. The entrances were shielded by a burlap curtain. A narrow board was placed across the kegs to sit upon. When everyone was back below decks they were addressed by their section mate.

Mr. Kyle, holding some papers, jumped atop someone's belongings. He proceeded to call the roll of the emigrants assigned to him, first, their name, age and occupation. With each "Aye" he made a mental note of the respondent. Most of the men were listed as either laborers or farmers, very few of them with any skills. The women were listed as wives or servants. The children by name and age only.

~5~

Very few of the Irish emigrants were tradesmen, most being either farmers or common laborers with little or no formal education. A book of any kind in a household was looked upon as a treasure even when no one in the family was able to read. The story was told of a destitute family in Clifden, County Galway that came upon a worn book of instructions on how to repair shoes. The book was treasured but went unread for twenty years until one of the sons was taught to read by the parish priest. The son taught his six brothers how to read with that same book. All seven sons became skilled cobblers each setting up shop in different towns throughout Counties Galway and Clare. There were no schools in rural Ireland. Under British rule, education of the masses was discouraged. The local parish priest was burdened with the tremendous task of not only being their confessor, but also their protector, spokesman and educator, many times himself controlled by a narrow minded bishop who, although against anything British, worked in liaison with them in preventing the development of mind and the dream of a better standard of living.

So, for the past six years, millions of uneducated, untrained, sick and diseased men, women and children swarmed to the shores of Canada and the United States. At first, the arrival of cheap labor was welcomed, but soon the unskilled jobs were filled and "No Irish Need Apply" signs went up. In New York and Boston, where most immigrants went ashore they were squeezed into the most depressed areas close to the docks where the work was. The living conditions in some cases were as bad, if not worse, than what they left, but few regretted leaving their homeland for here in this new, strange, bustling land, there was what they had been seeking; freedom of religion but most important, opportunity. The opportunity was slight, but it was there and many grasped it and held on tight. They made the most of it, being quick to learn.

From letters sent back to Ireland from early emigrants, Richard Walsh had heard of the waiting in squalor at Liverpool for passage abroad, and of the poor and crowded living conditions in New York and Boston, and was happy, but a bit apprehensive, to be going to another land called New Orleans. He and Rose had no further plans beyond landing in New Orleans. The excitement of adventure foreshadowed future concerns.

Rose, however, did have one concern, well, now two: The man with the scar, she supposed that was the man she cuddled, and her other concern, her unborn baby who was now kicking fiercely. She had not kept track of how long she had been pregnant as it did not matter. It seemed that she was always pregnant, Daniel being the first, born in 1843, then Mary in 1844. Mary died at eighteen months of Pneumonia. Then came Eddie in 1846. She had two miscarriages since Daniel and was somewhat fearful of a third. There was never any thought of postponing the voyage because of her pregnancy. She knew that there would be other women aboard who had aided in childbirth before. That's how it was done.

After the roll call Mr. Kyle repeated the Captain's instructions and asked that any valid complaint or request be brought to his attention. He asked for volunteers for water closet duty explaining that the kegs had to be emptied and washed out with salt water on a regular basis and the area swabbed with mops. When no one volunteered he pointed out four men and assigned them to the chore. When all four moaned their displeasure Mr. Kyle addressed them harshly.

"Quiet now! You'll be the lucky ones, now. There'll be some bloody jobs assigned later, lads!"

That first full day the boys explored every nook and cranny that they were allowed to get in and then some. The women went on deck to arrange their communal cooking facilities. Other passengers stayed below trying to arrange their belongings in order preparing for a long voyage. Word was passed that Father Healy would say Mass before supper and thereafter every morning at seven, above or below deck depending on the weather. Father Healy preached a short sermon giving thanks and praising those who in their hearts found reason to share their supper with those who had brought nothing.

~6~

As bed time approached, Rose became concerned about the sleeping arrangements. She told Richard that the baby seemed to be moving a bit more and would he mind if she slept on his other side so she could get up easier. He smiled and kissed her on the cheek as he held up a blanket so she could change into her night clothes. The boys dropped like stones in their bunk above. Richard undressed and crawled into the bunk ahead of Rose. Rose nestled upon her husband's shoulder and was almost asleep when she heard Richard, and felt the bunk sink a bit.

"Mate, my name's Richard Walsh. I hope my snoring doesn't keep ye awake now."

The man with the scar spoke after shaking Richard's hand. "Nay! I'll probably drown you out, I will. John Garvin's my name."

"Traveling alone, are ye?"

"Aye, my wife, daughter and two boys are already in the States. They're to meet me when we dock."

Rose pretended to be asleep, but strained to hear every word.

"Well now, John we'll be talking in the morning, goodnight."

"Goodnight, Richard."

Rose had not had morning sickness with this pregnancy, but during the night the ship seemed to roll and toss more than usual and she felt nauseated. She eased away from her husband and felt her way along to the ladder and ascended it to the dark refreshing night air. There, she felt better and moved toward the water closet. A cold mist covered her face. The sky was overcast and she saw no one and heard nothing except the waves smashing against the bow of the ship and the incessant creaking of wood and rope and flapping of sails. She entered the water closet and sat across the 2x4, her arms bracing herself as the ship rolled. She began to wonder if they had done the right thing. She remembered one summer when she was a little girl and she sat much like she was now, upon a stone wall watching her brothers running in and out of the surf as she admired the seashells she had collected and the rich green meadow behind her sprinkled with fat, healthy, chewing cows. Her thoughts came to an abrupt halt as someone drew back the burlap. First she thought it was another woman, but she could make out a silhouette of a man just standing there.

"Richard?"

"Nay, it is me, the one you so took a liking to last evening," John Garvin whispered as he reached for her.

"Oh, My God!" Rose shouted, then quickly adjusted her voice to a frantic whisper. "I didn't mean it. No, No! I thought you were my husband. Don't! Please! You have to understand!"

She tried to tear herself away from him but couldn't. He pulled her body against his, placing a leg in back of hers and forcing her to the floor. He was on top of her immediately and felt her protruding abdomen, but in his stage of lust and desire either didn't care that she was pregnant or it did not register. He only knew that here was a woman who had touched him lovingly, something that he had not experienced for a long time. He ripped her blouse open with one hand and cuffed her mouth with the other. Rose could only emit muffled noises but kicked her feet and squirmed back and forth to where her feet, and now his, protruded out on the deck from under the burlap. His pants and underwear were down around his ankles as he tried to settle her into position. His heart was throbbing, blood rushed to his face and he gasped for breath. He felt a powerful jerk at his collar, so powerful it lifted him off Rose. He was spun around and faced a shaded figure. At that instant he felt a numbing jar to the scarless side of his face, a crunching searing pain to his testicles as he fell sliding on the deck. Before he could even wonder what happened he was pulled to a standing position and felt a terrific impact to his mid section, bending him forward and then another jarring jolt to his head sending him up and over the bulwark. He did not feel or hear himself hit the ocean.

Richard spat after him, turned and went to lift his wife from the deck. Rose was sobbing quietly. Richard looked around to see if anyone heard or saw what had happened. He could see the frame of a sailor slumped over the ship's wheel that was secured by a line to insure a fixed course. Rose sobbed hysterically, "You can't just leave him out there. You have to do something!" Richard threw over a plank and told his wife, I hope it hit him on his bloody head!" They slowly returned to their bed without speaking and fell asleep holding each other tightly and slept until the boys converged on them early in the morning.

~7~

Mr. Kyle descended into steerage and began to call the roll as he would do every morning. When he called the name, "Mary Kay Cox" no one answered. He called the name again. A young red haired woman across the aisle nudged the woman next to her.

"Mother, answer him, now. Mother?"

The old woman was stiff, having died in the night. Mr. Kyle summoned two sailors to help carry the woman above along with her sobbing daughter. Father Healy would conduct his first funeral mass shortly after roll call and bless the body of Mary Kay Cox as it slid off a plank into the sea.

The roll call continued amidst the murmuring. When he called "John Garvin" no one answered. He called the name several more times without receiving an answer and he turned in the direction of Richard and asked, "Has anyone seen Mr. Garvin this morning? Come on, now, speak up, anyone?"

Richard volunteered, "I saw him go above last night. He said he wasn't feeling well."

"Well now, we'll have to look for him now won't we."

Rose began to tremble. Later, Mr. Kyle brought two sailors with him and asked Richard and other passengers if they could identify Mr. Garvin's luggage. Upon identifying and marking a crate and two large cloth bags, Mr. Kyle went topside, gave a description of Mr. Garvin to the sailors, and sent them searching the ship. Mr. Kyle surveyed the area carefully for any clues as to the disappearance of Mr. Garvin before going above deck.

Toward evening as Rose sat upon one of her bundles fondling her rosary. Two sailors started picking up Mr. Garvin's possessions.

"Did, —-did you find him", she asked.

"Nay, not a trace, there was. He must have fallen overboard. Don't know why though, the sea being so calm and all."

"Did he have family with him, do you know?"

"Nay, none listed, all alone he was."

~8~

By day four the passengers became more settled, establishing their territories and routines and sorting through their sacks and chests, pulling out what was deemed necessary for that day of the voyage. The first evening the chamber pots came out along with drinking vessels. Cooking utensils were unpacked although they were for the most part not used until food was distributed on the third day. Cooking was done on open iron grates in restricted areas above deck when the weather permitted. There were too few grates and too many women and no scheduling of cooking times which caused arguments and some fights. These conflicts started on the very first day of food distribution and continued throughout the journey. Battlegrounds and lingering friendships and enemies were established. Every fifth day food was issued in family lots, each family, regardless of size receiving the same: three pounds flour, two and one-half pounds biscuits, six ounces of tea, a short measure of rice, oatmeal and molasses and a gallon of fresh water. Those who missed the distribution or were near the end of the line when the food ran out received nothing and would have to bargain or steal from others to survive till the next distribution. The sea biscuits needed strong jaws or a lengthy soaking to be consumed.

Small children were taught and encouraged by some of their parents to scoot in among the women at the grate and snap up a morsel of food before anyone could grab them. This entertained the sailors who watched in amusement and made bets upon the success of each attack. Names were given to the regular poachers and soon odds were established. A red headed girl of about twelve was the best. She would approach one of the cooking stations every day wearing different borrowed cloaks and shawls. When she bolted from the cook with her loot the shawl fell off revealing her fiery red hair. "Little Red Fox" was her assigned name and always an odds on favorite.

Some of the more fortunate emigrants brought a supply of bacon or dried fish and when cooked provided heightened anxiety among all the others, especially the little thieves. Three meals a day were a rarity. No more than tea and a biscuit upon arising. They heated the water, many times the same water that had previously been used to clean themselves. A biscuit or two with molasses at midday and a concoction of rice, barley and peas which was boiled to an almost chewable mush for dinner. This was the days special, day in and day out for weeks ahead. The emigrants learned to expect nothing better, but as the days passed they reflected and spoke of their favorite meals of seemingly long ago, before the famine.

There were those passengers, too many of them, who found themselves unable to keep any food down, being consistently sea sick, often not able to reach the chamber pot in time, much less go up to the water closet. They grew weaker and the stench in steerage stronger. Those able would climb out of the putrid smell to the brisk, fresh air above deck as often as the weather allowed. One woman when asked why she never went above replied that she did once. She said that she relished the breath of fresh air but found that re-entering steerage was too much to bear, so she preferred to remain below decks for the remainder of the passage.

The Walsh boys, Eddie and Daniel had made friends with two other boys who, "Live over in the next row, two bundles down. Duddy's their name, Mom", said Eddie. "Michael and James" he added excitedly.

Richard went above as often as he could, becoming impatient with nothing to do with his hands. He watched the sailors as they scampered up and down the rope ladders and as they sat skyward upon the top sail yards working on the rigging while those below repaired sails and made more ladders. The mass of canvas, ropes, wooden mast and booms all with their individual purpose amazed him. He wondered how the captain and crew knew when and which way to turn and pull each sail and soon discovered the relation to manipulating the sails and yard arms and the captain or his mate manning the helm. For some of the sailors, this was their first voyage. They were learning the names of the parts of the ship as they worked with them. The sailors were a young and carefree lot and were always with song as they worked.

Several times a day passengers would peer over the side of the ship to determine if it was moving. No land was in sight. It seemed that the whole world had suddenly turned to greenish water with froth on top and that they were its prisoner. They lost all sense of direction, there were no markers. The movement of the ship was a constant up and down of the forward and aft and a rolling from side to side. It was hard to realize that any progress toward the promised land was being made.

The children would play games below deck, mostly of hide and seek, scampering to the numerous hard to get places, sometimes having to stay in a most fowl smelling place till found. The men busied themselves playing cards, exchanging tales and smoking their pipes, so much so that a cloud of smoke could be seen billowing out of the hold above deck.

~9~

On the morning of the seventh day the sea had calmed, the sun was rising off the starboard bow and was half way above a long line of clouds paralleling the horizon. The horizon appeared like a long stretch of land. Many passengers came on deck taking advantage of the lack of wind and the sure footing. The ship seemed motionless and to some below decks who had no sense of distance, it was thought and hoped that they had reached their destination. The orange and red sunrise was spectacular. Other than that first night aboard this was the first enjoyable part of the journey.

Father Healy said Mass upon a crude table arranged in front of the forecastle. He had previously heard confessions in the water closet aft having to redirect those anxious passengers to the closet forward. In hearing confessions in the previously cleaned water closet, Father Healy sat in the men's section and both men and women, one at a time, entered the women's section to confess their sins through a burlap wall. Word had spread throughout the ship that Father was hearing confessions and the lines grew quickly. Rose was among those waiting, Richard was not. He would confess his sins when he felt he had enough of them to make it worthwhile and only when he had finished judging his actions and thoughts, sorting them out as to whether they were actual sins and which ones he would confess and which ones he alone would manage to live with.

In watching the people pouring in and out of confession, Richard wondered what they would have to confess, having been confined to such a mundane life these last seven days. Then he realized that some of them had probably not had the opportunity to take part in the Sacrament before coming aboard with all the turmoil back home. There was no telling what awful deeds some committed out of starvation and desperation he thought. He also saw a young attractive woman in line whom he had noticed sharing more than one male passenger's blanket and giggling in conversation with the sailors. Her head was bowed, her hands pressed together in a praying position, her eyes full of mischief as she smiled at a sailor mending rope.

Richard waited for Rose to emerge from the confessional and walked along the deck with her. She found a vacated area to the side of the ship and knelt to say her penance. It seemed to take her a great deal longer than normal and Richard began to feel uncomfortable waiting for her. Others milling about also took notice of the length of the penance. When she finally stood, he rushed her along the rail out of hearing and asked, " What took you so long, Rose? You didn't go and tell him about—-, you didn't, now, did you."

"Yes Richard, I did," she answered with a smile. "I had to. I couldn't live with such a thing otherwise."

"Jesus!, Rose, what did he say?"

"He said that he understood why it happened, but that it was still a terrible thing and that he would discuss the matter with me again; and, Richard, he so wants to hear your confession, He——"

"I'll bet he does, does he! Did you tell him everything?"

"Yes, I had to." She began sobbing and Richard shielded her from the passers by.

"Well, now, I'll bet the good Father is having an interesting day with a collection of stories that would put any Seanchai to shame."

"Now, Richard. His last words were, 'Go in peace, my child,' and I do feel so much better now."

Although he knew that a priest was bound by his oath never to reveal anything heard in the Sacrament of Confession, Richard, from then on kept his distance from Father Healy. There were brief moments that Richard would feel Father's eyes upon him but he was always able to quickly shun any feeling of guilt.

~10~

Around three that afternoon, the sky was completely overcast with low, billowing dark clouds rolling toward them above the foaming and tossing sea. *Foley's Armada* was uplifted with each oncoming wave and tossed back and forth by the driving wind. The sailors scampered up the rope ladders to reef and furl the sails to cut down the risk of tearing them from their riggings, or even worse, snapping a mast. Cooking utensils rattled and clanged as they were toppled off the grates by the wind and the heaving of the ship. The burning coals were quickly doused. Mr. Kyle ordered all of the emigrants above to go below and asked Richard to help see that they did immediately, and requested that he return and lend them a hand. The passengers descended the ladders into the stench of steerage, cold and dripping wet, and as the ship pitched they tried to feel their way back to their area in the reduced light amid screams by the frightened. The mates had extinguished all but a few lanterns and yelled sometimes unsuccessfully over the roar of sea and cries of the passengers to secure all crates and bundles, preferably on their bunks, as water that was already streaming down the open hatch had begun to slosh across the steerage floor. Orders were given to extinguish all pipes. Richard returned above deck and then the sailors closed the hatch smothering the hysterical passengers in almost complete darkness. Rose and her two boys made their way through falling bundles and sliding crates and overturned chamber pots back to their bunks and once there, tried desperately to hold on to their possessions and keep themselves from slamming against the other bunks and bulkheads.

Above decks, the roaring sound of the sea and the wind all but silenced the orders being shouted at the crew by Captain Lynch and his mates. The Captain was at the helm with a rope around it and his middle. Richard was trying to secure objects on deck and helped the sailors straining with the sail lines. Monstrous waves crashed over the bulwarks and at times reached half way up to the main yard. The constant interruption of a wave of water pounding against the sailors bodies and the treacherous footing made the completion of the simplest chore seem impossible. Those up in the yardarms hung on tightly and furled the sails quickly. At one point the wind bent the masts like willow branches, snapping attached lines. Richard and another sailor were torn loose from their line and sent smashing against the starboard rail. As they spit out the salt water and gasped for breath and anything secured, a sailor working above on the fore-sky sail fell on the deck before them, his eyes open with a fearful stare and blood gushing from his mouth that quickly mixed with the white froth of the ocean on the deck. "E's a goner, lad. Grab a line if ye can and tie 'em down," shouted the sailor as all three were sent sliding across the deck to the port rail where they wrapped a rope around the still bleeding body. There was a faint crack and scraping sound as the forward water closet broke loose from its attachments, toppling over the barrels and spilling their contents on the deck.

The storm continued throughout the evening and subsided about two a.m. at which time the clouds and winds and high waves left as quickly as they came and it seemed that the ship had entered a different world. The sky appeared as a roof of black velvet impregnated with millions of diamonds. The air was still and humid.

Captain Lynch gave the order to his mates to gather their men and assess the casualties to his crew and the damage to his ship. With lanterns they walked the deck inspecting while listening to the muffled screaming and cries from below and those of their injured shipmates on deck. They returned to their captain and gave their report. Three crew members lay dead and two were missing. Two were seriously injured, being attended to by Surgeon Carey; that left six able bodied seamen and the four mates to sail the ship. As far as the ship itself, there was not enough light to see all the damage, but the masts seemed intact and if the hull was not damaged, there was no danger. The Captain told his mates to open the hatches and go below for further inspection and to assure "those wretched souls" that the ship had survived and that all was well. They opened the holds and started down the ladders only to be driven back by the stench that rushed upward. They wrapped pieces of cloth over their nostrils and descended again lighting the lanterns as they went and then stepping into a foot of water that came in through leaky hatches. The water sloshed back and forth carrying bundles, pots, clothing and feces. The people were hysterical, some praising the Lord, others pleading for divine mercy. When Richard and Mr. Kyle went below and met Father Healy in the quagmire the priest said frantically. "Mr. Kyle, we must get the wounded and the dead out of here now. I've counted four dead and at least two dozen seriously injured and I'm sure there must be more."

"We'll get them out Father. Help gather some men and we'll carry them up and then we must get back down here and bail out this mess!"

Richard rushed to find his family. He found Rose caressing their two sons sitting on the middle bed of their berths, reclining, as though they were sitting on an hillside, as theirs and the neighboring berths had torn away from their fasteners and were forced against each other resembling dominoes suspended in a partial collapse. Richard and another man righted the bunk and as they did, the body of a teenage girl with flaming red hair splashed upon the deck on the other side. Richard embraced his family and after examining them, relieved as to their well being, went around and picked up the girl and sloshed toward the hold with her in his arms. There, she was pronounced dead and left by the ladder until all the seriously injured were taken above. From all three holds the wounded were carried on deck and placed within Doctor Carey's circle of fully lighted lanterns. Next came the dead; six women, two men and four children. They were placed outside the circle and their faces were covered with pieces of their own clothing.

Every emigrant ship was required to carry on board: a scalpel, 1 blunt pointed and 1 sharp bistouries, gum-lancet, tenaculum, spatula, scissors, 2 probes, and curved needles, a case of tooth instruments, midwifery forceps and trachea tube. A set of silver and gum catheters, one amputating knife and cotton, one amputation saw, one hey's saw, tourniquet, a supply of silk for sutures and ligatures, Blue pills, calomel, balsam of Capiri, castor oil, cream of tartar, Epsom salts, spirit of hartshorn, Jalap in powder, laudanum, peppermint, Friar's balsam, and rhubarb in powder. Surgeon Carey was to use most of these before sunrise along with medications that the emigrants and crew brought themselves. Holloway's Pills was the largest seller on the face of the earth; guaranteed to cure liver and stomach complaints and thirty-six other ailments, including evilness, tumors and venereal disease. Whiskey was used as an anesthetic when he amputated two legs; one on a fourteen year old boy, the other on an old woman. The body parts were quickly thrown overboard.

Captain Lynch studied the stars and after reviewing charts in his cabin, determined that they were about 300 miles north, northwest of the Azores. After first light and a further assessment of damage, he would make his decision to proceed or head for the Islands for repairs.

Bucket brigades were formed by both men and women and for three hours emigrants and crew members carried the slop upward pouring the stinking contents over the railings until their arms felt like they would fall from their sockets. Their energy gave out leaving about two inches of slop still on the decks below. The buckets were set down by the weary. Almost everyone in steerage came up the ladders and into the fresh air soon to be warmed by a now rising sun. No one had slept. They emerged from the holds and melded together like three slowly moving streams, circling the makeshift operating area and filing past the bodies with every fourth or fifth person lifting the cover from a face then moving on.

In conferring with his mates, Captain Lynch learned that the ship had sustained a great deal of damage to the sails and rigging, but that all of the masts, yards and booms, except for the spanker boom were intact. With sail and rope repair and replacement and thereafter, a generous application of grease and fat to all masts, he would be able to proceed on his course as planned. He decided that the first priority was the burial of the dead and asked Father Healy to get on with it. After the burials there would be a rest period for everyone as the ship was becalmed anyway. A portion of whiskey was issued to everyone. Afterward his crew and any volunteers would take up the buckets once more and every man woman and child would be given a splashing bath of salt water.

The dead were wrapped in wet and torn canvas and one at a time they were placed upon a plank which was then balanced on the port rail like a see-saw. After Father Healy had blessed them and proclaimed their bodies to the calm waters and begged mercy for their souls, the board was tipped and all of the deceased, one by one entered their own world of "milk and honey".

~11~

Richard sat with his back against a mast nurturing his whiskey as did another emigrant to his side.

"Name's John Duddy," offered the man next to him. "Used to be O'Doud, but since they spelled it Duddy on the register, that's the way it'll be."

After the introductions, they learned that their sons had already made acquaintance and so did their wives. At Richard's effort to inject satirical wit by asking him how he was enjoying his cruise, John Duddy replied, "Oh Lord, frustrating it is. On land a man can run, hide or climb or go to a cave. The ground will always be there and not moving back and forth underneath ye. Out here, on this bloody board of a thing, with only deep water in sight, we're at God's mercy, we are! I'll be glad to be rid of this stinking ship, I will."

"Right you are. Where are ye goin' to after we reach this New Orleans?"

"Up a river called Miss something to a town in a County called Ill noise. We are to be met at a town called Alton. My wife, Catherine, has a brother out a bit from there in a place called Delhi. He and his family work a little piece of ground and he gets some work at a match factory. The wife's had letters from them telling her that the soil is rich and black as coal with no stones in it and with trees all over and running streams, and farmers always looking for good hands to work the land, and talk of railroads being built. And you, Richard?"

"I'm not sure, I've a cousin in a place called Hannibal. He wants us to come there. He's been there a year, now. He wrote us that he went up a river from New Orleans called Mississippi—"

"That's it, lad Mississippi."

"And right after reaching a St. Louie, they took another river to the left called the Missouri. Hannibal sets somewhere on the Missouri, that's all I know."

"Where ye from, Richard?"

"Renvyle."

"Aye, tis close to Clifden, is it not. Ye miss it now, don't you Richard."

The scenes of the people along the roads and the coffins stacked in front of Ryan's pub at Tully Cross flashed before him. "No, No, not now, John," he finally responded. "Tis' hard to believe such a thing could happen; that masses of people would die for the lack of food, mind you, and in such a beautiful land. It's almost that we had to pay that terrible price for living upon such a heavenly spot. The boring, peaceful beauty of it, John, even in the worst of weather. I'll never go back, for the good memories now are smothered by too many bad ones. One of my boys may sometime, if it's still there, or their children or their children's children."

"It'll be there Richard, but I'm like you, I won't go back. We're alive, our families are, or most of them, praise be to God, and we're goin to the land of opportunity."

"Aye", responded Richard, closing his eyes. Within minutes both men were asleep in the warm sun, exhausted, both dreaming of their homeland as it was when they loved it.

Two hours later the crew and the able-bodied male passengers began repairing the ship, some returning to steerage to bail out the rest of the water, after which everyone was ordered above decks, separated as to male and female, and given lye soap and ordered to strip off their clothing and wash themselves and each other. Several women, the ones who had been complaining the most of the sanitary conditions, were appointed to see that all females, regardless of age or infirmities were thoroughly washed. Some of the men who had refused to comply, stating that they had not taken a bath in their life and had never had any ill effects were scrubbed by the others with brushes and brooms and made a spectacle of. The temperature was in the lower sixties with no wind and the bright sun helped dry them quickly. The routine soon returned to normal; cooking fires were restarted, and after sunset, the passengers returned to the soggy, humid stench below.

Doctor Carey continued administering to the sick and wounded, watching closely his two amputee patients and delivering to Father Healy two others who died. Two days later, he would help bring into the world a boy and a girl. The boy was named Thomas Richard Walsh. His mother, Rose, came through the childbirth with no trouble. His father, Richard, received congratulations from his new friend, John Duddy. The girl remained unnamed as her mother, a Mary McManus, who was crossing alone, succumbed to the ordeal. Rose nursed the baby along with her son until another woman with milk became available.

~12~

Dr. Francis Thomas Carey was in his sixtieth year. His past had depleted his energy. He was somewhat callous of his patients sufferings and left him without a will to improve his self esteem. He was born in Dublin, educated there and in London. He returned to Dublin to practice. He married below his class to a beautiful young girl who worked in a pub near his office. His parents, who were strict Catholics, demanded that he get an annulment from the tramp or they would disown him. He refused and was relegated to treating only the poor people of the city with his fees, too many times amounting to, "Bless you and may God be with you, Doctor". His wife, Nell tired of the same and took up with a promising young lawyer. He received an annulment. He had become involved in one rebellion movement after another, all to be paid with prison terms for some and death for others and bitter defeat for all who fought to see Ireland free. He secretly treated the injured "soldiers" of these movements. He lamented his inability to help the poor people dying from starvation in the previous famine years and he hated the English Government for turning their backs on these people. He hated the English and the Irish landlords for doing the same, famine after famine. He ridiculed England for spending millions of pounds to build the Grand Exposition in London while his people starved. He gave up on Ireland ever being one country as his people had not been able to unite in their love for one another. Perhaps it was because everyone was so poor and destitute that there was always someone ready to grab at any opportunity for survival even if it required informing on those who were striving for unification.

He went to Liverpool and took up residence in the many pubs lining the docks where most of the Irish emigrants went by steamship to find passage to Boston or New York or Canada on what were to be called coffin ships. His drinking increased and so did the demand for his services, treating the lacerations of sailors that were inflicted in the many brawls. Word of his satisfactory doctoring reached a couple of ship captains of the Brookfield-Smith Shipping Co. and before long he found himself in the office of, and being hired by, a Mr. Bradford Smith. He remembered being told his responsibilities.

"Now look here, Carey, all we want you to do is to prevent cholera, dysentery, typhus and any other diseases from spreading to my crews. We collect our passage money up front so I don't give a bloody damn as to how many of these musty people make it ashore alive as long as my crew stays healthy! Understand? We don't run slave ships, getting paid to deliver live ones. Soap Carey! Soap. You'll have plenty of it. Make sure they use it. One other thing, if they're dying within a day or two of docking, let them, urge them to die. Declare them dead if you have to, we don't want any return passengers. And curtail your drinking as much as possible. The salt air will be good for you."

Dr. Carey knew that many of the slave traders treated their captured Africans as precious cargo as did the captains of the prison ships sailing from Ireland and England with convicted Irishmen to be used in helping to build Australia.

The Doctor had made twelve passages and was successful in that only three crew members came down with any disease. However, because of conditions, lack of supplies and concern, eight-hundred and forty nine passengers out of four thousand died, died even with all the medical treatment available to him. When he drank too much, he could see all of them being dropped into the sea.

Two years ago, Dr. Carey met Captain Lynch in a Boston pub. In a long conversation he learned of the humane treatment of passengers on *Foley's Armada* and their need for a surgeon. So, here he was, again losing patients to the deep and bringing into the world babies with little hope of surviving. He was always fighting a losing battle. His efforts seemed so futile. "Practicing physician", he thought. "With not much more skill than a butcher, but with a great deal more responsibility and remorse upon failure." He kept watch on his present passengers for an early sign of disease. He knew it was only a matter of time.

~13~

With patched sails and a rested crew, *Foley's Armada* crossed the fortieth parallel entering a warmer current and picking up favorable winds. With each day, the temperature and humidity rose. Below decks the heat was so bad that some of the occupants became delirious especially after hearing a man continually repeating, " We're going to hell, we are, we're doomed!". They were brought to their senses by the more stable passengers. There were days that dolphins swam with them, rising above and falling beneath the waves with a smooth rolling motion leaving not a ripple. Sharks approached the ship showing their menacing fins as they circled patiently as if they were awaiting another corpse.

On the eve of the twenty-third day fog surrounded the ship without warning. The sailors aft appeared as black silhouettes against the gray, the lanterns hung about the ship giving off a misty, quiet and peaceful feeling. Soon the sailors were blanked out with gray mist as were the light of the lanterns. No other ships had been sighted since leaving Galway Bay and the crew knew that they were still in the middle of the Atlantic. Even with such a dense fog they felt at rest and were becoming drowsy. The captain and his mates quickly alerted the crew to the possibility of a collision replacing their contentedness with a fear of the unseen like a blind man's first outing. Every man available was placed on watch to peer into the unseen and listen to the silence, trying their best to fight off the feeling of serenity and sleep. The ship's bell was rung at staggered intervals to alleviate the monotony.

Soon after the first watch changed, four hours later, singing was heard from out in the fog on the port side. The singing grew louder. The words were German. The ship's bell was rung frantically and the crew on duty shouted until their throats hurt. Suddenly a black mass appeared close on the starboard side and in another instant a slight nudge was felt toward aft and a ripping sound was heard accompanying the loud melodic voices. The uninterrupted singing soon grew faint and disappeared as did the last tone of the bell aboard the passing ghost ship as one would wait and relish the fading sound of the last soft note played on a piano.

The dawn brought with it a breeze that wiped away the fog and made the sails flap full except for the spanker sail. A large rip caused by the German ship released the wind as soon as the sail caught it. Some of the crew set to repairing the sail with needles and line. Just below the surface of the ocean was an abundance of kelp and other seaweed. They were now in the Sargasso Sea.

As the sun rose, so did the temperature and humidity. Many of the passengers emerged from below for relief from the stench. The man that earlier became delirious stood at the rail looking out at the floating vegetation with others. Suddenly he turned away from staring at the mass and bolted to and climbed upon the ratlines attached to the main mast. Before anyone noticed or was able to stop him he had scampered above to the top mast cap and stood there out of breath but shouting sporadically, "We're in the gates of hell! Listen to me. We shouldn't have come! We're all doomed, we're doomed, we are. There's no way out of this, repent! Repent before we burn to ashes! Blessed be to God!" A sailor edged closer and was about to reach for his leg when he spread his arms and shouted, "My guardian angel will take me away from here, he will" and he dove off his perch plummeting downward, bouncing off several ropes and spars, breaking his neck before hitting the deck like a limp sack of potatoes amid the screams of the viewing passengers.

The man was identified as Michael O'Rourke traveling with his wife, Hanora, and his four month old son, John. When Father Healy went below to carry the tragic news to Hanora O'Rourke, he found her seemingly unconscious and twitching. He thought that someone had already reached her with the news and she had fainted. He noticed that she was ringing wet with perspiration and that on the far side of her lay an infant under a blanket with only the top of its head protruding. Trembling, he pulled back the cover and the infant's blue eyes stared coldly and motionless through him never to blink or fill with tears again. The infant's mother was carried above to Dr. Carey who after doing the best that he could pronounced her dead two days later. With the heat from the sun being what it was, her husband and infant were buried at sea immediately.

In years to come, passenger listings of *Foley's Armada* would show, among many other emigrants, a Michael O'Rourke, age 37, farmer, wife, Honora, age 25, infant, John, no age, sailing in 1851 from Galway, Ireland to New Orleans. The listings would not mention that the O'Rourke family was buried at sea beneath a carpet of kelp along with all their belongings or that they had contracted a disease. Word of their death would reach Hanora O'Rourke's parents back in Ireland on the ship's return voyage, and Father Healy would break the news to her brother upon reaching the docks in New Orleans, but nowhere else in history would the death of these three emigrants be recorded nor the death of the next fourteen passengers to succumb to the deadly disease of cholera.

~14~

A few days later the ship emerged from the seeming grasp of the seaweed and sailed to the south of Great Abaco Island in the Bahamas. Gulls were everywhere, Brown Pelicans provided entertainment as they flapped fifteen feet above the ocean suddenly halting their flight and dropping into the water head first with their wings half folded. If they were successful in scooping a fish in their pouched bill they would dip their head while sitting in the water draining the water and then raise their head upward, swallowing the fish and take to flight again for another try. Awkward but successful fishermen they were.

Shouts of "Land!" "America! We're here!" went up at every approach to a small island only to be told that their destination was at least a week or two away. When they sailed into the N.E. Providence Channel, past Whale Cay and into the Straits of Florida slipping through the Florida Keys with islands laying all around them in the clear green and blue water, they were sure the sailors had lied to them. When they emerged from the Keys and once again sailed into water with no land in sight and lost most of the birds, they became despondent.

Three days later, at sunrise, everyone was ordered on deck. They were also ordered to bring up their possessions. At first they thought that they had finally arrived but in looking in all directions, they saw nothing but water.

The crew members rolled out a number of empty whiskey and pickle barrels and filled them with sea water. The men and women were once again separated and forced to remove their clothing, wash their garments and themselves with hunks of Lye soap provided. When through, half of the passengers smelled of pickle, the other half of whiskey. The crew then went below carrying buckets of sea water and bags of sand, with cloths across their nostrils to scrub best they could below decks and then attempted to dry the area with beds of burning coals.

That afternoon land was sighted once again. At least they thought it was land, not a cloud on the horizon. As they sailed closer they could make out what seemed like two islands overgrown with foliage. Gulls and Pelicans, both white and brown along with Terns, seemed to come out to greet them.

When the Captain ordered the anchor dropped and the sails furled rumors and questions abounded. The ship sat there. Captain Lynch used his telescope to survey the "islands". Another ship was sighted approaching from the starboard side and also weighed its anchor and gathered in its canvas. What was happening? Where were they? A smaller boat with black smoke belching from it appeared coming out toward them from between the "islands". The ship was a tug and its captain exchanged words with Captain Lynch, after which one of his men lofted a line to a sailor aboard and proceeded to tow *Foley's Armada* between the "islands", the mouth of the Mississippi River at its South Pass.

The anxious passengers lined the railings. They were told that, yes this was America, but that they had another day's voyage up the river, a hundred and ten miles, before they would reach New Orleans. What a disappointment, they thought. Were the crewmen lying again? This isn't what they pictured as America, the land of milk and honey. It must get better, they hoped.

The sailors had little to do now that the ship was being towed so they lined the rails with the passengers who were healthy and inquisitive enough to be interested in the passage up the Mississippi. When Richard heard that they were on the Mississippi he sensed that they were very close to their destination. Could it be that all of America is on or near this river, he thought.

Richard had once seen the mouth of the Shannon, but this, this didn't look like a river, rather an immense lake. As they moved up river the stream narrowed some and the color of the water changed from hues of green and blue to gray. The banks, still far apart were covered with low lying foliage. Upon small mud beaches alligators lay in wait, one yawning showing his long row of teeth, others slithering into the water. In small coves, they saw a long legged Blue Heron standing silently waiting for a meal to swim by. Large, flat, oval shaped turtles with pointed snouts piggybacked one another, while sunbathing on half submerged logs. Small green frogs sat upon lily pads. Above and between the mangroves flew Warblers and Flycatchers after the bees, gnats and magnificently colored butterflies. Gulls and Terns followed aft sometimes banking to follow another vessel being towed down river. Ducks paddled smoothly through the watery passageways, one unfortunately being pulled beneath the surface and into the large mouth of an alert alligator. Feathers soon floated away from the area. A Water Turkey soared high in the sky looking like a prehistoric bird with its long tail. Another perched upon a bare branch protruding over the water. Still another swam in the river with most of its body submerged only its head and long neck protruding, looking like a snake. Green snakes wrapped themselves around limbs and Water Moccasins squirmed off shore.

A Purple Gallinule swam to, and emerged upon, a mud bank revealing its gaudy color combination; a violet and purple head, chest and back and a pale blue patch on its forehead led by a red bill and supported by long, bright, yellow legs and feet. It cackled like a hen upon taking flight. The passengers had never before seen such living creatures.

Eddie Walsh pulled his eyes away from the river bank and asked Mr. Kyle, who was standing beside him, "Sir, are you sure that this is America?"

"Aye, Son, it is. It didn't used to be, lad, so I'm told. You see, now, this river has carried soil down from all over America for hundreds of years mixing it up and laying it down here, just a bit farther out each day making new land. Look at the water, lad. See how brown it's becoming. That's soil, it is. The water is good to drink after the dirt settles. Look up ahead, there. That's Pilot Town. The place is built on poles. The river's almost lapping their floor boards. This is the flooding season. It rains a lot in May and June."

The tow boat halted nearer the bank and as soon as it did an indiscernible, highly pitched hum, engulfed everyone aboard and scattered the frantic passengers immediately slapping themselves to no avail as mosquitos filled their bellies with their blood and moved away. Another wave descended, and another and another. The undulating sound and persistent biting of the attackers removed all reason from their victims. People ran, or tried to run away from them, but there was no place to go. It seemed that the insects knew that they were coming and laid in wait. Perhaps they did know, as many unsuspecting, blood filled human bodies had traveled up this river before them. Finally, after what seemed like forever, but was only ten to fifteen minutes, the crewmen aboard the tow boat threw up small nets for the passengers. They formed their own small mounds on the deck underneath the netting still screaming and slapping and scratching themselves. In an hour they moved out into the mainstream and proceeded forward. No explanation was given for the stop.

Dusk descended upon them and from behind the long shadows lining the shore were heard the noises of the birds settling in, the croaking of the frogs, the slapping of water made by fish rising above the water for some of the previously well fed mosquitos and other insects. Reddish eyes of the wildlife pierced through the increasing darkness. This was to be the immigrants first night in America although not one of them would acknowledge it as such. Most of the passengers were still awake as they passed beneath the flickering lamplight of Ft. Jackson on their left.

With daylight came muddier water, higher river banks and among the mangroves a scantiness of trees. Upon their long reaching branches draped a dull silvery moss. The river seemed to curve every hundred yards. Structures built on poles appeared more frequently. Barking dogs acknowledged their presence. Ships and boats of all sizes and shapes scurried up and down the river. The scent of the sea was gone and in its place was that of civilization, wood burning, fish oil, and a wiff of food being cooked. Anticipation mounted.

Under the late afternoon sun, after emerging from a long bend in the river, the passengers lined the rails and saw the tops of church steeples. As the river straightened they beheld an immense line of ships. First the Schooners and Packets side by side with their sails furled, looking like denuded trees, seemingly hundreds of them, and up river to them even more long, low-lying, steamships with their tall, black, ornate smoke stacks looking bold and massive, some belching black smoke that drifted eventually in every direction blotting out the view of the white domed buildings, and the many churches set behind a never ending row of warehouses. They had heard the sounds of the city for the last hour, now they saw where the noise came from.

The tug maneuvered *Foley's Armada* alongside another Packet that flew a German flag and was void of passengers. A ship with a French flag was alongside it. The day was Monday, June the second, a date all the passengers would remember. In a few years ships propelled by steam would reduce the crossing time considerably and with more comfort and safety.

The immigrants fondled their possessions in anticipation of going ashore. Conversations intensified, destination information, names and addresses were exchanged, promises of correspondence were made and hopes of continued friendships voiced, children were sought and corralled.

The Walshs and Duddys had developed a strong friendship over the last weeks. Eddie and Daniel were inseparable from the Duddy boys, Martin, nine and Joseph, six. Catherine Duddy had the attentive ear of Rose when she talked about settling in Delhi, Illinois, and the letters she had received from her brother, Bart O'Malley. Catherine carried the letters with her and read them to Rose whenever the opportunity came. If Rose had a choice, she would go with the Duddys to Illinois. She had not known Richard's cousin in Hannibal and it sounded as though anything could be grown on the land around this, Delhi. Catherine and Rose agreed to work on Richard to change his mind about going to Hannibal. Unknown to them, John Duddy had already convinced Richard to keep the families together, at least for a while.

~15~

New Orleans

The mood of the immigrants was subdued. Not like they had dreamed upon leaving Galway. Then, they could picture themselves applauding their arrival and kissing the ground upon going ashore to the land of their dreams. Some envisioned a large group of people welcoming them with open arms. They were in no mood for applauding. Their grand expectations had been pushed in the back of their minds by what they had endured. There they were, in family groups, projecting the faint scent of pickle and whiskey, clothed in damp cloth, some with shoes, some not, all still scratching and covered with red bumps. All were tired and hungry, hungry for something different and more filling than the slop that they had been eating. Only the children, those still healthy, showed any enthusiasm for their arrival. They were ready to run till their legs fell off after being so confined. Until they were set ashore, they overflowed with questions while constantly moving, unable to harness their energy and curiosity, and it was this excitement that brought back some of the faded dreams to those adults around them.

"Look over there, Father, at those men unloading that cart," said Daniel, pointing. "What happened to them, Father, they are all black, and that woman with that scarf around her head, so is she."

"I don't like them," retorted Eddie. "They look mean, they frighten me."

"They are from Africa lads, and I think they call them darkies, or niggers," answered Richard as they watched the two men empty a wagon loaded with hundred pound sacks of rice. One of the men wore a dirty, brown, felt hat, a billowing, faded, long sleeve white shirt somewhat tucked into a pair of brown trousers that ended at his knees with tattered strips of cloth. The other was a boy of not more than twelve. He also wore an oversized faded white shirt, pants with the ends rolled up above his ankles, held up by red suspenders and he wore a round straw hat. An old frail woman sat on one of the sacks weaving a basket with a straw-like material. The levee was a mass of Negroes of both black and lighter skin, Caucasians of all nationalities, Creoles, along with wagons pulled by teams of horses, mules and a few oxen. All the sacks, barrels, bales, lumber and hides placed at one end of the levee seemed to be needed at the other end producing a racket which was in constant motion, all amid the hot, humid afternoon air heated by the blazing sun. The noise of the commotion on the levee was muted often by the tooting blast of a steamship announcing its departure, arrival, or just plain letting off steam. The black smoke from its stacks would sometimes drift down upon the wharf bringing with it soot enough to choke one temporally with its dust covering whatever surface it fell upon.

Richard looked upon the mass of foodstuffs in his view and thought of the bare docks back in Galway and the starvation of his people and wondered why people anywhere had to starve when there were places like this with an abundance of food. First he thought that if Ireland had food, people would have stayed, but he quickly dismissed the thought as the lack of food alone was not the reason for emigration. Freedom was almost as important as physical survival. He held his infant son, Thomas, over the rail and said, "There you are, lad, your new country, you won't starve here, I promise you that."

The aroma of fish was everywhere veiling the lesser scents of various spices, Cedar, Pine and musty smelling hides. The one scent that reached the nostrils of nearly every man aboard was that of tobacco. Those with pipes grew anxious and busied themselves with cleaning their briars. The immigrants in the last few minutes had remembered why they journeyed so far, and they began to remember their wants and desires of this new land. Their immediate desires were first of food, any kind; water, milk, tea, ale and whiskey, clean dry clothes, a hot bath, and a dry sweet smelling place to sleep, and firm footing that did not move. That would take a good hour on land for them to retain their footing.

Captain Lynch stood at the top of the gangplank ready to bid goodbye and answer questions as best he could to those departing passengers who were being rounded up and set in motion toward the captain by the crew who resembled sheep dogs herding their flock. Below on the wooden dock awaited a variety of greeters; family and friends of some of the passengers, an undertaker, stepping down from his black draped wagon inquiring from one of the crew if there were any corpses aboard or if anyone was near that stage so that he might follow them closely. Two Urseline nuns, in their gray habit were standing with two boys, a girl and their mother. A smattering of well dressed con-artists were ready to sell passage on non-existing steamers. Pick pockets and thieves ready to be off with whatever possessions the immigrants lay unattended upon the dock were also on the dock. There were agents associated with rooming houses in the Irish Channel, ready to steer those looking for shelter to usually filthy, overcrowded, and always overpriced quarters. Money exchangers with accompanying body guards, ready to swindle the uneducated with whatever exchange rate they could get away with always did a brisk business.

The new Irish immigrants were always welcomed by the the citizens of New Orleans as well as the "established" Irish for only as long as their money held out. Once the new Irish began looking for work and posing a threat to the employment of the established citizens, they were strongly persuaded by threats, eviction and ridicule to move up river to find their own prosperity. There had been a strong movement by the "Know Nothings" for some years to curtail all immigrations and leave the job opportunities to the so called "Native Americans", not the Indians, but those who had immigrated prior to the eighteen forties. Wages dropped continually as labor was plentiful. An employer could always find someone to work for less than those he presently employed. If the employer was in the South and had money to purchase slaves he had no employment concerns. The immigrants from Europe tended to congregate with their own kind wherever they settled.

The Irish brought the small tract farmer, but mostly the laborer and the housekeepers; the Italians could fashion anything in leather, and had a passion for procuring and preparing fish and shellfish and vegetables, the Germans brought skilled craftsmen, metal workers and the knowledge of brewing. All of these people and their values were needed for the country to expand and prosper, but until they ventured out into the vast new land, they were not welcome where they landed. The immigrants came and would continue to come, later, by swifter ocean going steamships, through the ports of New Orleans, Boston, New York, Philadelphia, Halifax and others. Stricter immigration laws adding phisical exams and monetary worth followed. Those who could not pass the standards set were sent back to their former land. Immigrants kept pouring in and helped to expand the population of the country like the Mississippi river enlarged Louisiana. The country's soil flowed south with the river, the people flowed North, South, East, and West.

For the passengers aboard *Foley's Armada,* about to come ashore, there were few if any entry restrictions. New Orleans already had almost every disease that any of the passengers would have brought ashore, in fact, a passenger was more apt to be infected coming ashore.

~16~

The passengers began to debark and as they did they dropped their baggage upon the levee. They stayed put until they decided on their next move. First to find food and shelter, and then to decide where they were going and how to get there. Doctor Carey went over to the nuns, introduced himself and asked if their Order could help him get the sick to medical care. They assured him that they would help in any way that they could. At that point one of the Sisters introduced her companions, "Doctor Carey, I would like you to meet Mrs. Monica Garvin and her two boys and her daughter. They are here to meet Mr. Garvin, have you made his acquaintance? They have come to meet every ship from Ireland in the past week. Do you know if he is aboard this one?"

The doctor stammered. He turned and spotting Father Healy and called, "Father, Father Healy" and motioned for the priest to join them. "Father, this is Mrs. Monica Garvin and her children. They are here to meet Mr. Garvin."

"Oh," responded Father Healy somewhat startled. "Doctor, talk to the children for a minute, please, will you." Father Healy ushered the nuns and Mrs. Garvin aside and began, "Mrs. Garvin, your husband was aboard our ship, but—-but he's missing and it is assumed that he,— that he went overboard. It happened early in the voyage. I'm so sorry. You should talk to the captain, Captain Lynch, up there. He has your husband's luggage and will give you a written statement of his missing. I'm dreadfully sorry. I prayed for his soul. I did not meet him but I'm sure that he was a good man. I'm sorry."

Father Healy expected an outburst of sorrow and wailing, but saw none in either Mrs. Garvin or the Sisters. The older nun who introduced herself as Sister Marguerite asked Mrs. Garvin to join the children. She took the priest and the doctor aside and said, "Monica and her children ran away from Mr. Garvin and landed here six months ago. The boy, Charles is eight, his brother, Sean is ten, and their sister, Ella is twelve. Monica has been staying at the convent, and the children have been residing at the orphanage. Monica has been earning her keep by working in our kitchen and the orphanage. Over the last six months we have succeeded in instilling forgiveness in Monica's heart for the way her husband treated her and the children in his drunken rages. We were successful in giving her the Act of Forgiveness, but we have failed to remove the fear she, and for some reason, her daughter, has of Mr. Garvin. Two months ago, Monica received a letter from her husband stating that he had found them with the help of a private investigator and begged her for another chance. He stated that he would arrive in early June. We also feared for his arrival, but we prayed for the best, a reuniting and a new start. Now—-Now Monica must make a home of her own, somewhere, somehow, where the children can lead a normal life. I can only hope that now, Monica still has that forgiveness in her heart."

The doctor and priest were silent. Father Healy's mind was cluttered too quickly with the memory of the confession of Rose, an insight into the personality of John Garvin and the present predicament of the surviving Garvin family.

Doctor Carey looked over at Mrs. Garvin as she stood with her children as the other nun told, Charles, Sean and Ella what happened to their father. In Monica, he saw a slender woman of about forty five, erect posture with a look of frustration upon her otherwise very pleasant looking face.

"Well, Sister", started the priest," We have a couple of orphans aboard ourselves, and I had planned on presenting them to your Order's care. Their parents passed away during the voyage. I—-."

"Oh, Father, we will do what we can, we always do, but—-", she looked toward the Garvins and for some reason both the priest and the doctor started to feel a responsibility for the family.

"Sister, we have families in need of temporary quarters, and baths, and—-." started Father Healy.

"I will give you the names and addresses of such recommended establishments. Bring the orphans to me and Doctor, Father, perhaps you can think of a solution to the Garvins."

"A trade, so to speak", thought the Doctor.

The Walsh and Duddy family milled around their belongings once upon the dock, not knowing what to do next. They were hungry. They had money, English currency. Was it good and how much was it worth here? Who could they trust? Where do they go now? How do they get to Illinois? The children were restless, anxious to explore. Eddie said that he had to urinate. Daniel held his crotch and said, "Aye, Father." Richard took his two sons behind a board like fence behind which there was a shallow ditch. As Richard and his two boys returned, Father Healy and the doctor approached the group, with the Garvin family in tow. The priest held a scrap of paper upon which was a list of rooming houses that Sister Marguerite had given him.

"I have here a list of boarding houses. I think that you should look at them, unless of course, you have other plans", Father Healy offered. "Plans.", he thought. Suddenly he realized that he, himself, had none. Back in Galway, and throughout all of Ireland, priests had multiplied like rabbits and a smaller need for them arose as more and more of the faithful left for other lands. The Church decided that these souls may be leaving Ireland and the excess priests, especially the young ones, should follow their flock and nurture their devotion. The Church did not want to lose them wherever they ventured. He was the one chosen to embark on *Foley's Armada* and to follow those passengers that he determined most needed him and showed the most promise of propagating the faith. He had not thought of the details of his orders until now, and dismissed the thought temporarily as he introduced the widow Garvin to the Duddys and Walshs.

"I would like you to meet Mrs. Monica Garvin and her children. They of course were shocked and deeply saddened in hearing of the tragedy of Mr. Garvin."

Sympathies arouse from the group, Rose gasped with one hand on her heart, the other across her mouth. Richard's face was unemotional as he looked at the widow from a side glance. Father Healy, after making the introductions, seemed to glance encouragingly toward Richard and Rose when he elaborated, "They will need somewhere to start a new life."

"Where are you folks headed?", asked Doctor Carey, addressing the group. The doctor had no doubt that he would return to Galway on the return trip,— until he had seen Monica Garvin and had grown tired of serving aboard the coffin ships. Now he wondered if an oportunity for a new life for him was emerging.

"Illinois", boomed John Duddy. "We need to make arrangements for river passage as soon as possible, but first, we need to eat and drink and these vendors passing by with fruit and breads won't take our money."

The doctor and the priest, who for reasons unknown to themselves, started organizing each remaining group advising them and leading them to the closest bank, the few recommended boarding houses and then suggested that they all meet on the steps of the Cathedral the next morning after the 10 o'clock Mass. "You all will of course attend Mass, won't you," stated the Father Healy.

~17~

Father Healy was hungry and thirsty also, but he had a more burning desire for direction in his life as a young priest. After seeing his flock to their quarters, he headed to the Cathedral. There he had hoped to speak to the Bishop. After waiting for an hour he was ushered into a room and spoke to the assistant to the assistant to Monsignor Latour, a Father Archaumbault, who was very gracious. After the immigrant priest explained his reason for calling, Father Archaumbault said, "Father, I hope that you will forgive me for being so abrupt, but the fact is that we have no place for you here in New Orleans. New Orleans has no place for anyone, of any vocation. We have too many French, Spanish, Creoles, Mulattos, Germans, Italians, free Negroes, slaves, laborers, prostitutes, Kantucks, bankers, gamblers and yes, priests. What we could use are more Ursuline Nuns. They have been worth a hundred priests. Father—-"

"Healy, Father."

"Father Healy, you need to go up-river. You will be needed desperately to administer to the Catholic immigrants who have gone before you, those that came from Ireland with you and those that will surely come tomorrow and the next day. Urge those that you journeyed with to leave this city as soon as possible, lest they become stagnated. New Orleans isn't the land of milk and honey. It could be and may be someday if we could thin our ranks so this great city could instill some sense of order. Go upriver, Father, find your flock. It won't be difficult, believe me. Are you in need of funds?"

"No, Father, thank you, I am in need of purpose and to do God's will."

Father Archaumbault and Father Healy talked of the long voyage, the sickness and deaths, the conditions in Ireland, his admiration for Doctor Carey, the responsibility he and the doctor seemed to have acquired for the widow, Garvin, and the closeness he felt to some of the families, particularly the Duddys and the Walshs.

"Do these families that you speak of have a destination, Father Healy?"

"I believe some farmland near St. Louis, somewhere in Illinois."

"Then that is where you shall go. You will stay with us until your departure. I'm sure you will want to say Mass in the morning, Father. Allow me to show you to your quarters, they are rather meager and much used with the increasing flow of immigrant priests in recent years, mostly from Ireland, but many from other European countries. I am sure that you will welcome a bath and some clean clothes and a bite to eat later."

"Aye, Father, that I will."

Rose stood behind six other people in the hallway of Monahan's boarding house with her two reluctant boys, holding her infant son along with towels and a bar of sented, Lye soap waiting to enter the room with a bath tub. Eddie and Daniel took their baths first and when they emerged with dirty ears and dry heads, they were quickly turned around and admonished to wash thoroughly and quickly. When it came Rose's turn she slid into the still tepid water holding her infant son, Thomas, with his head over her shoulder. The water had not been changed for the last four baths. Rose soaped the baby and herself. She closed her eyes to the scum and relaxed except for her right arm around the baby. She had not felt this good since her last bath in their quarters on Squire Bentley's estate. It seemed so long ago.

At exactly seven thirty, Mrs. Monahan and her two daughters served dinner to her boarders, the Walsh and Duddy families and a half dozen other Irish immigrants who had resided there for several weeks. The newcomers were famished and beat the regulars to every pot. The new arrivals ate everything and later asked the names of most of the foods, the tomatoes, the peppers and watermelon and the pasta. Meanwhile Doctor Francis Thomas Carey had arranged for separate quarters for the Widow Garvin and her children and himself at the Magnolia Hotel and entertained them over dinner in the hotel's elegant Bayou Room.

~18~

After dinner the Garvin family retired to their room. When her children were sound asleep, Monica proceeded to go through her husbands luggage. Having emptied his clothing and toiletries, she came upon a canvas bag upon which was printed "Bank of England, Dublin Branch". Her eyes widened. Inside were coins, bank drafts and currency, and a scribbled note that she recognized as being in her husband's handwriting saying, "Place all the money in this bag and you won't be injured." Monica's heart beat at a rapid pace. She could not think or breathe. After gathering her composure, she counted the money. Over five thousand pounds! More money than she had ever seen. Her mind raced and so did her heart. She sat up all night clutching the money bag close to her breast, trying to hide it from eyes that were not in the room. She wrestled with the dilemma as to what to do with the money and whom to tell. She was sure John had stolen it, although on the other hand, she questioned that he had nerve enough to do such a thing so out in the open. Perhaps he stole it from a sleeping bank robber, she thought. He had never shown the courage to do something like this himself. He beat me and the children in private. He never hit us or used abusive language with us in public. He would have sexually molested my daughter, Ella, if I didn't walk in on him. He blamed me because I had not shown him the attention of a good wife. These thoughts raced through her head as she looked at the money.

She remembered that after she accosted her husband in the process of his vile, indecent act, Ella remained quiet and aloof from both her mother and her father. A feeling of distrust, suspicion and guilt flowed between mother and daughter. Only words of necessity were exchanged between them. His drinking and abuse worsened to the point that in his absence, she gathered up her children and left him.

~19~

New Orleans never slept. The sounds and scents pervaded every abode and the new immigrants lay in their beds sensing the city until all sounds and smells became so repetitious that the weary travelers drifted off, their stomachs full and their bodies nearly clean.

After an enormous breakfast, including grits and hominy, the Walsh family wanted to see as much of New Orleans as they could before going to Mass at the Cathedral. They walked through the dirt streets toward the visible steeples of the Cathedral. The nearer they came to the Cathedral, the more populated the streets became. Rose was told of the French Market and they decided to try to find that first. Ladies promenaded wearing with what Rose thought was an enormous amount of rouge and lipstick. They were dressed in bright blue, red, green or black flowing velvet dresses crowned with wide brimmed flowery hats below their ever present tiny parasol held with dainty laced gloves. Rose stumbled several times as she gaped at them with her mouth open. Richard also took notice, safely.

They could smell the market place from several blocks away and when they came upon the jumble of stalls they beheld one with caged or tied chickens, turkeys, geese and ducks, turtles and alligators with their snouts secured; another with fish of species they had never seen before. Wriggling crawfish, oysters, crabs, eels and snakes. Farther on were the fruit and vegetable vendors. The different types of food were matched by the different languages and dialects shouted by the vendors.

On their way back to the church they passed two gigantic hotels, the Saint Louis and the Creole, and noticed a small crowd around a pillared block. Someone else was hawking his wares. On drawing closer they saw a man in a black suit with a black hat describing an elderly negro man.

"Come on now, folks, I need a bid on this one. He's old, that's for sure, but at his age, he ain't gona run on ye!. His cotton picking days are gone, but if'in ye put a suit on him, let him grow a nice gray beard, he'd make a right nice butler or carriage driver. He came from the Morgan estate in Kantuck. Turn around there a little, Silas, show 'em how sprightly you can move."

Silas shuffled making a 360 degree turn without lifting a foot and had to hold on to the auctioneer who grimaced at the gesture.

"That's the oldest nigger I've ever seen on this block. How old do you figure he is?", asked one of the spectators.

The auctioneer heard that and shouted to the old slave, "How old are ye, Silas?" Silas, cupping his ear didn't hear what Aaron Frye the auctioneer asked. "Around forty- five, give or take a few," shouted the auctioneer. This brought a chuckle from the crowd and a smile to the face of Silas, who really didn't know how old he was, where he was born or who his parents were. He knew that he had answered to "Boy" when he was a child, then George when he was sold to a man named George Raddison about the time he could keep up with the other men in the fields. When he became too old and feeble to work the fields he was won in a card game by Silas Parker who owned a small section of land on the Kentucky side of the Ohio. Mr. Parker treated him well. His chores were in Mr. Parker's stables. Unfortunately, the breeding and training of fine thoroughbreds and particularly the habitual heavy betting by Silas Parker on his animals rather than focusing his attention to his sure money crop, cotton, led to his financial ruin and eventual suicide.

"Who'll give me fifty dollars. Fifty dollars, come on now."

Rose looked to Richard and asked, "Is that poor old fellow looking for work. Is this where people go to hire out?"

"To be sure, Rose, I don't know, I—"

"No lad", said a man standing next to them, "This is a slave auction. That old nigger is going to be owned lock stock and barrel by someone before this day is over. Ye, er new, arn't ye." Richard nodded affirmative. The old man was ushered off the block and the auctioneer called back for his next commodity.

"Did someone buy the old gentleman?", asked Rose.

"Gentleman!" scoffed the man next to Richard. "Nobody wanted him, but he'll be brought back up later." The man took enjoyment in educating the newcomers. "Aaron's a good one. He doesn't want to lose the buyer's interest. He'll throw in the old man with some salable nigger later."

A well proportioned middle aged mulatto woman reluctantly ascended the limestone steps to the block whereupon Mr. Frye, rubbing his hands together expectantly, continued to hawk his wares. "Sarah, here is a right fine buy. More fine qualities than I can reveal out here in the open. She's as strong as an ox, good teeth, and look at those hands, hard and calloused from picking cotton, straight back, and gentlemen, as I said, a right nice figure under all of that," pulling her dress up to show her ankles. "She came from the same estate as the old man. Here's a grand opportunity to pick up a field hand, good cook, nanny, or—-, who'll give me five hundred!"

At that point a girl of about twelve came running up the block with tears in her eyes grabbing the woman's skirt and yelling, "Mom, make them take me with you." Both mother and daughter looked over to the surprised auctioneer as the girl pleaded, "Please, suh, please, she's me mother!"

The auctioneer's assistant quickly drug the screaming girl back to the other waiting slaves as her mother stood erect with tears streaming down her cheeks. The child's screams became muffled.

"Well, that little gal has a lot of spunk, folks. She'll be up later. Just a little preview of what we got back there for you. Now, I got five hundred, who'll give me six?"

The woman was purchased by a man wearing a large brim straw hat, riding boots and rough work clothing. He paid the assistant with a stack of bills. He then called his giant of a slave that had been standing next to him to bind the woman's wrists and lead her off to the side of the group as the buyer waited for the next offering.

Eddie and Daniel heard, but could not see what was going on and kept jumping up and down and asking questions. Rose and her husband were awed by the proceedings. Richard lifted one of the boys after the other on his shoulders. While Eddie was upon his father's shoulder, the auctioneer brought out a negro boy of about fifteen. There was fear in the negro's eyes as he looked at the auctioneer and surveyed the crowd nervously. Mr. Frye started on his next offering.

"Lookie hear folks; name's Jobe. This here boy is perfect, all except he's missing both of his little fingers, probably cut off in an accident. This one's got a lifetime of good hard work in him, and he's already learned his manners, look here," directed Aaron as he removed the boy's shirt and showed the crowd the healed over welts upon his strong, broad, back.

"That boys' not broken", spoke the man next to Richard. "He's a troublemaker, look at those eyes. Common thief he is. That's why his fingers are gone."

"This here's a prime specimen," started the auctioneer. "Make a good breeder too," directing his comment to the man who made the previous purchase.

At this point Richard put the boys down and they passed through the group and into the stream of pedestrians going to and fro who were taking no notice of the commonplace slave market. Richard and Rose were upset with what they had witnessed but wanted to know more about this slave business. Eddie protested their leaving, wanting to know what happened to the black boy, stating that he looked mean and evil. Rose wondered aloud what would happen to the poor little girl who had lost her mother. Daniel whimpered at hearing his mother's concern for the girl.

The slave block was in full view of the people dining in elegance on the verandah of the St. Louis Hotel. Rose noticed Doctor Carey and Monica Garvin and her children rising from their table. She waved and was sure Monica saw her but she failed to show any recognition. She made a mental note to discuss Monica Garvin and the good doctor with Catherine Duddy. She knew it would be of no use conversing with her husband on such a matter, instead she gave her infant son, Thomas, whom she had been carrying since they left the boarding house, to Richard as they headed toward the Cathedral.

As they entered St. Louis Cathedral, they were astounded by its size, the beautiful statues, the gold trappings, the number of saint-like Urseline Nuns attending, and again from the diversely dressed parishioners with their muffled rumblings of so many different languages before the Mass commenced. Although Richard was impressed with his surroundings, he thought of the abundance of wealth this church had amassed and the seemingly unlimited supply of food available in this New Orleans, the first city of their new country. He felt somewhat guilty to be in this strange new world. He thought of those still in Ireland. He knelt down and gave thanks to his God to whom he had not talked for a long long time. The Duddys arrived and took a seat in the same pew. A little later the doctor, preceded by the Garvin family entered a pew toward the front. Other recognizable people from *Foley's Armada* were also seen. Father Healy was among several other priests who entered the Sanctuary in preparation for the beginning of the Mass.

~20~

The Isabella

After Mass the Duddys, Walshs, the Garvin family, and Doctor Carey, gathered. Soon afterward Father Healy arrived.

The priest said, “Doctor Carey and I, according to your wishes for accommodation, have secured passage for Saint Louis on the steamboat *Isabella*. The soonest booking that I could get was for this Friday. The ship leaves at five in the evening and is to be docked at the foot of First Street. Oh, and we, (the doctor and Monica Garvin and her brood) are going with you. Since we may not see each other until then I want you to have your passage tickets now. Here, Richard, the cheapest passage I could buy, the infant is free.” As Father Healy passed out the rest of the tickets he continued; “Let us bow our heads. Oh Holy Father we pray that you will watch over this little group and others arriving in this land so that we will safely complete our journeys and be able to find freedom and contentment and be able to spread your word in this Delhi.” Father Healy then prayed silently, “If it isn’t too much to ask Lord, let Delhi be in need of this humble priest, and also an old but spirited doctor, Lord.”

“If I might make a suggestion, Father,” spoke Doctor Carey, “I would suggest that between now and then that you familiarize yourself as to where the *Isabella* is to be docked. The advertisement stated that the passage upstream would take ten to fifteen days, so plan accordingly as to provisions if you will not be supping in the steamboat’s dining room.”

After the priest departed and the doctor, along with Monica and her children, left; Catherine and Rose got their heads together and gossiped fiercely about the widow and Doctor Carey. John and Richard walked ahead.

"Listen to them back there, Richard. I tell ye, there is nothing like a good piece of gossip to restore life and purpose in a woman."

Richard smiled and said "Aye, right ye are. Did you notice now the spring of a willow branch in that old man's step lately. He even looks younger. He has young ideas, John. It does appear that the thought of a made family agrees with him. I do hope that the widow Garvin is not out to take advantage of him."

"She seems a bit hard to figure now, doesn't she."

"That she does. Look at us, now, agossiping away faster the them back there."

They walked near the slave block again. Daniel came up to his father, "Can we stop and see what happened to that black thief? Can we?"

"No lad, we haven't the time, and listen, you're not to believe everything that man said. Go on now with the boys."

Richard explained to John what they had witnessed and John in disbelief walked with his head turning toward the crowd at the auction block. They arrived at the foot of First Street and looked for the steamboat Isabella to no avail. John asked a sailor aboard the ship next to the dock and was informed that the steamboat was scheduled to arrive from St. Louis that evening and would probably leave again Friday after unloading and reloading.

As they turned away relieved, Richard saw a dray pull up to the adjoining dock. Alongside rode the planter with the straw hat and upon the dray sat the bound Creole woman that he bought, without her daughter, and the frightened boy labeled a thief, the old man, Silas, and the planter's Negro, who displayed an authoritative air. The planter rode his horse upon the gangplank of the steamboat and the four Negroes, three still bound, followed.

The two men discussed what they knew and didn't understand regarding slavery and Negroes on their way back to the Irish Channel section.

Late Friday afternoon, the Walshs and the Duddys carried their belongings aboard the steamboat *Isabella* and were directed somewhat forward of the paddle wheel on the main deck to a small area next to bales of cotton. Next to the cotton was stacked fire wood for the boilers. Rose worried about the boys proximity to the water with no railing to prevent them from falling overboard, just spars supporting the main deck. She remarked to whoever would listen, "This boat doesn't look safe to me. If it rocks and pitches like the one we crossed on the ocean we're goners." They had seen other steamboats along the wharf, some looking very elegant with music coming from them and others that looked shabby, meant to carry lumber and supplies only. The *Isabella* fell somewhat in the middle. The steamboat that was next to theirs earlier, with the newly purchased slaves and their owner, was gone.

Richard and John had decided previously that they should conserve their funds thereby electing not to take cabins knowing fully what type of quarters, or lack of, they would have. They surmised that the trip up river would be more gentle and not take as long as their ocean crossing and more importantly that they would be in need of funds until they could earn some.

The boys were anxious to explore the boat and were waved on as their parents shuffled their belongings close to the bulkhead and sat down on the deck to watch the deck hands readying for departure. They watched men and women of high fashion ascending the gangplank followed by their servants, some of which were slaves, and some free blacks. Deck hands directed common laborers who migrated from one departing or arriving ship to another loading crates marked from England containing china, machine parts and cutlery from Germany, fine leather goods from Italy and silks and spices from the Orient, sugar and tobacco from the Carolinas, all of these goods being squeezed into available spaces some infringing on the main deck passenger's space.

A crude pen containing three geese and one containing two piglets were placed by the Duddy's luggage by a dirty, bewiskered, smelly old man. The man left the boat only to return quickly leading a goat which he tied to one of the spars. He then spread a tattered coat over the pen containing the pigs and sat down pushing his much soiled felt hat back on his forehead revealing rumpled gray hair. His beard was soiled with tobacco juice which he spit out haphazardly.

Richard nudged John, "Tis a shame but did ye notice, he's going to be up wind."

"Right ye are. It will remind us of home, it will. And did you notice that the spices and tobaccos went to the other side of the boat."

"I never thought that the smell of pigs and geese would someday be welcome", replied Richard. "The smell of this river is not to my liking." Garbage, paper, cotton wads, pieces of wood and some animal feces floated on the water's surface attracting flies and other insects along with mosquitos. It had rained throughout the spring as it always did in New Orleans producing mud holes, promoting a large crop of mosquitos, disease, fevers, flooded waterways and levee brakes. It was not yet learned that the mosquito along with filthy sanitary conditions fostered the dreaded yellow fever and other diseases.

The Duddy boy, Joseph, came running up to his mother, "We saw Father Healy and the doctor up on the next deck and got to see Mrs. Garvin's cabin. It's grand, Mum. You should see the swell clothes some of those people wear up there. And we saw the room where they eat, Mum, a big large fancy place with flowers and all. Then we were run out. How grand it was."

Joseph became aware of his new neighbor and his animals. He peered into the pens for a better look. One cage held six fluffy brown puppies.

"Hello there, young feller. Does yah like animals?" asked the old man smiling at Joseph and the adults behind him, spitting after every sentence. His smile parted his lips and allowed tobacco juice to spill out of his toothless head onto his once gray beard. "Name's Jake, Jake Collins. I'm on my way back to my little spread of land up North of Cairo, Illinois. Every Spring me and some other fellows build us a raft, put a little shanty on it, load it up with our corn, calves, porkers, chickens, cheese, fox, muskrat, rabbit furs, a couple of barrels of pickles and a couple kegs of the best darn whiskey you ever tasted and float down river to New Orleans. We can't float the remains of the raft back upstream, so's we leave it for wood scavengers and take the cheapest steamboat back home. I've a prize goat here to breed an so is those pigs and geese. My friends decided to stay and spend their money on the dance halls and women. Mine's going back into my farm. Where you folks from and where you a goin?"

As soon as Rose heard that Mr. Collins was from Illinois she was alarmed and certainly reluctant for this old dirty tramp to know that they had the same destination, but then she sensed a form of responsibility about him. John Duddy told Mr. Collins of their destination. Collins said that he had heard of St. Louis but never of this Delhi. He offered John and Richard a bite of his tobacco which they politely refused. Joseph was anxious to try some but his father refused for him. Mr. Collins offered the men a drink of his own makings of whiskey and they accepted not wanting to offend and thinking, as they soon found out, that it was strong enough to kill any germs coming from its maker. They agreed that they had tasted better back home, but this wasn't bad. After several swallows they also agreed that the smell of the animals and their keeper was deminishing. Mr. Collins started to tell them the ingredients and his distilling process.

At that moment a shrieking whistle came from both steam pipes, bells were clanged and a mate by the gangplank cupped his hands and tried to shout over the noise for all passengers to come aboard. Whistles and the ringing of bells could be heard from nearby steamboats and the sounding of pistons from all the noisy boats came alive. The *Isabella*'s stern moved away from the dock with the paddle wheels slapping the dirty water and the black smoke billowing from its two chimneys, and when clear of neighboring boats the *Isabella* backed out into the main stream of the Mississippi slipping downstream with the current until suddenly the pilot ordered full power and the boat quaked and groaned under the strain. The boat started to right itself and moved slowly upstream against the current. A number of other steamboats could be seen forward and aft of the *Isabella* maneuvering in the same fashion. It seemed that all of them were leaving New Orleans at the same time, early evening being normal departure for most scheduled steamboats.

Mr. Collins entered into a conversation with one of the mates and Richard and John talked about the differences between the *Foley's Armada* and the boat that they were on. The fact that there were no sails, no large waves, supposedly a much shorter voyage, better and more food and better quarters even though they had no beds. They agreed that the smell from the nearby pigs and geese and their keeper smelled like the sweetest flower compared to the stench below decks on the *Armada*. They also agreed that what they would most desire now was some privacy with their wives. They had none crossing the ocean, none at Mrs. Monahan's boarding house and none likely in the near future.

"Anyway, Richard, isn't it a bit too early for you and Rose?"

"Aye, it is, but not for long."

~21~

Within the next several hours the shore line became more distant as the river broadened; however, at times the deepest current brought the Isabella right up to the levee where those peering off the starboard side could see the vast plantations and their buildings five to ten feet below the river's surface. This amazed Richard. To him it appeared to be a bridge of water over land. Some of the workers in the fields stopped what they were doing to see the steamboat passing above them, some wishing that they were aboard, some wondering where the boat was going, some worried that the wake made by the steamship may erode the levee and some raised up and looked just to see something different than the drudgery they had been faced with for some hours. One plantation after another fanned out from the river on both shores and would from New Orleans to Natchez. Over the many years the river had supplied the rich soil. That soil grew an abundance of cotton, sugar cane and tobacco. Without the slaves to plant and harvest these crops there would have been no plantations.

As evening came the moon seemed to hide behind one small cloud after another. The sounds of water splattering and then dripping off the paddle wheels, and the never ceasing sound of the engine's pistons throbing, and the dogs on shore barking was to the Irishmen a symphony of the land of milk and honey. Later, the curse words to the pilot from a flat boatmen trying his best to avoid a collision on his way downstream could not be heard over the music, laughter and conversation emitted from the dining room until well past midnight.

Occasionally fires on both shores shone through the darkness indicating where there was a wood supply for those steamboats in need. The pilots of these scheduled steamboats were all experienced in running the river at night and were brought up to date daily on new or moved snags, submerged sand bars, existing sawyers, or an overabundance of floating debris. Even so the speed was drastically reduced and watches were always posted forward to look for problems and taking measurements of the depth of the water often. Metal fire buckets were extended on both sides of the bow to illuminate the water ahead.

At five in the morning, with just a hint of daylight off starboard, the engines slowed, the deck hands scrambled waking up all able bodied men on the main deck, and the *Isabella* turned toward a small fire on shore up ahead that was kept forever burning by an enterprising woodcutter. "Wake up, lads, here's where we earn a few coins," offered Mr. Collins, "we're goin to load up some wood for the boilers. The old boat has to take on fuel twice a day and some of the less prosperous plantations are in the fire wood business."

As soon as the boat was secured to the bank, roustabouts on board, including John, Richard and Jake, rushed ashore caring as much wood as possible. They stacked their loads as neatly as time allowed on the deck near the boilers. Black skinned, bare chested, free Negroes released temporarily from the boiler room were among the wood carriers. They relished the change from laboring in front of the sweltering boilers. When the boat took on as much wood as it could store, all hands returned on board. The sky was now much brighter and in turning around, looking back toward the shore, Richard saw a man riding a horse herding his Negroes away from the fire signal back toward the waiting fields. He was sure that the man on the horse was the same man that bought the slaves back in New Orleans. Richard kept his eye on the rider and as the steamboat powered itself into the main channel and headed upstream. The rider galloped his horse toward the shore, turned his horse up stream and down, prancing. He rode back to his slaves, looking at them briefly then rushing toward shore again before being lost from Richard's sight. The man on the horse was irritated by something. He seemed to be looking for something lost.

The early rising gentlemen on the boiler deck looked upon the stop for wood with interest and amusement and a form of entertainment.. Few if any ladies were out of their cabin at that hour. Lengthy preparation was necessary before their appearing in public. After the *Isabella* pulled away from the landing and as the entertainment was over, the gentlemen took tables in the dining room for breakfast. Dr. Carey and Father Healy sat together and in time were served bacon, sausages, ham, potatoes, grits, eggs cooked to their wishes, rolls, pastries, fruits, and the strongest coffee that they had ever tasted.

"Father, do you not find it inconceivable that we should be on this boat, going to a place far up-river, to a land we have never heard of before only because Catherine Duddy has relatives there?"

"Yes, that it does, Doctor, especially in your case. You had a position of respect, although I can understand your tiring of the pestilence surrounding you on every voyage. I had no definite plans upon leaving Ireland nor did most on board the ship. The purpose of most of those poor wretches was to leave the terrible conditions for something better, anywhere. And here we are, much more educated and intelligent than the Duddys and the Walshs and the Garvin family, following them. We seem to be drifting like a seed on wind with a blind faith that Almighty God is directing us. I also wonder why I still feel for some unknown reason, as I'm sure you do, some responsibility for their safe keeping. At the same time I'm concerned that there will be a place for us. 'Tis strange, but I find the uncertainty a bit exciting also, don't you? A new land, a bountiful land, a land with a future, action everywhere. Why I overheard two gentlemen last night discussing their plans to venture far west of here and hunt for gold. Gold, mind you! One said if they find the right spot, all they have to do is bend down and pick it up! Imagine that."

"Sounds as though you are becoming interested in material things, Father."

"Not at all. My job is with those who put material things before God, and it looks as though there will be a real need of my services in this land. By the way, Doctor, I have nothing but admiration for the benevolent interest that you have shown the widow Garvin and her children. You have been—-"

"I'm afraid Monica Garvin's decision to accept Catherine and Rose's invitation to come with them to start a new life is the main reason that I am here now rather than back in New Orleans and returning to Ireland for another cargo of hopefuls. I don't know if you have noticed, Father, but I feel like a young man when I am around her. I have been stricken with her quiet beauty. I may be an old fool, but for the moment I'm a happy fool when I can provide for her. I know that she has no love for me, Father. She's so quiet and somewhat mysterious, and her children seem so distrustful of everyone, yet they are very courteous. The mystery around her only enhances her beauty. I have difficulty in getting her to talk very much. She seems neither sad or happy."

"Perhaps this is her way of mourning. I do hope that you will allow sufficient time for her to mend on the loss of her husband before you advance your feelings."

"Although as I said, I feel like a young man. I know fully well that the feeling is all up here," pointing to his temple. "I don't have a great deal of time left, Father. What would you call a proper wait?"

"Well now, that's a good one. The poor woman lost her husband, his finncial support, and in a tragic way too, I—-"

"That was a somewhat strange happening now, wasn't it, Father. What do you suppose happened, the sea wasn't rough that night."

Father Healy's hand trembled as he raised his coffee cup to his lips and after supping, steadied the cup's decent with his left hand with the doctor's notice.

"I can't really say. He could have been delirious, sea sick and disoriented, or he could have been suicidal."

"Or there could have been foul play. Father are you feeling well?"

"Yes. I mean, yes, I am feeling well, and I suppose we can't rule out foul play. I say, Doctor, wasn't that a grand breakfast. Are we to expect the likes at every meal?"

"I do hope so. I wonder what kind of man Garvin was to deserve such a woman, and how difficult it would be for one to take his place. Is my love sick part of this conversation making you nervous, Father?"

"No, No," said the priest smiling embarrassedly.

"You're a handsome man, and young too. I'm sure you have had some strong feelings toward a woman from time to time, Father. How do you deal with that?"

"Oh, Doctor Francis Thomas Carey. As soon as the slightest hint of such a feeling surfaces, I pray, and pray and pray. Sometimes for longer periods than others. Usually constant prayer will abate the thoughts that men in my profession must suppress. And when that doesn't work I do some strenuous work. Now then, let's stretch our legs, shall we?"

They walked to the forecastle catching the humid breeze and watched the bow of the ship part the muddy water. Two well dressed gentlemen stood next to them enjoying their cigars. The men were engaged in a conversation regarding the pros and cons of slavery. They were without the Southern accent and from the gist of the conversation it was evident to the two eavesdropping immigrants that these two men, in theory, were against any human bondage but saw a total collapse of the South's economy, and the nation's, without slavery. Who else, they surmised, would work long hours for nothing, nary a one of the hordes of immigrants. They marveled, however disdainfully, at the similarities between breeding cattle to multiply one's herd, selling off the excess of the choice beef and the less desirable, and the fact that with slaves, an owner did not have to contend with the petty complaints and demands of a paid employee. They finished this particular conversation agreed that major changes and conflicts were on the horizon as the two men moved away from the priest and the doctor.

"Well, Father, here's a material problem for you. How do you feel about human bondage for the good of this country?"

"Ah!, An old problem for us Irish isn't it now, but ours was not nearly of this magnitude. We thought that we had it bad. Just think of what these slaves feel; and they must feel it, they're human beings! I feel that there is only one that man should worship and offer himself to, unconditionally, God Almighty, the One who created all of us—all of us!. And we are not slaves to Him. He gave us a mind to choose Him or not."

"Yes, Father, but imagine that you were one of these plantation owners who had purchased these Negroes, paid good money for them, counted on them to bring in your crops, help provide your higher status in this country, and someone told you that it was wrong for you to have this, this tool. How then must you feel?"

"Hmm, a strong question. If I were only doing what my neighbors, friends, and parents were doing, and have done, and the law of the land approved, I would question this person's reasoning. On the other hand I think that if I allowed myself, which I most probably wouldn't have, to think a great deal upon the right and wrong of it between myself and another human being, I would in my heart agree with that person, but for only an instant, and then for my conscience sake I would avoid the issue when ever I could."

"Well, Father, that's a very thoughtful and honest reply. We do tend to push some of those conscience tearing issues out of mind, don't we."

"Our waiter, back there; do you suppose he was a slave? He is dressed well, and is very articulate and courteous. He spoke French at one table and German at another. You know, Father I was almost tempted to ask him if he was a slave. How does one know?"

"I don't know. I've heard that some packet owners have slaves in the boiler rooms of their boats, others do not. Some of the Negroes, like back on the docks, are free and some are trusted slaves that are hired out by their owners. We are in a strange world; one of many languages and customs. I suppose as immigrants, our people are looked upon as only a step above these negroes and perhaps a step below them as unskilled laborers and field hands, expecting to be paid for their work."

"That Walsh boy, Daniel, he couldn't help but cry as he told me of his witnessing a slave auction before Mass last Sunday. Something about a mother and her daughter being separated."

"Monica and I could see it from our table at the hotel. A dreadful thing, yet she found it somewhat fascinating. Well, look, here she comes now. Father, I think I shall join her and her children for another breakfast."

It would be another hour and a half before the bus boys would gather up the food that was left and descend to the main deck to distribute breakfast to the passengers there, without the finery of silver utensils and china. Afterwards the deck passengers washed their containers by linking them on rope and lowering the collection into the muddy current of the Mississippi. These utensils were prized possessions, as were the chamber pots, still used discreetly behind blankets or bales, the contents thrown overboard near the aft of the boat.

-22-

After breakfast the boys scampered off to chase each other throughout the boat, running up the forward stairs, along the isles and back down the forward stairs, some descending on one side of the curving stairs trying to catch or escape the other, and becoming a nuisance to the adult passengers. Eventually they decided to form teams and play a form of hide and seek. Eddie broke away fast and found a place on the main deck aft behind some bales of cotton and kegs. He waited and waited for his pals to make it interesting by at least coming close which they did not. His friends lost interest in the game as the steamboat pulled toward shore and tied up rather loosely at a small dock belonging to the "Green" plantation, right south of the entrance of the Red River. Eddie's playmates watched the proceedings as two men left the boat with crates that they brought from New Orleans containing French wine and elegant china from Germany. Some roustabouts brought on board four bundles of tobacco and sacks of sugar. Eddie became impatient waiting in his hiding place and inquisitive and as he rose from behind the bales and kegs his eyes fell on two brown hands, with wrist tied gripping the end a lengthy rope looped over a spar. He recognized the hands first, each without their small fingers. Almost afraid to look at the face, he saw the evil looking young, thieving slave from the block. Jobe, the slave, had grasped the deck and was trying to climb out of the water. Eddie was frantic and began kicking at Jobe's hands trying to knock them free from the bottom rail. Jobe pleaded, "Please, Master, please help me." Eddie kept kicking, somewhat bewildered at someone calling him Master but still scared to death that this person would come and harm him, "Go away! go away! You're a thief and a slave, go away!" Eddie more frightened than ever ran to tell his father. Excitedly, Eddie came upon Jake Collins and his father in conversation over Jake's animals. "Father!, Father, I've seen him, he's trying to get on this boat! You've got to do something, come!"

"Settle down lad, seen who, where?"

"The slave we saw in New Orleans! He must have run away, the one with his fingers cut off, he's—-"

"Sh!', responded Jake quickly with his finger over his mouth and his other hand over Eddie's mouth. "If what the lad says is true, this is very serious. He's a runaway. I don't know what your feelings are about this slavery issue, Richard. You see, in this country the law is on the side of the slave owner. They passed a compromise law just last year allowing the masters to capture their runaways and provided for heavy fines and jail sentences for those among us who would harbor them, you see. Now I never thought this slavery was right and have been of some help in the past to these creatures. Evidently we have one hanging on the boat back there and we three now know it. What say you, Mr. Walsh? Do we turn 'em in? There may be a large reward for him!"

"We've got to turn him in, Father, he's evil!"

"Quiet, son. I'll try to explain to ye later, but from now on as long as I can help anyone from becoming a slave to another man, I will. I've seen enough of that. That lad was beaten badly, many times. He may be evil, we will know shortly. Now let's see if this lad is truly the same one. Mind you now, no one else must know, understand son? This is our secret, not even your brother or your mother, hear me?"

"Yes, Father, but——"

"Show us where this boy is, lad, very casual like, now, and remember what your father said, unless you want us all to go to jail."

Eddie showed disappointment and bewilderment for only a moment, then hurriedly grasp his father's hand and tried to run with him.

"Slowly, lad, cautioned Jake. Two men were talking at the rail and as they passed them, Jake said, "Look over there at that great plantation, Eddie, "Looks like a grand place. Now where was this big fish you saw." The two river men laughed.

As they came to the spot where Eddie confronted the slave, there was nothing. No rope, no slave. Richard and Jake looked at each other, then Jake saw the water drippings and what looked like puddles of blood leading from a rail a few feet away to behind the bales and kegs that Eddie had hidden behind. As Eddie stood watching for anyone coming by, Richard and Jake peered behind the bales and saw the slave squatting and looking up at them with the same fear in his eyes that Richard saw on the slave block. His hands were clasp as if praying. His wrists were bleeding where the rope had been tied. His knees were bleeding.

"How,—-How did you get here. How did you get away", asked Richard softly. "Don't be afraid, now, lad. We want to help. How did you do it."

"Ise slipped into the water way back there when the boat took on wood. I broke loose from the whipping post the night before and hid along the river in the tall grass, and when this boat stopped, Ise walked in the mud and swam out in the gray light to the river side of the ship and with my hands still tied together. I inched my way along to a spar where I managed with the length of rope to tie myself to a board over there. Don't make me go back, Masters, I'd a rather die!"

"Well, I expect you might just do that boy, if'n we don't get you fixed up," responded Jake. "Stand up some, and turn around."

The slave stood with pain and turned his back to the two men enough that they saw fresh thong gashes over his already scared back.

Eddie shouted, "There's the fish I told you about out there father!", hoping that the men that they had previously passed would hear him.

The men shoved the slave back behind his cover telling him they would be back soon, and joined Eddie at the rail.

Richard sent Eddie to find Doc Carey and tell him that his father wanted to see him right on, and emphasized that that was all Eddie was to tell the doctor except that his father would meet him at the foot of the stairs, forward, and reminded him once more not to breathe a word of this to anyone, his brother, mother, no one.

The *Isabella* finished her business of loading and unloading at the "Green" plantation. The port paddles were thrown in reverse turning the bow of the boat out into the current and with whistles shrieking and horn blasting and an order from the pilot for full steam ahead, the steamboat struggled against the water to regain full power, leaving the small dock quivering in its wake. Eddie found Dr. Carey in the dining room sitting at a table with the Garvin family. He did as he was told. The doctor excused himself and followed the boy down the staircase and up to Richard's side. Richard dismissed his son and drew the doctor away from nearby passengers.

"Doc, I don't know how to say this but there is a man aft that needs your help. He's a —-"

"Well, lets have a look at him, go on."

"No, first let me tell you. E's a slave. He's run away. I saw him sold on the block in New Orleans. Somehow he escaped from his new master, attached himself to this boat with a line yesterday and hung on in the water ever since then, until Eddie saw him an hour ago. I'm told it would be bloody trouble if we were caught helping him. He's bleeding around the wrist and all over his body where he's been slammed against the side of the boat, and worse he's been whipped severely on his back. Will you help him?"

"I'll do what I can, but what then, Richard, what then? This country has laws, yet—-. Take me to him. No first let me go and get my provisions. I won't bring my bag, too revealing. I'll be right back." Doctor Carey hurried up to his cabin, feeling self conscious with every step and getting angry at himself for feeling so. In his cabin he gathered the medications he deemed necessary according to Richard's description of the man's wounds and placed them in a cloth sack. As he closed the door to his cabin he headed for the stairs. He thought back to his conversation with Father Healy only hours ago as to what they might do and feel if they were personally involved in this slavery thing. Yes, he would treat this poor soul, but after that, would or could he brush the incident aside without making a commitment one way or another? One thing at a time, he thought as he met Richard and was led to the young slave. Jake followed them but not too closely and stood guard at the rail as the doctor tended to Jobe's wounds with an assist from Richard. Jobe's wet, tattered, clothing were removed and stashed away till nightfall when they would be slipped into the river. He remained naked until Jake returned later with one of his old shirts and a pair of trousers.

Jake, Richard, and the doctor stood together at the rail contemplating their plans regarding Jobe, wondering whom else they could bring into confidence. It was decided that Jake would bring food to him at the next mealtime. The slave must remain where he is for now and they hoped and prayed that the cargo hiding him would not be removed at the next docking. He would have to be hidden somewhere else or disguised soon. They worried about Eddie not being able to keep their secret. Richard would inform his wife, Rose. They worried about telling John and Catherine Duddy without being sure as to where their sympathies lie. The other children shall not be told. Doctor Carey would confer with Father Healy. Eddie returned to playing with the other boys, but his mind was on the slave. He hated him more than he had ever hated anyone before. He didn't know why. He was torn between his desire to be rid of this evil man and the fear that his parents and friends would be punished if he told anyone of their protecting him.

Doctor Carey entered the priest's cabin and told Father Healy about the new passenger. Father Healy listened intently and toward the end of the Doctors report asked, "Is the man Catholic? Oh, forget I said that! The Saints be with us, Doctor. This is a very dangerous situation. What does this Jake fellow say is to be done?"

"Jake Collins is his name. He's definitely against slavery and stated that there are numerous people who help runaway slaves escape to the North part of the country. They hide and comfort them along the way providing shelter until they reach a safe destination. He also stated that there are bounty hunters who make it a business of finding these runaways and return them to their owners, or occasionally do away with them. If captured it's the law in the Northern areas that they be returned."

"Well, we will have to find one of these persons who know how to help this lad, won't we?"

Richard confronted his friend, John Duddy with the problem. John had not been involved in any discussion on the matter of slavery. He looked upon the Negroes that he saw as just another strange looking human being inhabiting this fine new country. He had heard so many different languages and dialects, and seen so many different skin pigments since arriving and did not trouble himself with knowing or understanding more about them until he himself was settled.

"This is a dangerous and unlawful thing that you're doing from what you have told me. I want no part of it. All I want is for me and my family to settle down in this country and live a peaceful and bountiful life. I'm not going to risk that for some savage who has broken the law. He's taken you all in, he has! No, I don't want to hear another word of this deed. Think about what you and the others are doing, Richard. My family comes first, and so should yours."

"Aye, John, right you are about your family. I placed my family first back home, where I did things that I detested, and against me own people, in order that my kin would not starve. I'll never be able to forget that. Never. And I'd do it again, John. Before the famine, you and I fought as we could for our country's freedom. To have the right to worship, or not worship as in my case. To learn to read and send our children to school. To own books, man! To own land. We fought to be free of our slavery to the English rule. If the famines had not come, we might have won. Now, I don't know much about these black people, except a great many of them are in bondage. If I am caught and sent to prison, or executed, for that matter, I know that my family will not starve in this land. They will survive. I feel that I can afford to risk my skin to do what I can for this one singular person. John, I appreciate your frankness, and I will not try to sway you, but do say that you will not report us or hinder our attempts."

"You have my word, Richard. You also have my prayers. I hope that this mess will soon pass. We will be worried until it does."

-23-

None of the conspirators slept that night. With each stop to take on wood, cargo or passengers, Jobe and his band of amateur abolitionists would become anxious. The next morning after Father Healy said Mass at the head of the stairs leading down to the main deck with only a smattering of passengers present, he and Doctor Carey met for breakfast. They sat silently listening to the voices around them for any indication that any of their fellow diners would look favorably on their unlawful undertaking. They had the same waiter as the morning before. He moved graciously, almost feminine like. As before, he spoke many languages in conversing with the diners. He was tall and slender with light brown skin and when not carrying trays he would accentuate his conversation with rapid movement of his arms, especially dropping his right hand at the wrist joint as one of those fine ladies in New Orleans did when carrying their hand bag.

Doctor Carey motioned to the waiter to drop his head to within whispering level and bluntly asked, "Young man, would you tell us,— are you a slave?"

Father Healy choked on his coffee. The waiter broke out in resounding laughter. Amid his laughter, the waiter, moving toward the priest asked seriously, "Are you alright, Father?" The diners nearby chuckled slightly thinking a humorous story was told.

Doctor Carey frowned with concern at his partner, then smiled sheepishly at the waiter and whispered, " I meant no harm, sir. We're new to this land and wondered how one was to know which of your race are free and which are not. Please don't be offended." Father Healy recovering, nodded agreement.

Spreading both of his hands on the table exhibiting fingers covered with glittering rings he spoke softly, "Gentlemen, all you have to do is look at the Negro's face and his clothes and how he carries himself to know if he was born free, like myself. Those who have been slaves don't dare go anywhere far from home without papers to prove they are free men. The former slaves, may look like the ones who were born free, but they are always looking over their shoulder. One can almost see the past in their eyes: At least, I can. Most of the Negroes in slavery are on the plantations, or at the wood stops here in the South. Near all of the slaves you will find an overseer, black or white, with a whip, rod, or a rope in his hand. More coffee, Gentlemen?"

"Yes, please. The doctor here—-"

"Oh, you're a physician!"

"Yes, he is and a fine one too. We have heard about, and have been, what you might say, troubled, or ah, interested in slaves that run away." This time it was the doctor who fumbled nervously with his coffee. The nearby diners had left but their conversation with the waiter was at a whisper.

Smiling, the waiter asked, "Might you two gentlemen be thinking of taking up bounty hunting?"

"No, no! Nothing of the kind", answered the Doctor. "How, ah, how do you tell the bounty hunters from the people wanting to help the runaway?"

Trying to control a burst of laughter he said, "Well, you two have some odd questions. You're not bounty hunters, that's certain, but I don't believe you've made up your minds whether you want to be Abolitionist or in favor of slavery. Which is it going to be, gentlemen?"

"Well," ventured the Doctor, "We would like to talk to someone we could trust that is a, what would you call him, an Abolitionist who helps these runaways."

"Why, Doctor?"

"Why,—well ah, well, we may know someone who can use his services."

"You don't say! Gentlemen. We have talked enough on this dangerous subject, especially here." Speaking louder, the waiter asked, "more eggs, gentlemen?"

"No, thank you", responded Father Healy.

"Well, then, a good morning to you both. If you should desire service in your quarters, a cool drink before dinner perhaps, around four, send a boy for me, my name is, Alfredo. It would be my pleasure to serve you."

Walking away from their table and out into the cooler morning breeze at the bow, Father Healy asked, "What do you make of, Alfredo?"

"I don't know, but I think we shall order a drink at four in your cabin, and hope it's a refreshing one!"

The doctor and the priest decided later that they needed Richard at this meeting, if indeed it was to be a meeting. Father Healy went below to talk to him. Richard was amazed to hear how foolishly outspoken they were to this, Alfredo, a stranger, but agreed to be present. He strongly suggested that Jake, even though odorous as he was, be included. Richard also suggested the ruse of a card game.

As lunch was being served in the dining room the *Isabella* steered toward shore and docked again at what looked to be a large plantation. Cargo went ashore and replacements came aboard. More bailes of cotton were placed on deck close to where the slave was left. All members of the "Jobe Conspiracy" became anxious hoping the slave would be able to move from one cover to another if it became necessary. As the boat returned to the river's current and no shout of alarm was heard they returned to what they were doing.

-24-

Doctor Carey sat Monica Garvin at a table and arranged to have her three children seated at a table close to theirs, but not too close. Monica sat erect. She was dressed entirely in drab black, looking like the immigrant Irish woman that she was; wearing a shawl over her head, a long sleeve blouse, puffed at the shoulders, closed tight around her neck. She wore a skirt that reached down all but covering her black shoes. The skirt and blouse were not tight, but not so loose as to hide her trim, rounded figure. To the doctor she looked radiant. She smiled at him graciously as he sat down, her large blue eyes emitting a pleasant and satisfying feeling from her. She was beginning to like this kind old man. She had not been shown such attention since first meeting her husband, so long ago that it was but a faint memory.

"Well now, don't you look grand, Mrs. Garvin. What have you and the children been doing since I last saw you?"

"Doctor, please call me Monica. You have been so kind to us and I consider you, at the very least, my closest friend. I have come to sense, and I pray, that you do not look upon me as that widow, Garvin." Without waiting for him to answer, she continued, "The two boys have been romping all over with the Duddy and Walsh lot working up an appetite. I hope they're in good company. Ella, as you have noticed is the quiet one. She has found some books in the parlor about this United States and has engrossed herself in them. I spent a great deal of time this morning wondering about the future, Doctor. My, but it is warm and humid isn't—"

"Now, Monica, I would appreciate it if you would dispense with the "Doctor" and call me, Francis. Have you made any decision about your future, I'm very interested?"

"Well, Doctor, I mean, Francis, that sounds so odd, me calling you that. Well, Francis, I'm not a farmer. I have done some clerking and I am pretty good with needle and thread. I thought that I might find employment in one of the towns as a clerk in a bank or as a seamstress. I want my children to have an education."

"I have heard that this Saint Louis is a very large city. And it has a holy name, although, French. I have also heard that a few miles farther is Alton, and that it is a thriving community, although much smaller than Saint Louis. Either of them should hold opportunities for you and your children, but as of now I think I shall explore this, Alton. I would be most pleased if you did also. Please don't think me forward, Monica, I seem to have a bluntness lately in asking questions, but, financially, how did your husband leave you. Can I be of any help?"

Monica froze at the question and before her eyes was the knapsack back in her cabin lying open with the money spilling out of it. She started to speak, a stutter or two and the doctor quickly placed one hand on her shoulder and took her hand in his, "Forgive me. Please forgive me, I have no right to delve into your affairs, I've upset you and I'm sorry. I'm such a fool, I—-"

"No, no, that is alright", she almost whispered after taking a deep breath, "It must be this awful humidity, I felt a little faint. With your permission, I think I'll go out on deck where there's a bit of a breeze. Do you mind?"

"No, no, certainly not, but I feel that I should be with you. After all, I am a physician."

"Francis, I'm fine, really. Would you sit with the children for awhile, I'll back in a few minutes, —please?"

"Of course. Oh, by the way, I may not be able to dine with you this evening. Father Healy and some of the men want to have a card game of all things, and I've agreed to host it in my cabin. We're starting around five and I don't know how long it will last."

"Father Healy? Well now, he may not be so bad after all. Have a good time, Francis. I'll only be a few minutes."

When the doctor sat down with the children, Alfredo hurried to the table. "Is everything alright, Doctor? I saw the lady leaving. She looked rather pale." Monica's children expressed concern until Doctor Carey assured everyone that the heat made her feel a bit faint and that she would return after catching her breath out on deck.

"Alfredo, I'm to have a few friends in my cabin this evening for a card game at about five. I should like you to be there to, er, ah, to serve us, and to perhaps give us advise on a certain matter."

"At five, you say. I shall be there, Doctor. Now, would the young lady and two gentlemen care for anything else?" The children giggled and shook their heads negatively and Alfredo smiled and disappeared.

-25-

The sun was still high in the sky at five and so was the temperature and the humidity. The doctor's cabin was small, equipped for one person with one chair, a short narrow cot and a wash stand. One by one entered Father Healy, Richard, and Jake. The minute cabin window was closed for privacy. A kerosene lamp flickered shadows throughout the room. Within minutes the cigar and pipe smoke somewhat overcame the barnyard scent of Jake. Alfredo knocked at the door and was welcomed in. He wore a spotless white apron and a fluffy, white long sleeve shirt tucked inside his black trousers. His hands were gloved, white. He came in with a pitcher of lemonade and glasses and sat them on the table. His greased hair glistened. He held a pencil between his shining teeth, an order pad in his right hand and his left hand rested lighty on his hip. He smiled slightly as he quickly surveyed the occupants. Richard was quick to recognize his movements. Ireland had his kind also: the ones who were not ashamed of what they were. The ones who were ashamed were harder to spot.

"Gentlemen, how can I serve you?"

Jake started to answer, "We got a runa——"

Father Healy interupted, "Alfredo, supposing that we had run across a man like yourself—-"

"Not very likely," Alfredo toyed. "Excuse me, Father, please proceed."

"Suppose we knew of a man like you that needed help in finding a safe haven, a man who is on the run, so to speak."

"A runaway slave," blurted Jake as he spit tobacco on the floor upsetting Doctor Carey. "The poor niggers' been beat and cut and he's scared to death. We need to move him North."

"I assume he's on board?"

"Aye," answered Richard, "and we cannot keep him covered much longer, with all these stops and freight being moved on and off the boat."

"And I hear bounty hunters are aboard," added Doctor Carey. All four conspirators watched the waiter's face for any sign as to their wisdom confiding in him.

"Gentlemen," he paused. "Gentlemen I think you need a drink. What will you have? When I return with your order, I will try and have a solution to your problem, and an admirable one it is. While I am getting your drinks, bring this man here so I can meet him."

"In broad daylight!", exclaimed Jake.

"You'll figure a way", as he passed through the door smiling.

"How in the bloody hell do we know we can trust this, this…"

"Now, Richard, we must all trust in the Lord," interrupted Father Healy

"Bloody trust," stammered Richard. "There's a lot of disappointed trustees in this world, Father. Anyway, I got an idea. Give me twenty minutes. If our Jobe doesn't know how to trust in the Lord he surely knows how to take a chance. If that dainty fellow comes back with the law or some bounty hunters, send someone to warn us" and out the door he went.

Richard found Rose and told her of his plan. She sifted through her trunk and gathered the only other outfit she had and then nervously followed her husband toward Jobe's last hiding place. Shortly afterward, two women, both dressed in black, one with a veil draped down over her face, ascended the stairs and walked slowly along the cabin deck. Rose knocked. The door opened and the lady accompanying her went in. Rose turned and continued walking toward the rear of the boat, circling aft, and after walking the full length of the leeward side, winked at her husband as he was coming up the stairs. She went back to her encampment, taking her infant son from Catherine, a job well done.

Richard entered the cabin and heard Doctor Carey pronouncing, "Jesus, Mary, and Joseph!", as Jobe was disrobed down to his own worn trunks.

It was stifling hot in the small compartment. The port hole was draped and the only light was from an oil lamp setting on a small table beside the Doctor's bunk.

Alfredo was already there and he picked up the lamp and circled the slave carefully stepping between the feet of the occupants who had squatted on the floor, their backs against the wall. "Well, now, let me have a look at you. Ah yes, yes indeed, what a fine body. Look at those muscles ripple like a nervous stallion's," as he touched Jobe's back and shoulders with the tips of his fingers as though he was feeling a fine silk garment.

Richard spoke to Jake, "The boy may be better off where he came from than with this queer one!"

"Oh, my good man," replied Alfredo, smiling with a quick but gracious swirl toward Richard, raising the lantern to his face, "he doesn't fancy me, no, but you now, you with those deep blue eyes. You could arouse that special feeling in me." Richard lunged toward Alfredo staggering clumsily as Alfredo danced backwards.

Richard asked angrily, "What are we doing here, making a pact with the Devil, or better yet, the Devil's Sister!"

"Now, lads, let us be calm," responded the Priest. We are all here for a purpose. "Alfredo, can you help this young man," laying a hand on Jobe's shoulder.

"Yes I can," responded Alfredo in a more serious tone. "I can help him reach his freedom if he wants it bad enough and follows my every instruction. I have helped many others, and have failed with only a few."

Jake spoke, "I'm getting off at Cairo. Perhaps you can smuggle him off with me. I have heard of some runaways going ashore there and crossing up river around Kaskaskia on their way to St. Louis."

"That used to be a good route," said Alfredo, "But no longer. The bounty hunters have taken up residence there. Many ride horseback back and forth on the levee with one hand holding wanted pamphlets and in the other hand a pair of irons with a whip lashed to their saddle. I know because the last Negro that I set ashore there was among three runaways in chains that we brought aboard on our return trip back to New Orleans."

Doctor Carey spoke, "Well, then what is to be done?"

Alfredo turned toward Jobe, whose eyes still showed fear and distrust. "What is your name, Boy?"

"Jobe."

"Well it won't be from now on. I and everyone from now on will know you as, lets see,—-your name will be, now listen carefully, your name is Chris. Chris. That is your new name, your first name. You will now have two names, first name Chris, last name Attucks. Can you say that, Chris Attucks?"

"Crrr, Crissatuk. Crissatuk," said Jobe finally smiling.

"No, no. Chris, your first name. Now say it."

The two worked on the slave's new name until Richard again became frustrated. "For God's sake couldn't you give him a more simple name! Any name will do. Lets get on with it. The man wants to be free, he doesn't want a name!"

"No. This one is going to be my last. It's getting too risky. I've been saving this name. This one is to be special. Almost a hundred years ago in the city Boston there was a runaway slave named Crispus Attucks who was killed in what is remembered as the Boston Massacre. He was killed by British soldiers. That event was the start of the American Revolution. This uneducated, frightened human being is going to join others like him and somewhere, sometime do something worthwhile with his freedom." Everyone in the cabin, including Richard listened attentively. "What I propose to do with Chris Attucks here, (Jobe smiled) is to take him with me. He will work in the kitchen and also clean off the tables. He will always wear gloves, white gloves, and a hat when among the passengers, do you hear that Chris? I'll stuff the glove small fingers with wad. I have a dishwasher departing at the next stop. I'll be able to work him in. We must get him to St. Louis where we must find a way to get him ashore. He will need papers. Either a bill of sale listing someone fictitious back in New Orleans as the previous owner of him and one of you as the new owner or simply a paper granting him a free man. Preferably a sale document as I don't think he could carry off the ruse of being given freedom. Whomever of you being listed as the new owner of Chris Attucks will of course also have a document of freedom to give him after docking in St. Louis. How does that sound? Any questions?" The conspirators looked at one another and remained silent. "Well then gentlemen, it has been a pleasure to meet all of you. We have a risky job ahead. Keep our friend Chris here till nightfall. I will send down a busboy's uniform. One of you bring Chris to the back door of the kitchen and I will take over from there. If you should encounter him in the dining room or elsewhere, you are not to acknowledge your acquaintance. Now then, I had better return to my duties. By the way, we will be docking at Natchez sometime tomorrow at mid-morning to exchange passengers and cargo. It should take an hour or two. Good day gentlemen."

~26~

It was arranged for the doctor to keep Chris Attucks in his cabin until nightfall. Richard picked up the clothes belonging to Rose, and he, Jake and Father Healy left the runaway with a slightly bewildered and nervous doctor. Richard and Jake returned to their respective huddles on the main deck, Jake to his animals and Richard to his family, handing Rose's Sunday best back to her. The dress, of black linen, was the dress she wore when she was married and had not worn it since. She had saved it for only special occasions. She dusted it off, folded it neatly and placed it in her small trunk as though it had never left. John Duddy was sitting nearby and watched with controlled interest, glancing occasionally toward his friends as Richard told Rose of the happenings in the doctor's cabin. Richard knew John was straining to hear what was being said and wondered if he could trust his new friend.

Monica Garvin was also wondering if she could trust her doctor admirer. He had told her that he couldn't dine with her that evening as he was to host a card party. Her cabin was on the opposite side of the boat and on her way to the dining room she thought that she would drop by his cabin and help him prepare for his games. Upon rounding the bow of the ship and starting down the aisle, she saw two women wearing vails enter his cabin. She stopped abruptly, her face flushed. First there was a trace of jealously, then betrayal. She had thought that the good doctor was a nice and naive old man and physically harmless. Now she began to wonder if he had attributes that his years did not portray. He had been charming in a fatherly sort of way. She welcomed his doting and friendship. Now she felt a tinge of lust for this older man who evidently had younger feelings.

The next morning the doctor and the priest were at their usual table having breakfast, carrying on a normal conversation regarding the weather, compliments of the food, and intermingled with whispers about the previous nights episode. Alfredo had served them and seemed very abrupt, friendly yet not indulging in any chit chat, almost like this was the first time that he had waited on them. When they had cleaned their plates and had drunk their last cup of tea, Chris Attucks walked out of the kitchen all decked out in a white uniform with a little white cap and wearing white gloves. He approached their table and with his head bowed and a slight smile on his face began clearing off the table. He was clumsy, dropping a knife, then a spoon. A bowl slid off a plate and the doctor caught it before it hit the deck and he nervously placed it upon the table. Father Healy whispered, "Make two trips," motioning him away, "Two trips!"

The doctor wiped the mess off of his hands. When he finished and looked up he saw Monica Garvin approaching. She looked a little different, even more beautiful. There was a kind of enticing saunter in her walk, her hair was brushed back a bit exposing the lower part of her ears, and her black blouse was unbuttoned revealing the front of her neck.

"Good morning, Father. It is dreadfully hot and sticky again this morning. Good morning, Francis. How are you gentlemen this morning. I trust that your games last night were enjoyable? May I —-"

"Please do sit down," said the priest, "I was just about to leave. Please excuse me, perhaps the three of us and your children can have lunch today."

"Thank you Father, but I'm afraid that I can't get the little ruffians to behave enough to sit with adults. Unless of course you should threaten them with the punishment of Hell if they don't."

"Well, then I'll be off. I'll be saying another Mass down on the main deck by the Duddy and Walshs. Nine o'clock. Bring the children. You too, doctor. Oh, and I'll be hearing confessions in my cabin at sunset."

As the priest made his way out of the dining room he saw Chris drop two more dishes. Father Healy had to control himself in not going forward to help pick up the broken dinnerware; something that he probably would have done at a different time and with a different bus boy. He lowered his eyes, crossed his chest and left the room.

The doctor did not look at anyone or anything except Monica. His mind and body craved her and he didn't know what to do about it. Her eyes teased him, so much so he almost felt that she was looking at someone besides him. He was nervous and it showed. He could not control his feelings and he was embarrassed. He was sure his face was flushed. Was it his imagination, he thought, or does she really mean what she looks like she means, and what would that be. He fidgited.

"Francis, what is going to happen to you and to me, where are we going? Are we going to be together, and if so in what way. Do you and I have a future together?" She asked this leaning over the table toward him with her hands embracing his, and her eyes begging for a kind and favorable answer.

"This can't be happening to me," he thought, "not now, not even thirty years ago. What does she want?, I have nothing to give, except this passion she arouses in me and my desire to be with her always." His face flushed and his heart beat rumbled and his voice quivered as he tried to veil his nervousness and plea for time for his brain and body to recover in order to make an intelligent statement. He replied, "I, uh— I don't know exactly." He suddenly felt that he was back in County Claire in the middle of a stream playing the largest trout that was ever seen in all of Ireland on a light line, a line ever so light. "Monica, I think you are aware that your presence gives me a great deal of pleasure. I'm an old man, I—-"

"Oh, now, I don't know about that, Francis."

"Yes I am. I can think of no one else that I would want to spend the rest of my years with. However, you lost your husband only a short time ago. Your mind may be fuzzy yet. You haven't had time to sort every thing out, and I don't want to take advantage of you, my dear. Your future with me would be short. I am not wealthy by any means. I do have a promising profession however, even with my age, and I think I will be able to build a fair practice where ever I go in this new land. but—-"

"Now, Francis, she interrupted, you don't know anything about me or my feelings." She looked around to see if anyone was within listening distance. "Francis, my husband was a mean one. We left him and came to this country to be rid of him. My father, bless his departed soul, arranged the marriage or I should say the sale of me to him. Our family was on the verge of starvation and my folks knew that if I stayed healthy I would be wed to someone, so why not make a profit. John paid ten pounds for me. Money we later learned he stole from an elderly widow in a nearby town. My mother reluctantly agreed that I go with him, but only if we were married in The Church. We moved from parish to parish and town to town always an hour or two ahead of the law. When he was sober he could be half way pleasing. We had three wonderful children over the years. They weren't wanted at the time, or planned, but produced as The Church encouraged. I was beaten by him almost daily, and as the children came along, they were beaten also. As a good Catholic wife, I gave in to his lustful moments and tried to forgive him for the beatings as the priests of each parish we lived in, told me to do. The important thing was to keep the family intact they said, and to propagate the faith by having more children. John hated children but enjoyed his part in having them." Monica paused covering her mouth with her hand and with tears starting to well, continued. "One day, as I came home from working the bogs, I found him naked and in a lustful state, standing by the bed upon which lay my daughter, Ella, whimpering. He was drunk. I took the broom to him. He caught me and threw me against the wall. He quickly put on his clothes and kicked me before going out the door. The next morning after he sobered up, he told me that he was merely educating her. Two weeks later, Ella came running up to me where I was working the bogs. He had tried to assault her again. This time he was stone cold sober. He was gone when we got home. He was too mad and embarrassed to face me I suppose. I gathered up some clothes and what little money that was in the house and went to the neighbors and gathered up the boys. We've been on the run ever since. Somehow he learned that we were in New Orleans, and staying with the Sisters. I suspect that he asked The Church to locate us so that he could preserve the marriage and all that. I was told when his ship was to arrive. The good Sisters insisted, for the children's sake, that I go to meet him and give him another chance. I couldn't tell you, God forgive me, how elated and relieved I was upon learning of his loss at sea. I still can't believe it. So, Francis, my children and I have a new life, in a new land. We are free of him and the awful pestilence that has enveloped our former country. Now, do you understand my lack of mourning and the excitement that I have for the future?"

The old doctor paused before stating, "My dear Monica, I would be very pleased if you and your children would be part of my future. I have no staunch plans, except I think it wise for some unexplained reason to follow those two families down below, The Walshs and the Duddys, at least to the nearest town from where they plan to work for some relative on a farm. I think the town is called Delhi or Alton. Father Healy has spoken of it and I think he plans to inquire of his future there. Father and I have become very fond of each other."

"As we have become fond of each other, Francis? By the way, who were those two women I saw entering your cabin last evening, old man."

Who?, When?, —Oh, last evening, one was Rose Walsh and the other, ah, that friend of hers. They brought the cards and some small snacks for our games. They left right away, didn't you see them leave?"

"Why no, Francis, you talk as though I was spying on you."

-27-

Natchez

Around ten in the morning the boat pulled up to an opening at the dock in Natchez. The Mate announced that they could use every hand they could get to unload cargo and take on more including wood for the boilers. The dock at Natchez was crowded with passengers and cargo from other ships along with an abundance of local roustabouts, both Negro and White, looking for a chance to make a few coins. The Mate aboard the *Isabella* always preferred to have his own passengers do the work if there was a sufficient number of them. Duddy was anxious to go ashore and explore the town, having been forewarned of the dangers a stranger might encounter in Natchez-under-the Hill. After all he had been through, he thirsted for good Irish whiskey and some entertainment. He was told not to be long. Richard and the Walsh and Duddy boys helped where they could in the unloading and loading of goods aboard the boat. When it came time to shove off, John had not come back. Richard asked the Captain that he delay departing for at least another hour so that he could go to town and bring John back. His family was worried sick.

"One hour it will be. No more. If neither of you return we must leave."

Richard ran to the town and in and out of every tavern as fast as he could. Half way down the main street, he heard men shouting from an alleyway, one of the men demanding, "If you want to see the sun go down you'll give me your money!" Richard saw John backed against a wall pleading with the two men, one of them holding a large knife.

"Duddy, what in the bloody hell are you doing? Are these two lads your friends?"

As the two thugs turned to see who was approaching, Duddy hit the one with the knife and Richard kneed the other in the groin. Both men dropped to the ground and John and Richard ran for their boat.

When far enough away, they slowed to a walk. "Richard, you should have been with me," Duddy said out of breath.

"I don't think so. Look at you. You alright? Your breath smells like you are!"

"Richard, I'm excited, now listen. When I was having a whiskey, whew, let me catch by breath. Now then, I got into a conversation with these two chaps in this pub and they were talking about gold! Gold, Richard. They said all you had to do was pick it up! They were prospectors and they had a claim staked out West somewhere in California territory. They were going out to get some more. They said that they struck it so rich that they both had a mansion built up on the hill back there where supposedly all the rich people live."

"How much whiskey did you three drink?"

" You know that it only takes a few drinks to get the truth out of a man, Richard."

"Yea, and we both know that all it takes is a few drinks to get a lot of sheep shit out of some of them."

"Richard, we have to go out West, get our share of this gold before everyone else gets it. We can get off this boat and get on another where the Arkansas river runs into this one or even wait till we get to St. Louis and get on one that goes up the Missouri river. These men gave me a map of where the gold is!"

"Gave you a map?"

"Well I gave them a five dollar gold piece for it."

"The only thing that I want, John is land. That'll be my gold. I want to farm. Raise my own pigs, cows and yes, even grow potatoes, John. And I'll get that after working on this farm that you said we were going to. I heard that there were Indians, savages they are, out West. They would give some gold just to get that red hair of yours. Think of the risk to you and your family. No I'll have no part of that."

"I've made up my mind. You have time to think it over. Just think, you could come back with enough money to buy that farm and a big one, even with a house on it in only a year and perhaps less."

As soon as they set foot on the *Isabella* the boat backed into the current and headed for the next stop now loaded with bales of cotton for the factories in St. Louis and Chicago along with barrels of sugar and indigo and a passenger with wild ideas.

~28~

A man boarded a ship in Liverpool England giving his name as John Garvin. He had a hook fastened to his right forearm, a scar on the side of his face and his left ear almost missing. When asked what happened to him by a fellow passenger he said that he had fallen overboard from a ship going to America and drifted holding on to a board for what he thought must have been two weeks or more until a passing German ship spotted him and hauled him aboard, but not before a shark tore off most of his hand before he was picked up. The rest of it was amputated while he lay unconscious for days aboard the ship.

"My, the man said, and you're now going to give it another try."

"Yea, I've a wife and family waiting for me in New Orleans." The man took out his purse and offered Garvin a few shillings which he refused. Later as the man was standing at the rail talking to another passenger, Garvin passed him and removed his purse without the man feeling anything.

John Garvin's survival seemed a miracle to the crew of the German ship that picked him out of the sea. So much so that every crew member contributed to a fund for him. The ship landed in Bremerhaven and after a few weeks of mending, John Garvin entered one beer house after another telling his story and gaining a few more Marks and many free drinks. As he became well enough he made the docks his home and picked the pockets of many. Soon he had enough money to buy passage to Liverpool where he was able to find the only ship that was bound that month for New Orleans. His mind was on the money that he supposed his wife now had, but almost as important, revenge to the man who did this to him.

~29~

John Duddy and Richard had told their wives about the gold conversations that they had back at Natchez. Rose agreed with her husband that it would be folly to go chasing after something that they may never find. John's wife, however, listened intently to her husband's tale and could tell that he was more enthused about this venture than anything else other than his desire to leave Ireland. John's conversations with their children brought even more excitement. Richard's boys were excited about this "West" as well with the thought of seeing Indians.

John Duddy addressed Richard, "The Mate said that the Arkansas River is only two more days up stream. You can still change your mind." Jake Collins overheard some of the conversations but said nothing.

Richard knew that he was listening and asked Jake, "What do you make of this rush out West to find gold?"

"Well now, I've seen some men that came back and struck it rich. Yes Sir! I also seen a woman and with only two of her six children come back holding the scalp of her dear husband. The scalp was retrieved by the Calvary in a shoot out with some Indians." Catherine and Rose nearly fainted at this remark. Jake's habit of spitting tobacco after every sentence irritated the women. "You won't find me going out there, no sir. I'll take what little gold I get by trading down river and not with no Indians. That's enough for me."

Jake looked at John and said, "If"n you got your heart set on this, I'd advise you to take off from St. Louis. There you can purchase the supplies that you will need including the best guns. You're sure going to need them. You can get on another boat at St. Louis and go up the Missouri River all the way to Montana Territory or you can go out West from St. Louie with a wagon group or by Stage Coach but the Stage Coach will cost you some more money. By Golly, if I was your age, I would probably go. But not with a family."

John's enthusiasm did not retreat one bit but Catherine's did. John started counting his money and planing how they would travel. Their boys were still excited. The Walsh boys were pouting as their father and mother would have no part of this adventure. They foresaw their future toiling with farm work.

Soon the news reached Father Healey and Doctor Carey and the subject became a favorite conversation piece of theirs. At breakfast the Doctor asked, "What do you think of this wild idea that John Duddy is contemplating, Father?"

"I need time to think about it. I can understand the excitement, but I also see a bit of danger especially if he takes his family with him. On the other hand, I myself see an opportunity to convert the savages out there to Christianity, Doctor. Yes, I think that it would be a grand adventure."

"Oh, my, you're all the same. Converting, converting! Do you priests keep track as to how many converts you have made each year? Are there not enough where we are going for you to work on, or even aboard this vessel, without straying out into the unknown?"

"Why, I'm taken aback by your, is it anger, my good Doctor??"

"No, no. I'm just upset with the way this so called "conversion" is sometimes forced upon people or traded for with a hand-full of beads along with the teachings that the respondents don't even understand. And how long do they stay converted? I guess that I'm a little out of balance because Monica said that she did not want to supper with me today."

"Did she give a reason?"

"She said that we needed a pause. A pause!"

"Ah. a pause you say. You've been coming on too strong, old man?"

"How would you know, Father. Are you an expert on women?"

"If we keep up this conversation, we may come to fisticuffs, Doctor, and you will have to treat me for a bloody nose!"

That brought laughter and Doctor Carey relaxed until he saw Chris spill the remains of a plate full of rashers and eggs on a diner, bringing

Alfredo out of the kitchen immediately to clean up and apologize. Father bowed his head and made the sign of the cross.

The day proceeded with nothing noteworthy. The *Isabella* made a wood stop at dusk with Richard and John helping the roustabouts. While their men helped carry on the wood, Rose asked Catherine, "How do you feel about this venture for gold?"

"I have followed John all of my life. I'd be lying if I said that I was not fearful. But, Rose we have been fearful of everything that we have done since leaving Ireland, haven't we?"

"Yes."

A steamboat went by them at a fast speed causing wakes in its path to lap rather harshly at the side of the *Isabella.*

"Rose, the only other thing that I dread on this search for gold is that we will be on another boat, going up another river. I am so tired of water. Muddy water at that and this continual rocking back and forth. If I ever step upon solid ground I will never go on a boat again, unless, of course, years from now things change back in Ireland. Then I would risk it all over again to go back. We had such a beautiful land, Rose."

"That we did. Look at all the boats on this river. Where is everyone going so fast up and down river and why are they following each other so closely. What in God's name is so important that they go so fast?" Rose nursed her baby son. "I'll tell you what I dislike. I dislike these blokes passing by all the time trying to sneak a peek when I'm nursing my baby. I dislike our toilet arrangements. We had no room in our luggage for more than one chamber pot when we left Ireland and the only thing Richard was able too find in New Orleans was this small spittoon. It's so hard to clean! The men don't have to worry, they just go off the stern of the boat. When Eddie asked his father how and where he was to poop, Richard told him to just hang his fanny over the lower railing and go." Catherine laughed at that.

"We have no privacy, Rose. I'm going to ask John to see if he can get us a cabin on whatever boat we take out West if we indeed get on another boat."

"Is that a fiddle sticking out of your bag? Do you play, Catherine?"

"Have not for years. Once I played in all the pubs along the coast. Mostly in Doolin. That's where I met John. Happier times they were. I brought it along thinking that some day the troubles will be over and I'll pick at it again."

~30~

At daybreak they were going at a fair rate of speed when a steamboat passed them as many of them had before, the *Isabella* being one of the slower ones. About two hundred feet up river from them there was a loud explosion and the steamboat that had just passed them burst into flame and the blast sent most of what was above the water level skyward, some of which landed on the *Isabella*. Scraps of wood, searing metal, still red hot parts breaking off its stacks descended on the *Isabella*. A man's, it could have been a woman's, bloody hand thudded on the deck between Rose and Catherine. Catherine fainted. Jake threw the hand overboard. Everyone took cover for fear of anything, or any body or their parts, falling on them. The Captain of the *Isabella* slowed the boat as much as he could and the crew and some of the passengers looked for survivors in the water. Doctor Carey treated many of the survivors that were pulled aboard the best that he could with what he had. Father Healey tried desperately to soothe those who survived, but most were frantic not knowing what happened to their loved ones. Other steamboats tied up to the *Isabella*. They too had picked up survivors. A few boats continued their way upstream and down without the slightest hesitation, infuriating everyone. The dining room was quickly filled with the injured. Doctor Carey was assisted by Alfredo and the kitchen workers, including Chris who was told to bring pan after pan of boiling water. Chris never spilled a one.

It was decided by the Captains that the fastest ships would hurry on to Vicksburg for medical treatment for the lesser injured while the *Isabella* would travel only a few more miles upstream to St. Joseph on the Louisiana side of the river with their wounded. In tying up there, the wounded were put ashore for medical assistance and the Captain ordered the boat washed down. As they backed away from shore there was little evidence of blood splashed on the decks and minor damages were repaired. Catherine and Rose tried in vain to remove blood stains from their bags while they huddled closely for fear of another catastrophe.

Jake saw their fears. "Folks, this is a busy, busy, growing country and a lot of things happen. Some not so good. Why, one or two years ago a steamboat docked at St. Louis and caught fire, a boat that I had traveled on many times. The fire nearly wiped out most of the town! Nearly every steamboat tied up at the dock burned to the water. Why, boats run into each other, hit snags or go aground every day or blow sky high like that one back there. The bottom of this river is full of old wrecks from away down the Mississippi to New Orleans. I'll bet there's a fortune down there if'in you can figure out how to get it. When the river goes down a lot, which isn't too often, those old wrecks are gone over by enterprising people trying to salvage something or discover some gold or silver left in an unfortunate passenger's strong box. I was on the boat *Columbus* about a year ago when one of her tall black stove pipes fell to the deck. Flames and smoke shot everywhere. Eight passengers, two firemen and five others drowned. You can bet your bottle of booze and your bag of tobacco I was scared. The boat was towed to Cairo. There just ain't a better way to get from South to North and back, or in your case, Mr. Duddy to the West. Somebody once telled me that there were more deaths going between North and South by horse and carriage."

The *Isabella* stopped South of Vicksburg for wood and as they pushed past Vicksburg the passengers aboard the *Isabella* wondered about the wounded passengers that were aboard the unfortunate boat that blew up.

The next morning the *Isabella* pulled ashore at the small town of Napoleon which was almost on the Arkansas River. John Duddy was nervous. He wondered if he should get off the boat now and settle for one that traveled West up the Arkansas River. Time for a quick decision. Jake assured him once again that he stood a much better chance on waiting until they docked at Saint Louis. Gold had entered John's mind and would stay there until he got his share regardless of the consequences. He was in a hurry. He was afraid that by the time he would get to the gold fields there would be none left. He spent his days pacing the deck and grew aggravated with every stop that the *Isabella* had to make. He searched the boat for anyone who had any information whatsoever about this gold and when finding no one, grew even more testy. He wanted to be there, wherever that would be, now.

"John, you could jump overboard and swim to Saint Louis, but I think that you will get there faster by sitting down with me and having a smoke and letting this boat take you there."

"I can't help it Richard. Give me some of that tobacco." Jake offered a swig of his special concoction which settled all three of them down.

Father Healey came to Richard and when no strangers were around gave him the papers that he would need to bring Chris ashore in Saint Louis as a free man. The first paper was a bill of sale from Silas in New Orleans of a Chris to a Doctor Carey. The second a bill of sale from Doctor Carey to Richard Walsh for Chris and the third a document giving Chris his freedom to be signed by Richard and witnessed by Father Healy. Alfredo had supplied the papers and the language. Richard wondered if Alfredo received his freedom this way.

-31-

The *Isabella* passed Memphis and the immigrants surmised that the cities were becoming larger. When the boat stopped for wood at Ashport, Tennessee, Jake started getting fidgety with his animals and his cages telling everyone that he would be departing the next day. Upon learning of his departing, Father Healey and the doctor came down to wish him well and thanked him for all of his wisdom. Rose told Catherine, "I've grown to like that old man."

"Remember when we couldn't stand the smell of him?"

"I'm going to miss that too, I am!"

John Duddy tried to extract from Jake whatever information or suggestions that the man may have about this West and the best way to get there. Jake for the next twenty-four hours was the center of attention. The next morning as they stopped at Hayti, Missouri, Jake held court. "Ya'all need to take note. Forty years ago when I was a boy we had a terrible earthquake here. Yes, that's right an earthquake! And it was a strong one I tell you. It changed the flow of this here river and believe it or not, made it flow backwards for awhiles. Yes siree! Right here. It left a good size lake over there."

Late the next afternoon the *Isabella* docked at Cairo and Jake departed carrying his cages of chickens, dogs, geese and whatever else he traded for in New Orleans. He gave the Duddy children one of his puppies. He also gave his address scribbled on the back of a chewing tobacco label to Rose and told her that when they got settled he would like to hear from them. He said that he had grown interested in what their future held for them. He told them that surely in another day or so they would make it to Saint Louis. John and Richard helped him carry off all of his purchases. His wife was ashore sitting on a wagon that was hitched to the largest brown and white cow that Richard and John had ever seen.

Jake's wife was a round, short woman with stringy hair the colors of which matched the cow's. Her hair came down to her waist and her smile was as wide as the river. Her mouth was without most of her front teeth. She jumped off the wagon with the speed of a youngster and bear hugged her husband, spitting tobacco juice mid questions. "I heered 'bout another boat blowing up and I was worried, Pa. I've met the last five boats that pulled in here and ye weren't on them."

"Mable, I'd like you to meet these two fellers. They and their kinfolk came all the way from Ireland! This one's Richard and that there is John. Richard and his family are a going farther north in Illinois to do some farming. John here is headed for the gold out West."

"Well, that's so. And you got such a nice head of hair on ye, John. Wish ya the best in keeping it."

"Now mother,—-"

"I guess you done told him, Jake?"

"Yes'm."

Going back to the boat, John was upset. They turned to wave at Jake and his wife and as Richard rubbed John's head he said, "There goes a rich man."

The *Isabella* took on more tobacco and whiskey. Some of the tobacco was stacked in the space that Jake had occupied. Richard said that the air surrounding them was much better.

Alfredo wanted one more meeting with the doctor, priest and Richard before they arrived at Saint Louis. It was once again arranged to meet in the doctor's cabin. Doctor Carey decided that he would have to let Monica know what was going on. At lunch, he told her about the slave. Father Healy was present. Monica sat there silent, looking back and forth at the two men in disbelief. "Why didn't you tell me about this before, Francis?"

"He didn't want you to worry, Monica. We had not yet decided what to do or when to do it until we had that meeting in the doctor's cabin", Father Healy responded with the doctor nodding his head.

"The two women that went into your cabin. Were they involved?"

"Yes but there was only one woman, Rose Walsh. The other person dressed as a woman was the slave."

Monica remembered that when she saw the two women go into his room she was somewhat jealous and gave Francis a lot more credit for being sexually alive than he deserved. She was beginning to see him as she first did on the New Orleans dock. "Francis this is dangerous. You're too old for this. I mean—"

The old man pouted. "Monica, Father and I are not taking on the brunt of this. Richard Walsh and his family are willing to take the most severe risk. Father and I just helped set things up. I'm sure we can count on your secrecy until we get this poor soul safely out of bondage and through any problems that we may have in Saint Louis."

Monica again took her time in answering, frowning at the both of them. "Certainly, but I do not want to be involved. I have my children to worry about. I will help do what I can. Is that your slave, the one over there that just spilled coffee on that man?"

After Monica left them Father Healy said, " One conspirator gone, another aboard." Doctor Carey did not smile.

"Did you hear her. She now thinks of me as an old man. I think I've lost her. Come to think of it I think I've lost all my senses."

Monica thought some time about the slave matter and concluded that they were doing the right thing. She erased the impression of the doctor being old and replaced her thought of him as being adventurous. She wondered what would happen in Saint Louis with the slave. She also wondered what would happen to her and her children. What would they do. Where would they end up. And what about Francis?

That evening, Richard, Rose, the doctor, the priest and Alfredo met. Alfredo had a lot to tell them. "I want you to listen very carefully to what I have to say. We haven't much time. First, I want you to know how reckless that all of you are in taking on this endeavor and second, how much I admire you for doing so. When we reach Saint Louis, I will have Chris come directly to you, Mister Walsh and you will act as his owner. I will instruct him. He will carry your baggage and be at your side at all times until you deem it safe to issue him his papers of freedom. That may be sometime to come. It will be up to you as to when and where that will happen. Until that time you are to act like a slave owner. Bark commands to him and whip him if you deem it necessary. Your wife must do the same. I don't know how you propose to instruct your children. I leave that up to you. Spend only as much time in the city as possible. Look for a boat going to Alton. There will be many. There are as many bounty hunters in Saint Louis as anywhere on this river. Saint Louis is one of their last chances to spot a slave before he or she gets too far North. Be very careful again in Alton. Some fifteen years ago an Abolitionist named, Lovejoy, I just love that man's name!, was murdered. This Mister Lovejoy ran a newspaper and consistently printed articles denouncing slavery. A bunch of ruffians threw his presses into the river more than once, finally they killed him. So, there are still people in Alton who are for slavery but there are a growing number of them against it. I have been successful in getting two through Alton with the help of others. Doctor, and you Priest, are going with them surely. They could use all the help and collaboration they can get."

The doctor and the priest looked quizzically. "Well, Alfredo, we haven't thought of that. I would want to go to the Cathedral there and get some direction as to where I can serve."

"I was looking forward to setting up some kind of a practice in Saint Louis. I figured that more opportunities would be there." He immediately thought of Monica and her children. "Do you know how large Alton is?"

"Not nearly as big as Saint Louis. A small river town that is growing like all river towns. You could accompany the Walshs there and see for yourself. If the town does not meet your requirements it is only a short trip back. Remember, you are witness's on the bill of sale for Chris. Godfathers so to speak, gentlemen!"

-32-

Saint Louis

The next afternoon the *Isabella* arrived at Saint Louis. The captain had to wait for an opening at the levee. The boat went forward and then drifted backward with the current with the pilot forever watching so as to not bump into another boat. This back and forth made John impatient. Once the captain saw an opening only to be beaten to it by a sternwheeler. Everyone could hear the captain cuss. Finally they pulled ashore in the middle of what seemed like a hundred steamboats. John Duddy and family were some of the first to go ashore on the wide, long, crowded, sloping, cobblestone levee that was full of people, wagons, horses, and barrels, bales, and luggage. It seemed just as busy as when they docked in New Orleans. They saw no sign of the great fire that Jake Collins remarked about. John was anxious to secure passage on another boat going up the Missouri River. The Walshs waited for their slave and wondered how he would react. Nearly all of the passengers had left before Alfredo came to them with a rope around Chris' neck. Chris was handed over to Richard, he had brown work gloves on his hands to hide the amputations. The rope dropped and Eddie picked it up. When Richard started to pick up some of their belongings, Alfredo stopped him and nodded to him and then to Chris. "You, get those bags and be careful with them. You break anything and I'll be using the whip, you good for nothing!" barked Richard. Alfredo smiled and so did Chris. "And wipe that smile off your black face!"

"Yes, Master."

Alfredo pretended to give Richard some coins saying, "I appreciate your letting me use your slave in the kitchen. He wasn't worth much."

There were many people on the levee, some Alfredo suspected were bounty hunters. The priest and the doctor stood with the Garvin family off to the side observing as casually as possible the goings on. Rose walked over to Catherine. They had become good friends. "Rose, John wanted to run up and get passage on a boat as soon as he got on the ground. I told him,'John I'll not put another foot forward or go on another boat until you see to it that I and the children get a bath!' We are all so dirty, Rose. We were dirty back in Ireland living in mud hutches with dirt floors but not this dirty, not for this long a time."

John told Richard of his wife's demand. "Better do as she wishes, John. A gift of some of that perfumy water would be nice."

"Aye, we could use a bath also and some of that stuff ourselves. You should have asked your friend, Alfredo for some."

"Nay, he would have wanted to rub it on me. What an odd lot those kind are. But Alfredo is a good, caring man. Man or whatever he is, now. I like him", said Richard.

Father Healy walked up the levee to the Cathedral, a tall, elegant, limestone structure that they could see from a distance down river. Doctor Carey accompanied Monica and her children to an upper-class boarding house. He told her that he would be back in a few days, that he and Father Healy were going to Alton to look around. Richard found a small steamboat that made a daily run to Alton. The boat was a quarter of a mile north from where they had gone ashore. All but the Garvin family gathered where their baggage was dropped. Conversations of leave-taking ensued with the Duddys, hugs, kisses, hand shakes and a blessing from the priest.

The Duddy family went to look for, first a bath house, then supplies for their venture and then a boat to take them to their gold. John secured passage on a steamboat that would take him and his family up the Missouri River to Saint Joseph, Missouri, where he was told he could join one of the many wagon trains to the West or continue on the river to The Montana Territory. At a supply store he was given a list of everything that he would need if he was to travel out West to the gold fields. The list comprised of a good rifle, five pounds of powder, ten pounds of lead, a hatchet, a good large knife, a hundred and fifty pounds of flour, a hundred and fifty pounds of bacon, twenty-six pounds of coffee, thirty pounds of sugar, and enough warm clothes for two years. He couldn't believe what all was on the list and thought that one would had to have struck it rich to be able to afford all that. He was told that he could purchase it here in Saint Louis or at Saint Joseph but it would be much more expensive there. He bought a rifle, one pound of powder, a pound of lead, and a knife. He was running low on money. He made his boys give the dog Jake gave them to Eddie and Daniel. He had enough mouths to feed. Catherine was pregnant.

The doctor, the priest, the Walshs and their slave, Chris, proceeded to hopefully the last steamboat that they will ever have to board. Richard barked orders to his slave. The rope around Chris' neck was removed. Richard had to stop his son, Eddie from hitting Chris with the rope. On the way to the boat, Richard understood, if only slightly what it would feel like to be another man's master. What power, he thought and he seemed to sense a slave owners feeling of ownership and his wanting to be reimbursed for the loss of one's slave, his property. There was nothing to stop him from keeping Chris as his slave. He had the papers. "Ah, that's the devil getting to you, Richard," he thought as he grabbed one of the bags Chris was dragging.

-33-

The Piasa

They boarded a steamboat named the, *Piasa* and backing away from the levee, were once again going upstream. The boat was much smaller and the Captain more approachable.

The *Piasa* had no dining room or cabins. It carried livestock, people and supplies back and forth between Alton and Saint Louis and made the trip twice a day. Doctor Carey inquired of the Captain, a Mister Ripley, as to whether Alton had a hospital and if there were a lot of doctors there.

"You won't find a hospital, although I heard tell that there a thinking about building one, but not soon. As far as doctors, I've never found the need of one but I guess there are a few. The ones in town make a good living. The ones out in the country survive on what pigs, fowl, homemade bread, and sides of beef, that the farmers give them along with plenty of preserves. Taint a bad life though. If I was a doctor that's where I'd a go; out in the country. My wife and I have a little shack up river from Alton a mite farther than Grafton. A lot of river pilots live there. We could use you there, Doc."

The doctor thought of Monica. Would she be satisfied with a husband bringing in a few chickens and a pig for income. He doubted it.

Richard was nearby and asked Mr. Ripley if there was need of farm hands, ones with families like his.

"Have you done any farming, lad?"

"Yes. In Ireland. All me life until the potatoes rotted year after year."

"Oh, you're Irish are you. Well the farming around here is a bit different than where you came from. We grow a lot of grains: corn, wheat, oats, alfalfa, and the like. There is a friend of mine who is always looking for good hands. He's liable to meet us at the dock looking for workers and to pick up some supplies he's expecting. He's a good man with a large family. All girls. Six of them! His name is Howard Clarkson. He has a large spread a little out from Godfrey. He owns a few other small plots of ground nearby. Howard's a fair man, only wants a person that he can trust and a hard worker. I don't know if he's looking for a whole family though. If he's there when we dock, I'll point him out to you."

Richard thought that if this Howard Clarkson would hire him and his family, there would be no need to go to Delhi or Hannibal.

Father Healy was told at the Cathedral in Saint Louis that, yes there was a need for him here in the city, but more of a need across the river in and surrounding Alton. He should inquire at Saint Matthew's Church to see if they could use another priest.

It was a warm, late, sunny, afternoon in June when the *Piasa* glided in to Alton. Captain Ripley saw Howard Clarkson and motioned to Richard. Father Healey asked the directions to Saint Matthew's and Doctor Carey was told that the Franklin House was one of the very best in town. The Doctor looked forward to a long hot bath and rest from the voyage. Rose with her infant son on her lap, her two boys and Chris Attucks and the boy's newly acquired pup which they had agreed to name, Shep, sat on their belongings while her husband approached Mister Clarkson. After introductions Richard asked, "Mister Clarkson, I was told by the Captain that you were in need of good hands to work your farm. We, my family and I, have come all the way from Ireland looking for farm work, Sir. I've taken care of prize horses, cattle, sheep, and pigs I have, and the wife is a good cook and housekeeper and my slave, Chris there is a strong one—-"

"I don't take to anyone who owns slaves, Mister, what's your name?"

"Richard Walsh, and he's not my slave he nearly whispered looking around him for anyone listening. We picked him out of the river after he ran away from the man who bought him at a auction that we witnessed in New Orleans. I have ownership papers on him so as to evade those so called bounty hunters. I'm ready to give him his freedom whenever I think it is safe to do so, Mister Clarkson. I have the papers for that also. You can ask Father Healy over there and Doc Carey. They were in on it. I am anxious to turn him free. I just need to know how."

"My oh my. I'd like to hear the rest of that story. You want me to hire your whole family and your slave that's not a slave?"

"My wife and boys and Chris will work for you for a month with no pay except for somewhere to lay our heads at night and food for our bellies, Sir."

"Well now, I haven't had an offer like that from any of the blokes around here. I think I know where you can leave your slave for the time being until I find room and work for him. Help me load these supplies and you all climb into my wagon. I have a small cabin that my father built when he first came to this land. You and your family can stay there. It needs a bit of cleaning. I don't need a housekeeper with six daughters but we'll figure out something for your wife and that infant son of yours. Does your misses know how to keep a garden?"

"Aye Mister Clarkson, she does, she has and she will."

-34-

Clarkson's wagon was loaded with the supplies brought by the *Piasa*. The Irish family with their dog and the Negro climbed aboard and the wagon was pulled up one of the steep Alton roads by two of the finest horses that Richard had ever seen. As they came upon the African Methodist Episcopal Church near Godfrey, Mister Clarkson told Richard that this was a safe place for his Negro for the time being. Clarkson, Richard and Chris entered the church. There were other Negro men there. Clarkson talked to the man in charge, a white man who was a missionary of sorts, and there Richard signed the freedom paper granting Chris a new life. The white man who said that his name was Quinn said that they would take care of Chris and instruct him in the Christian way of life and try to teach him how to be a free man and all of the responsibilities that went along with being free. Clarkson told Chris that he would be back for him when he needed men for his harvest. He said, "Right now I don't have a place for you to stay. I have to find room for this man's family first. But when I do find living space for you, you can work and live on my farm and be paid wages! How does that sound?"

Tears of joy flowed down his face. He bowed to his deliverers. Addressing Richard he said, "Master, I'se don't know what to say. I don't know where you folks come from." Looking upward he said, "Lord, You brought them didn't you. I would do anything for you." A large black man named Shadrach placed his hand on Chris' shoulder and took him into another room to introduce him to other members of the church.

Richard heard the black man tell Chris, "You only have one Master now. The one we all have," as he looked upward.

As they pulled out of Godfrey and entered farm land, the immigrants smelled the clover and the soil from fields recently plowed and the sweet scent of lilacs here and there. In the yards of farm houses, they saw roses and peonies in bloom. They saw the golden wheat almost ready to harvest and the corn almost a foot high and oats in another field. "This is the gold that I'm looking for," Richard thought as he hugged his wife and took in the scenery.

"Look at all those ravens," Richard said nudging his boys.

"We call them crows over here, Richard, and a nuisance they are, but one of the smartest birds I know. I have a friend who captured one, split its tongue and taught it to talk. One thing you'll be wary about is snakes. We have some poisonous ones about. I know that you had none in Ireland because Saint Patrick drove them out."

"Nay, that's not the reason. It was too blamed cold for them there, it was."

"You said that you had worked with fine horses in Ireland, Richard."

"Aye, I had, before things turned bad. I trained them and raced them a time or two. We would have races along the beaches, we would. Oh, those were grand times, Mister Clarkson."

"He won a lot of ribbons, he did", exclaimed Rose.

"I have a couple of horses I'd like you to look at."

"Iv'e never seen a road the likes of this, boards laid down to travel on."

"A bright idea of one of our leaders, Richard. It's called The Plank Road. It won't last long. It's rotting now. We'll be on solid ground soon.

In an hour they pulled into a long drive leading up to Mister Clarkson's farm. When they stopped at the house, Mister Clarkson's wife and his six daughters rushed out to the wagon. "Mae and girls, this is the", He hesitated, "the Walsh family. I don't rightly know all of them but you all said that we needed help around here and I brought a bunch! Folks this here's, Marybelle, our oldest. She's a schoolteacher at our country school. She teaches the readin', ritin' and 'rithmetic, and there's Annabelle and Idabelle, Susiebelle, Josiebelle and our youngest, Jennybelle. We tagged on the Belles so as none of them would get the big head."

"I'm four, goin on five," Jennybell said.

The Clarkson girls asked the young Walsh boys questions as fast as a woodpecker pecks, while Mister Clarkson took his wife aside and told her of the Walsh family and of the Negro that they saved and where he figured the Walshs would live. In the old log cabin out back. "Well, Howie that place is a mess, so is the crapper. No one has lived there for years. How could you?"

"Well where are we going to put them?"

"In the barn for now. The girls and I will clean up that rat hole cabin in the morning. They don't look like they have had a bath in years! They brought a dog? And how do you know they don't have Cholera. You know there's been an epidemic going around brought on by people coming up from New Orleans."

"They look healthy to me, but they are dirty, Mae."

The immigrants slept that first night in the barn and they slept sound on solid ground that was covered with enough hay making a large cushion. Before dawn, Richard woke and nudged his wife and they did what they had not been able to do since leaving Ireland. A crowing rooster woke the boys and the baby as the sun rose.

Clarkson arose and went to the barn to see how his newly hired hands had fared. Before he got there, he saw both Richard and his wife on their knees at the garden spot turning over the black, rich, moist soil in their hands. He knew then that he had made the right decision in hiring them.

-35-

Kansas

John Duddy and his family traveled the Missouri River to the newly incorporated town of Westport near Kansas Territory. Catherine told her husband that she would go no farther by boat, and if he must go to the gold fields let it be by land so they debarked. John learned that a wagon train was forming but that it would take another week before it would be ready. John again could see the gold fields being picked clean before he got there. He never stopped to wonder why all the population of this community wasn't also going out for the gold. He thought that perhaps that if they had a map as he did, they would already be out there. In his frustration he went in to the nearest tavern, had a few whiskeys and started telling the man next to him of his problems. He spoke of his insistant wife wanting no more river traveling and his being anxious to get on with the journey. The bartender overheard the conversation and went to the end of the bar and relayed the conversation to an old, whiskered, red-eyed man with hair that was braided falling down his backside to his waist. The old man waited until he figured John, had just enough to drink and he went and sat beside him. "Friend, I hear that you're right anxious to get out to those gold fields. My name is, Joe Williams. I've done some scouting for the Army and have led many a wagon train out West, but I'm getting old and I'm cutting back if'n you know what I mean. My wife and I used to sow a large garden when we were full of energy. Now we just raise what we can eat. Let me buy you another drink. Charley, over here."

"I'll tell you what I have. I have a smaller covered wagon and a pair of healthy mules. The wagon is usually used by a cook but I'll fix it up so as there will be room to bed down and carry a few supplies. I'll make you and offer, friend. You can buy the whole lot for let's say one-hundred dollars or I'll take you and your party, how many are you?"

"Four. The wife and two boys."

"If I take ye it'll cost you five dollars a day until we get to Injun territory and then ten dollars a day. You'll have to buy yourself a good horse and saddle. I got them too."

"I don't have enough money to take you on. At least not for very far."

"How much money do you have, friend?"

"Don't rightly know. The good woman has the purse strings."

"I heard that you wanted to join a wagon train. One left two days ago. My friend, Amos Anderson took it out. I know his route and I think that we can catch up with that train in five days if we leave early tomorrow at day break. How about it? Let's get outa here and I'll show you the horse and saddle and the wagon."

The next morning before day break Joe Williams helped Catherine up into the wagon. She wimpered slightly. The boys clamored up and wanted to drive the mules. Joe had his own horse and John sat proudly atop his, smiling at his family, and off they went Westward with high anticipation.

Three days out, Joe said that they should over take the wagon train in two more days. That night, Catherine gave birth to a baby girl in the wagon with John and Joe Williams helping. They named the girl, Maggie. No telling where or when the baby would be baptised. Plans to catch the wagon train in two days were abandoned. Catherine would need some rest. On the fourth day they started again but at a much slower pace. Joe said that they would have to go faster if they were to catch up with the train in another four days. He suggested that they go on their own, following the trail and if they were not able to catch up, a newly formed wagon train back at Westport may catch up to them. He gave John the best directions that he could and told him that he would be collecting his money now. He wished the Misses well, kissed the baby, turned his horse Eastward and told John to look out for Indians.

They watched Joe Williams ride away disappearing over the crest of a hill and there they were, one lonly small wagon being pulled by two tired mules, a man up front on horseback with a holstered rifle and a wife, two boys and a new baby girl back in the wagon and no other humans or houses in sight. When the wagon stopped for the night there was dead silence until a wind came up and they then heard animals howl. John checked the supplies, the food and water were sufficient. He went to sleep that night knowing that when he found the gold they would come back to this Delhi by way of a fancy steamer, or if Catherine refused, a well appointed stage coach with all of them dressed in the very best clothes.

Right before the dawn appeared, Catherine picked up the baby, got out of the wagon and went behind some bushes to do her thing. She doubted that anyone could see her if she stayed by the wagon but she wanted privacy from whatever may be out there.

Dawn broke and John and the boys were awaken by loud hooping and squealing and the sound of hoofs beating the ground. He grabbed his rifle and came out of the wagon to see three Indians rushing toward him on two horses, two of the Indians rode one horse. Before he could raise his rifle an arrow pierced his chest and he fell dead beside the wagon. Both boys scrambled down to retrieve the rifle and both were hit by arrows, Michael in the neck and James in the back. They died instantly. The Indian without a horse took John's and then the three hesitated wanting the mules and wagon too. They conversed in their language and decided that all they had wanted to begin with was a replacement for the horse that was shot from under the younger brave by a white man at an encounter five days ago. They rode away still hooping and squealing. Catherine saw everything. At one time she screamed but fortunately her scream went unnoticed as it came at the same split second as one of the braves yell.

She wimpered and cried but showed patience in not running to her family until the savages were well out of sight and sound. She then came out from behind the bushes and went to her family carrying her baby daughter.

She sat on the ground with her dead husband and two sons surrounding her as she nursed her baby. She made no sound, just sat there staring out on the prarie until noon. She placed the sound asleep baby back in the wagon, pulled out the brand new shovel that John purchased to scoop up the gold with, and started digging graves. By the time the sun was setting she had placed her husband and her sons in the graves, covered them, and erected a cross made from stakes that John was to use to identify his claim. That evening she climbed back in the wagon and she turned the wagon Eastward. The baby began to cry. She brought forth from her baggage the fiddle that she played when she first met John in a pub in Doolin, a long time ago. She had not played the it since the start of the famine. Her grandfather taught her to play and now she played and sang with the words she had never sung before.

Oh let me go back, back, back

To that from which I came, came, came

Let it be like it was, was, was

Before the ground turned sour, oh so sour

The opression we could take, take, take

The starvation, naught, naught, naught

Take me back to the green green grass

The rushing streams, the glades, the stone walls

The ocean breeze and our own little patch,patch, patch

Tis too late now, now now

but there I'll forever be, my little Maggie.

She sang the same song over and over until the baby fell asleep.

The three Indians changed their mind and decided that they wanted the mules. When they crested the hill they heard the strange sounds coming from the wagon and were scared to death that unknown Spirits were around and silently but swiftly rode away.

A month later Catherine Duddy and her infant daughter, Maggie, appeared at her brother, Bart O'Malley's door step in Delhi, Illinois. She took the next year to recover from her ordeal. In the meantime she renewed her friendship with the Walshs who were not far away.

~36~

Saint Louis

Back in Saint Louis, after a restful night and a bath, Monica Garvin went to the largest bank that she could find to convert all of the money she had to American currency and open several accounts. When she entered the bank still dressed in her worn clothing and carrying a large soiled cloth bag, the receptionist was rather reluctant to direct her to her demand of "An officer of the bank". Mister Morgan, the bank's Vice President, was agape when she spilled out the contents of the bag containing the money. The sound of the gold and silver coins ringing on his desk attracted the receptionist and a few customers. The three stacks of English paper money was tied with pink ribbons. Monica told Mister Morgan that a wealthy uncle back in Ireland had died and willed her his small fortune. After securing cash and letters of credit and being wooed by several other officers of the bank, she smiled in a "so much for you" type of smile at the receptionist in leaving. From the bank she went to get her daughter, Ella. They went to the dry goods store recommended by Mister Morgan and his secretary and purchased several outfits for herself and Ella who was dumbfounded at her mother's unexpected extravagance. Monica had to shush her several times. They picked out new outfits for the boys. A stock boy helped them carry the purchases back to the boarding house where they attracted much attention from the residents there.

Doctor Carey arose that same morning and departed from the Franklin House refreshed. He went to the offices of a Doctor Schmidt and introduced himself. He told the doctor of his experiences and was startled to learn that Doctor Schmidt was wanting to retire or at least cut down on his work load. They had several drinks of the doctor's own concoction of blackberry brandy. After three hours of conversation Doctor Carey had a position in the offices of his new friend and benefactor Doctor Herman Schmidt. The next morning he took passage on the *Piasa* for Saint Louis and once there went directly to Monica's boarding house. When she came to meet him she was dressed in the latest fashion. He was flabbergasted and somehow wished that he had Father Healy along for support. He took her to lunch at the most extravagant restaurant recommended and over a glass of the finest French imported wine asked her to marry him only after he downed five glasses of the wine to gather the nerve. When she said "Yes" he downed three more, and with his rubbery lips wanted to know if she would come with him to Alton where he now had a practice and they could be married by their friend, Father Healy. When he said that they may have to get by on a meager sum until his practice grew, she told him, "I have some money, Francis. We shan't worry." He looked baffled and she said, "I had not told you. I had an uncle that left me a sum of money."

"Good, good for you," he mumbled. He told her that he had to return to Alton and find a place for them to reside and to make arrangements with Father Healy and, "Oh, my dear can we invite the Walshs to our wedding?"

"If you wish."

The good doctor, kissed her goodbye and walked out of the restaurant aglow but uneasy on his feet. The short trip aboard the *Piasa* made him queasy. He swore that if he was to drink in volumes it should be whiskey.

Monica walked back to the boarding house and thought to herself, "Here I am about to marry a doctor after being married to and being abused for years by a rat. Are the hard times really over?"

John Garvin stepped anxiously ashore in New Orleans and quickly went to the Convent. He talked to Sister Marguerite and was told that his wife had left. When questioned, she said that she thought that she had gone up river in the company of a doctor and mentioned something of a priest. Garvin vaguely remembered the surgeon and the priest aboard the *Armada*. Sister remembered hearing the towns of Saint Louis, Delhi, and Alton mentioned but she wasn't sure. Without lying, she said that she could be wrong but there may have been talk of her going back to Ireland. Sister realized that she had already given the man too much information but for the sake of The Church there was a remote possibility that their marriage would hold. Garvin rested overnight and booked passage on a steamboat going North. In debarking at Saint Louis he inquired at the Cathedral of the priest and learned of his next destination, Alton.

At breakfast at the Franklin House, both Father Healy and the doctor were in extravagantly good moods. The priest was told by the Right Reverend at Saint Matthew's Church that there was a need for him there. "My good doctor, do you know what this means.? It means that I will be able to say Mass in a real church and not secretly in someone's home like back in Ireland or aboard ships! What a joy. Now you look like a man that is bubbling over with something important to say. Out with it before you burst."

The doctor told of his meeting with Monica, his getting stoned on too much wine before he had the nerve to ask her to marry him and her quick, positive, reply, and their plans for the wedding. "Father, now tell me the truth. Do you think I'm an old fool for doing this?"

"I think you're an old fool for being so giddy. You're acting like a school boy. The Church would like it of course if you two were younger."

"So we could have children?"

"Of course, additions to the Faith, Doctor. But I have been with both of you and can tell how much you two love each other even though it be only a short time since she has become a widow. I would be very proud to marry you in my church."

~37~

The log cabin was made livable and Richard added on a room. The boys went reluctantly to school to learn the three R's from Marybelle Clarkson. The baby, Thomas, grew fat. Richard worked the fields with Mister Clarkson daybreak to sunset. Rose tended and expanded the garden. The Clarksons were Methodist and English which alarmed Rose until she realized that in her new country, freedom of religion was a given and no certain ancestry background was any better than another. Richard told her one evening, "They are not like most of the English we knew and if they don't push their religion we won't push ours."

After the first month, Clarkson told Richard how pleased that he was with their work and when it came time to harvest the corn he would go in and see if Chris Attucks still wanted to work for him. He and Richard expressed some doubt as to how good a worker he would be. Clarkson said that Chris of course would have to sleep in the barn and take his meals there, freedom for Negroes was one thing, dining with them, another. He also told Richard that in the months to come, if he and his family continued to "workout," he had a plan whereby he would sell them a small plot of land down the road. This stuck in Richards's brain more than anything else that had ever entered it.

Saint Matthew's was nearly empty. Monica and Doctor Carey stood below the altar with Ella beside her mother and Richard beside the doctor. Monica's two boys sat on one side of the aisle all dressed in their finery. The Walsh boys sat with their mother as she held her infant son, Thomas, on the other side. Mae Clarkson sat with them. Monica and Ella were decked out in the very latest fashion. The doctor had on a new suit. Richard wore his best, worn, hot, wool jacket with a white shirt, a bit ragged about the collar and pants with worn cuffs.

After the ceremony a carriage with a horse all decorated with flowers took the newly weds to their new home up the hill on State Street. Ella and her brothers had the choice of staying with Father Healy overnight or with the Clarksons. They chose the Clarksons.

Rose and Richard created their own garden patch and raised vegatebles that they previously never heard of, tomatoes, okra and different kinds of melons, strawberries and squash. Rose canned what she could. She helped Mae Clarkson and her girls can peaches and put up berries. They bought two piglets from the Clarksons, built a small pen and fattened them.

Richard and now, Chris Attucks worked the fields and cut timber and chopped wood for the coming winter. The Clarksons were looking forward to a bumper crop of corn, having already eaten and canned the soft sweet corn, the rest waited for the proper time to be shucked by hand and stored with the surplus taken to Grafton for sale and sent down river to Saint Louis.

John Garvin went aboard the *Piasa* and again, only because it was such a small boat, was able to talk to the captain regarding his wife. "No I don't rightly recollect a woman like that, Sir." When Garvin mentioned the priest, and the doctor and a man and his family traveling with them he said, "Why, yes, I do remember them. The man, a jolly nice chap, was looking for work among farmers and I was able to put him in conversation with Mister Clarkson."

~38~

Richard Walsh and Chris Attucks had been working through the hot days going through row after row of corn shucking the ears and cutting the corn stalks. They stacked the stalks in piles. They emptied each basket of ears into a nearby wagon. In the rays of the setting sun, Chris saw a flashing of something very bright in the nearby woods. It quickly went away. The next afternoon about the same time he saw it again and called it to Richard's attention. "The sun bouncing off a rock", Richard replied. Chris was to the rear of Richard and in the next row of corn. Right before dark he saw a figure of a man lurch toward Richard and bring him to the ground. Just as the man's hook was descending toward Richard's neck, Chris dragged the man off. He spun him around and hit him on the face so hard that Garvin fell to the ground with his hook imbedded in his chest.

Richard turned the man over and recognized the face and the scar. His mind envisioned that night aboard *Foley's Armada* and his foolishness in throwing a board overboard after him. "You saved my life, Chris!"

"You know this man?"

"Yea, I do indeed. T'is a long story, Chris."

"What we goin do wit him?"

"Well, for now lets drag him over in the woods, far in. We got to dig a grave tonight so the animals don't get to him. Chris, now listen, this is very important. You and I would not stand a chance in a court of law if the authorities learned of this. You especially. You must promise me that you won't mention this to anyone. You understand? No one! It's important that none of your or my friends or even my family know of this. No one."

That evening Richard told Rose that he and Chris were going out to see if their dog Shep would make a good coon dog. In the woods Shep was tied to a tree far away from the burial.

Two days later Richard and Chris took a wagon load of corn to Grafton. They told Mr. Clarkson that they would leave very early in the morning well before daybreak. Garvin's body was dug up, wrapped in a sheet and placed in the wagon under the upper layer of the corn. Before going to the grainery in Grafton Richard and Chris disposed of the body in the river. A week later there appeared an all too common article in the local paper, "Another body washed ashore near Alton. Hand missing. No identification or probable cause of death was made".

The next month after the harvest when all the wood was chopped and the grain put away, the Walshs went to Mass at Saint Matthew's in Alton. Confessions were held before Mass and at the urging of Rose, Richard, stepped into the confessional of Father Healy. "Bless me Father, for I have sinned. It has been awhile since my last confession." Father Healy immediately recognized Richard's voice and was inwardly elated that he was finally going to make a good confession and be in a State of Grace. Richard confessed all of his venial sins, his temper, his thoughts of other women, his drinking to excess on occasion, his cussing and using the Lord's name in vain.

He paused and the priest asked, "Is there nothing else, Ric—I mean, son. Is there not more?"

"No, Father, I think that's it."

Finally Father Healy became angry and frustrated. "Richard, what of John Garvin. When are you going to take responsibility and confess what could very well be called murder. When!!"

"Father, all I can say is that I did not kill him. This is the truth. He lived!" Richard was smiling.

"I don't understand. He never died of the ordeal? How do you know that?"

"That's the bloody truth it is. He did not die but is dead now to be sure."

"How do you know this, Richard. How do you know? When did he die?"

The priest suddenly remembered marrying his widow, or was it his widow?, to his good friend, Doctor Carey.

"When, Richard? When? When did he die?"

"You're alright Father. You need not worry. Now, Father what's my penance?"

~39~

Illinois 1856

For the past four years Richard along with Chris Attucks worked the Clarkson farm. Richard also worked some on a railroad being built nearby. The boys, Eddie and Daniel attended school. Their younger brother, Thomas would in another year. Howard Clarkson's passion was raising trotting horses. He bred them, bought them and raced them. His horses always finished well but never won. His friend David Pointer down the road would race him on the way to church on Sunday mornings with Pointer's wife following in a buggy and Howard's large family in a large wagon a ways back to keep out of the dust. Howard always came up short. That was before Richard started training and grooming the horses. He had a way with the animals. With Richard training them, Clarkson had developed a reputation of having the best sulkey horses around. Howard entered the horse that Richard deemed was the best of the lot in the Illinois State Agricultural Fair held for the first time in Alton. The horse's name was Dolly. Howard Clarkson told Richard two weeks before the race that if Dolly won Richard could buy the eighty acres down the road from him for a dollar an acre. He told Chris Attucks who helped Richard with the stable that he could buy a ten acre plot of ground over by the road to Jerseyville for a dollar an acre. The sulkey was prepared, and greased to the utmost. Dolly was ready and the race was on with the entire Clarkson and Walsh family in attendance. Chris was left on the farm and stewed for five hours until he heard the families singing and hollering coming down the road.

The next spring, Richard and his sons started building a house on their eighty acres of timber, ditches and weeds. They still worked for Howard Clarkson but not as much. Chris Attucks built a one room log cabin with Richard's help farther down the lane close to the road going to Delhi and Jerseyville.

In October on a Friday in the year 1858 Howard Clarkson, Richard and his two sons, Eddie and Daniel, drove two wagon loads of grain to Alton. When they reached the square they saw a large crowd of people assembling and red, white and blue buntings hanging everywhere. First, Richard thought that it was a circus. Howard informed him that there was going to be a big important debate by two very important people. In fact, one of them may end up being President of our country. Howard told Richard that these two men, one a Senator in the United States Congress, and the other a man from Illinois have been debating the slavery issue for some weeks now all over the state. This was to be their last debate. Did he want to stay and hear them? "To be sure! Do we have time?" Richard asked.

"These are politicians, Richard. They'll take all of your time if you let them."

Eddie and Daniel wanted to stay. They saw other boys and girls drinking from soda pop bottles and eating candy and were sure that their father would buy them some.

They gathered themselves into the crowd where they would be able to hear sufficiently as the two men were introduced, one a short portly man named, Stephen Douglas who was a senator and was up for re-election, and the other a tall, slender, dark complected person named, Abraham Lincoln who was a member of the House of Representatives and was running for Douglas' Senate seat. Senator Douglas started to talk first. After listening, Richard surmised that Mister Douglas was and wasn't for slavery but wanted the new states coming in to join the Union to decide for themselves. Mister Lincoln seemed to be against slavery as a whole and that the members who drafted the country's Constitution had meant to dissolve slavery eventually and that he was in favor of doing it right now. Each man was allotted time to argure his point; each one recieving spontaneous applause when their favorite hit on an agreed comment.

After an hour of this banter Richard said "You're right, Howard. They could go on forever. I'm for the tall one. He's sure an awkward, scragly man but I like the words that come off his tongue. Can I vote Howard?"

"No not yet. You have to be a citizen. We'll work on that."

Eddie and Daniel had been listening to most of the debate. Eddie liked, Senator Douglas and Daniel, Mister Lincoln. The boys were handed a wooden nicklel by men working the crowd. The speaker's faces were etched on them. They slept most of the way home.

On the way home Richard was troubled. He listened to the finer points of the dabate over and over in his head. He had a strange feeling about the tall, dark, lanky one. He felt that he was right in what he said, but sensed trouble in his eloquent words. He knew that somehow trouble always came with righteousness.

-Epilogue-

Lincoln lost the election but was later nominated for President. He won without receiving a single Electorial Vote from any of the Southern States. He was sworn in on March 4th, 1861 by the author of the Dred Scott Case, Chief Justice Taney. A month later the Civil War erupted.

Eddie Walsh left the farm and joined the Confederate Army. His brother Daniel sided with the Union. Both were killed in action in separate battles less than a year after their enlistment.

Doctor Carey tended the sick and wounded Confederate prisioners in Alton along with the returning Union wounded of Alton. Monica was seen wearing the latest fashions about Alton and Saint Louis where she had dress shops. Her daughter, Ella, entered a Convent, became a nurse and helped her step-father at the prison. Monica's son, Charles, became a doctor. His brother, Sean, became a common thief getting into trouble continusly in Saint Louis. When Monica died she left several hundreds of dollars to local charities.

Father Healy presided at the funerals of Richard, his wife, Rose, his good friend Doctor Carey, Monica and the remains of the Walsh boys. He married the younger Walsh boy, Thomas, to Catherine Duddy's daughter, Maggie, and lived to see Catherine move from Delhi to live with the young Walsh couple on the farm that his parents, Richard and Rose bought and nurtured. Two years after that, Father Healy died in a priest's retirement home on the outskirts of Saint Louis.

Thomas and Maggie reared three sons and four daughters having lost one at an early age. Maggie's mother stayed with them until she died.

Thomas and Maggie's sons and daughters would grow into the twentieth century with some of them raising another generation. And their story follows.

Book Two

≈

America

~1~

Jersey County, Illinois

June. 1927

Bridget Kelley stood between their white frame house and the weathered barn with her seven year old daughter, Gertrude, and her not quite three year old son, Joseph. They were feeding the Long Island Reds that they had raised from chicks on their eighty acre farm a few miles from Jerseyville, Illinois. Bridget rested the pan full of chicken feed on her protruding abdomen, in whose womb I was growing impatient. Gertrude held a smaller pan in her hand, and like her mother, strewed the feed in a sweeping arc so that it fell on and around the cackling hens and strutting roosters. Joseph begged his sister for some feed to throw. When he tried to fling it, most of it fell at his feet. He kept backing up as the chickens pecked at his toes.

"Give me some more," Joseph said to his sister.

"No!", Gertrude replied.

"Now don't be like that," her mother said.

"But he drops it, Mama. Look at that. They're pecking between his toes; he doesn't know how."

Joseph began to whine and turned toward his mother, pulling on her dress.

"How do you think you learned, big sister?," asked her mother. "Now Gertrude, give him a little more. There is no better way to learn anything than by doing it. Remember that."

Joseph smiled and continued to try. Gertrude frowned, but, with her mother, resumed the feeding. Bridget Kelley smiled under her round straw hat. She tugged at the neckline of her house-dress trying to fan her full breast. Her blue eyes were set wide above her high cheek bones. Although thin lines had begun to range out from the corners of her eyes and her thin lips, her posture on her small frame was erect. The other night, after they had gone to bed, her husband, Tim, told her that she was more beautiful now at age thirty seven and pregnant than she was when they courted. She doubted that, but his words pleased her.

Spring was fading fast and the days were becoming warmer. She hoped that it would not be another scorcher like last summer. The corn was up nicely; the wheat was half brown and half green and would be ready for Walter Hordack and his harvesting team on June the twentieth. That was always such an occasion; neighbors helping neighbors, food spread outside on makeshift tables, hard sweaty work with good fun, food and drink to follow. She worried about the coming of the baby and if it would interfere with the her preparations for the day.

"Well, if it does, I'll have my own little harvest," she thought.

Tim and Bridget Kelley desperately needed a good year for both the wheat and the corn after two poor ones. They were barely able to make interest payments to the bank the last two years and were told by Harry Blake, Alton Bank's vice president, that regardless of their friendship, a substantial payment on the principal was necessary this year or the bank might have to call in their mortgage. The Kelleys were hard workers. Their eldest son, Tom, was nine and already helping his father in the field and the barn. Most farmers counted on their children to help with the labor and favored having boys. One or two girls were acceptable, but any more were considered a burden. Three years ago when Joseph was born, in 1924, Tim and Bridget were told by Doctor Randall that they should not have any more children.

"Tim," Doctor Charles Randall said stepping out of the bedroom, "You have another fine son, but there will be no more, I warn you. We almost lost Bird this time. The boy's head did a lot of damage. If she has another, it will kill her, mark my words, Tim Kelley." Doc Randall walked to the wash stand.

"Is she all right, Doc? Tell me, I want to see her!", Tim said as he rushed toward the bedroom.

"Hold your horses, Tim", said Doc Randall grabbing Tim's sleeve with sweat dripping from his face. "She has lost a lot of blood and she's sleeping now. Maggie will be out with the baby in a minute after she cleans him. What Bird needs now is a lot of rest. She's not to turn a hand now, mind you, for at least a week. I'll be back then. If you need me before then, send Tom for me. Burn those bloody rags and towels. I don't know what we would have done without Maggie's help, Tim. She is getting up in years, but she can still put a lot of women to shame. I hope she can stay with you for a few days."

Maggie Walsh was Bridget's mother. She had come to be with Bridget and stay as long as necessary. Bridget's mother and father, Thomas and Maggie, lived on their own farm in the next county just a few miles away.

Tim Kelley's feelings were confused as he and Doc Randall walked toward the door. He was happy to have another son but deeply concerned about his wife. If he had to choose between them, it would certainly be Bird, regardless of what the church or Father John Clancy would say. He grew irritated, just thinking about it.

From the minute Doc Randall arrived, Gertrude and her older brother, Tommy, sat outside on a large limestone step. They were holding hands and had been sitting there for what seemed to them like hours, listening to the screams of their mother and the excited words of the doctor and their grandmother. Gertrude had sobbed throughout and held and squeezed her brother's hand. Although nothing was said, Tommy knew that he was to act like a man. He found it hard to grit his teeth and convey some sort of confidence to his sister. Swallowing when there was a lump in his throat seemed to help. He kept his jaw set, pursed his lips, and tried to get his sister to say the Our Father and Hail Mary with him. When the screams had subsided their worry had deepened. When they heard a baby cry their anticipation grew.

"Well, there they are, Tim. We couldn't have done it without these two guardian angels sitting out here." Doc Randall shaded his eyes for a moment from the bright sun. "You have a fine baby brother, kids.

Gertrude, you're no longer the baby of the family. You two are going to have to help your mother a great deal for a while."

"Is she," Tommy slowed his question, "Is Mom all right, Father?"

Tim quickly changed the concerned look on his face to a smile, but not in time for his son not to notice.

"Yes, Tommy, she has lost—-she needs a lot of rest now, so you two try to be as quiet as possible and help Grandma take care of things."

Maggie emerged from the house into the bright July morning holding Joseph. Her long snow white hair was tied in a bun. She was short and plump, and her smile, with her toothless gums showing, demanded, and always received, a return smile. Joseph was wrapped in a blanket, just his red face showing, his lips moving in a determined fashion. Joseph started to cry and that set off the nearby chickens to cackling and a rooster to crowing. Everyone laughed except Joseph.

As Tim and Doc Randall walked toward Doc's new Model T, they heard Gertrude ask, "Can I hold him, Grandma?"

"Tim, remember what I said. No more children. I don't care what Father John J. Clancy or our Pope says! No more children! I told your brother Mart the same after Marguerite was born and look what happened. I've seen too much of it, and I don't seem to be able to do much about it. Now I had better get home to my own. Send Tom after me if needed."

"Thanks, Doc."

As Doc Randall seated himself behind the wheel of his automobile, that looked like a top hat with wheels, Tim turned the crank. When the Model T started, it set off the chickens again. Tim turned and walked toward his now, three children, his mother-in-law and his wife in the bedroom.

That was three years ago.

With this pregnancy, Bridget had had very little discomfort so far and wondered why Doc was so worried.

Gertrude shouted, "Mom, look at Joseph, he's picking up chicken poop!"

"Stop that, Joseph", Bridget pleaded. "And watch that mouth of yours, Gertrude."

"What did I say Mother, what else can I call it? You should hear what Tommy calls it. He—-"

"Don't you dare! Here, move your brother back some, so that the feed doesn't end up in a pile at his feet."

"I told you he doesn't know how, Mom."

Tommy emerged from the corn field carrying a hoe, his perspiration showing through his blue coveralls and his shirt beneath. He was growing out of his clothes so quickly. Lifting his hat off his head to cool himself, he smiled at his mother and asked, "Mom, can I go over to the Whitfields for a little while?"

"Why?"

"Earl said I could come over any time and read all about Lindbergh in the newspapers they saved. Can I, Mom?"

"Are you finished hoeing?"

"Yes ma'am."

"All right, but be back in time for lunch. Take Mrs. Whitfield some of our turnips. Pick them fresh from the garden."

"Thanks, Mother," responded Tommy excitedly, running off toward the garden.

"Oh, and Tommy, ask Mrs. Whitfield if you could bring back one of the older papers for us to read."

Lindbergh's flight to Paris in his Spirit of St Louis had captured the interest and adulation of everyone in the world, especially anyone close to St. Louis.

Bridget emptied her pan and turned toward the house. "Come on, children, that's enough for today."

She took a few steps and stopped, dropped her pan and bent over in pain. Gertrude, startled, looked up at her mother.

"Mother! What's the matter?"

"It's the baby, honey, I think—-go and get your father, quickly. I'll sit over on the step. Hurry now, and then go fetch Tommy. Come here, Joseph, help Mommie."

It had been a torturous journey. Doc Randall was out of town. He had previously instructed Tim and Bridget to have the baby delivered in the hospital at Alton and had even suggested that Bridget stay with her sister Gertrude, in Alton a couple of weeks prior to the expected delivery date to minimize the risk. Bridget would not hear of it. Tim and his son, Tom, hitched their mare to the buggy, and the three of them traveled as fast as they dared over seven miles of deeply rutted dirt road and ten miles of pavement to Alton.

~2~

At ten after nine the next morning, Bridget Kelley gave birth to a ten pound, healthy, baby boy. She was not expected to live through the night. The family had gathered in the small waiting room, sitting at times in silence, numbed by the prognosis given to Tim and the rest by Doc Randall. He arrived early in the morning and had been with Bridget all the time. It was now nearly eleven. Tim was at his wife's bedside, trying his best not to weep. In one of her conscious periods Bridget laboriously discussed with her husband, the name for the baby, and how it was to be cared for. She could not muster the strength to discuss or even to worry about the other children. Tim had reluctantly agreed to have Bridget's Sister, Stella Muhm, take care of their new born son, Francis Leo Kelley. Stella and Bridget were very fond of each other.

Stella and her Husband, Emil, who was a successful salesman for a refrigerator company, lived in St. Louis since their marriage six years ago. Although having tried they were unable to have children. Stella was the oldest girl in the family and had taught country elementary school for several years before marrying.

Bridget asked the nurse to bring in her baby and to fetch Stella. The nurse returned with the baby who was asleep. Her sister, Stella was close behind clutching a handkerchief, manageing a smile under her uncombed auburn hair and reddened blue eyes. The baby was placed in Bridget's arms. Stella sat alongside them looking first to Tim on the other side for a hint as to why Bridget wanted to see her.

"Stella, I— We want you and Emil to take care of Francis. Tell me that you will," Bridget pleaded, smiling first at her son and then her sister. " Please say that you will, Stella."

Stella broke into tears, and found it hard to talk among her sobs. The request also shocked her. She had not thought of the baby or what would become of him. She and her husband had reconciled themselves to a childless marriage and had been living as such in an efficiency apartment in a building where children were not allowed.

"Stella. Please?"

Stella glanced across at Tim, who with his head buried in his hands stared at the floor, not responding.

"Stella?"

"Oh, Bird, Don't talk like that now, every—"

"Stella I haven't much time. Tim, here, can't take care of him. I want you and Emil to. Please now, tell me that you will, please?"

"All right, if that's what you and Tim want; we'll do our best, but—-"

"You'll make a perfect mother, Stella, I always told you that. Now here, take him."

"Oh—-Oh," She stammered.

The nurse took the baby from his mother and placed him carefully in Stella's arms. Bridget looked up at her son, Francis, in her befuddled sister's arms and smiled, satisfied, and closed her eyes, fading into unconsciousness.

The funeral arrangements were by Jennings Brothers in Jerseyville. A Requiem High Mass was celebrated at Saint Francis Xavier's Church and the Interment was at St. Francis Xavier's Cemetery.

The midmorning sun warmed those clustered around the open grave. The closed, gray, cloth covered, pine casket rested on supports, ready to be lowered. Muffled crying and sniffling mixed with a mocking bird's serenade from a nearby tree top. A gentle breeze carried the sweet scent of clover, but no one noticed. On one side of the casket stood Tim Kelley holding Gertrude's and Joseph's hands. Tom put his hands in his pockets, and stared at the ground. To their sides sat Mom and Pop, Bridget's parents. Maggie now showed all of her seventy-six years. In back of them stood, Stella and Emil. Bridget's other sister, Gertrude, and her three brothers, Martin, John, and Richard and their two cousins, Maymie and Marguerite. The Jennings Brothers stood off to one side, ready to assist in any way that became necessary. Doc Randall and his wife Ellie stood in the background. Father John

Clancy stood between two altar boys in their black and white garments at the head of the casket. Father Clancy had married Tim and Bridget, baptized their children and had brought the Sacraments to Mom and Pop Walsh when they became unable to come to church. He had been like family to most of those gathered. He was in his mid-fifties and had immigrated from Ireland some twenty five years ago, still possessing a strong Irish accent. He waited, with his head cocked slightly, listening to the mocking bird's song and then began to speak.

"Tis God's will that dear Bridget has been taken from our midst. He has a grander purpose for her in Heaven, we can be sure of that. Perhaps some of the answers lie with that baby boy back there in the hospital. We find it hard searching for a reason. It is not our privilege to know why these things happen, so let us not question, let us proceed with our lives in a way to please Our Lord and Bridget. Please join me in the Lord's Prayer. Our Father, who art in Heaven———."

Out of habit, everyone recited the prayer and several others after that. Tim, for the first time, began to realize that he had a problem with what to do with his children, not the baby, he couldn't have cared less about his new son; besides, Stella was going to take care of him, but what about Tom, Little Gertrude and Joseph?

When the ceremonics were over, Tim walked back to the waiting automobiles and buggies with Father Clancy. The relatives smothered the children with attention.

"Father, what am I going to do with the children? I can't take care of them on the farm! What am I going to do?"

Never before had Tim Kelley felt so weak and helpless. He was six foot two inches tall, lean and strong with long muscular arms and large calloused hands. He had thick black hair and bushy eyebrows. Tim Kelley was brought up on a farm and his education consisted of nothing more than six years of elementary schooling squeezed in among his chores. He had not ventured beyond Jersey and Madison County. He was the youngest of six brothers and five sisters, some having left home with no further contact. His brother Martin was the only known sibling that kept in touch. Their parents died years ago. His brother, Martin Kelley, married Bridget's sister, Peggy, and when she died, giving birth to his second daughter, Maymie, he took off for California, leaving

Maymie, and her sister, Marguerite with Mom and Pop Walsh. Martin Kelley did correspond with his girls and sent money for the them, but he never returned. Tim knew that he could not leave his children but slso knew that he could not take care of them on the farm.

"Father?"

"One thing at a time, my son. Where are you staying tonight?"

"With Mom and Pop, but they can't take care of the kids, they're too old now. They're good old souls. They raised Maymie and Marguerite as their own, and always gave shelter to anyone else that needed it. They always seemed to manage. I'm going to miss Bird so Father."

"I know, Tim. I know." Father Clancy turned back toward the grave and saw Tom still standing there.

"Come on, Lad," he said gently. Tom had been reading the grave markers in the family plot:

Thomas R. Walsh, 1851—- Wife Margaret Duddy Walsh, 1851—-

John Duddy 1821—-1851 Catherine Duddy 1820—-1897 Born Galway Ireland

Bart Kelley, 1830—-1910 Wife, Bridget Hines Kelley, (no dates) born Churchfield Co. Ireland

So many first names the same, Tom thought, and who were they? Tom turned and walked toward his father and the priest.

Father Clancy said, "Tom, your great grandfather and great grandmother, Richard and Catherine Walsh were buried over there by the corn field. The simple stone grave markers have weathered beyond reading, but they're there somewhere."

Relatives and friends, all bringing food of some kind, gathered at Mom and Pop's farm. Makeshift tables were set up on the lawn, a special one set for the family.

Mom and Pop were what was called, dirt poor farmers, as were most of their neighbors who worked small forty to eighty-acre farms. The Walshs raised chickens, a few geese, sold surplus eggs, raised a few hogs, had a dozen milk cows and two horses, and grew vegetables, and wheat and corn, all on only fifty acres of tillable soil, the rest being woods or badly eroded small gulleys. Very little of the farm products were sold, most being consumed by the family. They valued their freedom and independence and their opportunity to produce through their labors. They took pride in being self-sufficient. They thanked God for having survived.

The gathering was rather subdued at first, but in time the conversations grew in number and laughter was heard from some of the tables, except where the family sat.

When it appeared that everyone had finished eating, Mrs. Whitfield came over and offered to take the children to another table. Tom was reluctant to go as he sensed something was about to happen, but he moved off, lagging behind the others.

Father Clancy spoke. "Good people, times are sad enough, but I think you all realize that we have another very immediate problem. The children. What's to become of them? Stella and Emil have agreed to take care of little Francis, thanks be to God, but what of the others?"

Mom and Pop spoke in unison, "We can take——," before they were interrupted.

"No! That's out of the question", said Father. You have more than done your share over the years and God will surely reward you. Now it's someone else's turn."

Father looked around first at one, then another. No one spoke. Marguerite, now twenty three, blurted, "I would try to take one of them if I wasn't working in St. Louis, but I only have a sleeping room. I just don't know how I can, Father."

Maymie, her younger sister said, "I'm still at home here, doing what I can to help Mom and Pop. I don't know anything about kids. I don't think I could do it. Besides, I'm looking for a job in St. Louis."

"How about you, Gertrude?" asked Father.

"Oh, not me, Father, I'm engaged to Frank Ryan, and he don't like kids. We're getting married in the fall, maybe next week!"

Everyone looked surprised.

"And when did this happen, pray tell," asked Mom.

"Oh, Frank doesn't know it yet, but I'll pin him down to a date on our trip to Chicago this weekend."

This would be the third marriage for Gertrude, if it took place. She discarded husbands as quickly as whiskey bottles.

The only ones left were the men. Bridget's brother, Martin, was a bachelor and had a farm a mile away. Richard wasn't quite right since the horse kicked him in the head, and, John, a veteran of the World War, received a disability pension for being gassed, and spread his monthly check out among all the speakeasies in the surrounding counties.

"My, oh my!", exclaimed Father Clancy. "Unless someone can think of something else, I will ask Sister Benedict if they have room for them at the orphanage. At least they will be together, for the time being anyway." Tom, "Little" Gertrude, and Joseph frowned.

~3~

A week later Tim Kelley and his three children arrived at the Saint Agnes Children's Home in Alton and were welcomed in by Sister Benedict. The children were to remain for an undetermined period of time while their father continued to labor on the farm hoping to make a go of it without his wife.

Emil Muhm had driven up to Mom and Pop's from St. Louis to pick up Stella and the baby, Francis, and take them back to the three-room flat he had moved in to while Stella was getting pointers from her mother on how to take care of a baby. They drove back, Stella cradling Francis, successfully speaking the language of babies, and Emil driving slower than he had ever before, both happy, but apprehensive.

Mom and Pop Walsh sat on their screened, front porch watching the dust settle back on the road and the nearby foliage in the wake made by Stella and Emil's brand new 1927 Chevrolet. Maymie was in the kitchen clanging pots and pans. Their son, John, was in the barn removing the halters from their two horses and cursing with every other word.

"We're getting old, Pop," Mom said with a sigh.

"Yep. But I don't need to be told that all the time. I know I'm getting forgetful, but I'm not likely to forget that. Not with all these aches and pains to remind me."

"I didn't exactly mean that,—-Oh, I don't know what I meant Pop, I'm just getting so tired. We've been through so much and worked so hard. It's been an up hill struggle, all the way, hasn't it?"

"Yes, I guess it has, here lately anyway. I never really stopped to think about it until now. Anyway, Mom, We ain't ever had to pick shit with the chickens."

"Oh, don't talk like that! I'm not complaining. I've just never taken the time to look back on where we've been and what we've done, and

I sometimes wonder if we did right with our children. I don't know where we went wrong with Gert——"

"Or that good for nothing son of ours out there in the barn. Listen to him; he's calling those two mares sons of bitches! Where did he learn all that profanity. Not from me!. I'm learning it from him."

"The Army did that, it's not his fault——"

"What's that song, 'How you gonna keep them down on the farm after they've seen Paree?'. Well, He's back on the farm, but thinks he's still in Paree."

Now, Pop, John's a good boy He——"

"Boy ? He's what, thirty-seven years old! You and I can't take care of ourselves forever and he certainly ain't going to, and Maymie in there has her eyes on that railroad mechanic guy in Alton. As soon as he pops the question she'll be gone."

"Charles is his name, a nice man."

"Fergie, he calls himself, Mom."

"That's enough of that. Anyway, I'm not worried. We have each other. Our folks made it, and so did theirs."

"Just barely."

They held each other's hand. A gentle breeze crossed the porch carrying a faint scent of Cedar from a nearby grove.

"Have you ever thought about maybe going to Ireland where our folks came from, Mom?"

"Where in the world did that thought come from?"

"Well, have you?"

"No, I haven't, have you?"

"No, not until now. Remember how my mother and yours used to talk about Ireland?"

"Oh, that was long ago, I thought your memory was slipping."

"I remember them saying that they hated it."

"No, that isn't it at all, they hated the conditions, not the land."

"Who was it, your mother or mine, that said they owned land there?"

"Your mother, Maggie. You have something about it up in the trunk with your mother's things. We'll have to go through that some day, Mom, but I'm too tired now."

"Me too. It just breaks my heart to think of Bridget and the children, I want to hold and hug them and take care of them. It hurts so bad, it just..."

"I know, Mother, I know."

~4~

Frank

With my erratic education, and a shameless recall of my grades, I have calculated that since Adam and Eve there have been billions, if not trillions, of human beings that have lived on this planet and they all would have a story to tell. This is mine. It is no longer fragments of happenings and memory, with fiction mixed in, but will now be documented and out of my mind and into whomever invites the words into their brain cells.

I don't remember being born. I don't remember my mother dying and my father crying. I don't remember my two brothers and my sister being sent to the orphanage. My father was a farmer and couldn't take care of them and me and work the land at the same time. All of that and much more crept into my brain later, and the longer it remained there, the more it seemed that I did remember those particular events. The first thing I do remember is being on the kitchen floor at our home at 1723 Longfellow in St. Louis, Missouri. I don't remember my age at that time, I must have been about three or four. I had a fairly large and heavy toy truck. I shoved it off and it smashed against our brand new Frigidaire refrigerator. My mother, Stella, turned quickly from her chores and admonished me severely. The dent in the box was small, much smaller than that in my truck. My truck did not receive the tender caressing that the refrigerator did, nor did I.

I call, Stella, my mother and Emil, my father, because for all intents and purposes, they were just that. At that time, I either was not told or was too young to comprehend, that Stella was my aunt and Emil was her husband. They were Mom and Dad to me and were to remain so.

After the truck mishap, I remember a time when I absolutely believed that I saw the Easter Bunny in our bedroom. I had been told that he was coming, so I saw him. Our bedroom sat between the front living room and the only other room, the kitchen. Three rooms all in a row which was part of a four family flat: two up and two down.

Most of the houses on our block were old, made of brick, two story, three room flats, with a small yard in back between the house and the garages. The large, soot covered limestone, Immaculate Conception Church, where we attended, stood on the corner of Lafayette and Longfellow Boulevards. Across from the church was, what seemed to me, a very large vacant lot upon which all the boys in the neighborhood played. I had been told that I was not yet old enough to join them. According to the street maps, there was only one Longfellow Boulevard, but in a way, there were two. The block upon which we lived and that Longfellow on the other side of Russell Blvd. That Longfellow was the home of fine, large mansions, a few made of brick, most of stone, and none less than fifteen rooms. Many of the homes had ballrooms on the top floors. All of them were on beautifully landscaped, quarter acre lots. Running a slightly bent parallel to "that" Longfellow was Hawthorne Blvd., just as elegant, and the two boulevards merged right before running into Grand Avenue, some two very, very, long blocks later.

Mr. Livingstone and his wife lived upstairs from us. He worked on the railroad, or for the railroads. They were rich. They bought a new car every year, sometimes twice a year, and he didn't seem to have to go to work very often. He had something to do with train wrecks. He told Dad that he operated a big crane, and could be called out at any time. Sometimes he would be gone for days. They had a private telephone line and had to stay close to it at all times waiting for a train to wreck. I guess that's why he always needed a new car, for dependability. Sure seemed like a waste, only to be able to drive to work. We had an automobile, certainly not a new one like Mr. Livingstone, but it looked new to me. Nice and shinny black. Dad traded his Chevrolet for a used Ford. He drove it making his rounds selling coolers and refrigerators to grocers and meat markets. "We aren't rich, but not poor either", Mom always used to tell everyone. At the south end of our block, living in a larger more elegant house, lived a very old man who said his name was Colonel Brown. In warm weather he would sit in his rocking chair on his expansive front porch with his Union Army cap on his head.

Julia Siska and I would take turns sitting on his lap and listening to his stories about the war. If we listened well he would reach in his uniform coat and pull out lolipop suckers for us.

~5~

One fine spring day I was told that we were going to the country. We were going to visit my mother's father, "Pop" who lived on a small farm a few miles north of Alton, Illinois. He was having a birthday. I was told that all of my relatives would be there, or at least most of them. My grandmother, Maggie Walsh whom her children always called, Mom, died when I was two.

It seemed to take forever to get there with Dad driving and my mother beside him telling him how and how not to drive all the way. "Watch out for that car, you're going too fast, there's a red light up ahead. Mercy, mercy, Emil, careful, careful, watch it!" She was constantly slamming her foot on the floorboard and tisk-tisking between every word. If she were driving we would never have gotten anywhere as her foot would have been on the break all of the time. Mom did not learn how to drive and she didn't want to. She was satisfied in instructing Dad and making a nervous wreck out of us both.

The trip entailed going across the "Free Bridge" and driving through the towns of East St. Louis, Granite City, Venice, Nameoki, Rockford, Mitchell, and South Roxanna, and Wood River on Illinois Highway Three. Each town had railroad crossings and it seemed that at every crossing there were one or more rail cars blocking the road. As we waited for the engineer to hook and unhook box cars and get moving them back and forth but never far enough to free the crossings, we took in the black coal smoke from the steam engines along with slaughter house vapors of blood and manure. The smell of burnt metal came from the Granite City foundry and the strong scent of oil from the refineries in Roxanna. The oil smell made my mouth feel rubbery. It was a relief to finally see the caboose or the engine pass and the guard gate rise at each of these many crossings.

When we arrived in Alton, I was shown the hospital where I was born up on the hill. Alton was a series of steep hills rising from the

Mississippi River. All of the streets were paved with brick. From the hospital Dad drove down along Belle Street at Mom's request. Belle Street seemed to be two or three blocks of nothing but taverns. "The moral decay of the city" Mom called it. "There's their car" Mom said, tish-tisking. "I just knew they would be there. Gertrude will be half drunked up for Pop's birthday." Gertrude was my aunt, a sister of my mom, and a fun-loving woman, as I had heard someone describe her.

Dad drove on and parked the car in front of Saints Peter & Paul Church on State Street. Dad said rather nervously, with my mother suddenly silent, that we were going to stop up the street at the orphanage and see my brothers and my sister. "Your mother and I think that it is time that you met them. You see, we are not your real parents."

I started to feel sick. My heart was running. I had a hard time swallowing. I knew something was happening that frightened me and I wanted to jump out of the car but Dad drove on looking at me in the mirror.

"We love you very much, Francis and nothing is going to change, believe me, but it is time that you learned a few things." Mom said fidgeting.

I was told by both Mom and Dad very quickly, as though they had been holding all of this in for a long time and were finally relieving themselves of the information as to who my siblings were, and why they were living in the orphanage, and why I wasn't, and why our last names were different, and who my real parents were. I was told that my real mother was named Bridget and that she died shortly after I was born back in that hospital that they showed me on the hill. I may have been told some of this at an earlier date but I didn't remember or comprehend.

By the time we pulled up to the orphanage, my stomach had settled down. I crawled over into the front seat and was hugged and consoled by Mom and Dad. We emerged from the car and I saw this large, sprawling stone and brick building set back on a large lawn sprinkled with huge oak trees. We went up the long walk and Dad and I waited at the foot of the steps while Mom went inside. I could hear the voices of many children. I told Dad that it sounded like school. "It is a school, son. It's just that these children also live here. This is their home for awhile."

At this point, I didn't know what to think, was I going to be put in this orphanage? What are my newly found brothers and my sister going to look like. Have they been told about me, just now, or have they known about me for some time. I felt uncomfortable.

Just then Mom came through the door with three children, all of them holding hands. Mom put her one hand on my head and her other on each child as she introduced us to each other. "Tommie this is your baby brother, Francis. And Francis this is your sister, Gertrude, isn't she pretty? Little Gertrude, your hair is so pretty. And this is your brother, Joseph. We call him Barty because his full name is Joseph Bartholomew." Barty blushed. We looked at each other, smiling but saying nothing. Dad went back to the car and came back with a paper bag and gave candy bars to my brothers and my sister while Mom lined us up under this big tree and told us to smile. She raised her Brownie box camera and took our picture. I got the last candy bar left. I stood there looking around as Mom and Dad asked my siblings how they were, how they liked school, the food, if they liked the nuns and when Mom asked, "Has your father been out to see you?" I got confused all over.

My sister, Little Gertrude, spoke up, "He was here last Sunday and said that he would come again today. Father also said that he might be able to take me and Tommie home with him soon." Barty lowered his head and his eyes watered a little.

"Well", my Dad said, " Don't worry kids, it won't be too long until your father will be able to take all of you back home."

This father, would he be taking me with him? I guess Dad sensed my confusion and reminded me that my real father was Tim Kelley who lived out on a farm. We left soon after telling them that we would be back and that they, Mom and Dad, were so pleased that I finally got to meet them. I noticed that all over the lawn there were groupings of children with older adults visiting. I saw other kids looking through the windows, waiting for a familiar face to come up the walk bearing candy or for someone to come and take them home.

~6~

As we drove away from the orphanage, Mom proceeded to tell me who all was going to be at "Pop's", my grandfather's house. "Now, you're going to see Marguerite and Maymie." I smiled at this, I liked them a lot. "Your uncles, John, Richard and Martin will be there and you met your grandfather once but probably don't remember him. Your Uncle John was a soldier in the World War and got gassed in the trenches of France. Oh, and your Aunt Gertrude is supposed to be there."

I didn't rightly know if I liked my Aunt Gertrude. She she had the habit of tisk-tisking at just about anything that Mom or Marguerite and Maymie had to say. I heard someone once say that she was a loose woman. Her clothes always seemed to be tightened up to me, especially her dresses which were on the short side and of that ugly flapper style. I had heard somewhere before that she had a son, well an adopted son, named Jimmy Geeres, who was placed in the orphanage. She and a previous husband, Mr. Geers, adopted him. When they parted and divorced, Jimmy went back to the orphanage. Aunt Gertrude lived in St. Louis as did Marguerite. They both came to visit us often.

Maymie lived on the farm with Pop and kept house for him and Uncle John and Uncle Dick. She longed for the day that she too could leave. Marguerite and Maymie's mother died in childbirth when Maymie was born and a while afterward their father, Martin Kelley, went to California to seek his fortune, leaving the two girls with Mom and Pop. My Uncle Mart Walsh had his own farm about a mile away from my grandfather's. Martin Walsh was my mother's brother who had been to California a long time ago, made some money on the railroad and came back with enough money to make a down payment on his forty acre farm. I remember seeing picture post cards of him with his hat pushed upward and reaching for an orange off of a tree. One of the cards had his photographed face superimposed on a figure with a knapsack over one shoulder walking on a railroad track with "I'm coming by rail" printed alongside. I didn't seem to have any trouble having two uncles named Martin.

My Uncle John had a lot of stories to tell about the war and enjoyed telling them in the taverns in North Alton or down on Belle Street. Pop tried to get him to do more work around the farm but he always said that the gassing impaired his doing farm work and he had something more important to do. Maymie had a Model T that she bought from the mailman. Every Friday she would drive to Saint Louis to pick up her sister Marguerite from Shapleigh Hardware where she worked. Uncle John always went along to fix flats and, of course, have a few drinks here and there. If he got too drunk they would put him in the rumble seat. They would take Marguerite back to Saint Louis on Sunday afternoon.

Uncle Dick always wore a suit and never said much. My Dad didn't like him for some reason. Mom said that he was kicked on the head by a mule and wasn't quite right ever since. Dad told Mom that he didn't want him around me. Maybe he thought Uncle Dick would do me harm.

Dad drove on through North Alton and Godfrey and out into the countryside. We turned off the highway at a crossing. "Francis, see that school house up there," Mom pointed. I looked to see a small white building with a sign attached reading, Pembroke School. "I used to teach school there and so did your Aunt Gertrude. Mamie and Marguerite went to school there. Gertrude was their teacher. The school had only one room and all eight grades were taught." I had a hard time picturing Aunt Gertrude teaching.

"When am I going to go to school, Mom?"

"It won't be long." Her sentence ended abruptly as we came to an incline leading to a railroad crossing. "Emil be careful don't stop on the crossing, slow down, listen, listen do you hear anything coming? That crossing light doesn't always work. Amy Foster and her husband were killed here you know." With her hand still over her heart we crossed the tracks and descended on the other side. Another mile farther we turned down Lindley Lane. "Now," Mom said, "if we had gone straight, we would run into your Uncle Mart's farm." I gave a quick glance to where she was pointing. Off in the distance I observed the outline of a faded, white house.

The road that we were on was dirt as all of the country roads were and deeply rutted. Dad tried to keep the wheels out of the ruts. He said that when it rains or snows one wants to keep the wheels in the ruts, that way the car doesn't run off the road into the ditch. "Like you did when Mom died, I told you how to drive, but you wouldn't listen, we had to walk up the road in the mud and snow to Amos Lang's house and get him to pull us out with his mules," Mom ranted, tisk-tisking. I looked at Dad. He smiled slightly, chin up, didn't say a word. "Just look at that gully. It just gets worse every time we come up. Land sakes, when is John ever going to do something about that erosion!. Before you know it there won't be any farm left, just a big gulch!"

"Dick could help too," Dad responded.

"Dick isn't able," Mom responded. Dad smiled again. We turned in a drive of sorts and went up a hill and parked under a large Oak tree.

My cousin Maymie came off the porch to greet us and help carry things in. She bent down and gave me a hug. I liked Maymie a lot but I was beginning not to care for hugs. I felt that I was too old for that. They sure felt good but I didn't want anyone to know. From out of nowhere came this big goose honking and waddling toward me. She nipped at my leg and flapped her wings ferociously. I screamed and ran up on the porch and the goose followed. I opened the screen door quickly and let it "flap" behind me. When I turned around breathless a beautiful woman stood in front of me and said, "Don't worry, Francis, Matilda won't hurt you. She raises a lot of cane with strangers, specially little boys. My name is Sadie Fitzpatrick. I'm a friend of your Uncle Mart.", motioning over against one side of this large room where my three uncles were all sitting with the backs of their chairs tilted against the wall talking to my grandfather. "Francis, let me see your hands. My, look at those warts. How long have you had them?"

"A long time" I replied, embarrassed. "Someone told me that I got them because a toad peed on me."

"That's nonsense. After dinner I'll show you how to get rid of them."

As Mom and Dad came in, I could hear Mom whispering to Sadie, "A little girl friend of his down the street told him that."

"I don't have a girl friend."

Grandpa's house seemed to be one very large room. In the middle of this room was a massive black piano with stout legs. The top was covered with boxes of cereal, can goods of all sizes, candlesticks, kerosene lamps, books, jugs, stacks of cups, plates and what looked like a cookie jar. On the far wall was a wooden telephone with a black speaker and ear piece and a crank thing on the side. Near the south end of the room was a large black cast iron stove which Maymie was fussing over. When she saw me she asked, "Francis, would you like some goody?"

"What's that?"

"Oh it's something special, just a minute, I'll give you some." She handed me a small bowl of what looked like milk soaked bread. "Go on taste it." Soft, but not too soft, sweetened with brown sugar with a hint of cinnamon. I had two bowls of goody before my cousin, Marguerite ushered me out on the the porch. I looked for Matilda and relaxed when she didn't show.

"I'm going to show you how to make butter, Francis." Marguerite sat on a stool and proceeded to show me how to plunge this stick through an opening in this tall crock. She said that after awhile the cream inside gets thicker and thicker and harder to push and when it gets real thick I was to come inside and she would show me what to do next, but that I must not stop churning until it thickens. I sat there plunging and plunging and couldn't tell any difference in the consistency inside. I began to think that they, the adults, had found something to keep me out of the way or that my cousin Marguerite had found someone to do her chore. My arms were getting tired. I wanted more goody.

Just then an automobile drove up and my Aunt Gertrude emerged, not too gracefully with a cigarette hanging from her mouth and a bottle of beer in her hand. The man driving tripped on the running board and fell flat on his face with a beer bottle in one hand. Matilda came from under the porch, running, honking, flapping and attacked the man laying on the ground. "Get outta there you stustuffed old gruss" yelled Aunt Gertrude wailing at Matilda. "Get up from there, Fred. What kinda impreshion you gona' make on my father?" Both of them managed to get inside, giving me an embarrassed nod as they passed. I kept churning and tried not to laugh.

A few moments later my Aunt Gertrude came out of the house hurriedly and ran to the outhouse. I kept churning. Either the stuff was getting thicker or my arms were wearing out. All of a sudden I heard this piercing scream and in turning saw Aunt Gertrude bursting out of the outhouse hobbling with her under drawers around her ankles and hollering, "Snake! Snake! Jesus Christ!, There's a big black snake in the crapper! Get help! Help!"

I ran inside as Aunt Gertrude tried to get dressed while running toward the house. My Uncles John and Rich came out and burst out laughing upon seeing their sister still in disarray and cussing to beat the band. Uncle John went to the outhouse with a pitchfork and came out with a large black snake twined around the fork. It was alive and I watched him go off into the field and release it. Uncle John said that you should never kill a black snake that they eat the mice and rats around the house. I'm sure that my Aunt Gertrude would disagree with him. There was much laughter inside and a lot of cussing still from Aunt Gertrude.

I resumed my butter making operation and Grandpa came out and sat down beside me. He was shaking his head and nodding toward the screen door and he said, "I recon your Aunt Gertrude put on quite a show out here. She sure keeps things stirred up. Never a dull moment. You just about got butter there son. How old are you Francis?"

I replied that I was four and going to go to school soon. "How old are you", I asked looking up. He was tall and skinny and his white shirt was badly frayed around the buttoned collar that was too large for his neck, the shirttail being gathered in layers into his trousers. He fingered his large white mustache and smiling said, "Well now, would you believe I was born crossing the ocean a long time ago; neigh on some eighty years ago."

I looked at him for a long time. I didn't know people lived that long and I wondered how he could be born on water. "You see, Francis my father and mother came by ship from Ireland a way back then and I was born on the boat. When I was about your age my parents and my brothers and me moved to this very farm from a house up the road where my mother and father worked for the Clarksons. They raised enough money working on the Clarkson farm to buy this land. My parents built this house and farmed this land and your real mother,

Bird, and your mother, Stella, were born in this house along with your uncles and your Aunt Gertrude. Their mother and I had a wonderful time raising them. After they all grew up we raised Marguerite and Maymie when their mother my other daughter, Margaret died. So, Francis you're 100% Irish, remember that. Your ancestors came from Ireland. You be proud of that, and don't forget your brothers and sister, even though you're apart. Nor your real father, Tim Kelley."

"Oh, I forgot, your grandmother, my wife, Maggie, bless her soul, was a Duddy before we married and her parents came over on that same boat. So put that in your pipe and smoke it." Grandpa slapped his knee and laughed.

I was learning so much that my brain seemed about to explode when Grandpa said that the butter was done and I had better go in and tell Marguerite. I did and when I came back out Grandpa was smoking his pipe. A black and white shaggy dog came up on the porch and laid across Grandpa's feet. "That's, Shep. He's getting old like me. Shep's great, great, great, great grandfather was given to my two brothers and me when we came up river on a steamboat from New Orleans."

I had a hard time imagining him as a baby. Grandpa put down his pipe and blew out a bunch of smoke and we watched it curl and rise and flow up over the roof and out of sight. It seemed that his thoughts went with the smoke. "You know, that old outhouse over there has a lot of history to it. It's not a house that Washington or Lincoln sat in. Nothing like that, but an awful lot of folk sat in there since I was your age, yes siree."

Mom interrupted Grandpa by saying that dinner was ready. She brought my crock full of butter in with me and Grandpa. I liked him. I got to sit next to him. Aunt Gertrude's friend, Fred, was asleep on the sofa. I never found out anything about him. He slept all through our singing "Happy Birthday" to Grandpa. We ate fried chicken, mashed potatoes, corn on the cob, with my butter on it, hot bread out of the oven with my butter. I ate a slice of apple pie, gooseberry pie and rhubarb, all three with a glass of the creamiest milk.

The telephone jingled, quieting everyone, and Grandpa said that it wasn't for us, ours was three rings. Aunt Gertrude wanted to go and pick up the receiver and listen in but Grandpa wouldn't allow it.

After dinner when the dishes were done, Sadie Fitzpatrick took me out toward the side of the house under an old apple tree and asked me if I had a penny. When I said no she told me to go inside and get one from my Uncle Mart. When I returned she told me to rub that penny real good over all the warts, "real good" she repeated. "Now, close your eyes, Francis, and do exactly what I tell you. Make a wish that the warts go away and keep your eyes closed and throw the penny over your left shoulder as far as you can. Keep your eyes closed now and you must never, never go looking for that penny." I did what she said. I sure hated to part with the coin. I could buy some candy with it, but I also hated the warts. "I guarantee you that within two weeks your warts will be gone."

As we were about the leave for home I had to go to the bathroom. I opened the outhouse door and smelled the stink. It was a two holer. I looked down both holes for a snake. No toilet paper. The Sears catalog was about used up. The pages were slick. After doing my thing, I got up and looked down my hole and thought, I made butter today and now history.

A few weeks later, I remembered the pretty lady, Miss Fitzpatrick. My warts were gone.

~7~

That same summer Dad took me to Shaw's Garden. I got my first streetcar ride on the yellow #81 down on Park Ave. The seats were of woven cane. It felt good rippling my hands over the cane. The windows were open and I would watch the houses go by as the streetcar would rock from side to side. When the streetcar turned the metal wheels screached. Sometimes the long pole that touched the electric wire would give out with a loud crack and sparks would fly. I watched the people get on and off and the conductor every so often called out the name of the street when the car stopped.

The Garden was enclosed by a high stone wall. The Garden was free. We walked through a massive arch-way and upon doing so saw the Lily ponds with three plants in each pond. They had giant, round leaves with fluted edges turned up floating on the surface. They looked like very large green pies, each with a different colored bloom. Dad said that sometimes the plants got so big and so strong that a man could stand on them. I wanted to try it. "No, Francis, you're too big. They have to grow more." I felt big after that. I was impressed when he said that the Lilies were known as "The Victoria Regia" and came from the Amazon River in South America. A man from London, England, brought them here. Dad said that he read somewhere that down in South America the women washed their clothes in the stream and placed their babies on the large leaves. Dad also told me that the man from London, named Henry Shaw, had the Garden built, and that he brought specimens from all over the world, "Just for us to see, Francis."

Next we went to the Desert House. It was warm enough outside but it was hot and dry in there. I imagined cowboys and Indians peering from behind the tall cactus and large stones. Dad would name all the plants with words that were strange to me. "Look over there at that marvelous Sulcorebutia arenacea." All I saw was a round green ball with thorns wrapped around it and yellow flowers sticking out the bottom. "Look over here Francis, see that Cereus forbesii. We have some like that out in the country. After it blooms it has a fruit that is edible. Just don't eat the thorns."

"What does edible mean?"

"Edible means that you can safely eat it." Each and every plant excited him, almost as much as when he heard the Cardinals or Browns make a good play. We came upon a giant of a cactus and before I asked him he said, "That's a Carnegiea Giaantea."

"A what?" I asked. He repeated. It looked like a tall green chubby man with his arms sticking out and no head with long sharp whiskers all over him.

From the Desert House we walked up a path to a tall glass enclosed four or five sided structure with the statue of a funny looking man inside. Dad said that we were looking at the tomb of Henry Shaw. That was spooky. As we left the Garden I wondered why Mr. Shaw was there and not in the ground like everyone else. We walked a few blocks more and entered Tower Grove Park. I was getting tired and hungry but Dad said that he wanted to show me something. I could use something edible. Dad had been carrying a box. I almost asked him what was in it but remembered being told many times that children should be seen and not heard. I thought that he was going to rattle off some more strange names of plants as we passed numerous flower beds. We came upon a lake or more like a large pond. The pond had some small water lilies in it. There were some kids sailing small toy boats. They watched the warm breeze fill the sails of their boats and push them around the pond. Dad opened the box and brought out a small sailboat with sails and everything. He said that his brother, my Uncle Walter had brought it from the Goodwill Store and wanted me to have it.

"I also have two baloney sandwiches and some grapes. What do you want to do first, eat or try to sail your boat?" I jumped up and down and sideways and forgot all about being hungry. I gave the boat a push out into the water and watched it go almost out to the middle. I was excited. I thought of Grandpa crossing the ocean. My boat skimmed across the water and headed for a lily pad. It got caught, but in a little while the wind changed and away it went out to the middle and then it stopped. No wind. Dad said, "Wait a while that's what real sailors do when the wind subsides. The breeze will come back." We waited. I starred at my boat, even blew hard and waved Dad's hat. No movement on the sail. We waited. I stared getting hungry again. Dad said, "Let's eat" and we did. No wind. We waited some more... nothing. "Well". Dad said as he started taking off his shoes and socks. He rolled up his pant legs and walked out to get my sailboat. A couple of kids pointed at him and laughed. He came out of the water with awful black muck between his toes and handed me my boat. He sat down and washed his feet. We walked away from the pond, Dad still with his pant legs up, barefooted carrying his shoes and socks. I carried my boat in the box. "We'll do better next time," he said as we walked toward the streetcar stop. By the time we got to the streetcar stop his feet were dry and he put on his shoes and socks. I fell asleep on the way home. I told Mom how smooth my boat sailed. Dad smiled. So did Mom. He must have told her.

A few weeks later we went to Reservoir Park. We walked there. The Park has two small, shallow ponds. Dad brought the boat but he said that he was going to teach me how to swim. He said that I could take the boat in the pool with me, but first I had to learn to swim. I stripped to my underwear and looked around to see if anyone was looking and got in the water. Dad followed barefooted with pant legs rolled up. The water only came up to my knees. "Now what you're going to do is dog crawl. See if you can keep all parts of your body from touching the bottom. Keep your arms bent and paddle your legs like this." He was standing up straight and scratching like a dog do would digging. I tried it but my knees touched bottom. "No, you have to paddle your feet at the same time!" I paddled my feet and forgot to crawl, swallowed some water that now was pretty well stirred up. "Like this, Francis." Again he was scratching the air furiously and started to try to show me how to paddle my feet at the same time. He lost his balance and belly-flopped into the water with a big splash. He got up dripping and said, "Do as I say, not as I do." We both laughed and after a few more tries I finally was able to dog crawl back and forth across this small wading pool. He told Mom that I was a natural swimmer. She looked at him, still wet, smiled and wished to God that she could have been there.

Before my swimming lesson, Dad showed me around the Park. Across from Reservoir Park on Grand Avenue was this elegant apartment building called the Saum. Dad said that very rich people lived there. In the Park was a huge, metal statue of a black woman sitting on a throne on a large marble base. I crawled up and sat in her lap. Her body was smooth and when I rubbed my hand over her body it was as smooth as the hood of Dad's car. She did not have any clothes on. That didn't bother me. I liked her. I banged my knuckles on her thigh and it made a hollow sound. In the center of the park was the reservoir that took up most of the park. It looked like a fort with its high stone walls. Dad said that it held all the water for our whole neighborhood. Below it and not far from the beautiful black lady was an ornate stone water tower. Dad said that some years ago people were allowed to go up in the tower, but not now.

~8~

Gertrude

My sister, Little Gertrude started keeping a diary while at the orphanage with almost daily entries, some more revealing than others. No one knew about her diary.

April 5, 1932

Dear diary,

On this day, Father came to visit and took Tommie home with him. Joseph and I yearned to ask him when he would take us, but we didn't dare. I could see a tear in Father's eye as he kissed us goodbye. We hugged Tommie before he got onto Father's buggy and waved to them until they disappeared around the curve in the street. I went into the chapel and prayed that Joseph and I would soon be together with Tommie and Father. I cried too. I don't know if Joseph cried, but since he cries a lot I would bet that he did. I remember when Jimmy, our cousin was taken from here by Aunt Gertrude and her new husband. They went to Chicago to live and adopted Jimmy up there. Six months later Aunt Gertrude and her husband got divorced and Jimmy was brought back here. Tommie said that Jimmy told him that he was glad to be back. I couldn't imagine why. I used to think that our mother died on purpose. Mother scolded me for spilling some milk the day before she died. Sister Catherine Agnes told me why mother died. She said that a lot of women die in childbirth. Later on after talking to some of the older girls and learning how babies came to be I started blaming Father for my being here. I hope Mother and Father forgive me for thinking so. Now I sometimes blame my baby brother because he is alive and Mother isn't. I have confessed all of these dire thoughts to Father George and afterward feel so much better but some of the thoughts creep back and I have to confess them all over again. Joseph always complained that there was too much noise here and he is right. If someone drops a pan in the kitchen or a child squeales you can hear it all over. The lunchroom is always a madhouse. It is quiet through Grace and the meal but after that the nuns loose control until they blow their whistles 'til they are red in the face and everyone lines up to go to their classrooms, boys on one side and girls on the other. I never get to know any of the boys my age, only exchanging smiles and then blushing at that. At night after the lights go out there is always at least one girl who cries. Once, one of the new ones cried the whole night. It made some of the other girls cry along with her, remembering their first night.

~9~

Frank

My brother, Barty, whom I hardly knew, was staying overnight with us on Longfellow. He was to go with my father the next morning and get a pair of new shoes. Here was my seven year old brother, who evidently was taken out of the orphanage in order to be fitted for a pair of new Buster Brown shoes, and then to be sent back where he came from.

"Barty, come here and let me take another look at you. Emil, I think he needs more than just a pair of shoes, see about some socks. And, oh, look at this shirt, where did you get such a rag, Barty? Get him a shirt and some new pants too, Emil."

"I got the shirt from Richie Kramer, Aunt Stella, He out-growed it, and the Sisters gave it to me. You shoulda seen my old one." answered Barty to his aunt, who didn't hear a word he said as she twirled him around, tisk-tisking all the while.

I stood watching all of this feeling kinda perplexed. Here was this brother, in rags. Every stitch of clothing that I had was ten times better than his. I guess that was the first time that I felt better than someone else, "uppity", as Mom accused others from time to time. I didn't feel sorry for my brother. I was now beginning to feel jealous of him. He was getting the attention where before I had no competition.

"Mom, don't I need new shoes," I pleaded.

"Why, Francis, you should be ashamed. Emil come on, it's getting late. Klein's closes at noon on Saturday, you know."

"I'm coming. Where's my pipe? Oh, there it is. All right, Barty, off we go, come on. We'll be back in a couple of hours," answered my Dad as he went out the back door with my brother in tow, toward the garage.

My dad opened the garage door. He seated Barty in the Ford, started the car and backed out of the garage. He got out of the car and closed the garage door. As he went to get back into the car the motor died. The starter would not make connection as he tried to restart the car. He then went to crank the car. Many an arm was either bruised or broken while cranking a vehicle. A few tries only produced feeble chugg chug chug and a final wheeze. Dad took off his straw sailor hat, laid it on the hood and tried again. This time the ignition caught and suddenly the car lurched forward and with a thud pinned his legs against the garage door. He wailed. The car choked and stopped. Barty jumped out and ran in the house screaming for help. After calling the police, Mom called my Uncle Walter, he having read medical books and all. She was desperate. In what seemed like minutes an ambulance and police cars arrived, sirens blaring and red lights flashing. I was told to go out on the front porch and keep a lookout for Uncle Walter. Walter was my dad's brother. He was studying to be a doctor. Uncle Walter had a drinking problem. He had been studying to be a doctor for some twelve years. "One on, five off", Mom would say. For the moment, Uncle Walter was off. Off the booze and off studying. He managed a Goodwill Store down in North St. Louis. He brought my mother an old smelly bear rug from the store... the hide severely cracked and the bear's eyes kinda jellied over and in a trance.

I was a little self-conscious, standing out there on the porch waiting for Uncle Walter. All the neighbors were out looking at our house and wondering what all the commotion was about. I just knew something terrible happened to my dad and somehow also to me. I cried. Barty came out and helped me cry. Mrs. Schnur drove by in her silent running electric automobile. She always wore a black cape with a big stove pipe black hat on her head. She owned Schnur's Funeral Parlor which was just down the street on Lafayette from the Peetz Funeral Parlor. Mrs. Schnur didn't blink an eye at all the goings on at our house. She may have been thinking that she may be getting another customer. I worried about that.

"It was my fault! All because he was going to buy me some new shoes. It wouldn't have happened if it weren't for me", Barty sobbed.

I heard a screech of tires and a car swerved around the corner. As it got closer, I could see Uncle Walter standing on the running board, holding on to the car with one hand, and his brown felt hat with the other. He reminded me of Dick Tracy. He jumped off before the car stopped and ran to the garage.

"Wow!" I thought. "What a man."

Dad was taken to the City Hospital on Lafayette Avenue, almost downtown. Both of his legs were broken in two places. However, it was weeks before they realized that both were broken. They only set one. No one could say why they didn't know about the other one. They were sorry. They apologized. It was three weeks after his admittance that they decided to re-break his right leg and reset the fractures. Everything would be alright they said.

Brother Barty was returned to the orphanage, wearing the same shoes that he came with. Uncle Walter went back to the Goodwill to mind the store and read up on fractures.

Mom and I made two trips daily on the streetcar to see Dad. After three weeks of this we could no longer spare the streetcar fare. We walked every day. The hot, humid, days of the summer took their toll. Mom became more quiet, more cranky. She had less patience with me. I started to hear the phrase. "You know, money doesn't grow on trees". I got less and less of what I asked for. Soon it seemed I got nothing.

Dad lay in bed with both legs in a cast. He was in a ward with many other patients. His sheets and mattress often became wet with perspiration. He was despondent. The nurses gave him a straw Peetz Funeral Parlor fan and a used, felt bordered, fly swatter. The windows of the ward were kept open to catch any hot July breeze that may come along. He wanted to know how his Cardinals were doing. I told him not too good but they now had a good pitcher. His name was Dizzy Dean. "Dizzy? With a name like that he won't make it."

Sometimes on the way back home we would stop at Bettendorf's for groceries. Bettendorf's was about two-thirds of the way from the hospital, and we always arrived hot and tired. I liked Bettendorf's and

I didn't. I liked the way I could slide on the sawdust covered floor. The store smelled like raw meat, blood, fresh bread, oranges, and from a screen door opening to a small room that also opened out onto the sidewalk, I could smell wet chicken feathers. They didn't smell good. Chickens were sold alive, grabbed out of wooden cages by an old colored man. He and his wife, and sometimes their grandson, who was about my age, prepared the chickens. The chicken's neck was wrung. It was gutted and plunged into a tub of boiling water and then the feathers were plucked, all while the customer waited. "Fresh", they were advertised. "Bettendorf's had the best."

The thing that I didn't like was when Mom and the butcher confronted each other. I always wanted to hide somewhere or at the very least, to be seen as a stranger to my mother.

"Raymond, I want some Ox tails, the leanest you got and the cheapest. How much! Why that's highway robbery and you know it. What about soup bones? Oh, a couple of pounds. Get your thumb off the scale, Raymond. I don't like that. How about those spare ribs, how much are they? My Lord I can do better over at Henn's Market, which is just down the street from me. He delivers and also runs me a tab. Give me two pounds of bones for our dog, those are free aren't they? And I'll give you twenty cents for one of those fryers over there, the one making such a fuss. Yes, that one. Be sure that nig— a ah boy gets all the feathers off this time. I swear, everything gets higher and higher every time I come in here. You're not going to make a go of it if you keep this up you know. You'll be out of business in another month. You'll go belly up!"

"What's the name of your dog, Sonny?", Raymond the Butcher asked me.

He knew I was with her! He knew. Trapped again!

"Ah, Fido" I answered.

When we got outside, after stopping next door to pick up our chicken, and paying the old, smiling, courteous Negro two pennies for his trouble, Mom said, "I don't know what I'm going to do with you, Francis. You're embarrassing me. Last time we were in there you told the butcher our dog's name was Barney! For the life of me I don't know why on earth you picked the name Fido. Here carry this chicken."

"Mom, can I have a real dog someday?"

"No!, Do you think dogs, I mean money grows on trees."

I giggled. She frowned down at me and then laughed too.

"Mom, why do you fight so much with the butcher?"

"That's not fighting Francis. I was Jewing him down. You have to do that. It's a way of life."

I was beginning to learn more about "the way of life". I was also beginning to learn the names attached to people who were judged to be unpleasant to us because of our upbringing, fear, ignorance, or jealousy.

(Those names, which I now detest even when spoken in jest, or by one of their own, were used repeatedly in my so called "neck of the woods". Sometimes they were used in anger, but most of the time without thought that those named would have been hurt had they heard them. And sometimes they were just "The things to say". Sometimes saying those words made the sayer feel more important. I have my doubts that Samuel Clemens meant any harm in writing some of those words. They were part of the times. Part of the ignorance of those times. I truly believe that he loved some of the people that he used those words to describe. They were also part of my ignorant times, and will be used sparingly and purposely.)

July ran into August. The temperature and humidity rose. The Star Times said that this was one of the hottest summers on record. The walks back and forth to the hospital seemed longer. It seemed that Dad would never get out of that place. His boss, Mr. Breckenridge, came to see him right after the accident and told him not to worry about his job, it would be waiting for him when he got well. Of course, they could not pay him in the meantime. Mr. Breckenridge came again a month later and told Emil that he was sorry.

"We had to hire someone to take over your territory, Emil. I'm sure you understand. Your customers have to be served. They all ask about you. When you get back on your feet we'll see about getting you a new territory, although no one seems to be ordering right now. People are afraid of the future, Emil. This depression is terrible."

It was shortly after that that Dad developed a slight twitch in his facial muscles, and an odd sporadic grunting before speaking.

~10~

September came. My first day of school. Mom brought me up the two, long, wide terraces of limestone steps leading to the front door of The Immaculate Conception Elementary School located just a block from the church. As we entered the front door, I saw her. She was beautiful. She was clothed in a white robe of some kind with a blue shawl covering her head. She had a baby in her arms. Then I noticed a big menacing snake was wound around her bare feet. One foot seemed to hold it in place. She was the most beautiful woman that I had ever seen. I touched the statue, then the snake. The beautiful woman's toenails were unlike Aunt Gertrude's. They were not colored.

Mom called and ushered me over to a woman who wore somewhat the same kind of clothes that the beautiful woman wore. This woman was older. Her clothing was black all over except for a hood that had a white lining. She was ugly. I was later to learn that she was a member of The Sisters of Loretto Order. A Nun. "Sister, this is my son, Francis. He was five last June. Say hello to Sister Mary Elizabeth."

"Hello," I responded. "Who is that lady over there? And why is she standing on the snake?" Mom showed embarrassment for not having told her son about the Virgin Mary.

"The snake is the Devil, Satan, and the lady you refer to is The Blessed Virgin, Mary. You will learn all about her later Francis. Now, come with me and I will take you to your Kindergarten Class and introduce you to Sister Mary Clarice."

I was enrolled as Francis Muhm.

Mom waved goodbye, blotting her eyes with a handkerchief. I said goodbye and nearly twisted my neck off straining to see this statue of Mary, until Sister Mary Elizabeth, with my hand in hers, turned down the corridor toward my classroom. The room was bright. Boys and girls were sitting on the floor in a circle cutting strips of colored paper and making chains out of them. I was introduced to Sister Mary Clarice, who in turn introduced me to the group of kids. I sat in the circle watching. Directly across from me was a girl who was just as beautiful as the lady out in the lobby, only this one was my age. I looked for her snake. I thought all beautiful women had snakes. Anna Mae Young was the girl's name. She had light brown, curly hair with ringlets hanging down the side of her rounded, peach colored cheeks. She had blue eyes. She wasn't a bit fat like my friend, Julia Siska. I liked Julia too, but in a different way. Her Mom made the best potato pancakes. Julia and her mom and dad lived at the end of my block. I was getting hungry just thinking of Julia. In the last five minutes I had seen the two most beautiful women in the world. Anna Mae smiled at me from across the circle. I was going to like school.

At noon, Mom picked me up. Sister Mary Clarice told her that I did very well, except that she had trouble getting my attention. From school we walked to the hospital. This would be our routine day after day. It was a long walk, up Lafayette past the German House, a large elegant building, and then on past Lafayette Park which was surrounded by a high wrought iron fence, rusted in places. Mom said that a cyclone went right through the park some years ago and tore up most of the old trees and some of the homes nearby. Across the street from the park were three and four story homes that for the most part were now decrepit looking rooming houses or just boarded up and vacant. Mom said that a long time ago rich people lived in them and that on the other side of the park there were even finer houses that very wealthy people lived in. Now they too were rooming houses. I didn't know any rich people.

The leaves started falling from the Elms and Sycamores that lined our street. The concrete sidewalks were pushed up a little every year by their roots. Men and women raked the leaves to the curb and burned them. There seemed to be a lot more men without a job and nothing better to do. I thought it odd that they only did this on Saturdays. Mom said that they wanted people to think that they had a job during the work week. I liked the smell of burning leaves better than that of Dad's pipe. The air turned cold.

The windows at the hospital were closed, except for those in the TB Ward. I looked through the windowpaned door. The patients in the TB ward were heavily covered except for their cold red faces. The patient's labored breaths nearly crystalized. On our walks to and from the hospital my toes got numb from the cold. There were days every winter when the smoke engulfing the city was so thick that you couldn't see a hundred yards, everyone coughed. On rainy days my feet got wet quickly. I had holes in my soles. Mom would line my shoes with layers of newspaper. Dad had showed her how.

Posters and handbills were attached to every telephone pole and building promoting candidates for the coming election. I gathered Mr. Hoover wasn't doing so good. The streetcars had photographs of Franklin Delano Roosevelt plastered all over them. With a long strange name like that I just knew he didn't stand a chance. People wore buttons for their favorites. Songs were sung, slogans shouted. The unemployed and hungry favored, "FDR". I just knew that they had to shorten his name somehow. He didn't look like anyone I had known. He wore a big black hat. His smile showed a mouth full of teeth supporting a long cigarette holder. His chin and his nose were always pointed skyward. Anyway, he was elected President.

On November 20th, Mom told me that Dad was going to get to come home. He would have to use crutches for awhile and that I could be a big help around the house. No more cold walks to the hospital. Things were looking up. Uncle Walter came and the four of us celebrated Thanksgiving with one of Bettendorf's hens. Uncle Walter brought Mom a hand carved, marble topped lamp table from the store. With his words stumbling, Dad thanked God for our food, our togetherness and the election of FDR and the hope that he gave us. My Dad was very nervous and unsteady and seemed to kinda grunt when he got nervous which now seemed all of the time. It was because of the accident. After dinner I helped carry the dishes to the kitchen. Mom was there leaning over the sink with tears on her cheeks. When she saw me she said, "I got some onion in my eyes, Francis. Here, bring coffee to your uncle." Uncle Walter's eyes were red and his hand trembled as he drank his coffee. I thought it was because the house was cold. I was told earlier that we were saving the coal for the real cold weather ahead.

-11-

Mom and Dad always seemed so happy before the accident. Dad bought her a mahogany Victrola record player right after they got married and they would listen and dance to the music. Mom used to sing a lot. When I was smaller she sang "Rockabye Baby" to me and sometimes in the kitchen, "Mexacalli Rose" and "Twas on the Isle of Capri that I found her". I don't know if she sang with or without a beer. Dad made Mom beer in the basement. He had big jugs, dark brown bottles and a capping machine. When he made beer the basement smelled like molasses. Mom liked her beer and didn't think too much of Mr. Hoover, our former president because she said that he outlawed booze, but things would be better now. Dad did not drink beer, but once in a while would have a glass of wine. "Beer was never mentioned in the Bible but Jesus turned water into wine so on special occasions I will drink my Elderberry wine," he would say. Since the accident Dad wasn't able to go to the basement for awhile and the wine and beer making stopped but Mom "borrowed" some from Mrs. Siska. She heard that FDR was going to let the beer flow soon.

Dad and his brother, my Uncle Walter, grew up in Defiance, Missouri, a German community of hard working immigrants and their offsprings, mostly Lutheran in religion and strict and conservative in their ways. Their other brother, Oscar, was the first born and became a doctor with a practice in New Melle, Missouri. He died sometime before I was born leaving his wife, my "Aunt Martha", a son and two daughters. The two girls, Mildred and Edith graduated from Nursing School. They were pretty and both married before they did any nursing. The son became a dentist after attending St. Louis University Dental School. That was Harvard. Harvard would come to our house for lunch once in awhile. I was two or three then. I vaguely remember him standing over me hiding his face off and on with a newspaper and making me laugh. Dad's family was educated. Once in awhile, before Dad's accident, we would drive out to see "Aunt Martha". I liked her. She had a wonderful voice, a bit gravely with a German accent. We were never served food, just tea. Depending on the time of year, "Aunt Martha" would give Dad some blood sausage made by a Mr. Schroeder in town. It took awhile for me to try the stuff. "You don't know what you're missing", Dad would say. I liked it. The Muhms were not my real kinfolks. I guess that they were my adopted kin folks. It was said that they had "Class", what ever that was. I figured we didn't have it.

Mom never liked to go to Aunt Martha's but felt that she owed Dad as he became almost totally involved with her family. New Melle was an interesting little town. The bank was right across the narrow street from Aunt Martha's. It had been closed since early in the Depression. Aunt Martha had an outhouse with three holes! I wondered if more than one person used the outhouse at the same time. My Uncle Oscar had his office in a small building near the house. I was taken there by Dad one time and saw what looked like a very small baby in a jar of fluid. Dad said that it was a Fetus. I didn't know what that meant but the sight of it remained with me for some time.

When Dad met my mom, his strictness faded but not his conservatism. He took the instructions to become a Catholic and they were married in the Old Cathedral in St. Louis. A notice in the Alton Telegraph stated, "Miss Estella M. Walsh of Godfrey and Emil E. Muhm of St. Louis were married in St. Louis at the Cathedral by Rev. Tannrath, Tuesday, April 5th. Mr. and Mrs. R.W.. Sears of this city were the attendants. The bride is a daughter of Thomas R. Walsh, and is a young woman of many charms and accomplishments, with a wide circle of friends having taught school in both Jersey and Madison Countys for ten years but for the past ten months has been employed by Butler Bros. of St. Louis, where she held a responsible position. Mr. Muhm is a well known and successful business man of St. Louis as he is a member of the well known firm of the Harry Hussman Refrigerator Co. The bride was attired in a blue tailored tricotine suit with which she wore a small gray hair braid hat and a large corsage bouquet of Sweet Peas and Valley Lilies. The brides-maid was similarly attired in a blue tailored suit with her hat in contrast and a corsage bouquet of Sweet Peas completing the costume. The newly wedded couple will reside at the Statler Hotel while their new home is being fitted up." Mom was 28 and Dad was 40. That was six years before I was born.

~12~

Dad became the most devout Catholic in the family. He belonged to the Holy Name Society. I didn't know too much about the Society except that the men that belonged went to communion together every morning, ushered all the masses and most importantly, played Pinochle at school every Monday night. My dad had a talent of wiggling his ears any time that he wanted. This always made me laugh. I guess that was the only talent Dad had. He very seldom ever smiled. There was always a serious expression on his face with his chin raised and his lips pursed. I have a feeling that he did not look that way when he and Mom dated, however, photographs prove me wrong. I never once heard him say a bad word. His oft used phrases were, "Oh boy!, Holy Toledo!, Holy smoke!, Holy Mackerel or Son of a gun". Dad had many friends in the Holy Name Society. My Dad was a lot older than most of the other kid's fathers. He seemed even older since his accident. Dad put his crutches away and now used a cane. He had two canes, one for in the house and the other, with a nail protruding from the bottom, for his walks outside, so he could pick up stuff. This drove Mom nuts as she would clean out his pockets and find bottle caps, assorted pieces of paper, some coupons.

"Emil, why do you pick up this junk!"

"Cleaning up the neighborhood."

He didn't, or perhaps couldn't, play catch with me or anything like that. He seemed to enjoy watching me play with the other kids. Sometimes I got embarrassed with him watching me. No other dads watched their boys play.

Dad made friends with a man who came over from Germany recently who was studying Dentistry of a sort. He made false teeth in the old country and was trying to make a go of it here. His name was Krueger. Dad practiced his German on Mr. and Mrs. Krueger. They had a son who was a year or two younger than I. His name was Snookie. I don't think that was his real name. It was about this time that Dad started calling me "Snickelfritz". Only around me and Mom, thankfully. Snookie and I overheard them talking about someone named Hitler over in Germany who ordered books burned. I wondered if they were comic books.

We went out to visit the Kruegers. They lived somewhere near the Bevo Mill. Snookie and I played in the yard with a soft inflatable rubber ball. Before leaving, and out of sight of Snookie, I deflated the ball by pulling out the stopper and put it under my shirt. When I got home I hid the ball and was too ashamed to ever bring it out in the open less someone would discover my dastardly deed. I was a thief. In school, Sister Clarice told us that God knows and sees everything that we do and hears every word we say and He knows every thought that we think. I thought God and I alone knew where that ball was and as long as I don't bring it out no one else will know.

Mr. and Mrs. Krueger had strong German accents. They were members of The German House, that beautiful, ornate building up on Lafayette near Jefferson Ave. They were also members of the Bund and went to the Turner's Hall and other German organizations. Our neighborhood had a lot of Germans, some with accents and some without but still having ties to the "old country". The Kruegers and other friends of Dad, would visit a lot and play Pinochle. Mom didn't play. They spoke German while they played. Dad enjoyed their company and he got to brush up on the language. Mom couldn't stand to hear too much talk about Germans and Germany, and would have to interrupt once in a while with the virtues of being Irish, and how the Irish had spread themselves throughout the world and did this and that. Sometimes when they started singing German songs, she would go in the kitchen and sing "When Irish Eyes are Smiling". All this time me and Snookie, who were brought up to be seen and not heard, would be in another room enjoying the battle. Snookie never said anything about missing his ball.

There were a few Italians living in our neighborhood, but most of them lived on what I heard was "The Hill", and you didn't want to mess around with any of their girls or the Mafia would get you. I didn't know what messing around meant, but if it was liking someone or staring at them, or wishing that they would like me, like I felt about Anna Mae,

I wasn't in trouble because I knew somehow that she wasn't Italian. I did not know what she was and did not care. Ernie Foster was two years older than me and he looked Italian. I didn't like him. He would sneak up on me in the school yard with his middle finger bent and hit me on the arm and run away. Hit and run, hit and run. He never said anything. He just flew around like a bee with that finger poised like a knife hitting all the younger kids. Since he looked like an Italian, I made up my mind that I didn't like Italians.

-13-

The following weeks were like the weather, wet and cold and dreary except for school. School was Anna Mae. We were making paper chains again only this time they were to be hung on the Christmas tree in the lobby. When I went home I felt sad. Christmas would soon be here. I couldn't think of anything that I wanted. What was worse, no one asked me what I wanted. One evening, after supper I put on my hat and coat and went out back to the lot behind our empty garage. Christmas was a week away. I started walking around the cinder drive. It was snowing, and had been for about an hour. Large flakes came straight down. It was quiet. The snow that fell on the cindered drive melted right away but the ground in the center was covered and the lot looked like a large white oval with a black rim around it. I was feeling pretty low. I had heard my folks talking about moving to someplace cheaper. Mom said she heard of a house down on Lafayette with an extra bedroom. They could rent the room out. The rent Mom and Dad would be paying was lower than they were now paying. They could make a little money and Mom said that it was right across the street from school. As I walked, I saw the faint lights shining through the stained glass windows of the church and could hear the organ playing and the singing. I liked the singing and wished that there would be more of it instead of old Father Joe standing up there always asking for money. Whenever they had a Novena, Mom would take me. The purpose of a Novena, I was told, was to pray for something special, like the conversion of Russia or the Jews or the Africans, the end of the depression or something else big and important. You could also tack on prayers for your own special wants. Besides the singing, I liked the aroma of the burning incense and the booming lower notes coming from the immense organ with its dusty pipes that covered the entire rear of the church in the choir loft. When Mrs. Herman played and the parishioners sang, all in Latin, it produced an enthusiasm and joy in me that I had not experienced elsewhere. I couldn't understand what the words meant, and I doubt that most of the others could either, but they and I sang with a forceful, joyous voice, as did, Mr. Palmer, who always seemed to sit in back of us.

The snow became heavier. I looked up to the top of the church's smoke stack. I liked to watch the chimney swifts every evening coming back from wherever they go in the daytime to roost inside the stack. They would circle, chirping and screeching, and then dive one by one into the depths of the stack. I turned around to go back home. The snow was beautiful. As I started to open our back gate I heard a "Yap!, Yap!". I turned to see a small dog running toward me. As I hunched over and Yaped back the pup skidded to a halt, retreated a few yards and resumed his attack, barking. He then ran a circle 8, coming close but just out of my reach. This play continued until we were both tumbling in the snow. When I walked through our back door and into the kitchen holding the squirming and barking dog, I thought Mom would hit the ceiling.

"What in the world happened to you, and what in God's name have you got in your arms?"

I guess we did look a sight. I was covered with snow, the elastic on my knickers was down around my ankles, shirt tail out and we were both shaking snow off us. Dad came in from the living room excitedly grunting and wanted to know what was going on.

"I found this dog, Mom. Out in back. He likes me!" The dog barked. I shoved the pup toward Mom but she backed away, hands raised in defense.

"You take that thing right back out where you found him. Mercy, look at you!"

The dog jumped out of my arms and headed for Dad's pants leg. "Can I keep him, Mom, can I? I'll feed him, and take good c—".

"Certainly not! We have enough trouble putting food on the table now. Get that thing out of here and then you come back in here and clean up this mess. And get those wet clothes off. Well I say."

"Well I say" was a favorite family phrase. Aunt Gertrude, cousins Marguerite and Maymie all used it to emphasize their disagreement or ridicule of anything one of the others proclaimed. It always went along with the "Tisk, tisking".

While Mom was, "Well I say"ing, Dad had picked up the pup and gave it the once over. "It's a male, good colors. A Fox Terrier mix I would say. Won't get too big. And look he has a bobbed tail. Hard to tell if it was cut off or the dog was born with it." The dog was black and white with a little brown around its eyes.

"I don't care what kind of a tail it has, Emil, we just can't feed—"

"Take the dog in the back yard, Francis while your mother and I talk." As I went out the door I heard another, "Well I say". There wasn't any sense in me and the dog trying to get clean, so we played in the snow once more.

Inside, Dad picked up the broom and started sweeping up the mess. "Stella, I know how you feel, honey. But look, the pup surely won't eat much. He can sleep in the garage. It will give Francis some responsibility. He needs that. And besides, we haven't seen him this excited about anything, have we?"

Mom gave out one more "WIS" and sat down and started laughing. Dad thought she was getting hysterical and was alarmed until she managed between laughs to say, "That dog could make an honest woman out of me. All year I have been asking Raymond, the butcher for scraps for our dog! Oh, Emil, I guess we can manage somehow, My folks always did. I'll just tell Raymond that we have two dogs now."

When Dad opened the door we both bounded in creating havoc again. I was told to leave the dog outside. I was told also that I could keep the dog with certain conditions. I didn't care at that moment what the conditions were. I was elated and jumped up and down. Dad said that I could keep him as long as the dog did not belong to someone else. I hadn't thought of that. "Surely if he belonged to some other boy or girl you could imagine how they are feeling", Mom said.

A "dog found notice" would be posted all over the neighborhood and if no one claims him within a week I could keep him, provided that I would take care of him, feed and bath him, and make sure that he stays in the yard and doesn't dig holes, and another condition that I didn't think of or take relish in, pick up his droppings. I agreed and the next day the signs went up. I played with the pup with mixed emotions. I let up a little with my love and feelings toward, Bobby, that's what my Dad named him. Dad said that Mom could tell the butcher that

Fido and Barney either died or we gave them away. Dad told me that it would only be a "white" lie. I had never heard of white lies but I notched it in my memory for future use. I did and didn't want to get too attached to Bobby. I worried about losing him. Bobby didn't seem to miss his former owners. He only missed me when I was in school. I prayed that he came from nowhere, that no one missed him and that he would be mine. I asked Mom if the church had a Novena that we could go to so I could substitute Bobby for the Russians and the Jews. Not until February, she said, but that I could pray any time.

Christmas Eve came. One more day I thought. I got nervous. I thought of rushing out and tearing down all those "dog found" signs. Then I remembered what Sister Clarice once told us. "God sees and hears all." She always said that when she had to leave the classroom with no one to watch us. That evening after supper we gathered in the living room around the Christmas tree that Dad purchased at Bettendorf's only an hour ago at "close out" price. I helped decorate the scraggly tree with a paper chain that I made in school. There was only one brightly wrapped present under the tree. It wasn't there when I put the decorations on.

"Francis, that package is for you", said Dad with his arm around Mom.

I tore off the wrappings and was bewildered and disappointed when all that was there was worn, dirty cardboard.

"Turn them over," said Mom.

Four lost dog signs!

As I hugged my parents and ran out the back door to tell Bobby the good news, I could hear Dad saying to Mom, "Merry Christmas, Honey."

~14~

I was now in first grade. No more paper chains. We were now ready for the big important stuff. But always before the important stuff we had to learn about our religion, our Catechism. I guessed the one reason that we had to study religion was so none of us would have to ask who that pretty lady was that was stepping on the snake out in the lobby. This was hard stuff. We were learning to read and write and oh, the writing. For what seemed like hours we would draw ovals and then the up and down strokes, over and over again. The point of my pencil always got short and stubby and it was hard to draw this stuff as good as some of the others. I asked the Sister if I could go to the pencil sharpener which was located right next to Anna Mae's desk. She allowed me to go but only once a day. I looked at Anna Mae's drawings. They were perfect. We now had to stay in school all day. Arithmetic made my brain and my fingers sore. We were getting smart, or so we thought.

In late afternoons after school our radio had "The Lone Ranger" on and another one of my favorites, "Jack Armstrong, The All American Boy". I wanted to be like the "All American Boy". I pleaded with Mom to buy "Wheaties" so I could be like him. I also wanted to be like Charles Atlas whose advertisements I saw in magazines. He was selling something called "Dynamic Tension". I got to pushing and pulling my hands together thinking that was the secret. Mom started listening to some of the women's serials on the radio.

During baseball season, Dad would plead with her at times to turn the dial to the Cardinal games whenever they were broadcast, or the Friday Night Fights.

Dad said that the Cardinals were going to do all right this year, that they signed a rookie named Joe Medwick. The very first All Star game was played. Our Pepper Martin and Frankie Frisch were on the National team. Frankie Frisch hit a home run but the Babe hit one before him and the Americans won the game. It turned out that Dad was right about Joe Medwick. He ended up batting 306 with 18 home runs, but the team ended up 9 1/2 games behind. Dad said, "Better luck next time." He said that a lot. Every year.

Our radio brought the world to us. Dad and I listened to the broadcast when Primo Carnera knocked out this guy and then Dad read in the Globe three days later the man died. Dad said that Carnera was a giant and that no one would ever beat him. We heard Hitler on the short wave, shouting and ranting in a language that I didn't understand.

~15~

I was now seven going on eight. Time for our First Communion. I was anxious. I had seen the older kids and the adults go up to the communion rail at every Mass and be given the wafer, then coming back to their pew all holy looking with their head bowed and hands clasped heavenward. I wanted to know what it was all about! Sister Mary Rose said that before we could take communion we had to go to confession. She made us study our catechisms even harder and she tried to explain the difference between mortal and venial sins and how to prepare ourselves for a good and true confession.

Fred Jefferson raised his hand, and with a serious expression on his face, he asked Sister, "If someone used the word 'shit', what kind of sin—" The room roared except for the girls. Sister Mary Rose told Fred to come with her and out the door they went up to Mother Superior, Sister Mary Elizabeth. Mother Superior always gave several whacks on the hand with a foot long ruler for much less than poor Fred's unfortunate question.

We memorized what to say to the priest after entering the confessional and were told that whatever we confessed would never be told to anyone. "Not even our parents?" Kathleen O'Kieff asked. "No one.", Sister replied.

Our first confession was to be on a Saturday and our First Communion the day after. The First Communion was as big as a Presidential Election or a World Series. That's what Sister said. We practiced processions. We walked up the two blocks to the church, up the steps and down the aisle at just the right pace trying to look like angels, me in my slipping down knickers. I checked from time to time to see if the buttons in my corduroy fly were still holding shut. At the real thing, the girls would look like angels all dressed in white dresses with new, or looks-like-new, white shoes. The boys would still look like boys but with shiny faces, long white trousers, not a knicker in the bunch, and white shirts and black ties. Some of the families couldn't afford to buy new clothes and the Sisters would arrange for other families who had already had kids make their First Communion to loan the garments. Some, mine, had their old "Buster Brown" shoes dyed white.

The big day came for our first confessions. I remembered some of the adults always making their confession before Mass started. Some of them seemed to be in there a long time. From now on we would be marched up to church every Friday along with the upper classes for our confessions. It was hoped that we would not sin between then and Sunday when we would attend Mass and take Communion. We arrived at Church and the girls entered the pews near the front and the boys adjacent to Father Sullivan's confessional. Father Thompson entered his confessional down by the girls and Father Cronin had the middle one. We kneeled and said the Act of Contrition. I pondered as to what I was going to confess. I had bad thoughts such as looking at Anna Mae too often, or lying to my mother and father. Robert Finnigan said that his older brother always used that when he couldn't think of anything else, or not doing his homework. I settled on lying to my mother and father even though that would be a lie. Would Father Johnson know that I was lying? I wondered who Father Thompson went to for his confession. Who did Father Johnson go to and is being crabby a sin, and who did the Sisters go to and when? What in the world would they have to confess, sinful thoughts? All of these holy people were going to confession so that they would be in a state of grace, take Holy Communion and not go to Hell. I was a little confused about the meaning of being in a state of grace. Sister Mary Rose sent Ernie Foster into Father Johnson's confessional.

We could hear Ernie mumble, "Bless me Father for I have sinned. It has been,—I mean this is my first confession, I pushed my sister—",

"What did you say, boy", shouted Father Johnson. We could hear both of them perfectly well. Ernie repeated. "You pushed one of the Sisters! You should be expelled! Which Sister did you push?" We and poor Earnie could imagine Father Johnson's face all red and puffed out and his eyes bulging even though he was out of our view.

"My own sister, Father, her name is, Helen, she is twelve years old and she pushed me first, Father."

"Why in the world didn't you say so! Are you sorry that you pushed your sister, and will never do it again?"

"Yes, Father."

"Go now and get out of here and say five Hail Marys and five Our Fathers."

Every boy went in and told Father Johnson that they had lied to their mother and father. If they had sisters, they didn't mention it. The next morning we were all dressed in white and being in a state of grace, received our First Communion. Our relatives were in attendance and oohed and ahhed over us. Father Cronin placed the wafer on my outstretched tongue and it stuck to my upper mouth. I wondered why we didn't get any wine to wash it down. The priest did. The following Monday, Sister Mary Rose gave us a lecture on lying, especially to our parents. I, and others, remembered her telling us that no one but the priest would know what sins we told. We had until next Friday to think up some other sins.

~16~

Gertrude

Mom received a letter from my real father, Tim Kelley, telling her that he brought my brother, Joseph, and my sister, "Little" Gertrude home with him. Although Joseph was only nine, the nuns felt that his father, and his daughter, could take care of him.

Dear Diary

June 10, 1934. Our day has come! Father came for us in his buggy, loaded our few belongings. We were going home! We had been in the orphanage for seven years. I had mixed feelings. I loved most of the nuns and had made so many friends there. Some of my friends were adopted or taken home and some of them would not leave until they were eighteen. It was a long trip in the buggy. We stopped in Jerseyville for groceries. It is hard to describe how I felt when we came into the lane and saw our house. It looked like a castle. I almost forgot what it looked like. For a second, I expected Mom to come out and welcome us and then realized that she wasn't there and never would be. Tommie ran to greet us and wrestled Joseph to the ground. They almost rolled all the way to the door laughing.

June 11th. Father woke me at five O'clock and told me to fix breakfast. I told him that I didn't know how. "What did those nuns teach you all of these years?"

I told him washing dishes and clothes. He said "Well, as soon as you empty the slop bowls and wash up, I'll show you how to use the stove. " Slop bowls! We didn't have those at the orphanage. We had toilets with hot and cold running water and real beds to sleep in, not that sinking feather bed that I slept in last night. Tommie came into the kitchen with two buckets of water and told Joseph who was just rubbing the sleep from his eyes that fetching water was now his job and that later in the day he would show him where the well was. Father showed me how to build a fire in the large black stove and how to toast the bread over the flames without burning it. He said that the stove would be my ship and that I was the Captain of the Kitchen, after I learned a few things. Joseph and I were to gather eggs and feed the chickens. When he said that, I remembered that day seven years ago when Mother, Joseph, and I fed the chickens. After emptying the slop bowls, doing the dishes, and cleaning the table, I wondered when recess would come. It didn't. I bet that my baby brother in the city didn't have to live like this. That night I cried.

June 12. At breakfast Father said that on this day seven years ago our Mother died and that we should bow our heads and say a prayer for her. His eyes were watery when he lifted his head. He looked at me and sighed saying that I was now the lady of the house and that I did a wonderful job with breakfast. I felt important and grown up.

~17~

On July 1st, 1934, we moved to 2903 Lafayette. I didn't like it. Bobby didn't either. The back yard was small. There was no front yard. The front door was almost on the sidewalk. There was an upstairs, but you had to go out back and up an enclosed staircase to get there. There was only one room upstairs and that was were we would make our fortune. Mom would rent it out. We would be landlords. If the renter wanted meals there would be additional money. Mom put up pictures in the front room of The Sacred Heart of Jesus and President Roosevelt. She also hung a painting of a stream running through a woods. She got that from Wagner Furniture Store on Jefferson Avenue. She said that it reminded her of "up home". She bought a chair and they gave her the painting. It was so hot I slept on the floor of our living room with the only breeze coming from our black "Emerson" oscillating fan whose breeze I shared with Mom and Dad as they lay in the bed with just a sheet over them. Dad said that this was one of the hottest Summers on record and he was glad that it was about over. Mrs. Smith lived next door. She was old and fat. She gave piano lessons, twenty-five cents each. I was glad Mom said that I should learn the piano but that we couldn't afford it. Mrs. Smith lived alone and I never saw anyone come for lessons all the while we lived there. One day she came over and said that someone had left a bicycle in her back yard. It had remained there for a week and she had a hunch that someone had stolen it and in their getaway dumped the bike in her yard. She asked if I would I like to have it! Funny how I no longer viewed Mrs. Smith as old and fat. The bike was almost too big for me, red and white with big balloon tires, and a couple of dents in the fenders. Dad lowered the seat as far as he could but I still couldn't reach the pedals. I rode it standing up leaning off to one side to protect my testicles from the bar. I rode up the sidewalk to show my bike to my new friend, Avery. Avery was in the same grade as I and he lived with his grandparents. His mom and dad lived down in the Ozarks somewhere with his younger sister and two brothers. His parents wanted Avery to get a city education; and anyway they had too many mouths to feed.

~18~

Dad was doing better. He was happy as a lark. Our Cardinals won the pennant by two games. They then went on to beat Detroit in the World Series. Dizzy and his brother, Paul were the whole show. Dizzy won thirty games! They had a big parade downtown. Dad and I went. I think I got to see Mel Ott and Dizzy, but with the crowd, I'm not sure. Dad said to relish the victory because winning seasons never last. Relish, I thought that was the stuff some people put on hot dogs.

Sometimes Mom would take me downtown on the Southampton streetcar. The Southampton went right in front of our house. The streetcar would go straight down Lafayette, past the City Hospital and then twist and turn down this street and that with the iron wheels screeching with every turn until we got to Washington Blvd. We would go by tall massive, beautiful buildings, block upon block of them on both sides of the streets. Mom said she used to work in "that one" pointing to the Butler Brothers building. Upon entering downtown the streetcar would stop at the end of every block with people rushing on and off. The sidewalks were crowded with people. When we got to Seventh Street we got off. Sometimes we would go to Famous-Barr, a really big department store. When I was younger, Mom placed me in what they called a Nursery there. I liked that. They had toys to play with. Mom would go off shopping and come pick me up in an hour or two. I enjoyed watching the baskets flying here and there overhead on some kind of cable delivering papers or goods from one part of the store to the other. Every year at Christmas, Famous would decorate their windows on the corner of Seventh and Locust. They had an enormous "Lionel Train" display. This particular day we didn't go to Famous. We went through the Grand Leader. Mom said that some people called it Stix, Baer and Fuller. We then went out the side door and across the street to Lynn's Market.

Another thing that I liked about downtown was the policemen. There was one at every intersection directing traffic, waving the vehicles on or telling them to stop. The telling was done with their whistles and body motions. The streetcar's bells clanging, wheels screeching, horns and whistles blowing, fruit and vegetable stand workers next to Lynn's yelling, was exciting. The streets were crowded with people walking this way and that all in a hurry to get somewhere. Men wore suits and ties and straw hats in the summer, felt hats and overcoats in the winter. Their shirts were always white and their suits were black.

Lynn's Market had a small restaurant up on a balcony. The restaurant had windows so you could sit there eating your cheese sandwich and watch the women down below fighting over the best bananas, lettuce, or oranges. The women stood and waited for the produce man to wheel out a cart full of this or that and then they almost knocked him down trying to grab the best of the lot. I never knew that ladies could fight like that. Whatever was left after the raid was garbage. After lunch we went to the Union Market across the street. This was an enormous building with a lot of stands displaying fresh meats of all kinds, pig heads with apples stuck in their mouths, fish of all kinds with their heads on and their eyes staring at you. They looked alive. There were bakery products, cheeses, spices, live chickens, ducks, turkeys, and geese. We walked around every counter looking, smelling all of the different spices and foods, and listening to the men hacking their wares. I felt that I was taking a trip through foreign countries. There were samples at some of the counters. We went to all of them. The place was a hundred Bettendorf's rolled into one. Mom didn't buy anything, "Just looking", she would respond to the attendants. From the Market we would go back into The Grand Leader, and take the elevator. The female negro elevator operator announced the contents of each floor as she stopped and opened the door. She stopped on every floor regardless of whether anyone wanted off or on. She would reach out grasping the folding brass guard gate and then rolling back the door she announced the goods displayed on each floor pausing to see if she had enticed anyone to depart before going to the next floor. We rode to every floor, never getting off, just listening to the colored lady describing the merchandise. Mom never saw any of the items then but I kinda think that she could imagine what they looked like and I could imagine her saying to herself, "Some day, some day."

~19~

One day, the following Spring I came in from playing and Mom was crying. "Francis, Pop died. We have to leave and arrange for the funeral." We went to my grandfather's house and then to Gent's Funeral Home in North Alton. There was a lot of crying there and out at the cemetery. I didn't get to know my grandfather long enough. I liked him.

That summer, Mom rented the upstairs sleeping room to a man named Carpenter. Mr. Carpenter only stayed three months then Mom rented the room to a man named Hart. He was short and looked like Clark Gable. A lot of men tried to look like Clark Gable. Mr. Hart worked as a foreman with the W.P.A. He got real friendly with Mom and had her laughing and smiling when he took supper with us. Dad didn't like him. One Monday night I saw Mr. Hart with his arm around my Mom as they stood out on the back porch. He was trying to get her to go up to his room with him. I rushed back in the living room not knowing what to do or think. I wanted to watch but I was afraid. I heard Mom laugh and was relieved when she came in blushing and I heard Mr. Hart go up the stairs.

Monday evening after Mom and Dad and I and Mr. Hart ate the spare ribs and kraut with boiled potatoes, Dad went across the street to play pinochle with the Holy Name men. Mr. Hart helped my mother do the dishes telling her of his plans to head out to California after the depression was over. He told her that she belonged there, in Hollywood, with all those other movie stars. Mom laughed and blushed and rocked back and forth. Mr. Hart could make Mom smile and laugh. Dad used to be able to do that. I wished that Uncle Walter would come and stay with us and bloody this guy's nose, but I heard Dad tell Mom that he was on the binge again and that we probably wouldn't hear from him for some time. I made it a point to stick around when Mr. Hart was with my mother. She didn't mind but Hart did. He kept giving me pennies to go up to the store for candy.

A couple of weeks later Dad said that he was taking me with him to the school to show me off to his Holy Namers. Hart smiled at Mom as he helped clear off the table. I went with Dad so he could show me off to his pinochle players. After they oohed and ahad over me, I fell asleep as they seemed to be talking a foreign language in their card playing.

The next evening, Mr. Hart said that he had been able to put my Dad on with the WPA as a tool crib attendant. He was sure that he could handle it and the job paid seven dollars a week. Dad smiled, grunted and was nervously excited at the news. He would be working again! He went to the cupboard and brought out a bottle of elderberry wine that he had made and the four of us toasted. Mom smiled slightly but looked nervous. When Dad came home from work tired every day Mom would rub his legs. He still had to walk with a cane. Dad came home one evening and took my mother into the bedroom. As he closed the door I heard him say that he heard a couple men at work talking about her and Hart. Mom and Dad had a loud argument. I heard Mom say that all they ever did was kiss once or twice.

Hart never came home from work. Dad told Mom that he quit his job as tool attendant after he whacked Hart with his cane and told him that his things would be put out by the alley. Days later my mother and father had a talk with me. They said that they were separating and wanted to know who I wanted to go with. I cried and cried and told them that I wanted to be with both of them. After counseling with Father Johnson, they decided to stick together but things were never the same between them. Mom rented Mr. Hart's room to a man named Johnson. He worked in an office for the Frisco Railroad. He seemed quiet but OK.

~20~

Dad was unemployed again and one evening he came home from The Holy Name Society card games and announced that he had a part time job helping Clem the church's janitor. He said that sometime I may be able to help him. I had met Clem once with my Dad. Clem lived in the basement of the church and took care of cleaning it and the priest's home. It was decided that he needed help as he was getting up in years. Clem was very tall and skinny and smoked little cigars. Dad smoked a corncob pipe filled with "Granger Rough Cut". It stunk. It wasn't too long afterward that Dad started smoking "Little Stogies" just like Clem. They stunk too. All of the Holy Namers were ushers at the church. There were four Masses, at five, six, eight, and ten in the morning. Dad ushered at the ten o'clock and others if needed. We attended the ten o'clock Mass on Sundays. It was always crowded. Dad took his ushering job serious and with the long handled collection basket he started at the front of the church on our side and worked backward.

Since his accident it was embarrassing to watch him as he moved with a serious look on his face grunting occasionally. He was a little shaky with the offering basket missing some coins, allowing them to fall on the floor, causing people to bend over to look for them as Dad patiently waited for them to retrieve the coins. Some of them could not be found. Some of the people with hands closed reached into the basket and faked dropping an offering. I guess they were embarrassed not to have anything to offer.

The next Sunday on the way home from church Dad announced that the next day after school I could help him sweep the church. "And, Francis, Clem said that if you found any money on the floor that you could keep it. How does that sound?" I knew exactly which part of the church I wanted to sweep.

All day in school my mind was on my new job. I wondered how much I was going to find. I ran the two blocks after school to the church and met my Dad and Clem. Clem gave me two brooms, a regular one and a wide worn push broom. The push broom had soft black hairs. I was given a can of pink Absourine Sweeping Compound. He showed me how to sprinkle it on the floor. I liked the smell of it. Clem showed me how to lift the kneeling benches so I could sweep the entire floor. Dad had already started on the far end and with a wink and a very slight smile. Clem said, "Why don't you start on that side over there, the section where you and your parents usually sit." I went home with a dollar and five cents! Included was thirty cents in pennies. I guess times were hard. The next Sunday, I was still embarrassed but almost felt like cheering when Dad made the basket tremble and missed a coin or two. Dad never noticed any coins missing his basket.

~21~

My Dad got himself another job. He became a janitor in a four family apartment building on Russell and Nebraska. Mom told me not to tell anyone. Dad was happy and proud to be able to do things again and get paid for it. He collected all the newspapers that the tenants threw out and sold them. Also the return bottles. He got me a job as a dog walker. Mrs. Sanders who lived on the second floor had a long haired, black and white dog named Skippy that ate too much. Skippy was a house dog and needed to be exercised. I made arrangements to walk him before I went to school and afterward. For this I was to receive two dollars a month! I had to go up the metal stairs in the rear to get Skippy.

There was something wrong with Skippy. He had a growth on his left side. Mrs. Sanders said that it didn't bother him and I was not to worry about it. I walked Skippy around the block and over to Lafayette Ave. It always seemed that Skippy had to poop when we got to Lafayette. It was the busiest street. I guess he liked an audience. Skippy was always bound up and had a hard time pooping. He would hunch over and howl and sometimes scream as he tried to do his job. You could tell that he was in pain. I figured that a dose of castor oil or Milk of Magnesia would help, but it was not for me to tell Mrs. Sanders. People passing in their automobiles and people in the streetcars would look to see where this horrible sound was coming from. I turned my back from the street. I couldn't just let go of the leash and run away. I had to stick it out with Skippy. If there were any of my friends playing on the lot across from the church, they turned to look and laughed. I was so embarrassed. Skippy didn't care. He was trying to poop. Skippy and I walked in all kinds of weather. Skippy attracted so much attention with his pooping problems that I was ready to ask for a raise, but I wouldn't know how to explain Skippy's problem to Mrs. Sanders. She was a fancy lady. I started shortening his walks and taking him through the alleys so that when he had to do his painful pooping only he and I were around. I was glad that Bobbie had a yard to exercise and poop in, except for me having to scoop up his crap once a week and throw it in the ash pit. Everything went in the ash pit and everyone had one. They all were made of brick or concrete and had a small metal door at the bottom facing the alley. Inside them were cinders, cans, bottles and everything else except garbage. The city said garbage brought on rats. Some people threw garbage in their ash pits anyway.

When the boys started playing football on the lot across from our church, I would tie Skippy to the fence while I played. Mrs. Sanders appreciated my taking Skippy out for what she thought were longer walks. My two dollars was turned over to Mom and Dad for safe keeping. Perhaps they remembered my trading the genuine agate marbles that Dad gave me for those nice shiny glass ones.

~22~

Dad loved to listen to the baseball games, both the Cardinals and the Browns. He got excited every time he told me how the Gas House Gang won the pennant and the World Series. Dad would get so worked up listening to the games on the radio. Mom didn't have the foggiest notion who Dizzy Dean was except that she heard his name mentioned so often. She knew he was important. She said that he must be Irish. Dad tried to tell her more about him, but she had no interest in baseball or pinochle. One day some of the boys heard that Dizzy and his brother Paul were going to pay their respects to someone who died and was laid out at the Peetz Funeral Home. They didn't know who died but they and I were there when Dizzy Dean and his brother, Paul and some of the other Cardinal players walked in. We didn't get any autographs, but we all boasted that we saw Dizzy Dean go into the funeral parlor! When asked, "Who died" we answered, "I dono".

I hated winter. I was always cold. I was glad that I lived across the street from the school. Another thing about winter, I was always hungry. I liked the smell of vegetable soup cooking in the school kitchen. You could smell it all over the building and I could taste it as I sat in class. I could see the soup while waiting for lunch time, the redness of it, the tiny fat bubbles from the small amounts of beef and bone marrow floating on top like oil on a wet paved street, the oven fresh warm bread to sop it up with.

Another scent that came whiffing throughout the school occasionally was the smell of a burning cigar, Father Thompson's cigar, one of those big ones. He would drive the nuns nuts every time he showed up. He would go up to the third floor and stand at an open window facing out upon the school yard where all the boys would be standing below. Father told the nuns on these occasions that all of the boys and girls were to have recess, even if we had just recently had a recess. The girls merely played in their yard on the other side of the school gym which separated the boys and girls playgrounds. "Are you ready?",

Father Thompson would holler out as we boys would try to position ourselves for the best advantage. Father would throw out candy and gum with several flings. He roared with laughter at the scramble below, pointing out to the Sisters each struggle he deemed was worthy of their attention. Faces and arms would become scratched, dirt would fly, fights would break out and when the candy and gum had all been picked up a nun would blow the whistle and we boys would return to our classrooms loving Father Thompson. Soon the scent of cigar faded, the nuns were relieved that no one was seriously hurt, but forbade any eating of candy or chewing of gum in class. Mothers disapproved of Father Thompson's amusement when their boys came home bruised, dirty but happy, but his being such a good looking young priest, he was quickly forgiven. Fathers wished that they had had a priest like him when they went to school.

~23~

Father Thompson came to our classroom and asked who of us boys would like to be an altar boy. I thought that anything that he was involved in would be fun so I raised my hand. So did nine others. He said that we would have to study and memorize Latin and work harder on our Catechism lessons. Sister Mary Rose smiled and nodded. I began to have second thoughts as I was one of the worst ones in class for memorizing anything. In class I never raised my hand when Sister asked for answers. Number one, I didn't know the answer, and number two, if I did I would have to stand and the other kids would all turn around and look at me, and if they did nine chances out of ten my fly buttons on my used corduroy knickers would have popped out of their button holes. I once tried using a safety pin, but that showed too much. I lived in fear that Sister would call on me to answer a question. I flunked all oral exams and only did fair on the written ones. The Latin lessons progressed, and responding vocally in unison with the other boys, I managed to memorize the "*Et cum spiritu tuo*" along with the other responses. We were brought to the church and practiced the maneuvers of when to genuflect, make the sign of the cross, ring the bells just at the proper time, and not too long, bring and pour the wine and water to the priest and light the candles before Mass and put them out afterward. We learned to give the priest the finger towel while supplying him with a container for him to wash his hands We learned how to cross from one side of the altar with the Holy Bible after the priest read the Gospel, come down two steps, pausing exactly in the center, and turn facing the altar, genuflect and go up two steps and place the Bible on his left for the reading of the Epistle. Only the older boys got to light and carry the incense burner and serve at a High Mass, Funeral Masses, and weddings. Sometimes they got paid. You had to know your stuff to do that.

Father Thompson was the youngest and the newest priest. Father Cronin was blond and pasty looking but seemed alright, and Pastor

Joe Sullivan who was bald and old and always had a frown on his face, probably because of those tight looking glasses that seemed to pinch his nose, was "The Boss". Father Sullivan did the the nine o'clock Masses with the experienced altar boys. Father Cronin did the six and eight o'clock and Father Thompson, the rookie, was awarded the five fifteen Mass and he got me and Robert Finnigan. Finnigan was taller than I and talked like he knew everything.

On the day of my first Mass, Mom and Dad and I got up at 4:30 A.M. It was dark outside! Dad brought me to church for the big event. I searched the closet for vestments that would fit me. I found only one black gown that was okay but a little long in length. It had dried snot on the bottom where some boy had wiped his nose. A white cassock fit okay. I looked in the mirror and I was proud. I looked like a saint. Then I remembered that Sister said that pride was one of those venial sins. Or was it a mortal one?

Robert Finnigan grabbed the candle lighters as we were about to enter the Sacristy. I wanted to light the candles. Finnigan was the bully of the class. He was the tallest and was always threatening to fight. "Put up your dukes!", was his threat to anyone who crossed him. Finnigan's dukes were bigger than anyone's and the angry scowl that went along with them intimated all of us, even Ernie Foster. Robert and I entered the Sacristy with Father Thompson and took our places as Father stood at the foot of the altar and made the sign of the cross. Dad was out there among only a few early risers. Most of these men went to work on the WPA or the railroads after Mass after first stopping at a tavern for a boilermaker. The unemployed went out looking for work hoping to soon join the others for their own boilermakers. Finnigan got the bell job and rang them at the appropriate times. We both mumbled our Latin responses to Father Thompson. He turned slightly as though he had a hard time hearing us.

When it came time for me to bring the Holy Bible to the other side of the priest, I tripped on my extra long, dried snot gown and fell down to the foot of the altar barely managing to hold the Holy Bible in my outstretched hands. I thought I was Terry Moore making a spectacular catch in center field. Realizing what happened, I shouted "Holy Jesus!" I got up and gathering my composure carefully climbed the two steps and placed the Bible to the right of Father Thompson. Most of the parishioners that were awake and those that had previously nodded off had heard my un-Latin response to the episode. Father frowned at me but frowned even stronger at Finnigan who was laughing. My dad hung his head and I could hear him mutter, "Holy Toledo!" My next moment came when I brought the cruets of wine and water up to the priest with the tiny towel over my arm. We were trained to only let a very small amount of water and wine pour into the chalice. I tipped the cruet of water into the chalice and Father drank that. I did the same with the wine but he kept tapping the cruet and indicating that he wanted more. He did this until the entire cruet of wine had been guzzled. My mouth dropped open and I wondered if my contortions and stumbling all over the altar drove him to drink. I had never had a drink of that wine, but I suddenly wanted one. Before turning from me, Father Thompson winked.

Later in school, I knew that Finnigan told everyone in my class of the new altar boy's disgrace. Anna Mae would surely have heard it.

At recess I told Finnigan that I wanted to do the candles the next morning. "It'll be a cold day in Hell before I'll let you do that."

With my knees shaking, I told Finnigan, "I'm going to light those candles tomorrow". Some of the boys heard this and gathered.

Putting up his "dukes" he said, "You'll have to fight me to get those candles, squirt."

"I'll fight you if you don't let me." I just knew that he could hear my knees knocking.

"Name the time and the place, jack-off." A lot of the boys used that phrase, so much that I figured everyone in our school was a jack-off. I didn't know what a jack-off was.

"Tomorrow after church!", I shouted.

"You better show up jack-off." I wondered if he knew what a jack-off was. We Catholic kids sure knew our Latin but also how to cuss. Robert Finnigan must have seen a lot of gangster movies although I don't think jack-off was mentioned in any of them.

The buzz around school that day was about the big fight. That afternoon the other boys in the class were glancing back and forth at me and Finnigan. I tried to think of ways that I could get out of it. I could get sick or break a leg or arm or run away, but the more I thought of ways to chicken out the more mad I got at Robert for forcing me to fight him. I didn't sleep that night. The next morning Robert and I struggled with the candle lighters. He pushed me to the floor and quickly lit them just as Father Thompson entered. I was upset, and when we went out into the Sacristy after Robert had lit the candles to begin the Mass, I noticed a bunch of my classmates in attendance, Ernie Foster, Ean Fahey, Fred Merchison, and Charles Bench. At the five fifteen Mass! They never on their life got up so early. Father Thompson also took notice when they lined up at the communion rail eyeing both me and Robert. I had learned how to hike up my gown with a black belt so I wouldn't trip all over.

When the Mass was over Finnigan and I went out on the side lawn. The sun was rising and the boys had gathered.

"Okay squirt, you asked for it punk." Robert pushed me and I pushed back. He swung and missed. I swung and caught him square on his nose. His nose started bleeding. He looked at me, then looked at the blood on his hands and started crying. I began to cry too and I shouted that I wanted to light the candles. "Okay", Robert responded still crying and wiping the blood off his nose with his sleeve. Robert Finnigan turned and walked home. The boys slapped me on the back and congratulated me. I was still crying. So was Fred Merchison. I don't know why he was crying.

Ernie Foster never hit me with his knuckle again. Robert Finnigan and I became good friends. Robert quit being a bully. Ernie Foster started hitting Robert with his knuckle and running away. The attendance at the five-fifteen Mass increased. I guess people wanted to see who was going to fall on his face or get a bloody nose.

-24-

One day at recess a Sergeant Schumacher came riding up to the school yard on a shiny black "Indian" Motorcycle. He wore a black captains cap, a black leather jacket and shiny long black boots. He looked like someone out of the movies. The boys gathered around him and his motorcycle. In class, he gave a talk to us boys about starting a School Boy Patrol at our school. He said that in order to qualify you had to be at least eight years old. I told him that I would be nine in June. He said that we would not start until school started again in September. He showed us the magnificent white belt that went around the waist and crossed against the chest. We would get a badge too. He used Raymond Forcsh as a model. I saw Anna Mae looking goggle eyed at Raymond all decked out with his official uniform.

Our job would be to escort the school children safely across the streets on their way to and from school. The most busy street crossings would be assigned to the older boys, but those like me would be able to also serve. I immediately thought of at least two crossings that Anna Mae would have to cross. Wow, I, in all my splendor would get to escort her across the street. That's better than throwing your cape over a mud puddle. I saw someone do that in a movie. Upon leaving the school, Sergeant Schumacher throttled his motorcycle several times, upsetting the nuns, and with a salute to us rode off, out of sight, down Lafayette Avenue. I had another hero and the chance to be one myself, escorting Anna Mae safely across the dangerous streets of Saint Louis.

-25-

Our school picnic was usually the first week in June. Every year we prayed that it would not rain and that it would be warm so we could swim. Kids and parents would assemble on the boy's playground, picnic baskets in hand, waiting for the large green, double-decker buses to arrive and take us out in the County to West Lake Amusement Park. The most favored seat on the bus was topside in front. Those seats hung over the driver below and one felt like a captain of a ship at sea sailing over the roadways. The big boys always got those seats. The trip seemed to take forever as the busses, usually three of them. traveled at only twenty-five miles an hour at top speed. In the past years, I wasn't allowed on the roller coaster or the other big rides. This year I could if we had enough tickets. The school gave every kid five tickets, or I thought that they gave free tickets to every kid. Maybe we got them because we were poor, Dad's accident and all. Back then I used my five tickets for the Fun House where they had these three tall mirrors that curved so that in one I would look very tall and skinny as a mop handle, and the other making me fat, short, and bulgy, and the third with grotesque facial expressions. It was fun just to see how the other kids looked. The other thing that I liked about the Fun House was the large oak inverted, saucer which was mirror polished, with wires slightly embedded running all over it. As many kids that could scramble on it would wait until the attendant threw a switch and the saucer would rotate with increasing speed, and then the attendant would throw another switch turning on a slight but effective volt of electricity, and the kids screaming with delight, would release what tentative grip that they had and slide off into other kids before them, only to scramble on again for another ride. This year I wasn't even thinking of the Fun House. I wanted the roller coaster and the bumper cars. Father Thompson rode the roller coaster at every picnic, never getting out of his rear compartment, always holding up his hands skyward with every down hill surge.

Mom secured a picnic table spreading out everything that she would need for lunch, making me promise that I would return in two hours to eat. Off I went with my five tickets and five more that Dad bought. The roller coaster cost three tickets! I rode it twice, the second time sitting right in front of Father Thompson and raising my hands and screaming as the cars rolled up and down and curving, making the white wooden structure holding everything together creak and shake as if it was ready to fall apart. Soon I was out of tickets and returned to our table pouting. I watched other kids scurrying back and forth with tickets in their hands.

Dad got up and left limping along with his cane in hand and grunting. I buried my head on the table while Mom talked to the other mothers. When Dad came back Mom had lunch almost ready, baloney and peanut butter sandwiches, potato salad, and Dad fixed his specialty, radish sandwiches, pieces of bread buttered heavily with sliced radishes placed on the butter and salted. Back when Dad first fixed them I turned up my nose. Dad said what he always says when I didn't want to try a new food, "Francis, you don't know what you're missing." I tried them and this time, Dad was right. I liked them.

After lunch, Dad reached in his coat pocket, took off his straw hat and placed at least a dozen tickets on the table and gave them to me! Off I went, running.

When I was out of sight, Stella said, "Emil where in the world did you get those? You know that we can't afford any more."

"Stella, there's a rubbish pile out back where they burn everything including the used tickets." He emptied his pockets and placed a pile of tickets on the table, looking to and fro for someone watching.

Stella said, "Some of these are burned, singed on the edges", as she separated those from the better looking ones.

"I'm going to see if I can find some more."

"Emil, you're going to get arrested or thrown out of here if you get caught. Mercy, mercy!"

I was excited. I felt like a millionaire. I rode the bumper cars and drove like I owned the place. I kept Father Thompson company on the roller coaster and got him sodas and hot-dogs so he wouldn't have to get off. I wondered why he didn't have to go to the bathroom. Maybe he had some kind of a contraption under his garment. When I went to the Ferris Wheel and gave the man my ticket he looked at me and said, "Hey kid, where did you get this ticket?"

"From my Dad."

"Where did he get it?"

"I donno." He shooed me away and watched me until I turned the corner and headed for our table.

When I got back to our table Dad had already returned with a new supply of tickets. Mom had rejected most from the previous haul.

"Dad, that man at the Ferris Wheel looked at my ticket and looked at me kinda funny and asked me where I got the ticket. He told me not to come back."

Mom said, "No more rides today, Francis, here's your trunks, go swimming." I got as far as a "but" and was motioned away remembering, "A child should be seen and not heard."

I slept all the way back on the two-decker bus dreaming of the best school picnic.

~26~

One day I came home from playing with the kids and walking Skippy and found Uncle Walter and Mom and Dad all smiling. Mom said, "Francis, we have good news, we are so excited. You tell him, Emil."

"Francis, we are going to move. We bought a house over on Eads! Your new address will be 2838 Eads Avenue!" Dad's lips quivered and he grunted more as he spoke. I don't know which one of them was more excited.

I looked at Uncle Walter. He looked good, no red eyes. His hands were not shaking. I was told that Uncle Walter got his old job back at the Goodwill Store down on Hadley and Tyler street. He was going to help us move.

I couldn't figure out how they could buy a house when we were so poor. Mom told me that we would be renting the house and a portion of the rent would be held and applied to a down payment. Dad said that the house was three stories high and had nine rooms! He said that I could have one of the rooms for my own! He said that there was a nice fenced yard in the back where Bobby could run, and a two car garage.

"Are we going to get a car, Dad?" "No.", I was told. We couldn't afford one and Dad couldn't drive anyway but we would rent out the garage and all of the second story rooms and one of the third floor rooms. Dad seemed elated when he said that the house was over a hundred years old. I was almost afraid to look at it. Eads Avenue was two more blocks closer to "the tracks". I had previously learned that on the other side of the tracks was a large Negro neighborhood, somewhere in the vicinity of Compton and Market Street. I also heard it said that, "They don't want to be caught around our neighborhood after dark."

I didn't know many Negroes. I remember seeing some movie where these white hunters were caught in the jungle and led up to this boiling pot of water, only to be rescued at the last minute. That mixed up with my seeing those pretty and courteous elevator operators at Famous, The Grand Leader and the old man cleaning chicken at Bettendorf's, was about all that I knew about Negroes.

I worried that I may have to go to another school and never see Anna Mae or my friend, Avery. Dad said that nothing would change, just the houses. I got on my bike and rushed to tell Avery the news. He had been afraid to tell me for several days that they too were moving and also to Eads Avenue! In the same block. He was worried that he would have to go to the St. Vincent School and Church as the north side of Eads on that block was in that parish, but his grandmother worked it out so he could stay in our school. His grandparents, however, were supposed to attend St. Vincent's for Mass. St. Vincent parish was losing members rapidly as people were moving to better neighborhoods. There were still many homes in that parish that still had outside toilets.

Avery said that his grandmother told him that our new street was named after the man that built the Eads Bridge across the Mississippi, a Mr. James Eads, and that he once had a mansion on our street up near Grand Avenue. I remembered seeing the bridge when we went up to Grandpa's. I thought that it looked very old and massive and reminded me of a picture of the Great Wall of China in a school book. Avery and I rode our bikes down to look at our new neighborhood. Avery said that his new house also was over a hundred years old. It's a wonder that we didn't argue over whose was the oldest. His was also three stories high. The Hodgen School playground was at the East end of our block, a large fenced, paved, playground with basketball hoops. Hodgen was a public school. We didn't think that we were allowed to play there because we were Catholics and because one of the nuns told us once that we should never go into any church other than a Catholic Church. We figured that also meant schools and playgrounds. I wondered what those kids were like, the ones that went to public school. We rode down to St. Vincent's and saw that the WPA was in the process of building a bath house and an inside swimming pool on the Buder Playgrounds. Boy, that Roosevelt must be a great man! We are moving to new homes and soon there will be a swimming pool. Mr. Henn had a small grocery store up on the West corner of our new block. He didn't seem to like me and Avery sitting on his cast iron steps with our bikes laying on the sidewalk. From that point, we could see everything that happened on our block and up and down Nebraska Street.

Dad liked to listen to the Friday Night Fights with Don Dunphy giving him the blow by blow. He and I listened to the fight between Max Schmeling, the German, and Joe Louis who was expected to win since he knocked out Braddock and became Champ. Dad and Mr. Krueger liked the German fighter. Schmeling beat Joe Louis bloody. Dad said, "Well I guess that's the last we'll hear of him." Mr. Krueger was happy with the way the fight went but was very upset when Jessie Owens won all of those gold medals at the Olympics right in front of that Hitler. The Philco also had a short wave and sometimes we listened to the police calls. Most of them seemed to be "a domestic disturbance". Sometimes we were successful in getting Adolph Hitler making some kind of yelling speech. This was mostly when the Kruegeres visited. This guy, Hitler, was causing concern to a lot of people. Dad and the Kruegers' would play pinochle and discuss the speech in German. That would make Mom mad. If she was listening to the Victrola, she wished that there was a way she could turn up the volume. Mr. Krueger said that he and his family got out just in time but that he still loved his Father Land.

My cousin, Maymie, and her boy friend, Fergie, who tried to look like Clark Gable, came over to visit. When my cousin, Marguerite showed up, Fergie said that we should celebrate our moving. He was going to take us all to a nightclub. Dad didn't want to go but asked that they take me along. I think that he wanted Mom to be saddled with me. We all got in Fergie's car and went to a tavern or a night club of sort off Grandel Square. They had a dance floor and Fergie danced with Mom and cousin, Marguerite. Maymie said she couldn't dance. I was given a grape Nehi. They were drinking beer and having a good time.

The band took a break and the pretty waitress came and asked if we wanted refills. Fergie said yes and when she left to get their drinks, he said, "Now watch this carefully." He took out a silver dollar and placed it on the edge of the table were it looked like it was close to falling off. The pretty waitress came with the drinks. Fergie pointed to the silver dollar. She smiled, placed the drinks down, raised her right leg, with her skirt rising up to the middle of her thigh and placed her knee touching almost the middle of the table. She held on to the tray full of empty bottles with both hands. When she removed her leg the dollar was gone! The women burst out laughing and blushed. Fergie gave her a dollar bill. She winked and left. I looked under the table for the dollar and they all laughed at me. One of these days I'm going to figure out what happened to that silver dollar.

-27-

2838 Eads

We didn't have much to move. Uncle Walter borrowed a truck and got some neighborhood teenagers to do the heavy lifting. I stood on the sidewalk looking at our new home. The house sat on a two terraced hill and was three stories high with a steep, black slate roof. It had a front porch with railings. The concrete steps going up from the sidewalk to the house were a little out of kilter as a section broke away from the rest. The house was brick set on a limestone block foundation.

I ran up the steps, through the gangway and to the back yard. Dad had already quickly assembled two wooden gates with chicken wire to hold Bobby in. One side of the yard was nicely fenced with a seven foot high chain link structure. The other side of the yard was fenced with looped wire attached to weathered, and in places rotted wood stakes and rails. I soon learned that the good fence belonged to Mrs. Vick our new neighbor and the one falling apart was ours. Bobby was running along the fences smelling and peeing as he went and barking as if to say, "I'm Bobby and this is my yard". I looked at the garage in back of the yard. As I opened the door, which had one of four window panes missing, a hinge broke loose from the molding. There were cobwebs everywhere and when I brushed one aside, another would seem to grab me. The dust was so thick that you could smell it. Hot dust. I quickly left and went to the east side of the garage and found the ash pit which was half full. Ash pits were built in order to hold ashes and clinkers from the furnaces, and were to be emptied by the City from time to time. As years went by, people threw almost everything into them, including dog and cat poop, and the City ran out of the funds to empty them, so residences had to hire ash pit haulers to do the job.

I went out to the alley and observed how narrow it was. The alley was paved with brick with a telephone pole slightly jutting out here and there. An old shabby looking black man came down the alley in a horse drawn wagon shouting, "Rags, any rags, I'm the old rag man. I take anything you got." He must be a regular as some women came to their gate and gave him anything that they were going to throw out, broken lamps, old trash cans, bottles, beat up lamp shades. His wagon was loaded with junk. He nodded at me while his swayback old horse pulled the creaking wagon down the alley with him yelling, "Rags, glass, papers."

"Francis, come in here and be of some help", Mom yelled. I jumped up the steps to the back porch and ran through the kitchen, to the front door and up the walnut staircase to a landing midway to the second floor. Here was a door that opened to stairs going down to the kitchen. I was later told that the stairs were used by servants of the original owner some hundred years ago. The second floor had a bathroom that was above the servants' stairs. The bathroom had a deep white tub and a toilet. It was the only bathroom. There was a kitchen in the front of the house on the second floor. Next to it a living room, and beyond the tall, massive, oak, pocket doors, a large bedroom looking out on the back yard. Across the hall was a small bedroom next to the bathroom, with a window looking out on the back porch roof. I ran up the narrowing stairs to the third floor which had a small landing where you could look down through the staircase to the first floor. There was an old gas lamp sticking out from the wall. Next to it was a flanged pipe that ran all the way down to our kitchen. Mom later told me that it was used by the lady of the house years ago to communicate with the servants, and tell them to get down there and fix breakfast. They would use the staircase off the landing that came into the kitchen. They would do this so that the owners of the house would not be disturbed until the meal was prepared. She said she wished she had such servants. I asked her why they didn't just yell up and down the stairs. Mom said that would be improper and gross. She was sure getting uppity all of a sudden.

A very small, third floor attic room faced the front of the house with two small windows that opened outward. They were almost floor level. As I knelt down and looked out I could see over the houses across the street and hear the trains down in the rail yards which were about a mile away as the crow flies. I heard the locomotives heaving and shoving and banging the freight cars together, providing the rhythmic chug chugs like a symphony reaching a crescendo, and then receding only to start over again. The room in the back was much larger, though still with attic type ceilings. There was a rather large window sill, one could almost sit on it. I could see out over our back yard and over all of the garage roofs across the alley and the backs of the houses that lined Henrietta Street.

"Francis, where are you? Where ever you are and what ever you're doing? Come here this minute, you hear me"?

Down the stairs I flew, and when I got to the first floor Mom was standing at the opened front door directing Uncle Walter and Dad inside with a sofa. I was too busy to ask what she wanted. I said, "Hi, Mom", then ran down the dark steps leading to the musty dimly lit basement. Our washing machine was already in place directly over a drain. The duct work was round tubes coated with what looked like the same stuff that Dad's cast were made of and were only five foot off the floor. I touched one of them only to be plummeted with dust. A large coal furnace sat next to an enclosed coal bin. The bin had a small window to the gangway that held a removable board that was secured by a 2x4 held by brackets on the side. There wasn't any coal in the bin, only inch deep coal dust with a empty wheelbarrow and a shovel. Off to the side of the furnace was a small water heater stove with pipes that ran in and out of the furnace. When the furnace wasn't used and you wanted hot water you had to build a little fire in the stove. The windows in the basement were too dark with dust to see out. Off in the corner, somewhat enclosed, was a pantry where Dad had placed some of Mom's preserves, the rest of his homemade beer, and two of Uncle Walter's large medical books.

I opened the outside door off our laundry room and found myself under the back porch with stairs leading up to the yard facing Mrs. Vick's back porch. Bobby barked at me. I ran up the porch steps letting the screen door slam running into the kitchen where Mom was placing a table cloth on our red and white enameled table with folding sides, our only table. Mom gave one look at me, covered with cobwebs, and dust and said, "Francis! were on earth have you been, look at you. Don't touch anything, here's a towel and soap, go out on the porch and wash. Here use this pan of water and stop that dog of yours from barking. We'll get run out of the neighborhood before bed time." I cleaned up quickly and ran to the front door where Dad asked Mom where she wanted the library table, the one Uncle Walter brought us from his store. "Put it here in the vestibule, Emil." Vestibule? I never heard that word before.

I went through the entry to our living room, right off the "vestibule" and rolled the massive pocket doors closed, and did the same with the ones leading into the bedroom. Our Philco radio was already setting on top of the Victrola. Uncle Walter's musty bear rug was placed in front of the gas fireplace, the gas fixtures being removed years ago. I ran around the room wondering what to explore next when Mom and Dad rolled back the door, Mom grabbed me by the ear and lead me to the staircase, "Francis you sit right there on the steps and stay there. Children should be seen and not heard, and I've seen enough of your shenanigans for awhile."

She turned to Dad saying, "We can rent the front room on the third floor for at least three dollars a week and the one in back for four dollars, the sleeping room on the second floor for five and the three housekeeping rooms for fifteen. We can rent out the garage for say, five dollars a month and our own rent is only thirty. We must get some signs to stick in the window, and Emil, we will have to go up to Jefferson and see if we can find a cheap ice box, not a refrigerator, mind you, and some cheap beds. Oh, I'm so thrilled." "Yes dear", was Dad's response.

I remembered being promised a room of my own. Where would it be. The coal bin?

-28-

All of the houses on that block of Eads Avenue were like ours, three stories and nine rooms or more. Most of them were rooming houses, renting sleeping or housekeeping rooms to those who could afford the meager rates until they got back on their feet. I heard that phrase a lot, "back on their feet". There were "Room For Rent" signs displayed on a lot of the houses. In some windows the Ice Man's card showed how much ice the person wanted. That was so he didn't have to make an unnecessary trip up to the door. The sidewalks were pushed up in places by the roots of the Sycamore trees lining the street. I didn't like Sycamores. The smoke covered bark peeled off easily and whenever I climbed them I got my clothes all dirty and I caught it from Mom. We had a lot of smoke in the winter time. Some days it got so thick that you couldn't see a block away. Buildings were coated almost as much as the inside of a fireplace and it was hard to breath on those smokey winter days.

On Saturday evening the paper boys came down the sidewalk wheeling their wooden boxes stuffed with newspapers. I knew one of the paper boys, his name was George Clark. He was two years older than me. He told me at school one day that he got half a cent for every Sunday paper he sold. He said that there were territories given out and he had better not horn in on another boy's territory or he and his boss, who distributed the papers, would be sorry. He also said that if there was breaking news there were Extras printed and his boss would get him and his other carriers out of school so they could beat the other papers to the punch. I had heard them hollering Extra! Extra! at times like when Mussolini invaded Ethiopia, and that crazy King over in England gave up his throne for a woman. George sold the Star Times. Very few people got the daily papers but everyone wanted the Sundays. The other papers were the St. Louis Post Dispatch and the Globe Democrat, a morning newspaper. Dad liked the Globe as it had all the sporting results in it from the previous day.

One evening when my Aunt Gertrude was visiting and I was sitting on the front porch the Tamale Man came down the street pushing his white cart. "Tamales here. Get your red hots." The strange scent coming from his cart floated toward me. I rushed inside to ask Mom if I could have one and Aunt Gertrude said, "You don't want those, Francis, they're made with dead chickens!" I ugh'ed and went back to the porch but I sure liked the smell of those dead chickens. I could hear Aunt Gertrude laughing as my Mom tisk tisked. As the Tamale Man passed, the aroma from the cart made me hungry. The next Saturday night Dad went out to the street and came back with three tamales and explained that chicken soup, chicken and dumplings, and fried chicken were all made of dead chickens; didn't I remember how they rung the chicken's neck up at Grandpa's farm?

Mom said, "Hush, enough of that. Are we going to eat these or not?" We did and mine tasted as good as I thought it would. I wanted to keep the corn-husk that it was wrapped in.

Another day a man rushed his cart down our street, bells a-clanging and hollering "Knives, scissors sharpened." Women would run out with their stuff and he would sharpen their knives and scissors on a small grinding wheel that he operated by foot. Mom said he was an Italian from the Hill and that he only came around every two months. She said that a few years ago he had a monkey tied to his cart. She guessed that it had died.

The Ice Man came every day with his horse drawn wagon full of large blocks of ice wrapped in burlap. He looked up to the houses for Ice Signs, cards printed in black and white with 10, 20, 30,and 40 pounds printed on the sides. If he saw the "30" on the top he would use his ice pick in such a way to break out a thirty pound square of ice, hoist it on his burlap draped shoulder, enter the house and deposit the ice into their ice box. We kids would wait until he entered the house and rush to the wagon to scrape up small chunks of ice and then scatter when he emerged. The horse would turn his head and look back at us, stomping his hooves and swishing his tail trying to rid himself of flies. Coming out of the houses, the Ice Man would always holler, with a grin, "Get out of there!"

It seemed to be entertainment for some of the women on the block to keep track of how long the Ice Man remained in certain houses. I heard Mom say that Mrs. Wallace down the street heard from Mrs. Cassidy that one of Mrs. Owen's lady renters kept the Ice Man up there much longer than necessary. We kids didn't care because we got to eat more wet, burlap smelling ice. We, of course, had our Frigidaire and needed no ice but Mom bought some ice signs for the renters who would come. A couple of weeks later Mom heard from Mrs. Wallace, who heard from Mrs. Cassidy, that Mrs. Owen's renter was the mother of our Ice Man and he always stopped for lunch. The ladies had to look elsewhere for entertainment.

Days later we got more furniture, some from Wagner's Furniture along with a gift of an original painting of a countryside. That same day, Uncle Walter sent a boy with two bronze fishermen lamps. The lamps went on our library table in the vestibule. I thought that library tables were for books. Mom said that we didn't have any books. I was told that I could have the back room on the second floor for my own until we found a renter. Mom was to be the interviewer of any prospective renters, telling Dad that she was the best judge of character.

Sunday, after Mass, my cousin, Marguerite, and my Aunt Gertrude came to visit. Marguerite helped Mom fix the sauerkraut and spare ribs, mashed potatoes, fried potatoes, and boiled new potatoes. Mince meat pie was placed in the oven. I hated mince meat pie. Aunt Gertrude sat at the kitchen table, puffing on one cigarette after another and responded to just about everything Mom and Marguerite said with a "Well, I say", and a shaking of her head with a disapproving chuckle. Dad came in and offered her a beer and she said very little until the bottle became empty.

I liked Marguerite. No one called her Margaret. She wasn't pretty and wasn't ugly, kinda in between. She reminded me of F.D.R.'s wife, Eleanor, tall and gangly. Marguerite must have been color blind. She wore outlandish colors that always brought out a snide remark from Aunt Gertrude. Marguerite worked at Shapleigh Hardware Co. downtown and had been there since leaving the farm. She went to Mass every day, (thank God she didn't see me altarboying). She always ate Sunday dinner with us. She did not have a boyfriend. She liked her beer. Everyone in my family, except Dad, liked beer.

~29~

Avery had this friend, Leroy Grone, who lived a couple of blocks away. He wanted me to go with him to Leroy's house. Leroy had some books and magazines full of women. In Leroy's basement he showed us some of his "girlie" magazines and passed around a flip book. It was a small missal sized book with pages with worn edges. If you flipped the pages fast enough it was like a movie reel and showed a man and a woman "going at it" Leroy said. When his mom started down stairs Leroy grabbed the books and covered them with Popular Mechanics. I left Leroy Grone's house with new interest.

That night I took a bath in our bath tub. All of a sudden my penis grew and stood straight up out of the water and discharged a glob of liquid that scared me to death. I had just touched it as I had done many times before in washing, but this time I had such a pleasurable feeling, one better than scratching an itch, being tickled or anything else that I had ever felt. I was excited and thought that I might die right there. I saw the glob float and then sink slowly before me. I touched my still hard penis and another eruption occurred. Now I knew that I was dying! Mom called, "Francis, supper is ready, hurry up." I lay there, in the now becoming cool water, afraid to move and wondering now if I was a "jack off", or worse yet how would I get this thing to go down so I could go to supper. I thought that this must be what Father Thompson and Father Joe, in helping me make a good confession, asked me a couple of times, "Did you play with yourself?" I remember answering once, "No, I played with Avery, Frank and Fred and Ivan. Football, Father."

"Francis, you're Mom and I are waiting." I ended up in having a cold supper. Mom wondered why my future baths took so long. Dad merely smiled. I wondered if I was the only jack-off in the neighborhood. I never called anyone else one but I still wondered. I dared not ask anyone, not Dad or even, Avery.

That Friday the Sisters marched us up to the church for our confessions, boys in one group, girls in another. As I knelt in the pew I tried to think how I would confess what I was sure was, my mortal sin. Perhaps I could put it off till next Friday, or forever. I would make an Act of Contrition and then I would have to promise that I would not do it again. Sister motioned that it was my turn. My knees shook and I was sure that, Oh, my God, I had Father Joe. I trembled, “”Bless me Father for I have sinned. It has been one week since my last confession. I lied to my mother and father, (which I think was a lie but I never heard anything about lying to a Priest). I ah—I ah,”

“Come on boy out with it!”

“I ah, well you remember before when you asked me if I played with myself and I said, no I played football with,”—-

“Yes, I remember.”

“Well I really did it this time, Father.”

“How many times did you play with yourself, my son?” I was sure everyone outside heard him.

I whispered, “I think three times, Father.” I lied.

“My son, do you know what you're doing? You are wasting a life every time you do that. When you are old enough to get married and have a wife, each time that you do that under the Sacrament of Matrimony you will produce a little baby. Do you understand?”

“Yes, Father.” I lied again.

“Now go and say three Hail Marys' and four Our Fathers and promise me that you will not do this again.”

“Yes, Father.” When I came out of the confessional I just knew that everyone out there saw me as a jack-off. I further knew that I wouldn't be able to keep my promise to old Father Joe and that many more babies would be wasted. I couldn't help it.

~30~

Avery and I went everywhere with our bikes. Once I was outside the house, Mom and Dad didn't worry what I did or where I went. I always managed to be home for lunch and supper. After school a bunch of us boys rode over to play with Jason as we did often. We didn't know what his last name was. Jason was in a dirty wheel chair out on the sidewalk in front of his house. Something was wrong with Jason. He couldn't move his legs and he was always slobbering on himself. He couldn't make us understand him. He slurred his speech and was loud. We would taunt him circling him with our bikes. I guess Jason didn't know that we were making fun of him because he was always smiling and grunting loudly at us. Once I saw a woman look out the window of Jason's house. She must have been his mother. She looked very sad. I thought that I saw her crying. I don't ever remember feeling sorry for Jason. I do know that I couldn't look at him for very long. That troubled me, but I couldn't help it.

Another day some of us rode our bikes up to the Insane Asylum on Arsenal Street. Leroy Grone took us to a spot outside the high fence surrounding the complex. We looked through the fence and Leroy started calling. We could see this old woman in front of one of the open, barred windows dancing and twirling around in her white gown. Upon hearing Leroy shouting, she would stop, come closer to the window and lift her gown up to her chin, bearing what possibly at one time was a beautiful body. The woman would let out the shrillest laugh. Leroy applauded and told us to do so. The woman would turn her back to us and raise her gown again and then fade away dancing and twirling. A week or two later, Leroy wanted to go see the crazy lady again. We declined, but couldn't explain exactly why. We remembered Jason. We saw him fequently wheeling himself on the sidewalks around our school. We didn't taunt him anymore. We would remember him and the lady in the window for the rest of our lives.

~31~

I answered the door. A well dressed couple inquired of Mom's "For Rent" sign. Mom took them upstairs and showed them the housekeeping rooms talking like these three rooms were in the Waldorf Astoria. I had never seen the Waldorf, but had heard many use the name sarcastically. I crept part way up the stairs and could hear the tall man say, "We will only be staying a month or two. We have an airplane out at Lambert Field for repairs and we—-".

He has an airplane! He almost looked like Lucky Lindy. I made him my Mr. Lindbergh.

Mom was impressed and collected the first weeks rent, fifteen dollars! Dad wasn't so impressed. I think it was only because Mom had made the sale. I didn't get to see much of Mr. and Mrs. Smith. They told Mom that they were in the distribution business. Mom pretended that she knew all about that. They sure had a lot of men come visit them. None of them stayed very long. Mr. Smith would bring in a lot of cardboard boxes and carry a lot of them out. Several weeks went by and I heard Mom and Dad arguing.

"Emil, he said that they would catch up next Monday."

"But they are already three weeks behind. You could have rented to that other couple last week."

Monday morning came and Dad went up the stairs grunting and knocked on the door. The door opened slightly with his knock and Dad saw the dirty pots and pans stacked in the sink. The bed was stripped. My Lucky Lindy had flown the coop and without an airplane!

"Well if you think you can do any better, go ahead," Mom told Dad. " It's your turn."

-32-

One morning after breakfast as I was washing my hands in the sink, I saw this man standing behind our back yard gate staring at our house. Bobby was barking at him. The stranger just stood there looking at the house for a long time. I told Mom to come look. Mom quickly gathered up food on the table, threw in a banana, wrapped everything in newspaper and told me to take it out to the man. I was somewhat scared but went ahead. Bobby kept barking at the stranger. The man wasn't old. His face was drawn and weather-beaten. I gave him the food as he nodded to my Mom standing at the window. Mom said that there were plenty of folks like him down at Hooverville and that the country wasn't out of trouble yet.

The next day Avery and I set out on our bikes to find Hooverville. After a long bike ride, and stopping to ask directions, we found Hooverville way down in South St. Louis between the river, the railroad tracks and Broadway. Small curls of smoke rose above hundreds of shanties put together with smashed tin cans, pieces of metal and cardboard. It looked like a hobo camp that I saw in a magazine, except these people were not hobos.

Avery and I stared at the sight from afar until a man who was stirring something in a pot over one of the fires saw us and hollered, "What are you staring at, come over here and take a look at what I'm cooking." It did smell good. "Did you boys bring any food with you, if not you can't stay for lunch! Everybody contributes around here. Now, tell me. What did you come here for, to see the freak show." We kept our mouths closed and just shook our heads. We heard music coming from farther inside the camp, Rudy Valle singing something about "Brother can you spare a dime". I hated Rudy Valle. I was somewhat frightened. A few of the other men gathered around. A old, dirty man put his hand on my bike and asked another, "What you figure we can get for these two nice looking bicycles?"

A woman came out from one of the dwellings rubbing her hands together and smiling. "I heard you, John. Don't be scaring these boys that way, and, Cookie if they didn't bring any food with them, they can have part of mine. What's your names, boys and where do you live?"

"Mine's, Avery, Ma'am and this is Francis. We live on Eads Avenue."

"Well mine's, Mary Howell and this is my husband, John. Mr. Howell used to work in a shoe factory. He was a foreman and made good money until it closed up. We could no longer pay the rent on our flat, and John couldn't find work. I had no place any more to take in washing and we were just flat broke. We have a son and a daughter about your ages. Couldn't take care of them. They're with relatives. "

A whiskered man spoke up, "There ain't nothing wrong with being flat broke as long as you got your faith and a sense of humor. There ain't a man here that hasn't already been out there looking for some kind of work this morning. If he can't find any he tries to get himself to beg or go to the soup kitchen and bring back something to the community pot. Things are getting better though. The population of Hooverville has dropped considerably since this time last year, ain't that right, John."

Avery and I had a small cup of their stew and left. On the way up toward Broadway I saw the same man that came to our back gate heading down to where we had been.

~33~

September came and with it the pennant races. Dad and I listened to the Cardinal broadcast with France Laux announcing the plays. Dad got to hear them during the week, I listened on Saturdays and Sundays, or if the game ran late during the week and was still on when I got home from school. We just knew our Gas House Gang would do it again, although Dad said that they were getting old. I had many heroes, Joe Medwick, who I expected to hit a homer every time he came to bat and Terry Moore who glided all over center field. Mister Moore was not a slugger liked Joe, but he went six for six in one game when he was a rookie. They now had another young rookie named, Johnny Mize who could hit the ball a ton. Dizzy Dean was almost as popular as Lindbergh even with people who knew nothing about baseball. We listened to one of the Card's last games of the season. Johnny Mize was thrown out of the game by the umpire when he objected to a called strike. He was replaced by a guy named, Walter Alston who struck out in his first at bat. Dad said, "There's another one that we will never see again." Dad and I mourned as the Cardinals finished with a tie for second, five games out.

Sergeant Schumacher met with Leroy Jones, Finnigan, Ernie Foster and I in the auditorium and gave us our School Boy Patrol badges, and our bright white belts after a half hour of instructions. Boy was I proud! After Sergeant Schumacher left I looked at my assignment. I was to patrol the corner of Henrietta and Compton. I was deeply disappointed. Anna Mae did not go that way to or from school. She would never see me in my uniform. From the first day I pretended that my corner was the likes of Broadway and Washington, downtown. I blew my whistle when kids approached the crossing whether a car was coming or not. It got so that the older kids crossed without my telling them to, and a woman living on the corner hollered out the window for me to stop blowing that infernal whistle. I found out that Harry O'Shea had one of the corners where Anna Mae crossed. I tried to get him to trade with me. He said that he had a lot of other offers, but turned them down because he also wanted to escort Anna Mae across that dangerous intersection. I offered to throw in four agate marbles and he still refused. "Go back to your station, kid." Kid? Harry was only a grade ahead of me.

The nights were getting cold. Mom ordered coal. It was cheaper if the coal man just dumped it on the street rather than him wheel borrowing it up our terraced lawn and into our coal bin. She told the man that she had a strong son to take care of the coal. I came home from school after patrolling and walking Skippy and looked at the pile of black stuff and the terraced lawn that I was to push up the stuff. It took me two and a half days to get the job done with Mrs. Vick complaining that the pile of coal took up her boarder's parking place. Getting the coal into the coal bin was one thing. I had to go into the basement every so often and drag the stuff away from the opening in order to dump more in. Mom told me that next year they would buy the coal in July, it would be cheaper in the summer time. I was sweating profusely now, I imagined July. I got that word, "profusely" from Mom. She used that word often.

-34-

Frank Gordon and Charley Fitzpatrick told Avery and I that they had a super trick to play on old Mrs. Kowalski up the street. She was the widow woman that was always home on Halloween but would never turn her lights on or answer the door for the kids. The few times that she did answer the door she would slam the door on them after they gave their little performance without giving them anything.

Frank and Charley were older than us. They told us, or at least one of us, what we had to do. On Halloween night, Frank called me out of the house. I rushed by my Mom with a brown paper sack in my hand and off I went to meet up with Avery and Charley who were sitting on Avery's door step waiting for it to get dark. We had rehearsed this two times before. The hour came. We watched kids going up to Mrs. Kowalski's door, ring the door bell, do their little song, dance, or rhyme, and have the door slammed in their faces. "Go, Francis, here's the lighter, run now before any other kids come up."

"Yeah, go show her", Avery said. I gave him a dirty look and ran down the street with my bag and lighter and stumbled up her steps to the door. I lit the bag and rang the door bell and scampered back down and joined my comrades behind the bushes. When the door opened, she saw the fire and stomped on the paper bag full of the dump that I had taken late that afternoon.

The first scream was loud, the second was of a much higher octave and was mixed with sobbing. A neighbor man came over, looked at the mess, got her shoe off and took her into the house. We could see the man pick up the telephone. At that point we scattered like a flock of startled birds and ran to our homes, dreadfully regretting what we had just done.

I couldn't bring myself to confess this sin without telling Father the whole story. I knew it was a sin but I didn't know what kind. Probably a mortal one. That would mean Hell and Damnation for sure. I confessed,

"I lied to my mother and father" in hopes that would take care of at least part of the sin until I got enough nerve to tell the whole story. I got three Hail Marys and three Our Fathers. I said six Hail Marys and six Our Fathers.

I did not expect Frank to confess straight out. As I was saying my penance Frank was in the confessional. Father Thompson let out a loud laugh followed by muttering. Frank Gordon was in there for a long time. The Sisters were waiting on him to emerge and say his penance so they could take us back to school. We usually had a contest to see who could say his penance the quickest. Frank finally emerged with tears sliding down his cheeks and his hands pressed together, holy like. Sister Mary Elizabeth made the sign of the cross with her eyes closed after seeing him like that. We all waited twenty minutes for him to get through with his penance. That was a record. Father Thompson never came out but I swear that I heard a chuckle or two from that direction. I admired Frank, but wondered about him. I also wondered if he told Father Thompson who his accomplices were. Charlie Fitzpatrick and Avery were only in the confessional for a short period, so I know that they didn't confess what he did.

-35-

Dad rented my room out to a Mr. Greensfelder, a tall, thin, educated, looking man who said that he was a professor and between appointments whatever that meant. In his conversations with Dad, of which I overheard many, he would expound on his knowledge of nature and the environment. I knew what nature was, but not this environment stuff. I was moved to the third floor front. Mr. Greensfelder was a friendly sort and a week later he asked my Dad if he could take me out to Creve Coeur Lake for an outing on Saturday. Mr. Greensfelder and I took streetcars, transferring several times to get to the Delmar loop which seemed to be just outside the City limits. Not much was there. We then transferred to the Creve Coeur streetcar which took us out into the country with a stop in the town of Overland. From there the streetcar took us to the foot of a hill in Creve Coeur Park. Upon walking up the steps to the top of the hill, we could see the entire lake. Mr. Greensfelder said that the lake was formed by the backwaters of the Missouri River. He sure was smart. We ate our lunch looking at the view with the trees sparkling with their fall colors. Mr. Greensfelder explained how and why the leaves turned color. Something about the sap running this way or that. I forgot most of what he said. I told him that I had to pee. He said that he did also so we went into the toilet. No one else was there. I peed and he looked over to see my watchamacallet and said that I had a very fine one and would I like to see his. I didn't know what to say, but he turned and showed me his big long one. I got scared and ran outside and started looking for the streetcar to take us back. About five minuets later Mr. Greensfelder came out and apologized for frightening me and said that we should keep this as our little secret. I agreed. Anything to get started home where I could spill the beans on him. On the way back without much conversation, I couldn't figure out how to tell Dad. I decided that Mr. Greensfelder was a mite different than a jack-off. I did manage to tell Dad enough of the episode and the next morning before I got up,

Dad's renter was gone with Mom saying that the next interviews of potential renters were hers.

~36~

Thanksgiving Day came. Uncle Walter was missing again. Marguerite and Aunt Gertrude and her boy friend, Bud, joined us. Mom sent me to the Well # 1 down on Park and Nebraska for some beer. She put six empty bottles in a paper bag and as I started out of the door, she whispered, "Francis, three Hyde Parks and three Falstaffs and don't rattle the bottles". I thought of three Hail Marys and three Our Fathers and wondered what the Sisters, or God, or some shrink for that matter, would think of the workings of my mind. The Well # 1 was a neighborhood tavern and there were a lot of men there. Mr. Concoran, the head of Dad's Holy Name Society was there sitting at a table drinking beer, smoking a cigar and playing cards.

I told the man behind the bar that I wanted "three Hail—-, I mean three bottles of Hyde Park and three Falstaffs and would you please put them in two bags."

I gave him a dollar and he gave me change and a lollypop. As I walked out the door he said, "Hold them tight, now lad".

By the time I got to the foot of our steps the moisture from the cold bottles worked through the bags and one slipped through and crashed loudly on a step. Mom was at the door tisk tisking and looking this way and that. At the same time a man followed me up the steps looking and sniffing at what I had done. I heard him asking Mom about the rooms for rent. Mom motioned for me to go around to the back door as she led the man in. Marguerite was putting our Thanksgiving meal on the table, a goose accompanied by three kinds of potatoes, mashed, boiled and fried, dressing, cranberry sauce, and a mincemeat pie cooling on the sink.

Mom came in with dollar bills in her hand saying, "I just rented Mr. Greensfelder's room to this nice man and I invited him to share dinner with us. He went to get his suitcase, here he comes now. Come on in Mr.—I didn't get your name."

"Names Jacob Arnold, Ma'am. I'm a Baptist Preacher kinda traveling through looking for a place to preach the Gospel."

Aunt Gertrude started choking on her beer and between choking fits I heard her mumble, "Well I say". Mom quickly picked up the beer soaked bag of bottles that I had brought in through the back door and placed them in the refrigerator, bag and all, and wiping her hands on her dress motioned for the preacher to sit down.

Dad told Mr. Arnold that he had known several Baptist Preachers in the Defiance and Herman, Missouri area.

Aunt Gertrude's boy friend, Bud popped up, "I known one. He was a good drink—-"

"Hush", Aunt Gertrude said.

Mom said, "Mr. Arnold, or should we call you Preacher or what?"

"Mr. will do just fine, or better yet, call me Jacob."

"Well, Jacob", Dad said, "Welcome to our table, would you honor us by saying grace."

After dinner Mr. Arnold retired to his room. The beer came out of the refrigerator. Aunt Gertrude asked how Mom, a good Catholic, could bring herself to rent to a Baptist Preacher and that she may as well have rented to a Jew.

Mom, with a smile on her face, her cheeks starting to glow said, "We're all God's children, and I'll tell you another, yesterday I rented the back third floor to two young tap dancers. Marvin and Lillian Ginsberg! They are going to dance downtown at the Grand. They call themselves, 'Quick and Nimble'. She's the "Nimble." Aunt Gert choked.

Dad told me that the Grand was a Vaudeville and Burlesque theater. A kind of a mix between an opera and a musical with comedians and dancing girls. My cousin Marguerite joined Aunt Gertrude with a "Well, I say". Dad and Bud lifted their eyebrows and smiled at Mom approvingly.

My mother sent me for more beer with a dry double lined paper bag, again with a "Don't rattle the bottles."

In the days that followed, Mr. Arnold came down the stairs every morning before I left for school mumbling with the Bible in hand and left for parts unknown. When I came home from school I could hear "Quick" and "Nimble" tap-dancing as I ate my mayonnaise sandwich in the kitchen. It sounded like a machine gun only with rhythm and every once in a while they would both give it a big loud slam with their feet. When they left for work in late afternoon they would tap-dance all the way down the stairs and out the front door. At night after I was in bed in the room next to them, I could hear them discussing the night's performance, and being considerate, they practiced more steps without their shoes, producing barely heard thudding noises. Once in awhile if I couldn't sleep I could hear "Nimble" moaning with an almost whimpering sound along with the noise of squeaking bed springs like I made when I jumped up and down on my bed. I wondered if they were dancing on the bed. "Nimble" was very pretty. "Quick" didn't look anything like Fred Astair and I was glad because I didn't like Fred Astair. He wasn't my type of movie star. " Quick" and "Nimble" gave Dad two passes for the show. Dad grunted, smiled and thanked them. Mom frowned slightly, knowing that she would not be able to go, good church woman that she was. I looked forward to seeing "Nimble" come down the stairs on her way to work. She would wink at me or rub my hair as she and "Quick" went out the door. Our one bathroom became a problem now that we had all these renters and their different work schedules and my spending more time in there than anyone thought I should. I got hollered at a lot and the door would rattle often with someone wanting in. Dad and Clem went to the Grand on Saturday night just to check it out. Mom asked Dad if any of the Holy Name boys knew that he went. He didn't answer. I hoped that one of these days I would get to go to the Grand.

Preacher Jacob Arnold told Mom that he would be leaving the first day of the year, that he had done so well at a tent revival somewhere out in the county that a church in Wellston offered him a position. He said that he would never forget us and told me that I could come out to his church and be a server anytime. He surely hadn't seen me work. "Quick" and "Nimble" also gave their notice. They had a gig in Tulsa, Oklahoma. A gig is a word for a job, "Nimble" told me as she gave me a kiss. I got redder than Mom gets with a couple of beers. My watchmacallit woke up.

~37~

Christmas came. I got a BB gun. I couldn't use it until we went to the country. When would that be I asked? "When Spring comes and someone gives us a ride. I don't want you to ever kill any birds with it", Dad said. I aimed it at everything, even Bobby who just barked back.

I got a pair of boxing gloves along with a punching bag that Dad rigged up in the basement. He must have heard about my fight with Finnigan and saw me as the next heavyweight champion of the world. The gloves were red and had a faint, sweet, leather smell to them. I could get the punching bag to bang five or six times in succession but wasn't able to really get it going like I saw Joe Louis do in training on a newsreel. After a couple of weeks of this, Dad gave up on the idea of me being a boxer. He had told me of the great Jack Dempsey and his other boxing heroes. When Dad and I listened to the Friday Night Fights with Don Dunphey announcing the big ones, he really got excited. He would grunt and bob and weave and throw short punches in the air. I had a hard time trying to keep from laughing. He got just as excited listening to the Browns and Cardinal games. I could never imagine him taking part in any sport with all of his feebleness. I asked him once if he ever played baseball or boxed. "No, Francis, but one doesn't have to partake to be interested."

I didn't think much of this punching bag stuff. I wanted to get in a ring and show everyone my powerful right. I had muscles from hauling coal and mowing lawns, eating Wheaties and the pushing and pulling of my hands like the Dynamic Tension thing.

A couple of weeks later I talked to one of my classmates, Richard Fence, who said that he boxed down at the Buder Playground. He said that if I wanted to try boxing, he would give me a few pointers. We met after school at the gym. I brought my new boxing gloves. A referee said that he would judge the bout. I looked over at Richard. He was of slender build and at least three inches shorter than me. I always took him for somewhat of a sissy in the school yard as he didn't roughhouse with the rest of us. The referee yelled start. I was ready to throw my powerful right and finish the fight. Richard danced all around me and I had a hard time knowing where he was. I hit nothing but air. Richard had no trouble finding me. He hit me from every angle. I had not touched him. Between rounds he and the referee said that I needed to move around more and bob and weave. Okay. As I moved around and bobbed and weaved I found one of Richard's gloves hitting my face repeatedly like a woodpecker pecking at the telephone pole out in the alley. One more round and I gave up. I needed to learn more about boxing or not do it. Richard did not hit me hard, he just gave me a boxing lesson, one that convinced me to give my gloves to a scraggly kid who watched our "bout" laughing all the while. I liked Richard and respected him more than before.

~38~

Gertrude

December 20, 1936

Dear Diary

Winter is here and so am I. I cook three meals a day, do all the washing and make the beds. Barty carries the water from the well down in the valley and helps me with the dishes and takes care of the chickens. Tommy cuts timber and splits it into firewood and helps Dad with the livestock. We do all of this before and after school. School seems so different than at the orphanage. One room. Our teacher is Mrs. Cummings. The school has outside toilets. Dad hasn't the time to take us there or pick us up so we walk in the cold and the snow for miles. Christmas is coming. I cried myself to sleep last Christmas. We got socks and gloves. All the same color and size. None of our relatives came. The roads were too bad. We received presents in the mail two weeks after Christmas. We had nowhere to go and no one came to visit us. I sometimes wish that we were all back at the orphanage. Tommie calls the orphanage, "The Big House". Our relatives paid more attention to us then and we had friends our age there. We had Christmas trees, not the scraggly cedar tree that Tommie drug in. And singing. How I loved the singing. I know Father is doing his best but it seems that there should be more in life. We haven't been to church in Jerseyville in a month and anyway we can't all fit in the buggy. I wish that we could afford an automobile. I wouldn't care how old it was. An automobile would be a lot better than Father's buggy and old Rufus, our blind-in-one-eye horse. Tommie said that when he leaves this farm and gets a job that's the first thing he is going to buy, an automobile. Well not the first thing, he said. The first thing would be a big, grocery size, bag of candy. Tommie has a sweet tooth. He talks a lot about leaving the farm. I hope he never leaves unless we all go with him, but I don't know where we would go or what we would do. There must be something better than this. Tommie said that in another year or two he could hire out to the richer farmers at a dollar a day. Seems like a lot of money to me. No one knows that I write this diary. I'm running out of pages and I don't know how to ask Father for writing paper. I would like a new or a different dress, although I don't know what for. Last summer we did go to visit Grandpa Walsh. In his outhouse was this Sears and Roebuck catalog with all kinds of new dresses in it.

Dad never asks us what we want for Christmas. I remember when we used to write Santa a letter in "The Big House". The Sisters read them. A lot of the kids just wanted someone to come and take them home. Sister Lignatius told me that the day Dad came and got us.

~39~

On the day before Christmas Eve when his children were still in school, Tim Kelley came across his daughter's diary. It was time for them to be arriving from school so he only had time to read her last passage. He wept and got down on his knees and prayed to God for direction. He loved his children and knew that the life they had was hard. He couldn't afford an automobile. He could barely afford to make interest payments on the farm. All he could do was to keep the children fed and housed with their help until better times came. He prayed but no message came.

When the children came home from school, excited that there would be no school for a whole week, their Father said that he was going to go to Alton. No they couldn't go with him, he had business to conduct. He would stay overnight and be back late afternoon on Christmas Eve. They all wanted to go. He told them they had to take care of the animals and the house and to be good. They all wondered what their Father was going to Alton for and more importantly what he was going to bring back. Gertrude hoped that he would trade old Rufus and that weather-beaten buggy for an automobile. Tommie settled for a bag of candy. Joseph couldn't make up his mind what he wanted.

On the way there, Tim, who had originally started out with the idea of buying some presents, wondered if the Sisters would take his children back until he could better provide for them. He started to think of Francis and how much better off he was but he caught himself. He didn't want to think of his youngest son, the one he rarely saw. The one whose birth caused a lot of these problems. He thought again of his kids back home and couldn't bear the thought of them leaving him once again.

As he left Alton late the next morning, and after passing through Godfrey, it began to snow. Lightly at first. The automobile traffic was sparse so he was able to keep the buggy on the pavement most of the time. The closer that he got to Jerseyville the thicker the snowfall became, so much so that he rode the highway with the left wheels on the pavement and the others on the shoulder as to not get hit by a passing car. When he reached his road three miles from Jerseyville, he was glad to get off of the highway. He pulled off onto the dirt road which was covered with three inches of snow. Only seven miles to go. Tim could barely see what he thought was the middle of the road but Rufus didn't need to see the road. The old horse knew it by heart and despite which way Tim jerked the reigns he went his way and at his pace. When he was within two miles of home, a large buck deer suddenly jumped over a fence and in front of Old Rufus. The horse bolted. The buggy slid into the ditch throwing Tim out. He hit his head on a rock knocking him unconscious. Rufus struggled but was able to pull the buggy from the ditch and continued on his way with thoughts of a warm barn and dry hay.

Tommie was feeding the cows in the barn when Rufus pranced in with the empty buggy attached. He noticed the grass encased with mud and snow covering all of one side of the buggy. Tommie ran into the house hoping his Father was there.

"The buggy must have turned over and Father is out there somewhere! I'm going to look for him."

Gertrude was frantic. A sudden cloud of guilt engulfed her. Joseph started to cry. Gertrude started to put on her coat. Tommie told her to stay with her little brother and he went out the door with a flashlight and a lantern. Tommie went to their neighbor, Norman Morewise for help. He couldn't see ten feet in front of him, but he knew the way. Mr. Morewise and Tommie walked the road looking for Tim.

Tim awoke, still dazed, felt his head and felt the blood run over his fingers. He struggled out of the ditch and tried to get his bearings. The snow had fallen so fast and so heavily that all horse and buggy tracks were covered with six inches of new snow. He stood in the middle of the road and started walking. The wrong way. He hoped that the horse had stopped just up ahead, but with each step and no signs of him, he cried. He once again wondered if he did the right thing in taking his children out of the orphanage. He prayed to his wife, Bird to help him. His tears melted the snow flakes on his cheeks. He knew about how far from home that he was when the deer bolted and figured that he only had about a mile or two to go. After two hours of walking he realized that he must have gone the wrong way or he had been farther from home than he thought. He was freezing and he was wet clear through. The white out made him feel his way like a blind man without a cane in order to stay on the road. He walked and stumbled for what seemed like hours when he thought he saw a dim light up ahead. As he got closer he recognized Walter Evan's silo, the only one in the county. He then realized that he went the wrong way. Soon he was knocking on their door and when Mrs. Evans opened it, Tim fell in.

Tommie and Norman Morewise had just passed the point of the accident but were unaware of it as the snow covered all signs. Tommie put out the lantern and turned off the flashlight as they were of no use. The two men walked arm in arm, afraid of being separated. Norman Morewise was a short chubby man. He kept to himself, being a bachelor. He raised hogs and in some way looked like them. He also smelled like the pigs. Usually Tommie would try to stay downwind of Mr. Morewise on their infrequent encounters but he was glad to have him along. If they got separated in the blowing snow and wind, Tommie could hone in on him by scent if the wind was right.

Mr. Morewise liked the Kelleys and would see to it that they received a pork belly at butchering time. Once they invited him over to dinner when Bridget was alive. He came all cleaned up with his long hair all slicked back, and he took off his boots outside the door. He remarked how good everything smelled, especially the pumpkin pie and everything did until the scent of his boots outside crept under the door. It was still daylight outside but Bridget set a coal oil lamp on the middle of the table. The fumes from it, the pumpkin pie, and Norman's boots, produced a strange scent that would never again come into the house.

Tommie and Mr. Morewise trudged on trying to stay in the shallow ruts in the road until they too came to the home of Mr. Evans. Mrs. Evans answered the pounding on the door. When she opened it she saw two snow covered faces. When she ushered them through the door, Tommie started to ask her if she had seen his Father. Before he could say the words he saw Tim sitting at the kitchen table with a bandage on his head and with clean dry clothes on. He was spooning a bowl of soup very nervously. Soon Tommie and John's coats and hats and gloves were hung up and they too sat at the table. Mrs. Evans noticed a foul smell but thought that it may have come from the wet clothing.

Despite the condition of their visitors, both Mr. And Mrs. Evans were glad for the company. People seemed to avoid them. They supposed that it had something to do with the fact that they were so much wealthier than their neighbors. They had the best livestock, the very best machinery and wore the finest clothes. They employed a few laborers but had no friends or children. They looked at the three still shivering men sitting at the table conversing, smiling and for that moment wished they could enter their world, regardless of what their world was like.

After awhile the snow let up and Mr. Evans went out and hitched up his mules to his new wagon and the four men piled in and took off for home, Tim, Tommie, and Mr. Morewise dressed in finery that they had never known before. A live goose was secured behind them along with a sack of candies and one of cookies in Tommie's lap. Tim was feeling much better.

Gertrude and Joseph heard the shouting and talking and she rushed out to meet them. She threw her arms around her Father. Joseph did the same, crying. Gertrude burst out, "This is the best Christmas I ever had!"

Tim introduced Mr. Evans to his daughter and his other son and Mr. Evans graciously accepted a glass of "Old Grand Dad" and the three grown men toasted to new friendships. Mr. Evans told Tommie that come Spring he could use a strong one like him and would pay him well.

After Mr. Morewise and Mr. Evans left, Tim inquired of Rufus and the buggy. He put on his old jacket and went to the barn, stroked Rufus, gave him feed and untied the bundles still intact. Little Gertrude got her dress, a pretty blue print and some white shoes, the kind she made her first communion in. Tommie got six pounds of candy and some work gloves. Joseph got a cap, some gloves and a 22 rifle.

~40~

Frank

Two days ago our ton of coal was reduced to a shovel full or two and Mom ordered more. I came home from school and a pile larger than the first lay on the street half way in front of Mrs. Vick's house and ours. Between the coal deliveries, I had to take the clinkers out of the furnace, put them in a metal bucket and throw them in the ash pit. The ash pit was getting full. Mom said that she would get in touch with the Ash Pit Man. Even with the furnace going the house was always cold. Dad said that he read that this was going to be the coldest winter in a long time. I was getting more muscles shoveling coal. Mom said that I had better hurry up and get busy with that coal as she heard that it was going to snow. I managed to wheelbarrow half of that ton of coal up the terrace, turning the load as far sideways as the gangway would allow and tipping the coal down into the chute, then after every three or four loads I had to go down to rake the coal away from the chute opening making room for more. When it started snowing, I had to stop. Mom said that Mrs. Vick would be angry because some of the coal still lay on the street in her parking place. Mrs. Vick didn't have a car but her renter, Clifford Davis, did. Mr. Davis had been renting from Mrs. Vick for a good many years. "There was talk." I heard Mom say once.

The next morning everything was covered with snow. Dad said there was two feet of it. Everything on our street was beautiful and clean. That afternoon the smoke and soot from the furnaces made everything look like vanilla ice cream sprinkled heavily with black pepper. You couldn't see up to the end of the block for the smoke that hung over us.

~41~

Before long it was St. Patrick's Day. On that day my family let the world know that they were 100% Irish, the very best that anyone could be. Old Father Joe Sullivan had a green carnation hanging from a buttonhole of his cassock. He had his once-a-year smile on his face as he said Mass that morning. I didn't have school because Father Joe always closed the school on St. Patrick's Day. Mom fixed corned beef and cabbage with plenty of new potatoes. The Well #1 did a brisk business and I'll bet everyone there wasn't Irish.

That afternoon I was listening to the radio playing Irish songs when Mom came in and frantically said, "Go out in front and help your Aunt Gertrude up the steps and for God's sake shut her up. What will the neighbors think!" Aunt Gertrude had arrived or almost arrived. She made it to the bottom of the front steps leading up from the sidewalk and was singing badly and loud, "My Wild Irish Rose" with a green paper top hat askew on top of her head. She had started celebrating the day right after Father Joe commenced morning Mass. Having been ushered into the house and into the kitchen with Mom continually tisk tisking and "Well I saying", my Aunt collapsed into a chair and proceeded to tell Mom how to boil potatoes She reprimanded her for not being more enthusiastic about the day.

My cousin, Marguerite arrived later all decked out with more green showing than normal. She left the reds, purples and yellows home for the day. Throughout the day I was asked to resupply the troops with beer from the Well with warnings from Mom about rattling the bottles. After the first two trips, she seemed not to care. The head bartender got to know me. He told the other workers that it was alright for me to buy beer. Dad had given him a note saying so, which he kept behind the bar. My dad went to the Well once in a while just to talk to his card players. While the rest of my relatives celebrated, Dad, the German, remained in the basement frowning and puttering around with this and that. Later he walked over to Garavelli's Market to talk to the Italians. This went on every St. Patrick's Day. The rest of the year I would imagine our house was one of the dullest on the block.

Lent soon followed. How I hated it. First it started at school with the nuns asking all of us what we were going to give up. I heard the same thing at home, "Francis, what are you going to give up for Lent?" I felt like saying, rutabagas, parsnips, and spinach. "It has to be something that you really like," Sister Mary Elizabeth said. When she called on me without my hand being raised wanting an answer, I stood up checking the fly on my knickers to make sure that the worn enlarged button holes were still holding and replied that I would give up going to the Fox Theater to see movies. The kids all laughed because they knew that the Fox was the theater that had the first run movies and cost more than most of us could afford. Sister somehow knew this too and asked, "Does that mean that you are going to give up all movies for Lent, Francis?" There I was. I wanted so much to see a movie showing at the Lafayette and one at the Compton this weekend, one of those Saturday afternoon serials that the hero or his girlfriend is about to be run over by a train or they jump off a cliff only to be rescued the following week by simply avoiding that situation altogether. I was on the spot. Quickly in my mind I saw those forty days lasting two years without a movie.

I looked down to see if my knickers were still holding out and said, "Sister, I want to change my giving up from movies to a new pair of pants."

Sister thought a moment and looked over her class and the hand me downs that most of the kids were wearing and said, "That's good, Francis." She then went on with our Catechism lesson.

At home sitting on the back porch steps with Bobbie, I thought about Jesus and his suffering. I wondered what he was like and what he did when he was just a kid like me. I knew that he would not have done some of the bad things that I had done, but what did he do? Bobby answered my thoughts with his panting smile saying that he didn't know either.

Along with Ash Wednesday came the Stations of The Cross. We Catholic kids were marked. After getting ashes smeared on our foreheads, it was like we had a big sign pasted on the front of us saying we're Catholic. Someone told me that the Lutherans did that too. I didn't know any Lutherans. Walking on the sidewalk along Hodgen playground I spotted two kids with marked heads. Dad said that they were probably Lutherans or Catholic kids that could not afford to attend my school. We were marched up to church every morning during Lent to go through the Stations of The Cross. Father Sullivan wore his purple, and two altar boys moved with him from one station to the other, praying and shaking up the incense burner making me sneeze. These were experienced altar boys, not the kind that fall down from the altar holding the Holy Bible. Anyway I was "relieved of my duty" as an altar boy as a new, younger crop took over. I felt like a ball player considered to be too old to play the game but I wasn't disappointed because I didn't have to get up early.

Sitting at the kitchen table eating a mayonnaise sandwich after school, I heard the newsboys rolling their carts down the street yelling "Extra, Extra, Hindenburg blows up! Get your Extra here." Dad rushed out and came back with the paper showing this dirigible in flames. I had never seen a dirigible. Dad said that it was like a big balloon full of gas.

Avery and I went to the movies whenever we could. That was whenever we had the money. The Compton Theater didn't charge much but the movies were awful. We got tired of the Saturday matinees with the phony serials. The Lafayette Theater was better than the Compton but charged a nickel more. Leroy Grone swore that he could show us how to sneak in the back door of the Lafayette. We were afraid to try. I was given ten cents a week out of the two dollars a month that I got for walking Skippy. I was able to keep the money that I found when I cleaned the church. The rest Mom and Dad took and put in a "savings" for me. I never saw the money again or asked where it was or when I could have some more of my "savings". I figured that "savings" was something that was sent to heaven and you couldn't get you hands on it until you died. That is if you didn't go to hell. So, when I needed a dime or two I would sneak some change off the dresser. Mom and Dad never seemed to miss what I took. I still felt bad about it. Kinda. Me and Avery would walk up Longfellow Blvd. to the Shenandoah which showed the movies that the Fox had already run only weeks ago. One Saturday as Avery and I walked up Longfellow we marveled at the magnificent homes, all built with stone and with carriage houses and massive manicured lawns. Avery said, "Look at that one. I was told that the fourth floor has a ballroom! They have maids and chauffeurs.

Look over there. That one's for sale. It looks empty and kinda spooky. I wonder how much they want for it."

"An arm and a leg," I responded. My Mom used to say that a lot. I didn't know what a ballroom was but I wouldn't let Avery know. We went on and saw the movie, "San Francisco". Wow, what a movie! I was in love with Alice Faye. Clark Gable was still my favorite even though he reminded me of Mr. Hart. I didn't tell Avery about Mr. Hart. It was a family matter. I couldn't make up my mind which movie I liked best, "San Francisco" or "Call of the Wild" that we saw last year. Avery and I replayed some of the scenes coming back down Longfellow. As we passed the spooky house we saw a dim light that swayed back and forth in one of the third floor windows. All of the houses on Longfellow and Hawthorne had what Dad told me once were porticos, so in the old days when they had horse drawn carriages they could pull right up to the side door and get out without getting wet. "Boy, they must be rich I replied."

"Yep", Dad said. The spooky house had a portico but there were tall weeds growing through the cracks of the pavement. I told Avery what a portico was. He seemed impressed.

~42~

After Easter came Spring Training and a sudden increase in the talk of how the Cardinals were going to do, and who was going to do what. By July the infield at Sportsman's Park was mainly dust. The grass of Spring had been trodden on and starved for water under the hot St. Louis weather. Hopes for the Browns had long ago faded, but the Cardinals still had a chance. I had never seen a Cardinals game. Somehow our school, or someone in school, was able to get Knot Hole tickets to the Browns' games. Dad and I went to see them at Sportsman's Park. My only interest in the Browns was when the Yankees came to town and Babe Ruth played. Those were the only games that the Browns outdrew the Cardinals. Now we were going to see the Browns play Philadelphia. Dad and I took the Southampton streetcar to Grand, transferred and rode to the park. When I got off the streetcar I looked up at the high, seemingly six storied, black iron structure, and me and my Dad, with his straw sailor hat which was like all the other men's hats, went through the gates of the stadium. Our section was up high on the left field side and was full of kids and their parents with no one in the stands around us. The seats had green painted wooden slats that were encased in black cast iron with an occasional slat missing, and our section was behind two girders that blocked our view of a small part of the field. Ernie Foster asked his Dad if they could move down closer to the field since no one was there. He was told no, that he should be thankful for being where he was. Across the stadium in the upper decks of right field, behind a screen, were black people watching the game. They didn't have very good seats either. My thought was that they looked as though they were caged. I don't know why I thought that. Perhaps it was something someone had said. The only Browns player that I had heard of was Jim Bottomley. He should have been a Cardinal. Dad told me that Jim Bottomley would some day be in the Hall of Fame. "A Brownie?", I replied. Dad told me how great a player Rogers Hornsby the manager was, and about a player named George Sisler who batted 420 in the year 1920. He said that he saw him play once. Every time a Browns player came to bat I imagined that it was either Terry Moore or Joe Medwick or Pepper Martin, and when they took the field I saw Dizzy and Paul Dean pitching and Leo Durocher scooping up the balls at short stop. The only trouble was the Browns never matched my imaginary team. One thing that I could never figure out was that no matter how bad the Browns played, or what their record was, they were never booed! Dad told me that once a Brownie fan always a Brownie fan. The Philadelphia Athletics weren't very good either, so after eating a bag of peanuts and drinking a" Grape Nehi", I fell asleep in the sun. Dad woke me when the game was over and we scurried down to the exit. At the exit was a man handing out small cardboard containers of "Hershey's Cocoa". He gave me one and when I turned around the man was pushed over by the crowd. His samples rolled all over the floor. Dad pounced at the opportunity. I had never seen him move so swiftly and grunt so much. His sailor hat was full of the samples as were his and my pockets. He had trouble balancing his hat getting on the streetcar and paying the fare without spilling some of the loot.

"How was the game?", Mom asked looking bewildered as we came through the door.

"Great", Dad said.

"Who won?"

"We did. Or, no the Browns lost." We emptied our loot onto the kitchen table to the astonishment of my mother.

"Emil, what in the world did you do this time?"

That night, after a nice hot Hershey's Cocoa, I tried to sleep on the floor of the living room with an "Emerson" fan humming and swiveling back and forth producing only a hot breeze, and finally dozed off hoping that the Fire Department would open up a fire plug or two tomorrow, or I could go to Buder and swim. I dreamed that I got lost in that big black iron stadium and Terry Moore rescued me. Two weeks later when I came home from walking Skippy, Dad said that we were going to see the Cardinals! Mr. Mitchell of the Holy Namers gave him the tickets. Wow, the Cardinals! I would get to see my heroes. They were way down in the standings but I didn't care, I was going to see them! I watched Terry Moore roam the outfield. The temperature was over a hundred.

The infield was dust. Dad said that this is going to be one of the hottest summers on record. Dad bought me two sodas and a popcorn. The Cardinals won! What a day. The Cocoa man was nowhere to be seen.

Dad and I listened to the fight on the Philco between James J. Braddock and Joe Louis, the guy Dad said was sawdust after Schmeling knocked him out. It sounded like he was going to be knocked out again as Braddock knocked him down in the very first round but Joe Louis knocked Braddock out in the eighth round and was now the heavyweight champ. Dad, scratching his head, said, "Well I'll be a monkey's uncle!" Mom was pulling for Braddock because she heard that he was Irish.

~43~

I remember the first time that I went to Uncle Mart's farm. It was winter and very cold. My Uncle Walter and his lady friend drove us. Ethel was her name.

Mom said, "Wake up Francis, there's your Uncle Mart's place." I looked out and coming nearer was this two storied frame house that had just a tad of white paint left on it with smoke coming from the chimney. Everyone scrambled out of the car and rushed up the porch steps with caution not to step here or there on the rickety floorboards. We were to stay overnight. Old, almost rounded bricks, were warming on top of the kitchen stove. No electricity. No inside toilet. Several coal oil lamps placed around the room on any available flat surface.

I heard Ethel ask Mom, "Doesn't he ever clean this place! We're spending the night here?"

Mom said, "You're lucky that you are only going to be here one night. You're also lucky that there's not much light. Wait till morning and you'll be more impressed."

"Oh Lord, what has Walter got me into. I won't sleep a wink, and just the thought of me having to go outside and pee makes me have to go that much more and after that long ride, I have to go now."

"You won't have to go outside. We have chamber pots for both peeing and pooping. Here's one all cleaned and ready to use."

"You put it on the floor?"

"If you are good at stooping. Come in the next room. Some houses have a chair type that holds the pot, but not in this house. You squat, holding it behind you and do your thing. That's it. You have never been on a farm have you?"

"No, and you know what, I—"

"Go on in the other room, take this and do your thing. We'll empty it later."

From the kitchen, Ethel heard someone ask, "Stella, where is the pot for the soup?"

That was my first trip to Uncle Mart's.

The first week of August, Mom got a letter from her brother, my Uncle Mart, saying that the drought was so bad that none of his wheat amounted to anything and he didn't think that his corn was going to amount to anything either. It was so hot that his hens stopped laying and his ponds were going dry. He didn't ask for any money, but Mom and Dad wanted to go and see what they could do. My Aunt Gertrude and her now husband, Bud, drove me and Mom and Dad and Bobby and my "Daisy Air Rifle" up to Uncle Mart's farm. In North Alton we stopped at Homer's Blue Dell tavern for fried chicken and beer of course. I liked Homer's. They had juke boxes, pretty waitresses, and the best fried chicken I ever ate. Even though it was dreadfully hot, as soon as we left North Alton the freshness of the air was noticeable. I thought, this is what air is supposed to smell like. The air was full bodied. I knew that if I was blindfolded, I could tell when we crossed that invisible line going into fresh air. It wasn't just the air. I could hear things: every note of the singing mocking birds, the red breasted black birds, a cow or calf bellowing off in the distance, the wind through the trees. After awhile though I would take it for granted and not realize the gift of country until entering the city again.

Last May when we were up here the grass was green, the wild flowers were blooming, so was the pear tree. The pond and the well were full, and Uncle Mart was in a good mood, telling Dad how the wheat and corn was doing, and how it looked like he was going to have a good year. I took my BB gun and sat on the shore of the pond and picked off frogs as they sat and croaked between the cattails. I watched the beautiful dragon flies zip this way and that lighting on the water's surface. They didn't sink because their feet were like pontoons. I wondered what they were up to as their routine always seemed to be the same, hovering in one place, going back and forth horizontally, landing on water and taking off to land on a leaf by the water. I wondered about ants also. They seemed to work so hard back home running along the creases in the concrete sidewalk. They were always in a hurry running to I don't know where and back again passing other ones going in the opposite direction. They worked so hard. I wondered why. Dad skinned the frogs that I killed throwing the innards and heads out in the adjoining woods for "some hungry critter to eat tonight". Mom fried the frog legs in the skillet. The legs seemed to be alive as they jumped in the pan. Dad said that the nerves in the legs made them twitch. After awhile they stopped jumping. Boy, were they good! Just like fried chicken. It rained that night, a warm light rain. Before it arrived, you could smell it. The air felt wet, cool and fresh and after it started raining the scent all but passed.

The next morning before dawn Dad woke me and we went down in the woods. Dad said that we were going to hunt squirrels. By the time that we got in the woods, my feet were soaked from the wet grass, not uncomfortable, just a warm squishy feeling We sat down on the ground with our backs against a tree. Dad said to keep quiet and in a few minutes, right before the sun rose, the squirrels would wake up and start chattering. When they did, Dad chattered back. He did so by clucking out of the side of his mouth. He didn't grunt then but concentrated on his clucking. I guess he couldn't grunt and cluck at the same time. When it got light enough I could see the squirrels running all over the branches, up and down the tree trunks. Dad said, "See if you can pick off one with your gun." I drew a bead on one and missed. All the squirrels scampered out of sight to the other side of the tree. Dad waited a few minutes. He picked up several rocks and threw them to the other side of the tree. The squirrels came back to our side. I shot again and hit one but the BB gun wasn't powerful enough to kill it. I used up most of my BBs on that same squirrel until it finally fell from the tree, dead.

Excitedly I said, "I killed it!" Dad said that it probably died of a heart attack. He said that when I got a little older he would buy me a real rifle.

When the sun rose we went mushroom hunting. Dad said that many mushrooms were poisonous. The only ones that he knew that were not were the Morels and that is what we looked for. They looked like a brain on a cream colored neck. We were to look around dead and decomposed wood and near May Apples. He said that the Morels seem to like May Apples and rotted wood as their neighbors. Along with half a dozen mushrooms, I found two box turtles. Dad said that

I could keep them. He named them Carrie and Franklin. When I asked him who Carrie was he told me about a woman named, Carrie Nation and how she went on rampages pouring out whiskey and beer and how she was against drinking. I figured that she must not have been Irish. Dad skinned the squirrel, gave me the tail for me to tie on the back fender of my bike. We had fried squirrel and mushrooms for lunch. Sure beat a mayonnaise or radish sandwich. Bobby tried to get into the box holding the turtles on the way home.

That was last spring, now the pond was dry, the cattails were brown and a sound like the word "rush" emitted when a hot wind moved thru them. The surface of the pond was brown and the mud was cracked like a jigsaw puzzle. The corners of the pieces curled up. I picked up some of the thin pieces and stared at them. They looked like chocolate but tasted like mud because they were mud. The well was empty. We drank water from the cistern with the water accumulated from previous rains off the roof long ago. The water was bitter but as Uncle Mart said, "It's wet". He hauled buckets of water down to his cows and horses, he had to buy water from neighboring farmers who had newer and deeper wells. He had to buy river water trucked all the way from Grafton or Alton. Uncle Mart had no money left. Mom and Dad and Aunt Gertrude loaned him a hundred dollars. He signed an I.O.U. for it.

I went out to the hen house to see if I could fetch some eggs. All the chickens had their mouths open with their throats pulsating. They took dust baths to rid them of insects. They had no desire to lay eggs, only to drink and be cooler. They didn't have sense enough to venture out to shade under the trees. That old beat up brick structure was their home and they didn't go far from it.

None of us washed. Uncle Mart's towel, hanging on a nail above the wash basin by the front door, always smelled like it had not been washed in years. Now he had a good excuse. We used water only for coffee and cooking. We had brought plenty of store bread, jams, peanut butter, a hunk of salted cured ham, and beans, that is what we ate after the women set the food upon Uncle Mart's place mats, old newspapers, many pages so thick that when one was spilled upon he just removed it. Uncle Mart was thankful for the food and the money. Pulling away from Uncle Mart's, Mom remarked, "Mart works so hard on that old place."

"I know," grunted Dad.

"I wish that we could do more, I love coming out here." Mom tisked tisked.

Aunt Gertrude asked, "What do you say we stop at Homer Blue Dells on the way home? I'm parched." Everyone agreed. I wished that Uncle Mart was with us so he could have some fried chicken and a cold beer.

-44-

I was glad to get back to the bad air, and good tasting faucet water, and inside toilets, and my friends. The next morning I watched Bobby trying to get at Franklin and Carrie. He didn't know what to make of them. When they stuck their heads out of their shell he would charge barking, then they would retreat into their shell only to reapear when he stopped barking. I watched him for an hour until he finally gave up and came up the porch steps where I was sitting and took his usual position, his head shoved under my right arm pit and his paws lapping over the step.

I did a lot of my thinking out on our back porch steps with Bobby under my arm. He would talk and I would talk and we listened to each other. He and I wondered if and how, Anna Mae and I would ever get together, what I would have to do to make her notice me. She always seemed to talk to the smarter boys in class and laugh with them. I wished that I was not so bashful and was not afraid to talk to her. I just couldn't do it The last time I went up to Reservoir Park, I carved a heart with my initials and hers on the trunk of a maple tree on the south side of the reservoir in hopes that by some small, no, gigantic miracle, she would see it and she would know who FLM and AMY stood for. I know that I'm not smart like Bill Callahan or that smooth, Kenneth Taylor who is always saying something to her during class when Sister isn't looking. He carries her books after school. I was about to quit the school boy patrol. I didn't like any of the girls that crossed at my intersection. They were too young.

Bobby and I watched Franklin and Carrie slowly trudge to a grassy spot in front of the garage. It seemed like it took them forever. Almost like my sitting on the front porch and watching old Mister Schmidt trudge up the sidewalk to Henn's Grocery, one slow step after another. Would I ever get as old as him. Just then, Dad came out on the porch and asked me who I was talking to. I told him, Bobby. I thought he would laugh but he didn't.

"Let me show you how I've trained those turtles."

He proceeded to talk softly in a high pitched voice. Bobby looked up at him with his ears perked up wondering who he was talking to. Soon Carrie and Franklin turned toward him and started their slow but sure advance toward Dad as he stood in front of us. It took half an hour for those turtles to reach my dad. He placed two small leafs of lettuce before them. Dad winked and went in the house without saying anything. Bobby and I just watched them eat the lettuce. They ate just as slow as they walked, one chomp at a time.

That night it was so hot that I slept, or tried to, laying on the carpet in the living room with the old "Emerson" fan blowing hot air on me. I went to sleep remembering how I had to take that same carpet out in the back yard and beat it for what seemed like an hour, with the dust flying up with every whack, and me sneezing my head off and snot just rolling out of my nose and no handkerchief, just my sweaty forearm to wipe it on with my eyes watering.

The next morning Mom woke me and said that Bobby got out again. Mom said that I must have left the gate open while running through the yard. Bobby had gotten out before but always came back in a day or so, but I was worried because he had taken to chasing cars trying to bite the tires. He got bumped to the gutter in front of our house a couple of weeks ago. I talked to him about that but he didn't listen. Once before when he got out five days passed before Bobby came home all dirty, panting like he had been on a long trip and very hungry. We were glad to see each other. He never let on as to where he had been or what he had been doing.

~45~

The weather stayed hot through September. I don't know how the nuns managed, all wrapped up in their long dresses and that tight white collar around their necks with the black hood on their heads. We were hot enough sitting in the classroom. Sister Mary Elizabeth almost went out of her mind one morning because of the heat. None of us could correctly answer any of her questions in the Catechism lesson.

Wiping her brow of sweat and fanning herself she exclaimed, "I don't know why I put up with you children. You don't pay attention. I'm about ready to throw this book out the window along with all this terrible homework you brought this morning." She made one wide, wild sweep of her desk and the papers flew toward the window. I and everyone else was wide awake now. Next she said, "I don't know why I try to teach you! I'm ready to take a job in a factory and throw this collar, and hood out that window!" Wow, our eyes bulged. We sat motionless. There was total silence for a minute and then raising her head and taking a deep breath she said, "Harold would you please pick up those papers and put them back on my desk?" Harold was scared and stood as far from her as possible as he placed the papers on her desk. That being done she said, "Now turn in your books to page twenty nine." We all made sure that our homework was to her satisfaction the next day. All of us seemed to like Sister Mary Elizabeth a lot more than we had before.

Halloween came and us guys didn't want to do anything after what we did last year to old Mrs. Kowalski. Charley Fitzpatrick came up with the idea that we should gather up some flowers and lay them at her doorstep, ring the bell and run. We gathered up dandelions and stole mums from Mrs. Vick's flower box and Charlie ran up and placed them by Mrs. Kowalski's door and ran away not ringing the door bell. We then went begging the younger kids for some of their candy.

Thanksgiving came again and Uncle Walter showed up looking swell. He had some medical books with him and asked Dad if he could store them in the basement. He said that he got his old job back again at the Goodwill Store. Uncle Walter brought Mom two new pictures. I never knew whether Dad paid for anything that he brought from the Goodwill. One of the pictures was that of a wolf howling on a snow covered hill. The other picture was of an Indian warrior with what looked like rags on his body. His head and his horse's head were bowed down, and the warrior's spear almost touched the ground. Dad said the wolf was howling the call of the wild and that I should read that book. I told him that I had seen the movie. I don't think Dad had ever seen a movie. He said that the Indian showed defeat and tiredness, and is probably readying himself for his last stand, or he might be just giving up and is now ready to go to the reservation. I knew what a reservation was from seeing all those B Westerns showing the Indians coming out of the reservations to raid the wagon trains and all that shooting and arrow flinging going on with only a few getting killed. Terrible shots. I took a liking to both of those pictures. They brought both joy and sadness depending on what mood I was in.

Mom fixed a goose from Bettendorf's. Dad had some kumquats that he insisted that we try with a, "You don't know what your missing". Dad liked to go to Garavelli's market on Lafayette and Nebraska. He spent hours talking to Mr. Garavelli and his family about food fixtures, what brand they had and what was new and different. He didn't like Bettendorf's, "No character or ambiance", he said. I didn't know what he meant.

Gertrude

Diary

December 16, 1937

Today I am sixteen years old. Some of the girls I knew in the orphanage went to High School in Jerseyville. Rosemary was one and she writes me once in awhile telling me of her studies and of her boy friend. Oh, how I wish I had a boy friend, not that I would want to do anything nasty or anything but just someone besides Barty and Tom to talk to. A boy that I would like and he would like me. I wish that I had a girl friend that I could discuss things with. I get feelings and have no one, no other woman to talk to. My Aunt Gertrude, Aunt Stella, and Marguerite and Maymie aren't around. I would be able to talk to Mother if she was here.

Last month a nice man selling magazines came up the lane to our house while Dad and Barty were in the field. He said his name was Harry Brown. He showed me all the magazines with pictures of movie stars and models. I have never been to a movie. Harry Brown said that I looked a lot like some of the movie stars. He said that I had beautiful hair like Barbara Stanwick. I didn't know who he was talking about but he showed me her picture. He said if I subscribed to the movie star magazine, I would see and learn all about the stars. He left me a subscription form and said that he would be back the following week. I told Father about Mr. Brown and asked him if I could get one of the movie star magazines. He got excited and told me that those magazines were rubbish and sinfull. He wanted to know when Mr. Brown was coming back. The day Mr. Brown was to come back Father sent me with Barty to Norman Morewise with some bread that I baked and some eggs. Father met Mr. Brown and stopped him at our gate. I had come back and watched them out of their sight. Mr. Brown got out of his car and walked up to Father with a smile on his face and extended his hand to greet Father. Father raised his shotgun and in a loud menacing voice told him to leave and to never bother his daughter again or he would shoot him dead! I never saw Mr. Brown again.

Tommie has been working for Mr. Evans and getting a dollar a day. Soon he said he would buy a car. He would go with Mr. Evans to Jerseyville occasionally and when he did he bought the town out of candy. He brought me a box of chocolates for my birthday. There was one piece missing. He said that the factory must have made a mistake. We all laughed. We ate my upside-down cake and Tommie's candy. Tommie and Barty sang Happy Birthday, Father just grinned. I know that he loves me and doesn't want to let go of me, but I'm, as they say, coming of age, if not already past it. I need something to hope for. Out on the drive as Tommie was leaving to go back to Mr. Evans he handed me a movie magazine. I snuck it under my sweater.

~46~

Frank

Maymie and Fergie upset the whole family by announcing that they were going to California to live. Fergie said that his job on the Alton Dam had played out and that they were going to the land of milk and honey. He said that he was so glad to get off that frozen, windy, river. Fergie had bought himself a brand new Packard. It looked swell. They started singing "The Bum Song" as Dad played the record on the Victrola, along with "Big Rock Candy Mountain". I liked Fergie, and as I said before, he always looked like or tried to look like Clark Gable. After they all had a few beers, except Dad, they sang "California, Here I Come". I wished that some day I would go to California.

Maymie said, "We are going to visit my father in Turlock for a few days and get to know his new wife, and then go down to Fort Bragg where Fergie thinks he can get a job."

There were a few "Well I says" at first but as the beer flowed, some in the group were silently thinking of visiting them whenever they settled. While they drank and talked I put on the "Bum Song" again. I liked that. "Hallelujah!, I'm a bum, Hallelujah, bum again—-" I thought of the people down at Hooverville.

Christmas came. The church decided to start having Midnight Mass on Christmas Eve. We went. I thought it was great since we would not have to get up early Christmas morning. The decorations were all hung. The crib holding the Baby Jesus with Mary and Joseph and the Three Wise Men and the animals all around Him were off to the side. I saw Anna Mae up in front on the right. I wished that I could just go up there and wish her a Merry Christmas. She looked so holy and pretty.

Father Johnson gave the sermon. He was interrupted several times by mutterings and quiet laughter from the rear pews. It seemed that some of the men were drunk. They wouldn't have been if Mass was in the morning but they had celebrated Christmas earlier that evening. I had my doubts as to whether Midnight Mass would go over. I also wondered how much money fell to the floor on my sweeping section because of their condition. I got a real rifle from Mom and Dad for Christmas. A Springfield Model 15 from Shapleigh Hardware. Bullets would come later whenever we went to the country.

~47~

One evening at supper, Mom said, "Francis, your father wrote and said that he would like to see you." I looked across the table at Dad with my mouth open.

Dad said, "She means your father, Tim Kelley. In his letter he wrote that he would be pleased if you could come up for a couple of days and get to know your brothers and your sister better. You could bring your rifle and maybe hunt some rabbits!" There I was, perplexed again. I didn't mind the part of getting to know my siblings better but I again wondered if Mom and Dad were trying to get rid of me or if my real father wanted me to live with him.

I caught the bus to Jerseyville and there at the bus station was my father waiting. He was a lot taller than my Dad. He looked younger and stronger also. He carried my suitcase to his buggy and we started what seemed like a long journey to his home with Rufus trotting ahead of us. I wondered why I was there. We hardly spoke. He said, "Francis, you sure have grown. I would not have recognized you except for the pictures Stella sent us. I'm glad we are going to spend a few days geting to know each other."

I replied, "Yes Sir." At first I got a kick out of the buggy ride, but as I got colder and noticed the passengers in the passing automobiles smiling and pointing at us, I shivered because of the cold and I was embarrassed.

Tommie, Barty and Gertrude came running out to greet us. Tommie was home from his job with Mr. Evans. Gertrude started making supper. Barty was told to go to the well and get some water. I went with him, still shivering. "How far is this well?"

"A ways down the hill, watch your step this is a narrow path." Barty kept dipping a small bucket into this hole in the ground until the larger bucket was filled. When we got back to the house, Tommie was chopping and splitting wood for the stove. That night I shared a room and a piss pot with Barty and Tommie. My sister had her own room with her very own chamber pot.

Everyone was up before daylight. Gertrude fixed thick toasted bread that she had made along with hot cream of wheat and strong coffee. Everybody did their morning chores while I more or less watched. That afternoon Tommie was chinning himself from a limb on the apple tree. He stopped at forty five. Barty started. He got up to twenty before he dropped to the ground. Now it was my turn. I struggled to get my chin up to the limb and dropped after only three times. My arm muscles couldn't pull up the rest of my body. They laughed. Tommie said that it took practice. He said that they did it every day. "Gertrude can do it ten times", Barty said.

The next morning was Sunday and my father said that no work was done on Sundays, however Gertrude did the cooking and Barty hauled water.

After breakfast my father said, "Francis why don't you and your brothers go out and see if you can hit a rabbit or two with that rifle of yours and Gert here will fix them tonight." Tommie had a shotgun. I had not shot my new rifle but felt confident that I could hit anything with all of my experience with my BB gun. Tommie brought down two rabbits no sooner than we got to the field. I nearly stepped on one and it ran as fast as it could this way and that. I led it a bit and pulled the trigger and down it fell.

"Wow, Francis, that was a good shot. Got it on the run, and with a rifle", said Tommie. We brought back eight rabbits. Tommie and Barty showed me how to skin them and would I like one of the tails as a souvenir. I wasn't sure that I wanted to kill any more animals if I had to skin and clean them. I didn't like to look at their eyes while I ripped out their guts. The two that I killed were hung outside and kept cold for my trip back home. The stew was delicious.

The next day Old Rufus was saddled up and I left for home. My father said that he was glad that I came. I was to catch the bus on the highway. I just had to watch for it and flag it down. On the road to the highway, I held my rifle across my lap along with the two dressed, wrapped rabbits that I shot. Again I was embarrassed riding in the buggy as cars passed us with the people in them acting like we were some kind of a freak show. My father let me out at the highway intersection. He said that the bus would be along shortly and did I want him to stay until it came. I told him "No." and thanked him for a wonderful time. He turned around and started home. The rabbits were beginning to smell a bit. I didn't want any further embarrassment on the bus so I placed them on top of a mail box, before getting on the bus and heading for home sweet home. The next day I told Avery and the other boys about my trip and when I mentioned the buggy ride they all wowed! Maybe I missed something.

On his way back home Tim stopped to chat with a neighbor, Ted Andrews who was driving his car on the way to his mailbox at the highway intersection. "Well Tim, what brings you out this fine cold day?"

"I just dropped off my youngest son from St. Louis. He's going back on the bus. I hope he doesn't have any trouble. He shot two rabbits on the run with a rifle, can you beat that! I let him take them back to the big city. When you get to the highway, I'd be much obliged if you would see if he caught the bus alright." Mr. Andrews waved and drove off.

Mr. Andrews caught up with Tim before he got home. "Tim, here's the rabbits. Either your son forgot them or didn't want them but he was gone before I got there."

"Well, I'll be dammed. He'll never make a farmer."

Gertrude

Dear Diary

February 10th

What a snot, my baby brother. I'm not even sure he's my brother. What a spoiled brat! He was up here for a visit and didn't do a lick of work. Complained about everything! Can't chin worth a damn. Left good, fresh rabbits that I wrapped to spoil on a mail box. Father was disappointed.

~48~

Frank

It seemed to take forever for Spring to come but when it did Avery and I knew this was the best time to go ash pit hunting. Everyone had done their spring cleaning and had thrown the stuff that they didn't want into their ash pits. The pits would be full of stuff that the Rag Man didn't get and probably didn't want. Avery and I walked down the alley surveying the pits for promise.

"Remember what we found last Fourth of July?" Avery asked.

"Oh, yeah. The pink baby rats. They didn't even have their eyes open. We put them one by one under a tin can and blew them up with a firecracker inside."

"Do you have any fire crackers on you?"

"No, but I think I know where I can get some if we run into any baby rats."

"Oh lets' try to find some good stuff."

We started with the Schmidt's ash pit. Found a lot of beer bottles, Alpen Brau, Griesedieck, Falstaff and Hyde Park. Avery said that it looked like Mr. Schmidt had no favorites. I told him that it could have been Mrs. Schmidt. He looked at me kinda funny. He didn't know my Mom. A little farther down the alley we searched Mr. Woodhouse's ashpit and found wine and whiskey bottles. Dad had said that the Woodhouses never touched a drop of liquor, that they were teetotalers. I told Avery that and he said "Look over there in the ash pit next to this one." That pit belonged to Mr. and Mrs. Hogan who drank more than my relatives. Their pit had no whiskey bottles in it. We guessed that they too knew that one could find out about people by looking at their trash. We knew who tossed the whiskey and wine bottles into the Woodhouse's. We looked for soda bottles. We could get money for them. We would have to wash them first. Avery said that we would split the profits. I had started collecting soda bottles so I would have enough money to ask Anna Mae to go to the movies. We would even go to see Fred Astair if she wanted. I hated him but I figured that she didn't, as she was becoming so sophisticated. Anyway, Avery and I went from one ash pit to another. He got two Nehis and three Orange Crushes. I found four Dr. Peppers and a Coke. Avery dug up a Prince Albert tin and a Velvet. On top of a big rat,I found a pair of worn basketball shoes without the laces, but they still had the round ankle patches on them. I had eventually removed my round patches, little by little by picking at them. I figured that with some glue my tennis shoes would have patches again.

The weather warmed and the grass or weeds in front of our house grew. I was told to get out our mower and cut the grass whenever it got out of hand. We had an old push mower. Dad said that the blades needed sharpening and realignment, but if I just kept pushing it over the grass often enough it would all get cut. In the winter, I pushed our old wheelbarrow full of coal up the two terraces, now I pushed that mower up and down the terrace on both sides of the steps until I was soaking wet. My hay fever made me sneeze continually. My nose ran all the time, and my eyes watered and itched. I was about to go into a fit. I had three handkerchiefs in my pocket and they stayed soaking wet. I just let my nose run and occasionally swiped it off with my bare sweaty forearms. After I finished I went to my room and lay down until my nose stopped running and the sneezing stopped. After supper Dad asked if I had put the mower away. He said that the next time Tony came around with his sharpening cart he would have our mower looked at.

~49~

After dark I stood in the gangway looking up at a window on Mrs. Vick's wall, two stories up. It was a small window and appeared to be stained glass. I thought that it might be her bathroom window. I placed my back against our wall and my feet against Mrs. Vick's wall. I found that I could inch my way upward by shifting my butt upwards with my hands braced behind me and raise my feet at the same time. I was up about seven feet above the ground when Mom called. I hated the way she always called me.

"Frannnnnncisssss. Where are you and what are you doing? Supper's ready."

I carefully inched back down and thought that I had discovered something. If I got good at this gangway crawling maybe I could become a G Man or a detective. The next night I started up the walls. The higher I got the more frightened I got. My tennis shoes were worn smooth and I slipped a bit. I got all the way up to the window and when I stretched out to try to get a look in the window my left foot slipped off the wall and I let out a muffled yell. I heard Mrs. Vick shout inside that someone was outside her bathroom window. I heard Mr. Davis say that he would go out and look. I shouted, "Oh shit!", and tried to get back down as fast as I could, mostly sliding, scraping my hands and backside and falling the last seven or eight feet. I ran out through the back yard and into the alley with Bobby barking after me. I waited in the alley. I could see the flashlight beam going up and down the wall and Mr. Davis reporting to Mrs. Vick that he couldn't find anything and No, there was no sense in calling the police.

"It could have been a squirrel or a pigeon on the roof making that noise."

Mrs. Vick standing on the front porch said, "Well if it was an animal, I heard it cuss!"

I waited a good while and then went up the alley and came down the street and quietly went in the house and never again thought of becoming a G Man. I didn't rule out a private eye as long as gangway crawling was not involved. I told Dad the next morning that I could use a new pair of tennis shoes that my soles were slick.

~50~

A few days later, I came in the house all hot and sweaty from jumping garage roofs out back with the guys. Mom said that tomorrow morning she and I were going to Uncle Mart's to help him with the threshing, and for me to go upstairs and take a bath as we would leave early in the morning. Dad was to stay and take care of the place. We would be gone about three days.

Dad said that I would like it saying, "Men and women come from all around to help each other bring in the wheat. The women cook before hand and some of the men roast a pig while others set up their machinery. I wish that I could go."

Avery and I were supposed to go swimming the next day. I didn't show much enthusiasm.

The next morning Mom and I took the streetcar down to the Interurban Station and we were off on the electric railroad to Alton, going through all the small towns that we used to drive through except that we didn't have to stop at any railroad crossings. We were on our own railroad. One man got on holding a fishing pole and his minnow bucket. He got off at Horseshoe Lake. The train stopped for anyone along the line.

When we got to Alton, the train stopped at a small depot right alongside the river. We walked to the cab station, and there Mom started to haggle with some of the drivers to see how much they would charge her to drive us out to Uncle Mart's farm. Mom was good at this. I remembered trips with her to the butcher shops. I refused to go in there with her anymore. When she said that she would need help in carrying the groceries home, I would go but would remain outside until her haggling was done. I waited outside the cab office and overheard her say something about a very sick brother. I rolled my eyes. Out came my mother with a cab driver. "Two dollars now, that's all I'm paying you." She made, Jack, that was his name, stop at the grocery store in North Alton. She bought stuff for making pies and cakes and off we went, Jack complaining about waiting for her to shop. While they bickered, we passed Homer's Blue Dell without stopping. I was suddenly hungry. I could smell the fried chicken.

After we turned off the highway at the Pembrooke school we passed fields of corn, which mom said, "Already knee high before the Fourth of July."

I said, "What does that mean."

"That's just a saying. The farmers always hope that the corn will be at least knee high on the Fourth of July."

"That's right, son", Jack responded. "Finally it looks like these farmers are going to have good crops for a change. We've gone through some bad years. If they get their wheat in before a thunderstorm wrecks their fields they'll be happy."

"Watch the road there, Jack," Mom said tisk tisking.

There were fields of golden wheat looking alive as a gentle breeze made the stalks bend in unison and sway back and forth. It was beautiful to see. It was as if there was a conductor guiding their sway.

When we got to the farm, Jack informed Mom that it was a lot farther than she had let on. Mom went to the cistern, pumped a cup of cool water, and gave Jack a drink along with the two dollars.

"Here's a little extra", She said as she gave him a dime He drank the water and looked down at his open hand for what seemed minutes in disbelief expecting much more but not knowing what to say. He gave her a look as to notch her in his memory for the next time that she would need a cab. He nodded, looked around for her sick brother who just then came running up from the barn with a wide grin. Jack got in his cab and left shaking his head muttering to himself.

In helping to carry Mom's supplies inside I saw men out in the wheat field working with this big machine. Other men were starting a fire under a big black kettle. After setting the groceries on the table I ran outside to watch what was going on. I went out into the wheat field and watched. One of the men who was tall, sweaty, and sun tanned, with black, greasy hands approached me. I guess he could tell that I was a city kid. He said, "Tomorrow morning after the sun dries the dew, we will cut this whole field and separate the grain from the straw with that machine over there. We will also cut Mart's red clover. We're greasing up old Betsy now." "Old Betsy" almost looked like a locomotive. The men had it running. It ran on steam like a locomotive, belching and puffing as it turned a couple of wheels banded by a very wide leather belt. "Have you ever eaten wheat off the stalk?" When I said no, he pulled the end off of one and gave it to me. I chewed the grain. It was a little sweet. The kernels had a different taste to them. Different from anything I had ever tried. They smelled a little like flour and some of the cereal that I had eaten before.

I went over to three men by the black kettle. They had a fire started under it. The fire must have been burning for some time as the water in the kettle was boiling. "Time to whack that hog, George", one man hollered out to a man standing in the pig pen. I heard a loud smack, then a low squeal and George and another man wheelbarrowed a pig up to the kettle. The pig still had its eyes open but was deader than a doornail. The men lowered the pig into the boiling water and the smell was terrible. Like a dog or cat with wet hair only burnt. Quickly the pig was lifted out and the men proceeded to scrape the hairs off. They came off real easy. Then the pig was gutted with the entrails thrown in a pot. I almost threw up but couldn't stop watching. After the pig was washed with cold water, with its guts out and everything, the kettle was removed and its contents sloshed over the ground, some of the water being sprayed over the fire to reduce the heat. The men took the pig to the smoke house and hung it. "About four in the morning, we will start cooking that little rascal", George said.

Four in the morning made me think that I was back serving Mass. I hoped Uncle Mart didn't think I was going to have to get up then. Mom, I and Uncle Mart went to bed as soon as it got dark. I could hear the chickens clucking their last low muffled voices to each other, then silence until I heard a whippoorwill sing its song over and over again. I heard George talking to his friend outside for awhile longer until I fell asleep on the floor as a gentle hot breeze came through the window.

I was awakened before sunrise. People with horse and mule driven wagons came in from the road. I could hear women chattering and kids squealing. I looked out the window and tables were being unloaded.

George and his friend had earlier put the pig on a spit over a low burning fire. Mom came in the room and said that I was needed in the kitchen and to hurry up. The name "sleepy head" was thrust upon me from several women who I did not know. Bacon, ham, and eggs, were cooking on the big black iron stove and biscuits and bread were about done. I was told to bring in two buckets of water from the cistern after I washed up and brushed my teeth. Thankfully, Mom had replaced Uncle Mart's wash towel with a clean one. Afterward I watched the combine machine cut through Uncle Mart's wheat field followed by the wagons upon which the wheat stalks were pitched and brought to "Old Betsy". The wheat was separated from the stalks and poured into bushel baskets, and the wheat stalks funneled back onto another wagon until it was heaping with straw. Dust was everywhere. I began to sneeze.

About three in the afternoon the work was finished. The men washed themselvesas as best they could and sat with the women and children at the tables under the shade of several trees. A Baptist minister said Grace. I wondered if it was a sin to listen to him, me being Catholic and all. Uncle Mart stood up and thanked everyone for coming and helping out. Mom told me that her brother had helped two other farmers bring in their wheat two days ago and that was how it worked, one neighbor helping the other. Mr. Parsons who had a field a few miles up the road, the one that we saw coming in, would be next. After cutting his, all of the wheat in the county will have been harvested and the machinery would be put away for another year. One of the threshers, Amos Turner, would bring Uncle Mart's wheat to Alton. The Flour Company there would send my uncle a check. Mom said, "Now, Francis, aren't you glad you came?"

The meat from the pig was delicious. There were a couple of dozen different pies, cobblers and cakes, watermelon, fried apples, and many pots of different vegetables. My belly was about to burst.

Mom asked, "How would you like to stay here a few days and help your Uncle Mart put the hay away and help him with other chores. There's sure going to be a lot of good food left for you two."

"Aren't you staying, Mom?"

"No I have to get back and help your father out. I'm going to ride back to Alton with Mr. Turner and his wife. Here is a dollar. When you get ready to come home you can get a ride with the White Bakery man. He comes every Thursday. And you know how to take the Interurban to St. Louis and the streetcar home, don't you?"

This came as a surprise. I sure liked Uncle Mart and was kinda glad that Mom thought that I was capable of doing all of this. "How many days, Mom?"

"Only a few, Francis. If you get homesick you can leave whenever you want."

So, by that evening the only people left on the farm was Uncle Mart and myself. It was quiet. A couple of wagons full of hay were left by the threshers.

Uncle Mart smiled at me and said, "I'm sure glad that you are staying, Francis. I don't get much company. It gets lonely sometimes. Today was somewhat like Christmas. People pay a lot of attention to you and then the rest of the year, nothing. Tomorrow morning I'll show you how to milk a cow. How about that!"

I looked around the room. I couldn't see much as there was only one coal oil lamp burning between myself and my uncle. No radio and no electricity to hook it up to. No Emerson fan to blow air over me. No pop or ice cream. No bathtub, toilet was outside. Mom brought two new towels replacing the dirty, smelly, one on the nail. Dad won't have to worry about me spending too much time in the bathroom. I went outside and sat on the porch. I looked up in the sky and saw what I had never seen before, millions of stars just as bright as they could be. Where did they end I wondered, how far out did they go? Are there even some beyond those that I could see? I realized that there were stars up there all day long. My God!, I thought. I wondered where God might be out there among them. I thought of my grandfather and grandmother and my real mother. I wondered if they were out there somewhere. I wished that Bobby was with me so I could talk to him. Just then a dog came up and lay at my feet. The whippoorwill started calling. It was time to go to bed.

Before daylight Uncle Mart shook me and said it was time to milk. I could hear the cows bellowing. The rooster had not yet crowed. If the rooster could still sleep, I figured I could too. Uncle Mart thought otherwise. Out of the house we went, he carrying a big bucket in one hand and a lantern swinging from the other. I never ever left our house without some kind of breakfast. "Breakfast always comes later on a farm. We have to work up an appetite first."

I stumbled along behind him. The dog that came to me last night followed us. "That's, Shep. You remember he belonged to Pop. I took him when Pop died." The cows were gathered outside the barn bellowing and waiting to get in. They looked anxious like a bunch of women waiting for Famous-Barr or The Grand Leader to open their doors. Uncle Mart opened the door for them and they entered one by one walking along a feed trough to find their stall that had foder and grain that was put into it the night before. Two cats ran in and waited.

Uncle Mart showed me how to grab a cow's teat and how to gently draw the milk from its udder. He played a rhythmical tune using both of his hands drawing streams of milk into the bucket held between his legs. He turned a teat and sprayed a squirt of milk off to the side and the two cats bolted for the warm stuff. Now he got up and told me to try it. The cow kicked its hind leg and scared me. I grabbed one teat. I wasn't ready to be handling two teats yet. I squeezed and squeezed but nothing came out and the cow didn't like who was waiting on her. "Here look at my hands, Francis. Hold the teat gently and starting with your thumb and forefinger at the top, start the downward squeeze to draw the milk out, or better yet, go outside and watch the calf milk her mother for milk."

I went outside and watched a small calf, sucking on its mother's teats and pushing the bag upward trying to get more milk. I went back in the barn assured that I now had the hang of it. It took me awhile before I managed to get a stream going. The stream of milk slowed and I did what the calf did. I pushed hard on the cow's bag and the cow pushed harder on my shoulder and I flew across the stall.

"You alright, Francis?"

"Yea. I guess I wasn't considered family." Uncle Mart gave me a funny look. The other cows turned watching me while they chewed their hay. The cats also grew impatient. Uncle Mart took over and said that I could try again this evening.

"You see, the cows have their udders full of milk and they are anxious to be relieved of that pressure. It's like you having to take a leak and you have to hold it until you can find a place to go. Of course out here, you can go anywhere except on my garden." He laughed. "That's another reason, I can't leave this farm. The cows have to be milked. If they aren't their udders just leak and will dry up and sometime they get infected. It hurts them, Francis."

All that talk about having to pee made me have to so I went outside. Outside stunk. The cows pooped everywhere and there was a big pile of it off to the side. It was begining to come light and the roosters were crowing. I hoped that my uncle would hurry and finish milking. I was hungry. He finished with the last cow. All of the them came out one by one stopping, and lifting their tails and they peed and pooped. What a mess! I thought that if they would just squat when doing their thing, their rears wouldn't be so shitty. Uncle Mart's bucket was almost full. The milk was poured into a milk can that was later put out on the side of the road for the milk man to pick up. He said that last night's milk was ours and was kept cool in the cistern. Soon after breakfast, which was thick slices of bread passed over the fire until brown or black, lathered with butter and blackberry jam, strong coffee and hot cream of wheat cereal, we headed back to the barn to unload all of that straw sitting in three wagons. The straw was carried into the barn and spread on the ground for the cows and the horses. What was left over had to be pitched up into the hay loft. We climbed up to the hay loft and he showed me where the straw was to be "pitched" off to the side to make room for the red clover that the men cut which was drying out in the field. He said he would rake it tomorrow and we would gather it and put it in the barn later. Pigeons flew out from their perches up high near the roof. He gave me a pitchfork.

"I'll go down to the wagon and throw up the straw to the opening there and then you can scoop it up and pile it back there."

My uncle stood on top of the hay wagon and began pitching the straw up to me. I worked as fast as I could but couldn't keep the opening clear. He had to wait until I had made more room. The dust made me sneeze and my hay fever started up. I now realized where that saying "hay fever" came from. I kept pitching and sneezing, until all three handkerchiefs were soaking wet. My eyes watered almost as much as my nose. It was hot and the sweat and mucus poured from me. I gave up wiping my sore red nose and just let it run and drip. Uncle Mart knew he had a problem.

"Let's take a break, Francis and I'll come up there and you're tall enough that you can pitch the straw up to me. Alright?" I sneezed approval. After our break we switched places. At least I got a little breeze outside but soon the breeze just blew all the dust back on me. We went on all morning pitching those three wagon loads of straw into the barn taking water breaks. I continued to sneeze away the morning. My uncle didn't use handkerchiefs. When his nose ran he just bent over and placing a finger over one nostril, blew the snot out on the ground. I tried it but with hay fever, it didn't work. When we went in the house for lunch I told Uncle Mart that I had to stop the sneezing and runny nose, so I lay down on the floor for an hour.

When I came out on the porch, Uncle Mart said, "Come over here quick. Look down there on the field between the road and my barn. See it?"

"What?"

"That big buck deer! Right there." I looked over his extended arm and far off I could see this deer crossing the field.

"I haven't seen a deer around these parts for twenty years!"

That evening after milking the cows we ate some of the leftovers from the threshing day, more pork, dressing, sweet potatoes, watermelon and two pieces of pie, one blackberry the other peach, washed down with a pot of strong coffee. As my uncle sat there smoking his briar pipe, I noticed a red sore on the side of his mouth. He had bled a little and the blood dripped on the newspaper covering the table. I saw other dried blood spots on the ragged newspaper. "What's that sore on your mouth?"

"I don't know. It just won't heal. I've tried everything."

"Maybe you should have a doctor look at it."

"Nah, I don't have time for that. You go to bed now. I'll tell you what, you can have the day off tomorrow, how's that." I went to bed before he changed his mind.

The next morning as I brought in wood for the stove I saw a flock of crows. They looked lazy as they seemed to flap their wings just enough to stay in the air. They were headed for a particular field nearby. Every day before sunset they would return, flying over to the woods to roost. They seemed tired and too fat to fly. They made a ruckus going and coming. I wondered what they talked about. I had heard that you could capture a crow and make it talk like a parrot by splitting its tongue. I'm sure that they would rather be free and talk their own language.

I was intrigued by the big barn and went inside and climbed up to the hay loft. The dust from yesterday had settled and it was quiet except for some mice squealing down below. The pigeons had already flown outside but I found some of their eggs resting up by the roof on a rafter. It sure was hot in there. The eggs were dusty. I picked one up and it exploded in my face. The stink was awful and the egg was all over my shirt and pants. I came to the house, took off my pants and shirt, drew water from the cistern and proceeded to wash myself and my clothes.

"Been playing up in the hay loft, Francis? Got ahold of one of those old pigeon eggs, eh?" He seemed to get a big kick out of it.

That afternoon I wandered around the farm. It was only forty acres but seemed big to me. The sun was hot but clouds shaded me occasionally and there was a nice breeze. I walked down into a small valley where there were a few trees but mostly grass. I sat on a rock and looked around. For some reason, I started to get a hard on. I hadn't been thinking of any girls or anything and I would never, ever think of Anna Mae in that way but there I was so I popped it out, embraced it and let it rip. I looked around and saw no one. I was in a spot where no one could see me. Except, God. I remembered, another baby wasted. I wished that I had some control over getting hard-ons.

That evening after supper with my uncle smoking his pipe, I asked him some questions. I knew that in the past I was to be seen and not heard, but I felt that I was too old for that now and having shoveled coal, cut grass, pitched hay and wasted babies, I could now ask whatever I wanted especially since it was just the two of us. Besides, I felt more confortable talking to him than anyone else.

"Uncle Mart, how come you don't have a wife?"

“Well now, no one asked me that for a good while. I almost did take a bride once.”

“You mean, Sadie Fitzpatrick?”

“How do you know about her?”

“She got rid of my warts. She said for me to go and ask you for a penny. You remember that?”

“Yeah, I think I do.”

“Well, was she your girl and why didn’t you marry her?”

“You’re sure asking a lot of questions, Francis. Do you have a girlfriend?”

“Well, yes, I mean I wish that she was, but she doesn’t even look at me.”

“Did you tell her how you feel?”

“No but I carved our initials on a tree and had my friend Avery run back and forth in front of her house yelling that I loved her. I guess that sounds pretty silly doesn’t it?”

“Men do some silly things over women.”

“How come you and Miss Fitzsimmons didn’t get married?”

“Francis, she didn’t want to live on a farm and all I know about is farming. I don’t have anything else to offer her but this here farm and I owe for it up to my neck. Now end of that conversation.” He lowered his head and closed his eyes and told me to go to bed.

“Did she marry someone else”, I asked.

“No, now go to bed. Tomorrow, Lord help us, your Uncle John is supposed to come and help me move some cattle to another pasture. You can help.”

After breakfast we did the milking and when we were through we walked back from the road after setting out the milk can. Uncle Mart knelt down and asked me to kneel with him. I thought this was a funny place to say prayers.

"Look at this earth, Francis. Scoop up a bit. Smell it. Feel the warmth and the softness of it. Look how rich and black it is. No rocks. This will grow anything. All you have to do is hope that the Good Lord and Mother Nature will cooperate and let you take care of the land and the animals on it. This is why I can't leave this farm. Do you understand?"

I remembered Sadie Fitzpatrick and I didn't think that I would trade that dirt for her but I did not tell that to my Uncle.

About noon the next day the White Bakery truck pulled in the drive and Uncle John got out.

"Francis, I haven't seen you in a coon's age. You sure have grown. How old are you? Where's my brother?."

He shook my hand and headed for the house. He wore a brown felt derby hat cocked to one side and had street clothes on. Spats on his shoes. He was short and slender. Looking back he addressed the White Bakery man, "Thanks for the lift, Forest. Give this boy one of your crumb cakes on me."

Forrest shook his head and gave me a crumb cake all wrapped in cellophane and took out a small note book and wrote 15 cents under a page that had my Uncle John's name above a long list of IOUS. As Uncle John went up the porch steps he wavered a bit and I could see a whiskey bottle sticking out of both of his back pockets. I realized that this was Thursday and Forest would not return for another whole week. I was certain that the crumb cake wouldn't last a week and I wondered if I would.

"Well, brother, you got any cold beer in this place?"

"You know damn well I haven't. I thought that you came to help me, not get drunk."

"I can get drunk tonight. I'll help you tomorrow. I don't see any young pretty girls around here either, Mart, when you gonna get yourself one?"

"I didn't see you bringing any with you. How's the gals on Belle Street treating you?"

"Just fine, brother. I left them crying as usual, wanting to know how soon I'd be back. I can see why you ain't got any women here. This place is filthy."

"You should have seen it a few days ago before Stella cleaned up a bit."

"Where is she. Went home overwhelmed by the dirt I suppose."

"Now, did you come to complain or to help?"

"To help, brother, just as I did twenty some odd years ago when I helped this country win a war and it looks like there gonna need me again the way that Hitler's going. I thought I killed all the Germans back in France."

"Francis, did I ever tell you about my war experience?"

"No you haven't because you ain't seen him much over the past years, but I got a feeling he's gonna hear about them now."

Uncle Mart said that he had work to do and left me there with my Uncle John. After learning how old I was, how I liked school and how many girlfriends I had, my Uncle John began to tell me of his Army experiences. He began by taking two swigs from one of his whiskey bottles and told me how, when he wasn't much older than I, he read that his president, Woodrow Wilson, needed brave men to fight the Kaiser, and that he rushed to Alton to join up. He said that he was one of the first in the whole county to enter the service, and happy he was to do so. He said that since he was such an expert marksman they sent him overseas with very little training. He told me how rough the sea journey was and how he was the only soldier aboard that whole ship that did not get seasick. He said that he fought the Germans in the trenches in France for months, killing so many that he lost count until the Germans used gas on him and his buddies and they had to retreat. After catching his breath, he advanced in the trenches all through France killing more Germans. He said that after the war, when he and his buddies received a heroe's welcome in New York City he met a movie producer who wanted him to star in the movie "All Quiet on the Western Front" but he turned him down saying his Mom and Pop needed him back on the farm. After that, and draining all that was left in the bottle, he fell asleep in the chair.

Uncle Mart came in and looked over at him, smiled and shook his head and asked, "Did he tell you how many Germans he killed?"

"Yeah."

"And did he tell you about being gassed?"

"Yes."

"Well he's been trying to convince the Veterans Administration of that for the last fifteen years. What else did he tell you?"

"He told me that he almost made a movie, that some man in New York City wanted him to star in it."

"Well now, that's a new one! I'll take care of him. You go out and see if you can gather some eggs, and then you can help me out at the manure pile, but put these boots on before you go out there."

What we did out in the feed lot was shovel the wet and semi-wet cow pies in to a wheelbarrow, then pushing it to the small mound of manure, and dumping it or pitching this crap on top of the pile. Uncle Mart told me to go in the barn and "collect" the horse manure from their stalls and stack it in a separate pile outside. He said that the horse manure was good for his roses, and the cow shit would be spread out over his fields as fertilizer once it dried. If I had a choice of picking up shit I would prefer the horse's. The cows came out splattering all over the ground. Their tails and rear ends looked and smelled shity.

"Francis the day after tomorrow we'll clean out the pig pen." He didn't see me grimace. The only thing that smelled worse than cow shit was pig shit. I could smell it from afar even without the wind blowing my way.

That evening after supper, Uncle John started on his other bottle.

"You won't be of much help to me tomorrow if'n you keep that up."

"Just a nightcap brother. Don't worry about me, I've herded cows with Pop for many a year after you struck out on your own leaving me there with him, aging and all."

"As I recall you left him alone a lot while you did your carousing in Jerseyville and Alton."

"Just a break once in awhile, brother. That's what you need. A break once in awhile. I can fix you up real good."

"I'll bet you could and I'd probably have to go to the doctor afterward knowing the type of women you run with."

"If you don't see a doctor about that sore on your lip you'll have a different problem. Getting back to me fixing you up, nothing ventured nothing gained I always say."

"Enough of that talk. You're gonna give the boy some of your ideas. Stella wouldn't like that."

"You and Stella still blame me for losing Pop's farm. It wasn't my fault that the barn caught fire. I did my best to keep that farm going and never got any credit for it."

Uncle John had just about drained the bottle of whiskey and was starting to sob.

"Well, John, let it rest. Let bygones be bygones. Now lets all go to bed. Big day tomorrow."

I got the feeling that every tomorrow was a big day for him.

The next morning after the milking and breakfast we three walked down to the lower pasture with Shep at my side. The crows were "cawing" loudly and Uncle John was singing some Irish ditty and slapping me on the back and winking as we walked. Our job was to drive about two dozen cattle from the pasture they were in up the hill to a fenced area that held more grass.

"Did Francis tell you that we saw a deer the other day. A big buck."

"You two drinking? Sorry, Francis, just that their ain't been any deer around here for years."

Uncle Mart got on one side with me in the middle and Uncle John on the other side as we proceeded to shout and wave our hands trying to get the cattle to move where we wanted. One cow roamed away from Uncle John. "Get back there you lousy son of a bitch! Damn it to hell get over there." I heard more cuss words than I ever did on our play ground back at school. I tried to remember some of them.

"There you go again, bother, calling that cow a son of a bitch. Don't know a bull from a cow!" All three of us laughed. The next morning my Uncle John left with the milk man. I liked him. He was exciting even with his bull, his singing, drinking and his continual farting.

"Here comes another big bomb, duck!", he would say before letting loose with one of his farts. I didn't count him as one of my heroes but I liked him. He made me smile.

~51~

Uncle Mart must have sensed that I was growing tired of all this farm work and asked me if I would like to go fishing.

"Yeah! but I don't have a fishing pole and where would I go?"

"I'll fix you a rig. You walk down past your grandfather's farm until you come to the Lindley Bridge. There's a nice pool underneath it and from what I've heard it's got some nice catfish."

I was excited. I had never been fishing.

"You may run into Richard Attucks down there. He fishes there every day. Sometimes never putting his line in the water. He just likes the place. He's a Negro and by the way he has a link to our family."

"You mean that we are part Negro?"

"No no, Francis. What I mean is, that as my father once told me, Richard Attucks is the Great Grandson of a Chris Attucks. He was a runaway slave that was rescued on the river when your great grandfather and your grandfather, who was just a baby then, came up the Mississippi from New Orleans after crossing the ocean from Ireland a long time ago. If you see him tell him I said, hello."

I wasn't interested in meeting any Negro. I wanted to fish. I walked for about an hour before I came to the large pond. I pulled out a worm from the tin can Uncle Mart gave me and stabbed it on the hook and threw it in the water and waited, and waited. I was beginning to doubt that there was any fish in this pond when I heard a "plop" at the other side of the pond. I saw this large snake swimming toward me! He didn't like me being there I thought. As he got closer I got scared. I had heard of Water Moccasins and heard that their bite could kill you. I let go of my fishing pole and turned to run. As I turned a big black man stood in front of me. I yelled thinking that I was between a killer snake and a black man that was going to kill me!

"Don't be afraid. I'm sorry that I frightened you. That's only a water snake, son. It wont hurt you. You from around here?"

He waved his arms and the snake changed direction. When I stopped shaking, I told the man who I was. He told me that he was Richard Attucks who lived down the road and that his father named him after my grandfather. He told me about his great grandfather being rescued by my great grandfather and his friends a long time ago. He said that he had a son about my age and the next time that I visited Mart, we two might get together and play. We didn't catch any fish, but walking back, I felt good. I wondered how true his story was.

The next day I told Uncle Mart that I would be leaving if that was alright.

"Sure, Francis. You've been a big help to me. I hope that you will come again and spend some more time with me. Maybe I won't work you so hard. If you get up early you can go with the milkman."

"I think I would like to walk to North Alton. I like to walk." That evening we sat at the table eating our supper. Not much was said. Blood ran from the corner of his mouth where the sore was.

"You should have that looked at."

"I will, Francis, I will."

The next morning I left and started walking to North Alton. When I got to the highway I looked up at the old Pembrooke School, now empty. I tried to imagine my cousins, Marguerite and Maymie going to school there and being taught by both my mother and Aunt Gertrude. After walking the nine miles to North Alton, I rode the bus to the train station. I collapsed on a seat of the Interurban and slept all the way to St. Louis.

~52~

Two new kids moved onto our block. Jimmy Knox was three years younger than me. I could boss him around and he didn't seem to care. His father was a big shot at some bank downtown. That's what Jimmy said. The other kid was a girl. Her name was Gloria Lamb. She was two years younger than me and since she couldn't find girls to play with she kept showing up wanting to play with me, Jimmy and Avery. Me especially. I couldn't get rid of her. She wasn't ugly. She looked like Alice Faye may have looked when she was a child, but she was too young for me. I liked Alice Faye. Mom made me play hopscotch with Gloria.

"Mom, what will the fellas think, I'm 11 years old!" She said that I should be nice to her. Gloria drew the lines on the sidewalk with chalk and showed me how to play. I hated it. I finally got Jimmy to take my place. He didn't like the game either, but I told him that he would be doing me a big favor.

~53~

Dad rented the third floor rear to this middle aged couple who came from Germany. They spoke German and English. Their name was Lieberman. His name was Samuel and his wife's name was, Sophie. They told Dad that they were Jewish but were German citizens. They said that bad things were happening in Germany, especially for the Jewish people. Their parents and his brothers and sisters were still over in Germany, somewhere, and they were worried for them. Dad was delighted to practice his German on them but somewhat doubted their story of persecution. Although he had heard and read of such things, he did not want to think that such things were happening in the home of his ancestors.

Mom rented the second floor housekeeping rooms to a couple who acted as though they came from the Ritz. Mom said that the woman wore a big flowery hat and although it was fairly warm out, she had a fur stole wrapped around her shoulders over a beautiful silk dress. She carried a suitcase with fancy stickers pasted on the side from many countries. She held a silver candelabra in one hand and a beaded purse in the other. The man also carried a suitcase but much larger and of brown leather. He wore a straw sailor hat. He wore a tailored blue suit with no tie. They both had a dejected look to them although the woman spoke beautifully. Mom could tell that she was highly educated. Dad tried to pry some information out of the man who said his name was Mr. Wallace McDermott but all he learned was that they had lived at the Saum Apartments on Grand avenue for a good many years and that they had no children. Mr. McDermott said that his wife's name was Violet and would it be alright if their colored cook came every afternoon to cook for them. Dad didn't blink an eye when he said, "Of course."

The next day was Sunday. Aunt Gertrude and Bud came to dinner along with cousin, Marguerite. I of course was sent down to the Well #1 the evening before with a bag full of empty Hyde Park beer bottles. Mom fixed sauerkraut and spare ribs with plenty of boiled potatoes.

Any time, Mom fixed sauerkraut and spare ribs, my saliva would turn salty just thinking of them. Mom proudly told everyone that she had rented the rooms and that all the rooms were now full except the third floor front.

"A Jew!", Aunt Gertrude shouted and tisk tisk tisking. "For crying out loud. Well, I say! The next one will probably be a Nigger."

When she was told of their dire circumstances, Aunt Gertrude quieted down just slightly. Bud popped up and said, "Speaking of Niggers, I heard that they are going to try and move into this neighborhood." He had everyone's attention as he continued, "I heard that next Saturday they are going to form a gang and move across Chouteau Avenue and march all the way up to Park carrying signs demanding equal housing."

Aunt Gertrude lit up a smoke and gulped at the Hyde Park while nodding her head. Bud continued,

"Ever since that boxer, what's' his name..."

Dad said, "Joe Louis."

"Yeah, ever since he started whipping all these guys, them Niggers found themselves a hero. They need to stay on the other side of the tracks where they belong."

Cousin Marguerite came in and having heard most of the conversation said,

"Stella tell them about Mr. & Mrs. Ritz."

"Shh, I'm sorry I told you. You tell them."

"Well Mr. and Mrs. Mc—"

"Shh they'll hear you."

"Well, they have a colored cook that is going to come in and do their evening meal!"

Aunt Gertrude tisked tisked after every gulp of beer with Bud laughing. She slapped the table spilling some of the juices from the sourkraut on the table and replied, "You're sure going to cause an uproar in the neighborhood, Stella. I wish that I could hide behind the bushes across the street this week to see the reaction when all these people come and go. Well, I say."

All that I tried to remember of that conversation was that there might be a race riot down around Park Avenue. I was excited. A race riot right here in our neighborhood. I looked forward to it with excitement and the fear of the unknown. Saturday came and I started walking toward Park Avenue and as I approached Compton and Park I could hear shouting and saw some men running toward the intersection with baseball bats. The shouting grew stronger with the words Nigger and Coon being yelled along with,"Go back where you belong!" A group of black men caring signs, some of which were now torn to shreds turned the corner onto Park chanting "Equal rights and Equal housing!" over and over. I sheltered myself up on the steps leading to a vacant house and soon a colored boy about my age ran in and sat down beside me. I looked him over as he did me. He looked scared. I know I was. The palm of his hands were almost as white as mine. He was thin and muscular and bare footed. We watched the grownups as some of the white men hit the black men with whatever they were carrying. Father Thompson came running down Compton yelling something and shoving his way into the middle of the fray. The white men seeing him and realizing what they were doing, dropped their sticks and bats and just backed away. I turned to the boy aside me and asked his name.

"Nnn—Nathaniel."

"Mine's, Frank."

I hadn't used, Frank before, but "Francis" sounded too sissy like.

"What did you come here for?", I asked.

"Came to see the excitement. See that man over there with the red scarf on his head. That's my uncle."

"Where do you live?."

"I live down across the tracks close to Market Street. I gotta go now, my uncle's calling me."

"Ok, nice to know ya."

Nathaniel nodded and ran toward his uncle and the other black men. I went home after stopping by the confectionery and getting a triple decked ice cream cone. I was confused. I had heard the word "Nigger" often along with the phrase, "If you give them an inch, they'll take a mile." Or "work like a Nigger". I also heard the word colored many times. My Dad called Joe Louis the best colored fighter he had known and possibly the best heavyweight of all, after James J. Braddock and Max Schmeling. Mom and Dad never said anything bad about the Rag Man or the chicken plucker over at Bettendorf's, but I still remembered the black savages in some of the Tarzan movies. And then I remembered the fine colored woman running the elevator at The Grand Leader. I also remembered Mr. Attucks up at Uncle Mart's. If I saw a colored man or a boy on the street, I felt a slight fear of him, but never a colored woman. I didn't know why. I was also a little leery of men with beards.

Sunday morning after Mass a colored woman rang the doorbell. When Mom answered, the woman asked if Mr. and Mrs. McDermott lived here. The woman had two large shopping bags. Mrs. McDermott hurriedly came down the stairs and introduced Mom to Mary their cook. Mary bowed slightly and followed Mrs. McDermott up the stairs. Mom opened a Falstaff and proceeded to fix pork chops. About an hour later, after Marguerite came for dinner, an aroma of fried chicken, like we had never smelled before, penetrated and overcame the pork chops. We all sat down to the pork chops. They were good but we ate mostly in silence sniffing more than usual and wishing that we were eating with the McDermott's.

After dinner, Mary came down the stairs with her shopping bags folded and she had tears in her eyes.

"Mrs. Muhm, I can't stand to see how those two have to live now. It's just too much to bear. They were on the top of the world just a short while ago and now they have nothing. Nothing!"

Mom brought her into the kitchen and sat her down at the table. She found out that Mary had been cooking for the McDermott's for ten years. That they were very wealthy, had no children, and drove a new Lincoln every year. Mr. McDermott was an investment man of some kind and when the market crashed he got out just in time to save half of his investments but they have been living on that and only that for the last eight years.

"Mrs. McDermott used to be so full of life and generous. They had so many parties in their fancy suite at the Saum and now she just doesn't seem to realize the fix that they are in, or doesn't want to. She used to send me to the very finest butchers and grocery stores for supplies, but now she says that Kroeger has the best of everything, and that they are on diets so they don't need much. She keeps telling me that she never has the right change on my pay day and to remind her next week. They give me the money to buy groceries and food to take home to my family but that's all. I don't know what to do. They have been so nice to me over the years, but I'se gotta have some pay. I could go all the way out to Clayton and University City and clean house and cook for those rich folks but that's too far. I got no transportation. I think that Mrs. McDermott has been selling or pawning some of her jewelry. They have fallen so far, Mrs. Muhm. I hope you'll be nice to them."

Mom nodded and helped Mary to the door. Mom was dying to ask Mary how she cooked chicken, but thought perhaps another time. Mom was now worried as to whether the McDermott's would be able to pay their rent. The next morning as Mom was hanging out her clothes, Mrs. Vick came out on her back porch and said, "Well, Stella, I see that you folks must be doing alright now with a colored maid and all coming to work for you."

Mom was flustered and without much thought said, "I guess so. Easy come and easy go." Mrs. Vick tried to pry out the story but Mom just kept changing the subject.

Within a week, Mary had two job offers from women on our block solely due to the aromas emanating from 2838 Eads.

I surmised that things must be looking up for our neighbors. I know that Mom and Dad were doing a little better with renters and Dad said that he may be eligible to get a Social Security check some time in the future. We weren't rich but Mom changed her weekly order of beer from The Well # 1 to two Budweisers and three Hyde Parks. Dad and I still kept our jobs, me walking Skippy and helping Clem clean the church, and Dad doing odd jobs for Mr. and Mrs. Sanders and cleaning around the apartments and gathering used newspapers and selling them just like our rag man did. He would save the used Saturday Evening Posts for us.

~54~

Until the Liebermans and the McDermott's came, Mom was having more trouble keeping the rooms rented. People were getting particular and would leave saying something like, "It's not exactly what we were looking for." I guess we were lucky to have Mr. and Mrs. Liberman from Germany. It was a good thing for us that things were not so good for them over there, and that the McDermott's were down on their luck. Mom put up another photograph of F.D.R. right next to Jesus and The Sacred Heart.

My Cardinals were not doing too good. Dizzy Dean broke a toe in the All Star Game last year and was traded to the Cubs of all people. Johnny Mize and Joe Medwick were still hitting the ball over the fence. Dad said that the Cardinals signed a rookie pitcher that they thought would go far but he injured his arm and was assigned to be an outfielder in the minors. Stanley Musial was his name. When Dad mentioned his name I thought of Stan and Laurel. Dad said what he always said when things didn't go just right, "Win some and lose some." Terry Moore wasn't playing as much as he used to but I still liked him. Dad said that the Cardinals now had three good new players signed. A guy named Slaughter, another Cooper, a catcher, and a pitcher by the name of Max Lanier. Dad told me of a pitcher that the Cardinals brought up from the minors. Frankie Frish got so disgusted with his pitching staff in one of the last games of the season that he told this rookie to show him what he had. The guy went to the mound without taking any warm-up pitches and got clobbered. Dad said we'll never see him again. I asked his name. Dad said with a laugh, "He calls himself a preacher, Preacher Roe! He better start preaching to himself. We won't be hearing about him anymore."

~55~

I went up the rear black metal steps to pick up Skippy for his walk. My footsteps made a dull clinking ring as I climbed. Mrs. Sanders came to the door with tears in her eyes. She told me that Skippy had died. They had taken him to a veterinarian and he was put to sleep. "He was in so much pain, Francis. He liked you so much. He was always so happy to see you when you came to walk him. I miss him so much."

"What was wrong with him?"

"He had a tumor and the Vet said that it just kept growing until it shut off his intestinal track. I miss him so." She cried so much that I had a hard time to keep from crying.

All I could think to say was, "I'm sorry Mrs. Sanders." I turned around and went down the stairs. On the way home I remembered how I cheated him on his walks, tying him to the fence while I played with the boys on the lot, and how I pulled him along trying to get him and myself out of sight from the passing motorist and streetcar riders on Lafayette when he had trouble pooping. I remembered how he screamed.

When I got home I told Mom and Dad. Dad said that he was going over to see Mrs. Sanders. I went out back, sat on the porch steps and called Bobby to my side. He nuzzled under my arm. I stroked him, hugged him, and petted him, and we sat there for an hour until Mom said that lunch was ready. I was perplexed again. I didn't dislike Skippy but I was never fond of him. He was my job and I did not do it well.

Jimmy Knox and Gloria showed up and so did my cousin, Marguerite. Marguerite wanted to take our pictures with her new Brownie camera. Bobby also got in the picture. Gloria said that she would like a copy. Ugh! Gloria was then asked to take a picture of just me and Marguerite.

~56~

I was out in the alley with the boys when Mom called me. I hated the way she would call, "Francisssss." The guys always laughed. When I went in the house, Mom asked me to take the garbage out to the ash-pit. I told Dad quietly how much I disliked my name. He replied, "How would you like mine, Emil Ewald?"

For the last few years we boys would climb up onto the garage roofs and jump from one roof to the other. We got the idea from watching the Tarzan movies, except he swung from tree to tree. We had become good at it with only minor accidents. The roof on Mom and Dad's garage now had a spring to it. I guess that it was from us landing on it so many times. It was almost like landing on a sponge and made for a softer landing. We liked that. Mr. Nelson's garage next door was too far for anyone of us to jump from, but a tree grew to the side with a limb jutting out just in the right place for us to tie a rope on to it so that when we swung out, holding on and yelling the Tarzan yell, we would let go and drop onto our garage roof. This same tree grew long cigar like pods that we tried to smoke when they ripened. They weren't very good. The cigarette butts thrown away on the sidewalk were better.

The only problem in jumping from the Nelson's garage roof to ours was that you had better let go of the rope as you came over our roof or you would swing back into the walk way between the garages and have to drop down ten feet. Jimmy Knox had been pestering us to let him try all summer. Gloria watched us from the ground wishing that she was a boy. One day Jimmy pestered us again, and when we told him that he wasn't big enough he pulled out a quarter and said that if we would let him swing he would give us the quarter. Gloria told him that if he tried it she would run and tell his mother. One of the guys went down and held Gloria and nodded that Jimmy could be Tarzan. We told Jimmy that he had to hold the rope tight as he could while we pushed him back and forth like on a swing to give him enough height and surge to get him over the gangway and above our garage in which sat Mr. Woodhouse's new convertible squeezed in at an angle in order to fit. Jimmy gave out a loud Tarzan yell and sailed over the gangway. He dropped at the perfect time and landed on the roof and fell thru it. He ended up sitting in the back seat of Mr. Woodhouse's convertible along with tarpaper and pieces of roof covering him. Jimmy's screaming didn't sound a bit like Tarzan's yell. Most of the boys scattered. Gloria ran to tell Jimmy's mother. I ran in to tell Dad. We got Jimmy out of the car. Dad had Jimmy walk around until he was satisfied that nothing was broken. Mom took him in the house to tend to scratches on his face, legs and arms. Mrs. Knox rushed in all upset until she saw that her boy was alright. Jimmy asked me if he still had to pay the quarter. I got a dirty look from the adults while I shook my head, "No." to Jimmy. I was sent out to the garage to clean up Mr. Woodhouse's convertible. I took my time because I was fascinated with the automobile and hoped that some day I would have a car. Dad said that he would get a roofer and that garage jumping was over. Mom tisked tisked and said, "Well, there goes the garage rent". Gloria sent Jimmy a get well card.

~57~

September came and school started again. School had a new custodian, an older Italian man who did not speak much English. His name was Mr. Fagnanny. I thought that was a funny name and wondered if that was his real name. Whenever the kids would greet him with, "Hello, Mr. Fagnanny", he would smile and wave.

Sister was teaching us how to diagram sentences. I hated that. Why couldn't she just let us write like we talked? Why do some words have to be called objects, nouns, pronouns, predicates, and verbs? And all these periods, commas, colons and semicolons, dashes and quotation marks. Why do we need them? Pronouns. Are there anti-nouns? I got rapped on my hand by Mother Superior for that one. And I ain't never gonna say ain't in front of any nun.

My Cardinals finished 17 games out. Dad said that they went "Belly up", whatever that meant.

On Sunday Father Joe announced that there would be a social in the school hall the following Friday night. We all knew what that meant, because we had one every year about this time. The church always needed money. At the social they had gambling, card playing and the one I liked, The Wheel of Fortune, a big wheel with sections marked off where you could place your bets, a nickel or dime and hope that the wheel landed on your spot. There were hot dogs, soda pop, cotton candy and kegs of beer. The women brought pies. I looked for, Anna Mae but she wasn't there. Mom and I played The Wheel of Fortune. Dad entered a pinochle game. I won seven dollars on The Wheel. I figured that was three and a half months of wages for walking Skippy. Sergeant Schumacher was there and I heard him introduce his Captain to Father Thompson. There was a big crowd so I guess the church made a lot of money.

The days got shorter, the Sycamore leaves fell and the wind blew them down the street and the sidewalk. They made a hollow scratching sound until they found a resting spot. The furnaces and the kerosene space heaters started up. The lucky people had kerosene heaters. They didn't have to haul in coal, just carry oil cans, The smoke from the coal furnaces filled the outside air and covered everything with a black smudge. Coal was delivered and I pushed it up the terrace to the coal chute. As long as there was a fire in the furnace there was hot water for bathing, washing clothes and dishes as the water pipes threaded through the furnace.

~58~

The temperature stayed below freezing all the month of November. I came home from school one day and Dad said that Bobby got out again. Mom said that I must have left the latch unlocked. A week went by and no Bobby. I would look for him every day when I came home. Two weeks passed. This was the longest he was ever gone. I started praying for his return. I even lit a candle at church. The scent of melting wax and burned wicks penetrated my nostrils. It was a remembered kind of smell.

When I came home from school a couple of days later, Dad was on the sidewalk in front of our house talking to Mr. Smith who lived down on Eads near California. They stopped talking when I got close. It was freezing cold and I was anxious to get up the steps and inside. Dad said that Mr. Smith may have found Bobby.

Forgetting about the cold and everything else I shouted, "Where?"

Mr. Smith started walking away and Dad said, "Francis, I think he's — dead, but we're not sure that the dog Mr. Smith saw was Bobby, we're going to look." My heart seemed to stop and I had trouble breathing. I started to dislike Mr. Smith and asked Dad if we could go look now. "He's, or the dog is, up on Eads near Jefferson, don't run so fast, I can't keep up with you." I waited for Dad to catch up at the end of each block. I was aggravated that he took so long, limping and grunting.

When we got up alongside Nash's Drug store I saw this dog laying in the gutter. The dog was still and splayed out with his hind legs extended far back and his front ones forward as though he was running. I got closer. Bobby's eyes were open staring at nothing. His mouth was open with dried frozen blood hanging down. Tears formed and streaked down my cheeks as I picked him up. I told Dad that I would take him back home and bury him. Dad had tears too. Bobby was stiff as a board. He was hard and cold and heavy as he lay across my arms on the way home. Dad offered to carry him part of the way, but I knew he would have trouble handling his cane and Bobby too. He put his hand on my shoulder as we walked slowly. People passed us and looked and turned around to look again after they passed. I was not embarrassed like I was with walking Skippy. And now, I wasn't embarrassed to have Dad along either. It started snowing real heavy. I struggled to say, "It snowed the night I found Bobby, remember, Dad?"

"I remember."

Dad and I placed Bobby on the ground back by the ash pit. Mom had fixed supper. Hot vegetable soup along with a lot of hugs. After supper Dad and I got a pic ax and shovel from the basement, broke through the frozen ground, and buried my dog with the snow covering us and the ground quickly. I said a Hail Mary and told God that Bobby deserved to be in Heaven and asked him why he had to die?

Mrs. Liberman and also Mr. McDermott told me that they knew where I could get another dog.

"Thanks, but I don't ever want another dog."

~59~

Avery came by the next day and wanted to go to the movies. "The Lafayette has Dracula and Frankenstein tomorrow night, ya wanna go?"

I told him about Bobby. He said that he was sorry. He said that he never had a dog. I felt kinda sorry for Avery. The Lafayette Theater was like the Compton Show, old and usually running B minus movies but it was cheap. Both Avery and I had seen both of these movies before but we were older now and knew that we wouldn't be as scared as the first time we saw them. We were wrong. The movies over, we walked over to Eads Avenue and down past the gutter that Dad and I found my dog. Avery and I were so busy talking about the scary parts of the movies that I didn't even realize that we had walked past the spot. I was glad that Avery asked me to go to the movies with him that night.

Gloria came over and gave me what Mom called a sympathy card. I kinda wanted Gloria to find another friend and I kinda didn't.

~60~

Thanksgiving came but no sign of Uncle Walter. He had not been heard from for over a year. No one ever knew how to reach him except at the Goodwill Store. They said that he had just up and left six months ago. Mom and Dad talked about what to fix. Mrs. McDermott overheard their conversation and suggested that "Their Mary" do most of the cooking and we would all eat together. One thing led to another and it ended up that the McDermott's, Liebermans, Marguerite, Aunt Gertrude, and Bud, Mom and Dad and I and Mary all sat down to a meal that was a mixture of Kosher, "Soul food," and Mom's goose. Dad offered everyone some of our "Hershey's Cocoa", trying to get rid of it but they all declined. He then brought out some Elderberry wine. Mr. Leiberman brought a bottle of Manechevitz. Aunt Gertrude brought a mixture of Hyde Park, Alphen Brau and Falstaff beers and I had a Grape Nehi. Mrs. McDermott had on white gloves and a fancy dress. I sat next to Mary and asked her what her last name was.

"Washington, Mary Washington, Francis. Thank you for asking."

"Do you know a boy named Nathaniel?" Everyone stopped talking and listened to us.

"Why yes I do. I have a Grandson that is two years old. His name is Nathaniel."

"I met this boy named Nathaniel a few months ago down at the Race Riot on Compton and Park but he was my age."

Mrs. Washington didn't say anything. Mom quickly asked Mary if she wanted any more goose.

"How about more of your delicious dressing, Mary?"

Everyone started talking to Mary and handing her food. Mary Washington put her arm around me and asked, "Did you and this Nathaniel like each other?"

"Yes ma'am."

Mom asked me to go down to the Well #1 and get six more Hyde Parks. When I got back, Mary Washington was leaving. She said that she had to go home and cook a large Thanksgiving dinner for her own family. When the wine and beer bottles emptied and dishes were washed and put away, everyone went home or to their rooms full and contented.

On Christmas Eve Uncle Walter showed up. No one ever asked him where he had been. Dad always assumed that he was on a binge. This time it would have been a very long binge but he looked great. He said that he had been out in Nebraska taking medical courses. He brought Mom a canary in a bird cage and for me a big beautiful sled. I had never seen anything like it in the hardware stores. It was made of wood, painted black with metal runners fastened to long round cane like wood curled in the front to a figure six. The bed of the sled was painted with flowers. Mom quickly placed it in the corner of the living room by our scraggly tree saying that it was not meant for outside, just for show. We had oyster stew for supper. We had that every Christmas Eve. I again looked for pearls. Every New Years Eve Dad would bring home pickled herring and black eyed peas. I of course heard the "You don't know what you're missing" when I hesitated. When we came back from midnight mass, Uncle Walter was gone. No note, nothing. He always seemed like a flash of a wonderful dream. He was someone I desperately wanted to get to know better, but somehow felt that he didn't want me to know much about him. Only the good stuff.

Two weeks into the new year on a Sunday, we had a heavy snow. When Mom was over talking to the neighbor and Dad was at the church helping Clem, I took the sled Uncle Walter gave me and carried it to the top of the side terrace at my school. Away I went downhill. I was headed toward a big Maple tree and when I tried to turn the sled, I realized that the runners were not flexible and in a split second remembered what Mom said, that the sled that I was now on was just for show. I collided with a the tree. The sled was in a dozen pieces. I had a knot on my head and a big gash on my hand with blood gushing out. I ended up in the Emergency Room of City Hospital where a doctor stitched up my hand. I told Mom that I was sorry that I broke her sled. Gloria wanted to see my hand. Wouldn't you know it, I got another sympathy card! The next day, with my hand bandaged, Avery and I stopped at Henn's Market and Garavelli's to pick up cardboard boxes. We went up to Reservoir Park and with the cardboard boxes flattened spent the whole afternoon sliding down the slopes on them. Much better than Mom's fancy sled, I thought.

~61~

Avery and I did everything together. We went to the movies, rode our bikes all over town. We played horse on the lot with other boys. I was always the horse. I carried him. We couldn't be beat. I stayed on my feet and Avery pulled the other boys off their horse. Avery was my best friend. One day after playing and winning horse again, Stanley Phillips and his rider, Earl, were looking at us kinda funny. We overheard Stanley use the word "queer" in his sentence while pointing at us. We laughed and went on with the game.

Days later Avery came over and we went to the basement where we had somewhat of a clubhouse. We had nailed some orange crates together and made a small table and two orange crate chairs. We were in the process of making scooters out of our old roller skates by nailing them to a two by four which we would fasten to an orange crate. We would attach wooden handlebars across the top. As we sat there I asked Avery, "Do you think we are queer?"

"I don't know. I don't think so."

"What's a queer, I asked." I knew what a jack-off was now. Could I also be a queer, I wondered. "What do they do?"

"Well they both take out their pricks and—- lets go outside."

We went out the basement door and stood at the bottom of the stairwell, under the back porch. He took his out of his pants and I did the same. Both of ours lay limp.

"What now", I asked.

"Well I think one of us has to be like a female and one of us the male and the male puts his into the female's mouth."

"Ugh, I don't want to be the female!"

"I don't either!"

Just then, Mrs. Vick stepped out onto her back porch and saw us standing there with our wing dings hanging out and shouted, "What in the world are you boys doing! Why I—." We buttoned up quickly and went back into the basement. Avery said that he had better go home. At least we felt that we were not queer but didn't rightly know what we were.

That night I stayed in my room and heard Mom and Dad discussing a conversation that Mom had with Mrs. Vick. I heard Mom tell Dad that he was going to have to do something. The next day Dad asked me if I would like to go to lunch with him over on Lafayette. I said yes. Lunch with my dad? I thought that was queer, or I meant different. I figured he was going to give me a lecture on queers. I had never been in this restaurant and was unaware that Dad had been there.

After sitting down, a pretty waitress came over to take our order. She said her name was Sally. She said, winking at me, that I was a real handsome lad. I blushed. She sat down alongside Dad and brushed his remaining hairs back, kissed him on the cheek and asked him, "Whatya have today, Champ?"

I about choked ! Dad told her a hamburger. "Is this your son, Emil honey?" When Dad said yes, she said, "Why Emil I may have to give you up for your sexy son here. What's your name tiger?"

"Frank", I said as I looked at her legs coming out of her short skirt. I admired her high heel shoes, not the ugly kind that Mom always wore.

"And what will you have, Frank?"

"A hamburger", I said as she stroked my hair and rubbed my leg. My penis was aroused.

Dad was grunting faster and louder than normal. He kept his eyes on me rather than Sally. I watched Sally. She talked and laughed with the other waitress as she waited for our order. I overheard one of the other waitresses say, "Sal, I never knew that you had such moves." They all giggled.

Afterward Sally came swinging over and said, "Open your mouth, Frank baby. I'll give you a treat." She placed a chocolate kiss on my tongue and said, "Sweets for the handsomest man that I've seen in a long time."

Our bill was thirty two cents. Dad left Sally a two dollar tip!

Walking home Dad said that it would probably be good if I didn't see Avery for a few days. I didn't ask him why. I asked him when we could go back and see Sally and how long he had known her and did Mom know about it. Dad smiled and said that Mom knew about it but didn't answer my other two questions.

Two weeks later when Avery and I walked up Longfellow to see a movie at the Shenandoah I asked him If he had ever been to the Lafayette Cafe. He said Yes. His grandfather took him and there was this waitress named, Sally!

~62~

In February we got a package that was almost falling apart from Maymie and Fergie in California. Two oranges, an avocado, a half dozen nuts in the shell and some figs with a note enclosed wishing everyone a Merry Christmas and apologizing for being so late. Mom said that was just like Maymie, always late. She said in her letter that the temperature was in the seventies and that Fergie had a job at Fort Bragg and that they went to the beach Christmas Day. That California sure sounded good. Maybe some day I would go there.

Dad had been trying to teach me pinochle. I wanted to learn how to play poker like some of my friends but Dad said poker was a sinful game. I wondered how any card game could be sinful and then I remembered Leroy Grone wanting to play strip poker with some of his neighbor girls. Dad said that he thought I had become good enough to play as his partner. He had arranged a game with Mr. Lieberman and Mr. Krueger and they would teach Mr. McDermott as the game went on. Mom baked some cookies and made a big pot of coffee. Mr. Lieberman brought a bottle of wine and an "Orange Crush" for me. Before the game I was sent to "White Castle" to get ten hamburgers. Mom gave me two coupons that she had cut out of the paper that read five for a quarter. I liked them almost as much as the tamales. They came in small castle shaped boxes. I was so tempted to eat one or two on the way home and tell Mom that I dropped them. When I got home, I told Mom that the ten White Castles wouldn't go very far. She agreed. She made some peanut butter and jelly sandwiches and said that we would eat the hamburgers before the games got started. The castle boxes were empty five minuets after she said that.

I felt pretty important since I was to play with the grown-ups. We played up on the third floor in Mr. and Mrs. Lieberman's room. The ladies all gathered downstairs with Mom. I don't know what they did, probably listen to one of those heart throb radio programs that Mom liked. Snookie, (I wish that I knew what his real name was) stayed home.

Maybe he figured out by now that I stole his ball. The Lieberman's room was neat but somewhat crowded with us men there. They had a large candle holder sitting on the back window sill and a short wave radio next to it. The radio was tuned to Germany and Mr. McDermott and I could not understand a word that was spoken. Mr. Lieberman and Mr. Krueger helped Dad understand a lot of the words since they were spoken too fast for him. Mr. Lieberman noticed my and Mr. McDermott's disinterest and went over and turned the radio down.

"When did you leave Germany?" Dad asked.

"June 9, 1936," Mr. Lieberman replied. "My wife taught school and I had a small tailor shop. We saw the handwriting on the wall. On April 30, 1933 the SS troops came to my wife's school. They went through all of the books. They carted most of them outside and set fire to them. Right in front of her students and the other teachers. The teachers were told that other books were on the way and that they were to teach from them and no others. About a week later I started losing customers. People would come in and pick up their clothing. A lot of the clothes were just brought in a day or so before and I had not time to even start working on them. A sign was put outside of my shop telling everyone that I was a Jew, which they already knew. They were told not to do business with me. I have a brother, Silas, who had a good clerical job at what you would call City Hall. He and six other Jews were told that they were no longer needed. His boss told him that if he was Silas he would leave Germany as soon as he and his family could. He said that Hitler was trying to rid Germany of Jews. When my brother told me that, I still couldn't believe it. What had we done, I wondered. We paid taxes like everyone else. My brother's boss said that the people were being told that Germany was in such bad financial shape because of us Jews."

"What did you and your brother do?" asked Dad.

"We waited. Waited for things to, what do you say, blow over, get better, but it got worse. My wife's mother and father were forced out of their home. A home that they had paid for and had been living in since they were married. They were loaded in a truck with other Jews in their neighborhood and were told that they would be, I think they used the word, relocated to better housing. They knew that this was not true because all that they were allowed to take with them was what they could carry."

"What happened to them?" asked Dad.

"We do not know."

"What's your bid, Sam?" asked Mr. Krueger wanting to get on with the game.

"Samuel told me when they moved in here that they did not know where his or his wife's relatives were, right?" Dad asked.

"At that time I did not know. We have received several letters from my brother Silas since then."

"I have the last one that I received right over here, I'll get it and read it to you." Mr. Krueger sighed deeply. He laid down his cards and shuffled his feet.

"It's in German of course so bear with me". "Dear Brother, I am writing to you from somewhere still in Germany, but where I will not say. If you get this letter it will have been mailed for me by my new friend, Fritz. I won't tell you his real name because if this letter falls into the wrong hands it may cause him trouble. He is not Jewish but is against all that is being done here. I have tried to get information on our parents and those of Sophie's but all that I have been able to learn is that they were moved somewhere close to the Polish border. I have been on the move continuously, mostly by foot and at night headed always to the east trying to get out of Germany. Just a few more miles and I will have made it. Things are terrible for us here, but for the Germans, they are excited and full of hope. Most of the Germans seem to worship their Fuhrer and if I wasn't Jewish, God forgive, I think that I too could get excited with all the marches, patriot songs, and Swastika flags waving everywhere. I don't think that the people realize what is happening. It is their hope for better times. I think that they do not even think of the cost. The cost and suffering of other people to have those better times. You and Sophie left just in time. I hope that we will all be able to meet again soon in America. Pray for us."

No one spoke for awhile until Mr. Liberman showed me the envelope and asked me if I would like the stamp. I said yes. He tore the stamp from the envelope and gave it to me. Hitler's picture was on it. It was a dull red. He said that he had others and I could have them. He then asked, "Who dealt that hand?"

Mr. Krueger asked, "How did you get out of Germany?"

"Sophie and I knew that we had better leave the country as soon as we could so we took what little gold that we had. A friend of ours made gold buttons to replace the ones that we had on every piece of clothing that we owned. He even made shoe buckles out of our gold. We started moving East and then South to France. The French people were very nervous. We got to Paris right before Hitler invaded the Rhineland. When that happened we sailed for England. I worked in a tailor shop there until we had enough money to come to America. We thought that Hitler would invade England. We wanted to go as far inland in this country as we could afford. So, believe it or not, here we are on the third floor of the Muhms and glad to be here."

I looked at the buttons on his sweater. He saw me and said, "No, Francis, the gold is all gone. Just ordinary buttons now. I will have to start all over." They all laughed and we resumed the game. I had another hero. What an exciting life he has had. He doesn't know what happened to his mother and father or his other relatives. Now he and his wife live in this hot, small, third floor room in our house.

~63~

The canary that Uncle Walter gave Mom for Christmas didn't sing. It just pooped and scattered seeds. I was given the job of cleaning the birdcage. I was shown how to cut newspapers to fit the floor of the cage, and how to take out the dirty papers without spilling all of the poop and the seeds on the floor. After awhile we ran low on newspapers, since I still used some of them to put in my shoes to cover the holes. Dad whistled to that bird for two weeks but it did not sing a note. It just pooped and ate. One morning Mom said that the bird was dead. Aunt Gertrude came over she proclaimed that Dad drove it nuts and killed it with his continual whistling. Mom told her that Dad almost drove her nuts. I was glad the bird died. Two weeks later, Mrs. Nelson next door brought Mom one of her canaries. She said that the bird's name was Valentino. Valentino sang continuously from the time Dad removed the cover in the morning until he put it back on in the evening. Valentino seemed to eat and poop twice as much as the first bird. Dad started whistling to Valentino. Mom told him to stop it. Dad said that he was only trying to learn its language. "Learn my language, Emil, stop it!" Dad grunted and pouted.

Aunt Gertrude came over to see and hear Valentino. She told Mom, "I just saw Mrs. Schultz scrubbing her limestone steps, and in the rain, mind you."

"Those scrubby Dutch, there's more to life than that. Clean, clean, clean. Some people just wear out what their cleaning," Mom replied.

I thought of Uncle Mart.

~64~

Gertrude

Diary April 4th

Tommie surprised us all. He drove up our lane in a car honking and honking with a big grin on his face. He said that he bought the car! I don't know what kind it is. It looks great. He made Father get in the front with him and me and Barty in the back and away we flew over the pasture toward Norman Morewise's home. That's the first time I heard Father laugh. He laughed every time we went over a bump. Tommie got Norman Morewise's attention with all the honking. Out of his pig pen, he came to see the automobile. Tommie shoved him in the car next to Father. Boy did it stink in there. We circled Mr. Morewise's boxcar home a dozen times bouncing up and down scattering the chickens and it seemed that all the dogs within miles started barking. After letting Mr. Morewise out we headed home and Tommie pulled up slowly next to old Rufus and gave him a honk. Tommie said that he was able to make a sizable down payment on the car and would have it paid for in six months. He brought us candy and Father a supply of tobacco and he gave me an Alton Telegraph to read and the newest movie star magazine.

~65~

Frank

I was being moved again. This time to the third floor front, the top of the house and hot. The only thing that I liked about the small, low ceiling room was the small double window. It opened but not wide enough to climb through. I could look over Gloria's roof and see the clouds of black and white smoke made by the locomotives down in Rankin Yard. On a quiet day or evening I could hear the huffing and puffing of the engines and the slamming together of the freight cars. I had to move up here because Mom had put a "For Rent" sign in the window trying to attract a renter for the second floor rear room. My room! I did a lot of dreaming and thinking in my new room. I thought of Anna Mae and I started thinking about religion. My religion. The Sisters poured the Catechism into us every day, twice a day. I wondered about Heaven and Hell and what they were like. Purgatory really puzzled me.

In my Missal there were prayers for the dead. If you said them, they were good for a certain number of days or even years. Something like a reduction of sentence for the dead who never made it to heaven. Those people in a holding pen. How do I know which of my dead relatives and friends are in Purgatory? If I knew that my mother, Bridget, and my grandfather and grandmother were in Purgatory, I would say that was not fair, but I would sure pray for them anyway, just to be sure. And how long would they be in for? If they were in Purgatory, were they told for how long? Could I pray for myself if I was to go there. Could I earn points ahead of time. How many and what kind of sins must a person have, to be told, "No you can't go in yet, you need to have people pray for you down there." And who decides the score? Does someone up there keep tabs on how many days of indulgence does "Joe Blow" have and how many more does he need to get in. Is he told what the score is? Is it hot or cold in Purgatory or just plain dark? Things were a lot simpler when I didn't start thinking. And what about all of these other people in the world that have never seen or heard of any kind of a church. Those who can't read like those in Africa. Are they doomed from the start? If not, boy, they must need a whole lot of prayers.

We are told that unless you are baptized you will never get to Heaven. There must have been millions, no, trillions of people that have lived and died ever since God created humans. There aren't enough people living who know how to pray for their souls. We would need a lot more people to pray for their souls. What is the cut or the passing grade to get into Heaven? And another thing, what about people who went to other churches, those Protestants and Jews like the Liebermans and those people that Mom calls those "Holy Rollers that go to that church a couple of blocks away. Boy, they always sound like they are having fun, shouting and singing. Mom says that they roll on the floor. Sounds like fun to me. But are these people doomed to Hell because they aren't Catholic. If so I don't think it's fair. I don't exactly know what my soul is. I kinda think that it may be close to having a conscience but I'm not sure. If my conscience is "clear" does that mean my soul is OK. My conscience is never clear.

With all of this thinking and doubting about my religon I always got nervous, so much so the first time I was very afraid that God would say, "Enough of that, Francis! Your days are over!" My heart beat real fast and I started sweating. I was afraid that God would strike me down, but God didn't kill me that first time. I still think that He's saying, "Don't go too far with all of this doubting, Francis." But I'm not sure of that. How far can I go?

~66~

One day when Mom was downtown and I had come home from school and was eating a couple of Dad's radish sandwiches when the door bell rang. Dad beat me to the door.

"Is this the Muhm residence?" a lady asked Dad. "My name is Freida Robbins. Friends of mine out in California gave me your address and said that I might find a room for rent in your home."

"Well we do have a small sleeping room for rent." Dad replied. "Who was it that gave you our name?"

"Lillian Ginsberg. We worked together for awhile out in California. I'm looking for a quiet place for only a couple of weeks."

"I don't recall a Lil—."

"Dad", I interrupted, "Remember Quick and Nimble."

"Yes, I should have mentioned those names. Do you have a room available?"

Dad started to grunt at a faster rate. I shouted, "Yeah." Freida smiled at me. She was pretty but her clothes were kinda plain. I looked outside and she had a taxicab waiting. We rarely ever saw a taxicab on Eads Avenue. Dad said, "Let me show you the room" as he hobbled up the staircase with Freida behind him and me behind her. I was there to help. I didn't want Dad to mess this one up. After they agreed on the price, Freida asked me If I could help her carry in her luggage. Mrs. Vick watched and so did Mrs. Schultz. Freida had an awful lot of clothes and a lot of hat and shoe boxes.

When Mom came home we both told her that we had rented the room. Paid in advance. Mom said that she was stopped by Mrs. Schultz who asked, "Who was that floozie that she had taken in now!"

When Dad introduced Freida Robbins to Mom she told them that she worked in the same theater where Quick and Nimble worked and that she was a dancer.

"Oh a tap dancer," Mom said.

"Well, no, not exactly, Mrs. Muhm. You have never been to a Vaudeville Show, have you?"

"Oh my, I think that I know what you do. I'm afraid—-"

"Oh, Mrs. Muhm, you will never see me around here with my show clothes on. I go to church nearly every day. I'm a good Catholic girl. I don't smoke or carouse around. I'm hoping that I can better myself in show business. I need a few breaks. Quick and Nimble said that you had a good, quiet, homey place here and I hope that you will let me stay for my two weeks run. If you're' going to church tomorrow morning, I would like to go with you."

Dad still grunting asked her, like he knew all about show business, "What's your stage name?"

Freida blushed and giggled, "Tiger Lil."

Another, "Oh my", from Mom but she said that she supposed that it would be alright for two weeks. Dad gave out with one of his few smiles. I was racing downstairs to go tell Avery when Mom grabbed me and said, "Don't you dare tell anyone, especially your Aunt Gertrude!"

The conversation was on the second floor hallway and the Liebermans and the McDermott's heard everything. A week ago Mr. McDermott and Mr. Lieberman said that they thought that they would be leaving soon. That's why Mom went downtown looking for a job. Now, they had changed their minds at least for the present they said, perhaps for the next two weeks.

The next day after school, I rode my bike all the way downtown to the Grand Theater. There on a big poster was our Freida known as Tiger Lil. The large colorful poster featured Tiger Lil with a scant outfit on with brown and black stripes, bare legs and high heel shoes. She was curled up as if to strike out from the poster. She had a brown and black hat on that had ears. The large printing below her picture said, "This is one pussy cat that you don't want to miss!!"

I stood there straddling my bike when a man came out of the theater and seeing me goggling said, "Boy, get outa here, you're too young to be looking at that. What would your mother say."

I started to ride away when another man came out and said, "Boy, you looking for a job?"

"What kind of a job?"

"We need a boy to sell candy during the intermissions."

"You mean in there, with Fr—Tiger Lil?"

"Yeah, in there but no, you won't be allowed to see the show. Just sell candy. If I catch you peeking at the girls or listening to the jokes you're outta here. You want the job?"

"I go to school but I could do it on Saturdays and maybe some nights."

"Nah, no nights. You be here Saturday morning about ten and Harry will show you the ropes. You'll get one percent of what you sell and you have to be quick on your feet and know how to make change. You got any talent like dancing or juggling?"

"No sir."

"That's too bad. Be here at ten Saturday. Come in the side door and ask for Harry."

Wow! I got a job in show business and me being a pretty good peeker, I'll bet I get to see Freida do her thing whatever that is. Wait till I tell Dad.

When I told Dad of my new job he started grunting and his eyes lit up. "We won't tell Mom." He now knew for sure that Mrs. Vick and he and Mom had nothing to worry about me.

The next day Dad went to the restaurant on Lafayette. He had a cup of coffee and left Sally a fifty cent tip.

I couldn't wait till Saturday. I came home from school Friday and started to clean the bird cage. Somehow Valentino flew out lighting here and there. I couldn't catch him. Mom and Dad tried also. He just kept chirping and flying from our reach. With Dad whistling continuously trying to catch his attention, Mom finally said, "Just leave him alone and leave the door of his cage open and maybe he will go back in where his food is." That sounded like a good idea to us. Dad could call turtles but had no power over Valentino.

That evening before dark, we heard a scream from Freida's room. I ran down the steps. Freida had her door open pointing inside and said, "There's a blooming bird flying around in my room. I can't stand this!" Valentino was perched on a lamp shade. I guess he was tired out from flying all day so he let me grab him and take him out the door. Freida kissed me on the cheek and thanked me for coming to her rescue!

I blushed and said, "I'll see you tomorrow."

Saturday morning Mom went downtown to apply for a job at the Grand Leader. I rode my bike downtown to my new job. I met Harry. He was an old man with a handlebar mustache and looked to be three hundred pounds with a big belly leaning out over his belt. I thought he must eat his own candy bars. He gave me a cart full of candy, some of the brands I had never heard of. He told me that today only I would have the center aisle. He repeated that I had to be fast and holler out "Get your candy, hurry up before the show resumes!" I was to do this during the intermission. I was told that some of the men would get up to go to the bathroom while others would remain in their seats. I was to catch the "Gents" returning from the toilet and sell them candy.

I stood on the far side from the ladies dressing rooms where the jugglers, dancers, and comedians entered the stage. Before the "Girls" did their thing I was shoved out the side door and not let back in until their act was over. I had to figure out how I could see Tiger Lil. I remembered how Leroy Grone and some other guys would sneak in the back door to the Lafayette Theater. Sometimes they got caught, but not always. I never had the nerve to try that but this was worth the risk if I could figure out a way.

The man who introduced all the acts finally said that there would be a fifteen minute intermission after which, "What you all have been waiting for, Tiger Lil!" There was an uproar. All the lights were turned on, Harry shoved me out into the crowd.

Most of the candy was a nickel so I managed to make change easily. It didn't take very long to make it up the aisle and back. Harry would announce that they all had another chance to get that favorite snack so up the aisle I went again. I thought that I spotted Mr. Foster over on the other aisle. He plays cards with Dad after their Holy Name meeting. I don't think he saw me.

Some of the men had overcoats draped over their laps even though it was hot in there. After the fourth trip the crowd was getting impatient. The fifteen minute intermission lasted twenty five and the men chanted, "We want Tiger!" over and over. Harry motioned for me to come back stage where he took my money and candy and sent me out the side door to wait for him to let me back in. I could hear the band playing and the men howling. Our Freida evidently was giving them quite a show. I couldn't see it.

After Freida finished I was let back in. I was told that my commission was thirty two cents. I could have any one candy bar that I wanted. Just then on the other side of the back stage, Freida opened the door to her dressing room and hollered to Harry that she wanted a candy bar.

"I'll take it to her", I shouted.

Harry smiled and said, "OK, Buster go ahead."

I went over to her dressing room, knocked on the door and said, "candy bar."

"Come in, I hope you got the kind that I like." When I entered here was Tiger Lil with heavy make-up on. Her silly looking hat was on the dresser and her high heel shoes laying to her side. She was plucking her false eyelashes off. She didn't look a thing like our renter, Freida. When she saw me she said, "Francis! Is that you, Francis? What in the world are you doing here?"

I gave her the candy bar and told her that I too was in show business. I told her how I got the job.

"Does your mother know?"

"No ma'am."

"Well, we are going to have to tell her aren't we?"

"I guess so. Dad knows but told me not to tell Mom."

"Well now, we have to get her permission, OK? How much did you make today?"

"Thirty two cents and a candy bar."

"That's terrible, I'll talk to Harry about that."

At first Mom was very upset but Dad said that Freida had nothing to do with me getting the job. I told her that they wouldn't let me see the show. Freida apologized to Mom for possibly being a bad influence on her son. She said that as long as I was in the theater, she would personally take care of me. Mom said OK. I liked that part where Freida was going to take care of me. Mom also liked the idea that her son had the gumption to go out and get a job on his own. She didn't know the real reason for me wanting the job.

Mom cornered me and said, "Don't you dare tell your Aunt Gertrude!"

~67~

I sure had a lot of secrets to keep lately. I only had one more chance to see Tiger Lil on stage doing her thing and that was next Saturday. I remembered how the men looked in the audience and how they were dressed. Friday night, when Dad was out at the Holy Name Meeting playing cards, I looked in his chifforobe and took a pair of pants, his winter felt hat and an old shirt. In the dresser drawer he had an old pair of glasses. I took them. Out on the porch he had forgotten or left one of his corncob pipes. On Saturday, Freida's last show, I showed up with a shopping bag containing Dad's clothes. I left the bag outside. After I sold my candy and was shoved out the side door I quickly dressed and went around to the entrance wearing my father's clothes. I went up to the window and proclaimed in the deepest voice that I could muster, "I would like a ticket to the show."

Mable Morgan who was the cashier looked up. She quickly digested who was in front of her and said, "The show is already underway, but if you still want to see it that will be thirty-five cents, please, Sir." She put a lot of emphasis on the "Sir". I handed her the thirty five cents that I had made selling candy and went inside. I could hear Mrs. Morgan laughing uncontrollably. I sat in the back row by an old bald headed man eating the candy bar that I sold him. I felt good about that. Out came Tiger Lil. Wow!! Soon I wished that I had brought Dad's overcoat!

I couldn't see too well with Dad's glasses on and the man in front of me kept standing up and shouting along with others, "Take it off, Tiger, take it all off!" I thought that she had taken enough off already but if more was to come, I had to see better. Off went Dad's glasses. I moved slightly into the aisle. Tiger Lil was about to drop another piece of clothing. I stood there with my eyes bugged and my mouth open. Just then someone grabbed me by the back of my neck and drug me into the lobby. It was Harry.

"You're fired Frankie boy. I don't want to see you around here anymore. What would your mother say."

What would my mother say, I thought as I rode my bike home with Dad's clothes in a bag hanging on my handlebar. I had another secret to keep.

Mom and Dad asked how much I made and I told them that I quit because Harry would not let me see the show. "Well good for this Harry", Mom said.

Monday Freida Robbins packed her bags and left. She waited until I got home from school. When the cab came, she asked me if I would help her out with her things. On the way down the steps she whispered, "Harry told me that you saw my show, Francis. What did you think?"

"Wow!"

She rustled my hair and said, "Maybe the next time I perform it will be in Hollywood and you will be old enough to come and see me."

Off went the cab down Eads Avenue leaving me at the curb wondering how I could get older faster so I could go to Hollywood or get into the Grand without getting thrown out. I don't think Avery or Leroy Grone believed me when I told them of my being in show business and seeing a stripper and that she lived in our house, but I didn't care whether they did or not.

At the end of the week both the McDermotts and the Liebermans moved out. Mr. Knox, Jimmy's father, got Mr. McDermott a job at his bank and Mrs. McDermott said that they were going to move back into the Saum. Their cook, Mary Washington, told Mom how happy she was for them. Most of the people on our block did not know the McDermotts, but they all knew Mrs. Washington. They and we would miss the food and the aroma that her cooking produced. Mr. Lieberman, who worked part time at Weil Clothing Co. on Washington Avenue doing alterations, was promoted to head tailor. They were going to move to an apartment in University City.

Rooms for rent signs went in the window.

That Friday the nuns marched us up to the church for our usual confessions. "Bless me Father, for I have sinned. It has been one week since my last confession. I lied to my mother and father." "Three Hail Marys and four Our Fathers and you must learn to tell the truth, my son."

I didn't think sneaking into the Grand was a sin; I paid my way. I could have asked Sister in class whether it was a sin, but thought better of it. Although if I did that, Anna Mae might think that I was someone to be interested in. After Tiger Lil, I lost interest in Anna Mae, at least for awhile. My interest was in older women. Mom said that I had to stay in that third floor room so she could keep my old room clean for showing. It was hot everywhere in the house but more on the third floor right under the roof.

~68~

Gertrude

July 14th

Dear Diary,

Today is Barty's birthday. I baked him a cake. Angel food. Put some whipped cream on top of it. Father and I sang Happy Birthday. Up until last year, Barty didn't know when his birthday was. Father told him that he was a firecracker and he thought that he was born on the Fourth of July, but he wasn't sure. I'm going to miss these two. I answered an advertisement in the Alton paper for a homemaker. Tommie placed it for me. This family wanted someone to live with their mother and do the cooking and cleaning for her. They would pay a dollar a day with room and board. When I talked to Father about the job and the fact that I had already applied and that I got the job he was very upset. So was Barty but as I told him later, there had to be more to life than what I had experienced.

At the supper table yesterday I blurted out, Father, I've taken the job in Alton. I am to start next Monday. You've what, he said. What do you mean? Barty raised up from his meal with his mouth wide open in shock. I told Father that the job pays real well and I get room and board I told him that I could be home one day a week and I could help pay for things around here. He didn't let me finish. He said, You'll do no such thing, Daughter. You got a job right here and this is where you are going to stay. Who do you think is going to do the cooking, laundry and cleaning around here. No, I'll have none of this, Gertrude and that's that ! I had never before argued with Father but I was determined to be out on my own. I told him that my mind was made up. I wanted to be around people I wanted to see what the world has to offer out there. I told him that I loved him and

Barty very much but I was a woman now. I have feelings like a woman. I told him that may be hard for him to understand. Besides, I said, Barty here can do the cooking. He's seen me do it often enough. Barty said, I can't cook and I don't know how to wash clothes.

I told him that he could, and you will because I won't be here. You will learn or starve to death. I may have been too angry but I stood my ground.

I told Father that the farm was loosing money and he knew that. We have all worked so hard and for what. Tommie is giving you some money from the job he has and I can do the same. You can start taking it easy. I told him to sell some of the cattle and hogs and just raise enough garden vegetables and slaughter enough meat for yourselves. Tommie and I will help you make interest payments to the bank. You won't have to worry and I can have a life without this farm. I blurted all this out at once. No one spoke the rest of the day.

~69~

Tim remembered how he felt that Christmas when he read his daughter's diary. He wondered then if he was doing the right thing by keeping the children with him. Nonetheless he couldn't stand hearing what his Gertrude said, so he got up from the table without finishing the meal. So did Barty. Gertrude remained seated, staring at her dinner as tears rolled down her cheeks.

Sunday, Tommie drove up, loaded his sister's suitcase in the car. He waited until she hugged and kissed her father and Barty. As they drove down the lane toward the road, Tim and the only son he had left watched until they were out of sight.

The Kelleys were all together at home for Thanksgiving and again at Christmas. Tommie and Gertrude gave their father two sets of overalls. They gave Barty a stocking cap and a new pair of shoes. Tim listened to all the news and their experiences. Barty counted his days until he too would leave the farm.

~70~

Frank

We had a somewhat strange and quiet Thanksgiving and Christmas. Uncle Walter did not show. Cousin Marguerite moved in with us and took the third floor rear room. I was glad of that. Marguerite paid her rent just like any of the previous renters. She got tired of the rooms that she had down on Caroline Street. The house had an outside toilet and no hot water. She said that she did not know why she ever moved there in the first place.

Mom got a letter from Maymie saying that she was coming for a visit. She would be here for St. Patrick's Day. Mom was excited. I thought that I was going to get my old room back but Mom said Maymie would take it. She wrote her brothers Mart and John about the visit and offered them a room if they could join us for Maymie's visit. She did not write her brother, Dick because she did not know where he lived. Dad didn't like him.

Mom would drag me along occasionally to Jefferson Avenue when we would meet my Uncle Dick without Dad knowing it. We would see him standing outside of Nash's Drug store. These meetings would always be on a Friday night with a group of men and women wearing their Salvation Army uniforms playing their instruments. I was always told to go over and listen to them while Mom talked to my Uncle Dick who got kicked in the head by a mule a long time ago. At times I saw her give him money.

The day before St. Patrick's Day my Aunt Gertrude and Bud went out to Lambert Field to pick up Maymie. I wanted to go too so I could see all the big airplanes but Mom said that she had things for me to do. I was sent down to The Well for beer. I had to make several trips. She also told me to get a bottle of "Three Feathers" for my Uncle John. Uncle Mart wrote and told Mom that he could not leave the animals. Uncle John had never been to our house. I'm not sure that my Uncle Mart had ever left the farm for anything. At first Fred the bartender, refused to sell me the whiskey but his boss told him that it was OK with a warning to me, "Don't open it until you get home, and don't rattle the bottles!" The men at the bar and sitting at the tables laughed. How did they know? A lot of those men were already wearing green.

This year, St. Patrick's Day fell on a Sunday so the Well would be closed. We went to Mass, just as usual. Although it was Lent and we were to fast, our Pastor, Joseph Sullivan, gave us special dispensation for eating meat. He said nothing about drinking but he didn't have to.

Aunt Gertrude said, "Those poor lots down at St. Vincent's can't celebrate until tomorrow."

Our neighbors watched as I made several trips to the tavern and back the day before. They just knew that the Muhms, with the German name, were about to have an Irish blow out again. And on a Sunday! I figured that some would be tisk tisking while others would be wishing that they were invited. Dad was sent to Garavelli's for some corned beef and cabbage.

Mom told him, "Plenty of horseradish. And get the fresh kind, you know the kind that comes from over around Highland, Illinois. That's the best. Oh, and new potatoes and plenty of carrots and some small turnips."

"How about some rutabagas?"

"No!", both Mom and I shouted.

As he went out the door on his walk to the alley, we could hear him mutter, "You don't know what you're missing."

Our house had been kinda quiet and empty since the McDermott's and the Liebermans and my favorite, Tiger Lil, left. Mom did not seem too worried about the money coming in because she got on at The Grand Leader, working in the Infants Wear Department. She said that if she got on full time, which she thought that she would soon, she would get a discount on everything in the store, even clothes for me and

Dad. She said that she would be paid a commission for what she sold. Mom had been practicing her sales pitches on us with all the "Dearies" Would you like some oatmeal, dearie?" At first I didn't answer because I didn't know who she was talking to. "Francis!, Dearie!" It got downright unbearable until Aunt Gertrude made her come to her senses.

Maymie arrived and got out of Bud's car wearing a large, felt, black hat. She looked like a female Napoleon. My Uncle John arrived later in a cab. He had the cab wait. Mom gave him money. He went down, got his suitcase out of the cab and paid the man. He had liquor on his breath but was all smiles and telling jokes. I couldn't see them, but I knew eyes were poking through the lace curtains of our neighbors.

When we all went to Mass, except for Uncle John, I saw a lot of strangers at church. Marguerite said later that many of the strangers were from St. Vincent's. They figured that if they came to the "Irish" church that they too could celebrate.

After church, Uncle John came down to the kitchen with no shirt, just wearing his long underwear with his pants held up by red suspenders. He got a glass out of the pantry and poured it half full of whiskey and asked Mom, "What's for breakfast?"

"Whatever you want to fix yourself, John. We have already eaten."

"Well, what kind of hospitality is that? And to your own brother." He winked at me, slapped me on the back, went to the Fridgadare, got out two eggs, broke them and poured them into another glass and drank them down in one gulp with an "Ahhh" at the end. He went back up to his room and didn't come down until he could tell by the smell that the corned beef and cabbage was done. By that time Aunt Gertrude and Bud had arrived. Mom and Dad and I, and Maymie and Marguerite, were all at the table with a bottle of beer before them except for Dad and me. I gave him one of my Nehis. After the meal and a few more beers the table was cleared. Dad said that he was going up and talk to Clem for awhile. He knew what was coming.

Maymie went upstairs to her room. When she came down, she had on her big black hat with a hat box under one arm and a shoe box under the other. Everyone had some green on. Marguerite did manage to have some green on along with just about every other color. When

Aunt Gertrude saw Maymie's hat a "Well, I say" came out between puffs on her cigarette and swigs of the beer.

"Where on earth did you get that?"

"I won it at Santa Anita, betting on Seabiscuit last year! I won a hundred and fifty dollars. This hat cost me twenty-five. A few of us girls go to the track every week. Fergie doesn't know it and their husbands don't either!"

"Well, I say."

Mom asked, "What do you have in these boxes?"

"I brought these snapshots that I've been keeping for years and I thought it would be fun to go through them again. We're not getting any younger you know. Look at this one. My first car. I bought it for three hundred dollars from the mailman. Remember, Marguerite, we got three hundred dollars each when our Aunt Nellie died."

"Yes, I saved mine until Uncle Dick needed some money, so I gave it to him. You remember Mom telling you that the Model T would be a waste of money because you wouldn't take care of it. She said that because you never cleaned the buggy. I always had to do it."

"I don't remember that. What would we have done without that car. I took care of Mom and Pop while you worked in St. Louis. I went to get you every Friday and brought you back every Sunday with John along to change the tires."

"What do you mean," John said, "I took care of Mom and Pop too!"

"Yes, you and Maymie here used the car to go carousing around Alton from one speakeasy to another. Your uncle, here was a bad influence on you."

"Now that's not fair. I gave her an education!"

"Where and what kind, up at Hine Woodhouse's place in Godfrey where all the drunks hang out?"

Mom sensed trouble coming and started singing, "My Wild Irish Rose". All of us chimed in.

That over, everyone wanted to see some more pictures.

"Oh look at this one," Maymie continued. "That's Betsey and Rudy and their colt. Mart and John are holding them This was taken in front of the orchard. Remember, Marguerite, that's were you and I would hide when there were chores to do or when we got into trouble."

I asked, "Why was Uncle John all dressed up?"

"Oh he was going to a dance that night. Every Saturday night some farmer would open his place for a dance. You remember, John, they had a wooden platform that they would drag from one farm to the other. Someone would always show up with a fiddle and that's all it would take. Some of the men brought their own booze."

"Yeah and boy was it strong. It would sure cure what ailed you. Can't get it anymore", Uncle John said. He and Bud got in a separate conversation concerning booze.

I asked Maymie, "Did Uncle Mart go to the dances?" I thought of he and Sadie Fitzpatrick.

"Oh, yes indeed, he went. But there was only one suit in the family you see. It belonged to Pop. He let the boys use it for the dances but they had to take turns. Pop was the tallest and Mom was kept busy taking up the pants and letting them out. Once in awhile, not very often, they would take me and Marguerite to the dance. Remember? We would sit in the grass watching all the ladies all dressed up in their finery. We would wish that we were old enough to wear beautiful dresses and dance on the big board."

I had a hard time imagining my Uncle Mart wearing a suit and dancing.

Dad came back from visiting Clem. He thought that the celebration would be over.

"Here's one, talk about women's finery look at this one with Stella."

"Oh my, they wouldn't be able to sell that now at The Grand Leader!", Mom laughed.

"Watch out, John you're spilling your drink on the table." Maymie said, "Here's one, Gertrude, if you don't look like something the cat drug in!"

"Oh, look at this one, Gertrude you and little, Jimmy Geeres, two years, three months old written on the back."

"That was right after we adopted him," my aunt said.

"Yes and about a year later, you shoved him back in the orphanage," Uncle John slurred.

"That isn't true, it was two years later, and what was I to do. Ralph divorced me, leaving me with nothing. I had to take him back. You're mean, John!."

Aunt Gertrude started crying. Mom gave her a fresh beer.

Maymie only made a small dent in the amount of snapshots that she wanted to show us. She shuffled for one that would not bring forth an argument. "Lookie here, John. Here you are leaving for the Army."

"Well, I say," Aunt Gertrude responded, fully recovered. "Look at how dapper he looks, suit, overcoat, tie, new hat, and what looks like a brief case. He's about to knock out the Germans with just his looks!"

Maymie brought forth another. "This one, he's home on furlough, remember. Look at him, short haircut, khakis, not too dapper. Oh, and this one is a prize, John holding the American Flag with the whole family around him. See there's your mother, Bird, Francis standing next to our Mom and in front of your father."

I held the photo for some time. "Oh, Francis you and Emil will get a kick out of this one." Dad came to the table, Maymie brought forth a large tinted photograph of two streetcars with men standing in the front of one of them.

"That's our father, Martin Kelley, in the white shirt leaning out the middle front window. Look, It's the Grand Avenue streetcar with a Bellefontaine one in back. Look at the sign on the cowcatcher!, 'Take this car for Baseball To-day! St. Louis American League vs New York."

Dad studied it with me.

"That's a great photograph, Maymie. Francis, I think the game they are advertising was when the Browns played New York in the World Series."

"Our Browns, Dad?"

"Sure way back then they were pretty good."

We heard the rest of them arguing over if the photograph was taken before Marguerite was born or after and why Martin Kelley eventually left his daughters with Mom and Pop. Dad and I wondered about the ball clubs advertised in the photograph. Mom started singing an Irish ditty but before Maymie put a lid on the hat box, she showed us a photograph of Gene Autry riding his horse, Champ. She showed us his autograph on the back.

They sang a few more songs, drank more beer, then, one by one, they shuffled into the living room to fall asleep wherever they could, another Saint Patrick's day celebrated. Dad sensed the quiet and warmed himself up some corned beef and cabbage. He told me, "Each year they finish celebrating a little earlier. They are getting old, Francis."

I asked him, "You didn't clean the church, did you?" "No, I left that for us tomorrow."

Maymie left to fly back to Fergie in California wearing her black hat. She told everyone to come and visit them. I wondered if I would ever get to.

-71-

A week later the weather turned cold and windy. Dad said that March was going out like a Lion. When the wind stopped, our street and the whole city was covered with smoke so thick that I couldn't see the end of the block. Our Mayor got the politicians to pass a smoke ordinance which Dad said meant that we would have to burn more expensive coal. The tree trunks and buildings have been coated with a soot like substance for years. When it snowed it did not take long for the white stuff to look dingy. One of the papers said that St. Louis was one of the dirtiest cities in the country.

Dad and I were hopeful that this would be the year that our Cardinals would do it. We lost Dizzy two years ago but got this pitcher, Curt Davis. He won 22 games a year ago and hit 381 for average. A pitcher! We still had Johnny Mize and Terry Moore and the new long-legged short stop, Marty Marion. We couldn't wait until the season started.

Dad said that our country was gearing up for war. He said that our people did not want war. They had enough in World War One which he said was supposed to be the war to end all wars. He said that most people didn't think that we should get into it. He said that our President wanted to help our Allies but Congress would have no part of it. Dad said that Mr. Lindbergh made a speech telling the American people that we should stay out of the war. He said that Lucky Lindy, my hero, accepted a medal from Hitler. Dad said that Mister Lindbergh wasn't thought of too much after that. Now that England and France declared war on Germany, Dad said that he knew that we would get into it. I didn't understand a lot of all this politics. I just wanted everything to be the same, or did I. I couldn't make up my mind. I wasn't having what you would call a very exciting life.

-72-

My grades at school were getting worse. Sister Mary Agnes said that my mind wasn't on my studies. She said that if I didn't improve very soon I probably would not graduate with the rest of the class next year. I guess she got the idea of my mind not being on my studies from the time she walked up the aisle and asked me a question about geography. I forgot what the question was. I looked at her and said, "Huh?" I guess that I had answered her that way more than once. She made me stay after school and write on the blackboard twenty-five times, "I will not say 'Huh' again." It took me awhile to write it. She walked up to me and asked, "Francis, are you done?" I answered, "Huh?" She shook her head and sent me home. I went home knowing that I was the dumbest thing alive.

I had been taking my report cards home with all the "Fs" on it along with a note from the Sister showing concern. Mom and Dad took turns trying to help me with my homework until they finally had an argument as to which one of them was teaching me the right way. I told them that it wasn't their fault that I was just plain dumb and nothing could be done about it. I told them that I didn't want to go to High School anyway. I asked Mom how far she went in school.

"Well, I finished elementary school. But that was different then."

"But you were good enough to go on and be a teacher, weren't you?"

"Well, yes, but I was only allowed to teach the first grade. Your mother and I both taught at Pembroke School. Later, I took courses and received a certificate to teach the older children. But those days were different, Francis. We didn't need a lot of higher education unless you were going to be a doctor or a lawyer and no one thought that women should go to high school, at least not up there in the country. You are growing up in the times of opportunity, Francis and you need to learn all that you can."

"How much of this education did you get, Dad?"

He stammerred and grunted before saying, "Elementary school, but your Uncle Walter and I gave up the chance for any more education because of our brother, Oscar. He was the bright one and he went on to be a doctor. We didn't have the opportunity that you do, Francis. You need to apply yourself and get your money's worth from every teacher you have."

"Mom, how much did Uncle Mart have?" I was trying desperately to find a way of getting out of school.

"Your Uncle Mart did not finish elementary school and neither did John or Dick. They were not given the chance because they were needed to work the farm with Pop. Now if you want to spend the rest of your life pitching hay, slopping hogs and spreading manure I'm sure you can get a job for life."

I remembered my pitching hay and working with Uncle Mart. I told Mom and Dad that I would try to do better. My grades improved just slightly, but I would have to say that my penmanship improved tremendously. I practiced forging Dad's signature. I got so good at it that I forged his signature on the next two report cards. They were gems! Perhaps I could be an artist. Mom and Dad asked me a month or two later when I would get another report card and I told them that evidently Sister Mary Agnes felt that since I was doing so good, one wasn't necessary. Father Thompson asked me in the confessional why I always lied so much to my mother and father, This time he asked me what I lied to them about. He caught me so off guard that I told him the truth! One of the few confessions where I told the truth. There was a long pause before he gave me more penance than anytime before. Boy was I dumb! But I knew that I was still safe because he wasn't supposed to tell anyone what I or anyone else confessed. I don't think I could ever be a priest. I couldn't keep all those secrets. Nevertheless I was scared that my parents would find out somehow so I really paid attention in class and my grades improved. I learned that Johnny Jacobs brought his report card home but was afraid to show it to his parents. He buried it in his back yard. The only problem was that his dog dug it up the next day and his father got it. Johnny got it after that!

Mom and Dad received a letter from Sister Mary Agnes asking them to come to her classroom for a conference to learn how I was doing and to bring me along. The jig's up! I developed all kinds of illness that day but Mom and Dad dragged me there when I could have been playing cork ball or bottle caps in the alley with the guys.

"Mr. and Mrs. Muhm, I have been wondering why I had not heard anything from you in answer to your son's terrible report cards. I hope that it is not because you don't care."

I slouched down in the seat as far as I could hide and prayed to God that this was just a dream and wasn't happening.

Dad said, "Well, we didn't know that he was still flunking. I don't remember getting a report card. When was the last time we got one, Stella?"

"I'm not sure."

"Well, here are the last two, Mr. Muhm. They're signed by you are they not?"

Dad started to grunt, Mom looked at them and asked him, "Why didn't you tell me about this, Emil. I'm so embarrassed, Sister."

Sister looked at me and I started to cry. I had to fess-up. I told them that I had forged Dad's signature. That I did it because I did not want them to worry. I thought that if they did not know the bad news it wouldn't hurt them. I told them that I was now doing better. My parents did not know what to say.

Sister Mary Agnes looked at me still sobbing uncontrollably and said, "Francis, haven't I and the other Sisters always told you that God sees everything that we do and say."

I nodded and thought, yes but Father Thompson isn't God and he broke a rule. Sister said that I had been improving very much and that if I kept it up I wouldn't have any problem. She also told them that she had taken a handwriting analysis course at the convent some years ago and had become very good at it. So much for my becoming an artist. On the way home, I told my parents how sorry I was and this time I didn't tell them a lie. I wasn't allowed to play after school for a week. Dad told me that my forgery fooled him but I should never try it again with him or anyone else or I would soon end up being a jailbird.

-73-

Gertrude

Dear Diary,

I have been working here for Mrs. Moran for almost a year now. It doesn't seem that long. Father is still on the farm. Barty left for a job at a bakery in Alton, so Father is by himself. I wish he would get a telephone but he's stubborn. I don't make much money taking care of Mrs. Moran but it sure beats life on the farm. Inside toilet. Real toilet paper, a bathtub, and hot and cold water. No pumping or carrying water from the well. A fine gas stove to cook on and the best part is that I have met Mrs. Moran's nephew, Johnathan. We have gone to the movies together and for long walks. He has a car. We drove out to Father's several times. Father seems to like him and I like that. There is only one problem, he's divorced. He told me that right away. He knows that I'm Catholic. I told him that I wasn't a very good one. He said that he did not care and that I was his little angel. His little angel! That's a lot better than what I've always been called, "Little Gertrude". I think we love each other. I know that I love him. Another problem. Johnathan thinks that we will go to war soon and that he will have to go in the Army. I worry about that and for Tommie also. Johnathan said that we would worry about that when the time comes. I wish I could feel that way. I do the worrying for both of us.

-74-

Frank

Soon it will be my birthday. I'll be a teen-ager. That sounded good. The day before my birthday, Dad came home from the Holy Name meeting with two tickets to the Cardinals game! Wow, what a birthday present! The Globe the day before my birthday said that the Cardinals traded Joe Medwick and Curt Davis to Brooklyn. To Brooklyn! They got a lot of money and four players in return. I was so disgusted that I didn't want to go to the game but then again, I did. Baseball was just like slavery as far as I was concerned. They better never trade Terry Moore! I was still complaining to Dad as we rode the Grand Avenue streetcar to the game. When we crossed the Grand Avenue Viaduct, which Dad proudly said he and the other W.P.A. workers helped build, the streetcar stopped at the North end of the viaduct. A lot of Negroes got off. I saw large posters tacked on nearby telephone poles proclaiming "Kansas City Monarchs vs St. Louis Stars, Today Only" Streams of people, all black, walked down the hill under the viaduct and out of sight.

"Where are they all going?"

"To see the ballgame. The Kansas City Monarchs are one of the best Negro ball teams in the country, Francis."

"I didn't know that black people knew how to play baseball. I'll bet that they don't have any players like Dizzy or Terry Moore."

A man sitting behind us said, "Son, they have a pitcher that you wouldn't believe. He's better that anyone that I've ever seen, black, white or yellow—."

Dad interrupted him, "Satchel Paige."

"Yeah."

If he was so good, why didn't Dad tell me about him.

When we got out to our seats at Sportsmen's Park way up in the stands on the left field side, I looked over to the screened in section in right field where all of the colored people sit. The section was almost empty. I pointed that out to Dad and asked him about this pitcher, Satchel Paige. "I have never seen him play but I heard that he is really something. But we will never see him in the big leagues."

"Why?"

"Because he's black, Francis."

I don't know why, but that seemed to be a good reason. The Cardinals, without Medwick, won the game. The Hershey Cocoa man wasn't there to give out free samples. The next morning I looked at the sports section and couldn't find any mention of those Black teams or that funny named pitcher, Satchel Paige. I wondered why.

-75-

Dad came home from his Holy Name meeting and told us that "There was big trouble at church. "I think that we are about to see the last of Father Thompson."

"No!. Why? What has that poor man done now. It's because he's young and good looking and all those rumors isn't it?", Mom complained.

I had not heard any rumors. I did notice that his confessional always had a line of mostly women waiting for him to hear their confessions. I and all the kids liked him. Some of the nuns did not, but that was because he smoked that cigar and threw out candy from the top floor of the school to us boys. He told all the nuns to either send us home early or let us spend the rest of the day at recess. Mr. Dailey told Dad that he had heard that one of the members of the church told Father Sullivan that his wife wanted a divorce because she was in love with Father Thompson. When Dad asked who this man was, Mr. Daily told him that the man's name was a secret. The man said that there were other wives in the parish who felt the same way and that The Church should not have someone, especially a Priest, creating evil thoughts and feelings of lust. That was a new word for me, "Lust". I'll have to look it up.

Mom said, "That's a bunch of rubbish. He can't help it because he's good looking. I think it's just time for him to move on. They all do that. Rotate. He doesn't need to leave with all of those lies following him. Good Lord, you mean all the priests coming in have to be ugly."

That Friday when we all were ushered up to confession, Father Thompson's confessional was empty. I had a choice of Father Sullivan or Father Chronin. I didn't like the idea of a strange priest coming in. No telling how strict he would be. We might get that Father Schmidt, who was the very hard of hearing priest that Alan Norman told us about at St. Michael's. We would have to yell our sins to him so everyone could hear. I never thought that a priest could be one of my heroes, but Father Thompson was close to Terry Moore and Dizzy. Well, not quite that close, but up there. I would miss him.

~76~

Cousin Marguerite had been living with us for sometime now. She worked downtown at Shapleigh Hardware. She got tired of waiting for the streetcar every morning so she bought a car. She did not know how to drive. She took lessons. Many of them. Six different instructors quit her. Aunt Gertrude told us with Marguerite there, "They all ended up out on Arsenal Street, stark raving mad!"

"I know how to drive, It's all of those other crazy people out there that shouldn't be on the streets!. I haven't had an accident or killed anyone, have I?"

"Well, I won't ride with you", replied Aunt Gertrude.

"Well, I wouldn't ride with that drunken husband of yours either." And so went the conversation.

During the day there were plenty of parking spaces on our street. When people came home from work the spaces got filled quickly and those that were left required a driver to parallel park. Times were getting better. More cars. My cousin flunked parallel parking with every lesson, but that did not stop her. She would drive around the block for however many times it took for a large enough space to open up so she could just glide in. Well, "glide in" may not be the right way to say it. Once she ran out of gas and had to be pushed to the curb over on Henrietta Street. Another time she had to park four blocks away after circling our block a dozen times and not finding a big enough space close to our house. She walked the four blocks. When she got two houses away a man pulled out leaving an opening right in front of our house. Boy, was she mad! Last week a policeman came to the door asking who owned the car down the street with the front end parked up on the sidewalk and the back stuck out in the street. She told the officer that someone probably had pushed her car that way to make room for their own. She named off a bunch of Irish policemen that she knew downtown and asked what part of Ireland he was from. He said that he was Dutch. She got off with a warning.

A week later, Aunt Gertrude and Bud were over. Marguerite came in huffing and puffing with her hair hanging straight down, barefooted, carrying her wet shoes, her clothes soaked, cussing about another run in with the City. Mom tried to calm her down.

"Well, I've finally done it. You two, (meaning Mom and Gertrude) outta be happy! I ran into a damn fire plug!"

"Where?"

"What the hell matter does it make, where! Up on Grand and Penrose, damn it. They had no business putting that thing so close to the street!"

"Are you alright", Mom asked.

"Do I look alright?"

"You look like you could use a drink", replied my Aunt. "How's the car?"

"Just a dent in the bumper. That's another thing. They should build those things better. Why a dog could knock one of those fire plugs over with a strong piss!"

Dad came in the door catching part of the conversation. "You knocked over a fireplug?"

"Good God, yes, Emil. How do you think I got in this shape, swimming in the Mississippi ?"

Cousin Marguerite usually didn't get this worked up about anything but this car of hers was kinda making her a different person.

"Well I say. I'll bet that was a sight to see. I wished I was there with my Brownie," laughed Aunt Gertrude.

Our kitchen was full of laughter dry towels and wet beer. Mom asked if I would go to the Well for more beer. I asked if I could go later as I didn't want to miss anything.

After drying off and changing into dry clothes and drinking a few beers, Marguerite continued, "That water shot up as high as this house. It stopped all the traffic. There must have been a dozen cops. Three fire trucks! I just sat there in the car watching the rainbow until this one fireman opened the door and asked if I was alright. I told him, yes and close that door, you're getting me all wet, I'm watching the rainbow."

"Did any kids get to play in the water?" I asked. She ignored my question.

"They had the nerve to give me a ticket!"

A week later a letter came from the city. My cousin was fuming as she read it to us. It was an itemized bill from The City of St. Louis, Department of Public Utilities, Water Division:

Material $21.16
Labor
2 foreman 6 hrs. @.85 $5.10
5 laborers 19hrs.@.67 1/2 per hour $12.83
5 laborers 19hrs @.55 $10.45
1 truck 4hrs. @ 1.25 $5.00
1 dump truck 2 hrs. @1.25 2.50 35.88

Total $57.04

We had to hear how she was going to get a job as a foreman with the City. "That's outrageous! Highway robbery!"

~77~

Mom seemed much happier lately. We didn't have many renters but Dad was getting a small Social Security check and she was working a few days a week at The Grand Leader. Marguerite wanted Mom to ride to work with her but Mom told her that she would rather take the streetcar and besides they had different starting times. Mom told Dad and me that she would be a nervous wreck if she rode with my cousin. She used to be a nervous wreck riding with Dad when he had a car. Mom had made some friends at the store and she told my aunt that she felt like she had a new life now, being out of the house and earning money again. She said that she did not feel guilty leaving home to work now that I was grown up. She said that she was sick and tired of housework. "Emil can take care of that now."

Mom made friends with another salesperson by the name of, Grace Mullanphy, who worked in the same department. They would stop for a beer after work at this small tavern downtown on Locust Street. The tavern served food. Ted, the owner had three tables set up just for the women while the men stood at the bar to eat and drink. Mrs. Mullanphy and Mom would go there sometimes for lunch. I met her friend there one Saturday. They had the best ham on rye that I ever ate. They dipped the thin sliced ham in what seemed like tomato soup and placed it on special rye bread.

"My, what a good looking young man you have, Stella. I bet you have a lot of girl friends, Francis." I lied and tried to be nice to Mom's friend all the while wishing that I was somewhere else. I guess she was just trying to be nice. I thought of Anna Mae and wished that I could truthfully say that she was my girl friend. Mom sensed that I was getting embarrassed but that I was willing to put up with all this, "faulterall" and "rig-a-ma-role" as Mom would call it. She ordered another ham sandwich and an Orange Crush for me. As I said, Mom seemed much happier getting out of the house and meeting people.

It wasn't long before Marguerite joined them for lunch. I don't know what my cousin did at Shapeleigh Hardware, but she usually took two to three hours for lunch. Maybe she needed that much more time to find a parking space. Grace Mullanphy became like family. Mom would come home from The Grand Leader all tired out and tell Dad and me about her day asking what we did.

"Well, I made the beds, did the dishes, washed some clothes, and fixed this supper. How do you like The Grand Leader?" Dad asked.

"Wonderful, Emil. I'll take over tomorrow and the next day. I'll be off."

"Dad, tell her about the new renters," I said.

"Oh, yes. I rented the second floor east room to a couple of young ladies from Poplar Bluff. They got a job somewhere in North St. Louis making bullets."

"I hope that you told them no men."

"Yes, Stella."

These two bullet makers from Poplar Bluff were real pretty. I asked for my old room back, the one right across the hall from theirs and Mom said OK. I decided that someday I would have to go to Poplar Bluff to see if all the girls down there were that pretty. They dressed plain like and wore long slacks and wore no hats, unlike just about all the women that I'd seen. I don't know why women wear hats. They seem to get bigger and bigger with all kinds of things piled on top and hanging down on the side. The ones that Cousin Marguerite wears always brings out a comment from my aunt.

~78~

The next day my Uncle John called and told Mom that he had brought Uncle Mart to the hospital in Alton. The sore that he had on the side of his mouth got bigger and was starting to make him sick. Mom left right away and took the Interurban to Alton. Dad said that he guessed that it was cancer. We should be prepared for the worst. I was upset but did not know what to do. Dad said, "Pray" and that Mom would be coming home the next day. Mom was home when I came in from school. She had been crying. She said that the doctors said that the cancer had spread so fast that there wasn't anything that they could do except try to slow it down. She said that it was probably caused from his smoking that pipe for so many years. Dad put down his pipe causing us to glance at him.

Friday afternoon I asked Avery if he would like to take a bike trip with me to Alton.

"Sure, how far is it?"

"I don't know. Probably take us all day to get there and back. We better take a lunch. I'll meet you at seven in the morning, OK?"

"Yeah, do you know the way?"

"Yep."

The next morning I got up early and told Mom and Dad that Avery and I were riding our bikes out to the Zoo and won't be back for awhile. Avery told his grandparents the same. I had three baloney sandwiches and Avery brought one and an apple and off we went.

"What if we have a flat, Fran?"

"I guess we walk till we come to a filling station. I don't know how to fix a flat, do you?"

It was a beautiful morning. The Mississippi River was wider than I had imagined as we pedaled across the long curving "Free Bridge" and into East St. Louis. We followed Highway Number Three which ran close to the Interurban tracks and the Mississippi going through Nameoki and then Mitchell where we stopped to have lunch although it was only ten. Avery said that he thought that Lewis and Clark started their trip up the river from around here a long time ago. Avery was a lot smarter than me and read a lot more so I guess he was right. Next was Hartford and Roxana where the refineries almost made us sick. We were both excited about our adventure and the peddling was easy as there were little or no hills. When we got to Wood River we were thirsty. Avery forgot to bring some money. I had taken twenty five cents off the dresser. I figured that my parents wouldn't want us to die of thirst so I felt that if it was stealing, it was like venial stealing, not mortal. I bought Avery and me a cold root beer and we pushed on through East Alton. When we finally got to Alton, Avery was excited as he had never seen the Alton Dam or the lake or the tug boats. We watched one go through the lock and then I told Avery why we had come to Alton.

"To visit my Uncle Mart. He's in that hospital up there on top of the hill. He has cancer. He is the one that I spent some summers with. I told you."

We went to the hospital to see my uncle. The nurse at the desk asked if I was family. When I said yes, she asked if Avery was. I said no. She told me that I could visit him for only a few minuets but that Avery would have to wait in the lobby. I walked into the room and Uncle Mart was in bed. He had a large bandage covering the side of his face and half of his mouth. Blood was showing at the corners of the bandage. He was surprised to see me and smiled. He asked with difficulty, "Who did you come with, Francis, Stella?"

"No. I came with my friend Avery. He's down in the lobby. They said that he wasn't kin."

"How did you two get here?"

"We rode our bikes, Uncle Mart. How do you feel?"

"Well, real good right now. You two rode bikes all the way from Saint Louis! Does Stella and Emil know?"

"No. I didn't want them to worry. If I asked them to let us do it they would have said no."

"Well I'll be a son-of-a-gun!"

"How are you going to get back?"

"On our bikes. How long are you going to be in here?"

"Oh, I guess a day or two more. Your Uncle John is out there minding the farm. I don't like to think about that. I'm anxious to get home. I miss the farm."

"I think that you better let the doctors take care of you and get well first, Uncle."

A nurse came in and my uncle told her, "This is my nephew, my sister's boy, Francis. Guess what. He and his friend rode up from St. Louis on their bikes just to see me. I wouldn't mind meeting his friend if you can manage it, nurse."

"From Saint Louis. On your bikes. Are you staying overnight?"

"No ma'm."

"Francis said that they are going to ride back this afternoon!"

"Does your mother know that you did this?"

Why does everyone always ask that, 'Does your mother know this or that or what would your mother say'. If my mother and my father knew everything that I did they would have had what they call a nervous breakdown a long time ago. Leroy Jones used to say, "What they don't know, won't hurt them." He used that for everything that he did that he shouldn't.

"Francis, do you remember Sadie Fitzpatrick?" I nodded. "She was here this morning. When she walked in she said, "Well you finally moved in to the city."

I said, "Yes. Now, do you want to marry me?"

"Only if you intend to stay in the city.", she said.

"She would liked to have seen you.", he said.

Before Avery came up to the room, Uncle Mart told me to go to the closet and get his billfold. He gave me a gold twenty dollar coin and told me that it was a present. He showed me where he had scratched his initials on both sides, “M W”. He said that he earned that years ago working on the railroad out in California and he had been saving it for someone special. He told me not to spend it but to keep it to remember him by. I didn’t know what to say except, “Thanks.”

Avery came to the room. Uncle Mart said that he was glad to make his acquaintance and that any friend of mine was a friend of his. The nurse told us that our time was up and that the patient needed rest. We shook hands. Uncle Mart pulled me closer and gave me a hug, winked at both of us and waved as we left the room. I quickly turned around, stuck my head in the door and asked my uncle, “Don’t tell Mom that we were here.”

“I won’t as long as you two are careful going home.”

Outside I told Avery that we could go home by taking the short-cut over the Lewis and Clark Bridges. He was all for a short-cut. We were both getting tired and hungry and our legs ached. I thought about that cab driver that Mom hired that day to drive us out to Uncle Mart’s. I wondered how much he would charge us to take us to Saint Louis. I had twenty dollars. I figured if he recognized me he would take all of it. Going over the Lewis and Clark Bridges wasn’t bad but after that there was one steep hill after another. We peddled up the first one and then walked beside our bikes going up the next.

“I saw some bikes last week that had more than one speed,” said Avery.

“What good is that?”

“The one that I saw had three speeds. Frank Long has one.”

“Well, his parents are rich. Everything he has is the best.” I looked back at my rear wheel and saw the tail from the squirrel that I had killed with my BB Gun years ago still hanging from my rear fender.

“Those three speed bikes make it easier to climb hills. I watched Frank riding his. He has to peddle a lot faster, but it’s easier. Your legs just go around three times faster and the bike goes three times slower. When I watched him, it looked like he was peddling to beat the band but not getting anywhere”, panted Avery.

"Well, right now I want to get home three times faster than we're going. Boy, my legs hurt and my butt is sore!"

"So's mine!"

We got home after dark and were tireder than we had ever been, hungry but too tired to eat. We both lied about our day at the Zoo. I fell asleep worrying about my Uncle Mart. Avery stayed away for several days. I guess he thought that I might come up with another wild idea. I do know that neither one of us rode our bikes for awhile

~79~

September came and we were back to school. I was now in the eighth grade. We had Sister Mary Agnes again. She let me know that I had better buckle down if I wanted to graduate next June.

I think by then all of us kids got to see "Gone with the Wind" even though The Church forbade it. Me and Avery figured out that the movies to see were the ones that The Church didn't want us to see. The Church ruled a lot of movies as "Objectionable". I don't think any of the nuns ever got to see a movie. I thought of Dad saying, "You don't know what you're missing". I doubt if any of the priests ever saw a movie. Avery and I argued over which one movie that we saw was the best. I voted for "Lost Horizon" and Avery liked "King Kong". I know that the nuns or the priests never got to see "Tiger Lil". What a pity. Anyway, it seemed that the only thing most of us boys remember about "Gone with the Wind" was Rhett Butler's line, "Frankly my dear, I don't give a damn". We repeated it to one another frequently and silently to Sister when she would ask us questions such as, "Don't you want to graduate? Don't you want to improve your knowledge? When are you going to finish this or that?" Or her question to me and a handful of others, "Do you want to be a dumbbell all of your life?" Frankly my dear—-. Oh, we had fun with that line.

Besides all of the movies Avery and I saw, we read just about all of the comic books. My favorite was Superman. I guess that I read the Superman Comics so much that I started dreaming that I could fly. Well, not like a bird and not with a cape, but in my dreams I would soar just above the utility wires and everyone would look up at me. When I wanted to go faster and higher I would just do the breast stroke like I was swimming. People would look up and say, "That's Frank!" In a few of the dreams Mom would shout, "Francissss, you come down from there," and I would wake up. I asked Avery if he ever had such a dream. He gave me a funny look.

It took awhile for Sister Mary Agnes question to sink into my numbscull, "Don't you want to graduate?" I realized that Anna Mae was a shoe-in to graduate and if I didn't, she would be gone next year and I would still be here.

President Roosevelt signed the Selective Service Act. Everyone worried, if we wrere going to get in the war? My brother, Tommie was twenty-one. How soon would they draft him? Our German friends were worried. Some still had relatives in Germany. We listened to FDR's fireside chats with more interest. In October we listened to Edward R. Morrow who reported right from London as the bombs were falling. We also heard Mr. Kaltenborn reporting of the war in Europe. We were sending ships loaded with supplies to England and other countries. England stopped and searched many of them. I guess they thought some of the stuff was going to Germany. English ships were being sunk by German submarines. Dad said that a lot of young men were getting married whether they wanted to or not just to get out of the draft.

~80~

Sunday dinner at our house. Aunt Gertrude, Bud, and Marguerite ate with us. Dad did most of the cooking. During dinner, Aunt Gertrude shocked us by saying that she and her husband were getting married!

"You're already married!", Mom exclaimed.

"Yes, but not in The Church. Justice of the Peace. We want to get married in The Church. Emil here has been bugging us for years to make it right. We already talked to Father Cronin and Bud here has taken the necessary lessons to convert to Catholic. We just haven't told anyone until we were sure that we could do it."

"But,— what about all the other marriages, Gert. What about them?", Marguerite asked. "The Church frowns on divorce, you know."

"Father Cronin said that they didn't count because I was never married in the eyes of The Church. He said that The Church doesn't recognize any of them and it was just like I was living in sin with each one."

Bud raised his eyebrows and laughed with a beer in his hand. "Anyway, we set the date for a month from now and we would like you, Marguerite, and you, Francis, to stand up for us. Would you please? And Marguerite, please wear something nice. Don't look like a scarecrow."

We both said yes. Marguerite agreed with a frown. I felt important but then wondered if I was their last choice. I was once again puzzled about the rules of my church. Marguerite and my Mom had a long discussion about Bud and Aunt Gertrude after they left and agreed that my Aunt was acting kinda strange lately. They felt that she was fearing death and afraid that she was going to Hell. She had made funeral arrangements last year at Schnur's and stopped by there regularly to make changes. They figured that she was driving Mrs. Schnur nuts.

The following week, Mom said that I would need a suit for the wedding.

"Who all is coming," I asked.

"Just family, but you have to look nice. I already talked to Mr. Silverstein down at the store. You are to come down there Saturday morning and get fitted. You can use the same suit for your graduation if you don't grow too much in the next few months."

"If I don't flunk out.", I thought. Sister Mary Agnes has been on me something terrible, saying that if I don't shape up and fly right, I won't pass and she will be stuck with me again for another whole year or maybe even more. I hated the thought of that more than she did. I met Mr. Silverstein, a nice old man. He thought that I would look good in dark blue. I didn't care as long as the pants had a zipper. I was tired of those buttons popping loose. He placed one end of a cloth tape on the floor and shoved the other end up my crouch. I jumped.

"Haven't been fitted before, Son? You want cuffs or not?"

I looked at him kinda funny and he said, "Cuffs."

"The suit will be ready one day next week. I guess your mother will pick it up." I was glad to get out of there.

A week before the big wedding, Mom said I needed a hair cut so up I went to Joe's Barber shop next to Zahner's Jewelry Store on Jefferson Ave. I liked to go there especially on Saturday. He had the football games on the radio and he never fiddled with the scissors for what seemed like hours cutting my hair like some other barbers. Notre Dame was my favorite but I started to get interested in the Army team. I liked the Navy better than the Army but Notre Dame best of all. That day Notre Dame was playing Navy. It sounded like there were more Irish players on the Navy Team than there were on Notre Dame's. It was a boring game. The Irish beat Navy 17 to 7. One day I would join the Navy and see the world. When I got home I had coal to shovel. We had different coal now, the kind that was supposed to make the city cleaner. It was just as heavy as the old stuff. Mom said that the Mayor promised that we would all be getting gas in the near future and that there would no longer be coal furnaces. Dad said that that is all well and fine, but who pays for putting in the new furnaces.

When I got through shoveling, I sat on the front porch waiting for the fun to start. Marguerite was due to come home. I wondered how many trips around our block she would have to make in order to find a proper parking place. I tilted my chair back and leaned against the wall like my uncles used to do up at Grandpa's. A baluster was still missing where I had pushed it out by accident a couple of years ago. Dad said he would show me how to fix it. He always wanted to show me how to do things stating, "I won't be around much longer, so you better learn how to do this." Whenever he said that I got mad. I didn't like him saying that. I wanted him to always be there and told him so. He got so that he couldn't do too much and I guess I got lazier as he got older.

I looked forward to the Poplar Bluff girls coming home. They always smiled at me and mussed my hair up on their way through the door. I had tried to look under their door to see if I could catch them undressing but the opening between the bottom of the door and the floor wasn't large enough for me to see anything except bare feet or the bottom of someone's shoes. The keyhole was blocked with their key. I nearly got caught one evening when one of them rushed to the door to go to the bathroom. I stumbled all the way into my room. The Poplar Bluff girls got home before my cousin. They knew how to parallel park. Marguerite was on her fourth go around. My cousin came walking around the corner carrying two shopping bags and wearing the wildest looking hat on her head. She must have parked blocks away. When she got close to home, three cars pulled out right in front of our house. I heard her cuss.

~81~

Wedding Day. We all got to the church at seven thirty in the morning and rehearsed at the side altar while Father Joe was conducting Mass at the main altar. Father Cronin looked at me and said, "This won't do. He's too young."

Aunt Gertrude stepped down and went to Dad saying, "Emil, you got us into this now and your going to have to get us through it."

Dad grunted loudly. He rose up and replaced me at the altar with his cane at his side. The one without a nail at the end. We got more attention than Father Joe doing his thing. He was trying to conduct Mass and he was visibly upset by the rumblings of my family. Aunt Gertrude had on a dark suit and Bud the same. Marguerite wore a dress with every color under the sun under her new hat. I looked down at my fly and was pleased to see that the zipper worked. I smiled when I realized that I got all of these new clothes for nothing. Mom and I were in the side pew along with Grace Mullanphy. When it came to the part where Bud was supposed to place the ring on my aunt's finger, he couldn't find it and got very nervous. Aunt Gertrude looked at her hand extended ready to receive the ring and exclaimed looking at him, "It's still on my finger, dummy, you never took it off!" Dad grunted nervously. Bud took a deep breath, took the ring off and then put it back on. His deep breath exhale made Father Cronin cough several times. When they departed the church before Father Sullivan finished his Mass, I threw a pocket full of Uncle Ben's rice on them. We all walked down Lafayette passed where I used to walk Skippy. A streetcar came by and people looked at our procession.

I heard my aunt proclaim, "I need a drink!"

"So do I," answered her new and old husband.

"You already had your share!"

I heard Dad say to Mom, "Ah, wedded bliss."

~82~

FDR was elected again. This time the race was closer. A man by the name of Wendell Willkie ran against him. I liked this Mr. Willkie but not as much as FDR. Clem, up at the church, retired and moved to be with his daughter in Iowa. The new janitor said that in two weeks he would not need Dad to help him clean the church. Dad wasn't too upset about it but I was. I had no Skippy to walk and now, no coins to sweep up on the days Dad ushered. Perhaps Dad was upset about it after all. On the next two Sundays he was overly nervous in stretching out the offering basket down the pews, almost tipping it over on two occasions and failing to catch more coins than usual. I silently cheered him on while Mom hid her face in her hands. I gathered more money after those two Sundays than ever before, but after that I was out of work. After sweeping the floor, Dad told me that I was old enough to contribute money to the church. I was shocked. When I asked him how much he said ten percent of whatever I made. I picked up two dollars and thirteen cents cleaning the church the next day so the next Sunday I put twenty one cents in the basket when Dad passed it down our pew. He didn't drop a cent. I wondered if I was going to have to contribute ten percent of what I sneaked off the dresser.

Thanksgiving came along with a greasy goose on the table along with mincemeat pie and three kinds of potatoes. Dad bought a couple of pomegranates at Garavelli's. No one wanted them. Too strange looking.

"Why on earth do you bring all this stuff home, Emil?" Mom asked.

"To broaden your taste and education," Dad replied somewhat disappointed.

After the mincemeat pie I felt sorry for Dad and opened the strange looking pomegranate. After tasting it, I liked it. "Something like cranberry sauce only sweeter", I said with my mouth all red.

Christmas was coming and Dad suggested that I buy everyone a gift. On previous years, Dad gave me a small amount of money to buy Mom a gift. At first I hated the thought of spending my hard earned money on someone other than myself. I remembered one of the Sisters saying, "Tis better to give than to receive". When I heard that I thought she was crazy. I took the street car downtown ready to play Santa Claus to my family. First stop was Woolworth's. I was fascinated by the demonstrators throughout the store, one man showing the crowd around him how this tool of his could peel potatoes, tomatoes and apples in a jiffy. I bought one for Mom. I bought a handkerchief for Aunt Gertrude, and a box of candy for Marguerite. I went to the drug store and bought a can of "Prince Albert" for Dad and two placemats for Uncle Mart's table. I bought a pack of "Lucky Strike" for Bud. The clerk asked who all of this was for and I told him, Christmas presents. "It better be", he replied. I spent a dollar and ninety seven cents and had more than a dollar left. I still had the twenty dollar gold piece that Uncle Mart gave me. It's funny but I enjoyed that Christmas almost better than any other except when I got Bobby. That was the best. I got clothes for Christmas and was happy. Happy to see my family happy.

~83~

Six months before graduation. If I make it. Mother Superior or someone up high thought that we all needed to "express ourselves" better. We were told that a speech therapist was to start giving us lessons, "One on one" starting the first of next week. We guys silently gave the "Rhett Butler" reply. Monday morning after Catechism a young, shapely, blond woman, wearing a tight skirt and a white blouse doing its best to hold back her breast walked in the room and Sister introduced her as Miss Madelyn Smith who has two degrees in speech and education and is volunteering her time to make us more confident in speaking to an audience or anyone else. She would also help some of us to be better able to give oral answers to the Sister's questions. Sister Mary Agnes looked directly at me. Miss Smith wore black patent leather high heeled shoes. The girls were smiling and enthralled with her looks, hoping that some day soon they would look like her. I looked around at the boys and most of them were twisting their necks to get a better look at this angel from Heaven or whatever she was that has just come into our dull classroom.

Well, the "one on one" worked for the girls and for a few of the boys, but the rest of us were just so taken with her looks and movements, especially her lip and mouth motions that we either blushed throughout our sessions or developed a hard on that delayed our exiting from this private room that she had us in. Miss Smith lasted a week. We were sorry to see her go. We all asked where she went. I couldn't get her or her high heeled shoes off of my mind.

~84~

A couple of days later in class, Sister Mary Agnes smiled at me. I didn't know why. For the first time I really looked at her. She had a beautiful face. Round cheeks, blue eyes, no glasses and a nice complexion. I wondered what she would look like if she wore clothes like Miss Smith. I wondered how she slept at night. When she and the other nuns went back to the Convent after school, did they take off those tight collars and hoods. Did they have hair or was their head shaved. I wish that I didn't wonder so much about everything. It made my brain sore.

A few days later I went home and snuck into Cousin Marguerite's room. She had a pair of bright red high heel shoes. I stared at them and wondered how a woman like Miss Smith or Tiger Lil felt wearing shoes like that. I wanted to know more about women like them so I could understand what makes them tick and maybe then I would know what I had to do to make girls like me. I put on the red shoes. My first thought was how uncomfortable and silly they felt. I took a step and fell to the floor. I quickly took them off and backed up. I didn't learn a thing about Miss Smith but decided that I still liked high heel shoes a lot, except on Cousin Marguerite and myself.

While our minds were still on Miss Smith, Father Cronin came to class and told us about our future as good Catholic boys and girls. He told us of the Catholic High Schools that were available to us. He said that there may be scholarships available to the brightest students. He said that upon graduating from one of these schools some of the graduates could enter into the priesthood or the girls could become nuns. He just wanted us to think about these things. When Leroy asked, "How much does Christian Brothers and South Side Catholic cost and are they just for boys?," Father Cronin answered, "Well, that's a good question. Yes, there is a tuition. Your parents can call the schools and get that information. And yes, South Side Catholic and C.B.C. are for boys only."

I knew that whatever the tuition, Mom and Dad couldn't afford it, and anyway, no girls? And me a priest? What would I do with this thing between my legs and my thoughts about high heel shoes, but boy, would I like to hear other peoples confessions!

All of this talk about High School and graduating made me realize that these kids that I have been with for nine years are soon going to scatter. I worried about that. Was Anna Mae going to go to one of those high schools for girls? Would I not see her again? When I overheard Anna Mae talking to Eileen O'Hara telling her that she would be attending Roosevelt High School I was glad. I was afraid that she would become a nun, her looking so holy all the time. I later learned that all the kids living west of Nebraska Street were to go to Roosevelt and the ones east of Nebraska were to go to McKinley. I did not know anything about either school except that I heard that they were Public Schools, not Catholic, and I lived east of Nebraska. I would have to go to McKinley High School. When I told Mom and Dad that we should move to the next block they questioned why. I told them that I wanted to go to a better school, one with an indoor swimming pool and a nice football field and a track. I wanted to go to Roosevelt. They said that I could probably make a special request and see what happens. I didn't tell them about Anna Mae.

We were fitted for caps and gowns. I got the feeling that Sister was going to pass me. We were told to go up to Zahner's Jewelry Store and be measured for our graduation rings and for those of us who could not afford one were to see Father Cronin. The day arrived and we had our pictures taken with our two priests standing on the side. We were given diplomas and a blessing with all of the nuns applauding. We were given ten minuets to talk to each other and then sent to change into our clothes. We were dismissed for the day. For the year. Forever! I received special permission to go to Roosevelt. I wanted to go there because Anna Mae was going there even though for the last nine years she barely looked at me. Avery was going to McKinley. Avery and I spent most of the summer riding all over the city on our bikes or on the streetcars.

Uncle Mart got out of the hospital and went back to the farm. Dad said that his cancer had grown and it didn't look good. I went up and helped him load manure into his spreader and pitch hay into the barn.

I changed the bloody newspapers on the dining room table. When I got home, Mom said that he belonged back in the hospital but he would have no part of it. His friend, Sadie Fitzpatrick, tried to get him to let her come in and cook and clean for him but he refused.

September came and I started High School. I was nervous. I rode my bike to school every day. I liked Roosevelt High. The school had a wonderful quarter mile track and an inside swimming pool. There were at least fifty kids in each of my classes and I never once saw Anna Mae except when she got into a car with some guy after school. I was flunking every single class. What a dummy.

~85~

Thanksgiving came around again. All of the usual relatives were there. The Well would not let me buy and bring home beer anymore. I guess they thought that it was for me. Dad was asked to go with me to get the supply. I would carry the bottles. Mom didn't trust him with his nervousness. Dad said Grace and asked God to be with us all, and also with Uncle Walter, wherever he may be, and with Uncle Mart and for my brother, Tommie who was facing the Draft and surely war. We made a wish that all of us would be together again next year. The door bell rang and Dad went to answer it. A young man with a large cowboy hat on, wearing purple boots, introduced himself.

"My name, Sir, is Sonny Newberry. I come from Texas. Well, that ain't just right. I was born in Texas but I've been out in California for awhile."

"Well what can I do for you, Mr. Elderberry,"

"Newberry, Sir. A young couple out there that I did a show with said that I was to look you up if'n I ever passed this way. You see, I'm on my way to Tennessee and I need a room for only a couple of weeks. You may remember them, the Ginsbergs—."

"Oh, yes Quick and Nimble."

"Is that what they called themselves? That's downright cute."

Mom came to the door to see what was taking Dad so long, and learning who he was and who sent him. She invited him to dinner.

"Well, now Ma'am, I didn't want to disturb your Thanksgiving dinner, I should have known it were about eating time."

"Nonsense come in, there's plenty and we do have a room for rent."

"Well I do declare, that's right nice of you," he said taking off his big hat and bringing his guitar to the front of him.

"Where is your luggage?"

"Oh, I put it in a locker down at the Greyhound Station. I ain't got much."

Dad found another chair. When he came into the kitchen he laid his cowboy hat on top of the refrigerator and leaned his guitar against the wall. Mom introduced him to everyone. He shook each and everyone's hand with a "Pleased ta meet ya". I heard Aunt Gertrude whisper, "Well I say".

Sonny, that's what he told me to call him, was real likable. He said that he was a Country Western Singer and when I asked him what that was he said, "Well, Frank", (I told him to call me Frank), he said, "Country Western is just a kinda glorified cowboy singer."

~86~

Gertrude

Dear diary,

I have been so happy working for Mrs. Moran and going out with Johnathan. We have become very close. He is so kind. We have been driving out to see Father often. Barty is still working in Alton. Johnathan and I picked up Barty, went out and got Father and took both of them to Homer Blue Dells the last two Sundays. Father really enjoyed their fried chicken He said that it was almost as good as what I used to make. Barty dropped his mouth open when he heard that and then we all laughed. Johnathan wondered what we found funny. He had not had any of my fried chicken. But maybe, just maybe one day. One thing that I'm worried about is this cloud of war hanging over us. Will John have to go?

After fixing Thanksgiving dinner for Mrs. Moran, Johnathan and I loaded up his car with a big goose and groceries. We picked up Barty and headed out to the farm. On the way through Alton, I asked Johnathan to stop across the street from the orphanage. I looked up at the building and could see, hear, and feel, everything that happened there to my brothers and me. I looked up at the building for a long time. When I told Johnathan that we could go now, I was finally saying goodbye to the place.

Johnathan and I fixed dinner with Barty and Tommie helping. We were once again together along with a new guy that I loved very much. I remembered the Christmas that Father almost got killed coming back from Alton with Christmas gifts for us. I miss being here on the farm, sometimes, sometimes.

~87~

It seemed that Sonny sang and played his guitar every minute that he was in his room, except before eight in the morning and after nine at night; Mom's rules. He played and sang with the windows open when it was warm enough and when that happened the two short haired Pointer dogs next door howled their hearts out. I didn't like those dogs, a male and a female. They were forever going at each other and once in awhile they would get locked together for days with him inside her. I did not like our neighbors either, they would play their radio with all of this hillbilly music blasting out. Their dogs would howl when a yodeler came on. Now we had our own "Country Western", or "Cowboy", or "Hill Billy" Singer, Sonny. He sang with an entirely different sound than he talked with. All twangy and holding on to the notes for so long and with a suffering, miserable look on his face with his eyes closed.

When I asked him why he sounded different, he said, "Gee, Frank, I guess that's what it's all about. Most of the songs are about suffering and heartache, like loosing a girl friend."

I thought of… Oh, I don't want to think about her anymore. Maybe I could write a song.

Avery started bringing his clarinet over to try and play with Sonny. Helwig and Arlene, who lived across the street and played their accordions, joined Sonny and Avery on Sunday after church and dinner. They played and sang out on the front porch. The neighborhood, including the Pointers got to hear music that they had never heard before.

Mom and Dad and I were in the living room one Sunday listening to the radio that was turned up as loud as it would go because of the music out on the porch, when suddenly someone came on with a special report. Pearl Harbor had just been bombed by the Japanese. Ships were sunk and men were killed. We called the musicians in to hear the rest of the terrible announcements. Everyone was quiet.

The next morning Sonny said good-by. He was heading back to his hometown in Texas to join up. School was canceled. Cousin Maymie called long distance from California to tell us that everyone out there was scared to death, and that balloons were spotted overhead, and that they thought that they were going to be invaded. Here, the paper boys ran down the street three times that day and night with different Extras and pictures of Pearl Harbor. I had never heard of this Pearl Harbor.

It was a warmer than normal day for December. I was worried. I took a walk up to Lafayette and stood across the street from my old school just looking and remembering. I walked up the two blocks to our church. I stood and looked at the church and the vacant lot across from it. I walked around to the lot behind our old house on Longfellow and remembered Bobby. I came back and sat out on the front porch looking through the space missing between the rail supports wondering what was going to happen next and somehow realized that I had had it good up to this point. But things were changing.

THE END